Praise for the novels of Karen Harper

"Harper…has a fantastic flair for creating and sustaining suspense…[the] deft knitting of fact and fiction enables Harper to describe everything from wilderness survival to supernatural lore with the kind of detail that convinces readers anything is possible."
—*Publishers Weekly* on *The Falls*

"Her deft juxtaposition of the cast of creepy characters and a small-town setting…makes for a haunting read."
—*Publishers Weekly* on *The Stone Forest*

"A glimpse into the lives of the modern-day Amish…Harper's choice of setting and lifestyle for her heartwarming characters adds a fresh twist."
—*Publishers Weekly* on *Down to the Bone*

"While the story moves quickly, the mystery builds slowly and hooks readers as Harper gradually introduces one clue or suspicion after another. The characters are well drawn; readers suspect nearly everyone."
—*School Library Journal* on *Down to the Bone*

"Mystery, intrigue, love—it's all here. Don't miss this fascinating and exciting story."
—*Rendezvous* on *Shaker Run*

"With a wonderful feel of suspense and a well-plotted story, Ms. Harper delivers a fabulously frightening late-night read."
—*Romantic Times* on *The Stone Forest*

"There are enough crimes and suspects in this action-filled romance to satisfy everyone."
—*Ohioana Quarterly* magazine on *Down to the Bone*

"Exciting, dramatic and spine-tingling."
—*Rendezvous* on *The Baby Farm*

KAREN HARPER

DARK ANGEL

MIRA®

ISBN-13: 978-0-7783-2809-4

DARK ANGEL

Copyright © 2005 by Karen Harper.

www.MIRABooks.com

Printed in U.S.A.

In loving memory
of my father,
Robert Kurtz.

And as ever,
to Don.

AUTHOR'S NOTE

The Amish don't believe in ghosts, but they are haunted by certain hereditary illnesses. Natal Accelerated Aging (NAA) and Regnell Anemia in the book are fictional, but are closely based on real genetic diseases. Dr. Mark Morelli's clinic is inspired by, but in no way based on, two clinics in Amish country where doctors are diagnosing and treating debilitating and, in many cases, lethal gene disorders. These facilities are overseen by Dr. Heng Wang at the Deutsch Center in Middlefield, Ohio, and Dr. Holmes Morton in Strasburg, Pennsylvania. We owe a debt of gratitude to the Amish, who, though they choose to live in a horse-and-buggy world, are willing to contribute to the study of cutting-edge, futuristic medicine that will benefit everyone.

Prologue

Tears froze on her face. Clumps of clouds hid the stars, and the sharp wind clawed at the buggy as Leah Kurtz turned her horse into the driveway. She climbed down and tied Nell to the hitching post, trying to keep her black cape from flapping in her face. Even at a fast clip on ice-etched, deserted rural roads, it had taken her nearly a half hour to reach the isolated house of her lifelong friend, Barbara Yoder.

Leah was frantic to see her. *Fading fast,* the Wengerd boy had said when he'd knocked on her door just after midnight. *Asking for you. Real desperate, she is.*

Everyone knew Barbara was seriously ill, diagnosed during her recent pregnancy with what the Cleveland specialists called Regnell anemia, named for some Swedish doctor who'd discovered it. First pregnancies took a lot out of women, but Barbara's extreme fatigue, nosebleeds and bruising had turned out to be a lethal form of leukemia. A husband, a one-month-old baby daughter, and years of life ahead of her: Leah could still not accept that the woman who'd been closer than a sister for their twenty-six years was going to die.

The wan light of gas lanterns inside silhouetted a stocky woman at the window. Barbara's parents were dead, but that looked like Sam's mother, Mary. As Leah rushed up the walk, the old, two-story house seemed to sway in the wind, but it was only her tears blurring her vision. Swiping at them with her gloved hands, she climbed the familiar steps. The howl of wind sounded like a woman's shrieks. Fresh snow, still stuck sideways on the porch posts, made it look as if ghosts guarded the door.

Despite her panic, sweet words popped into Leah's head: *"O Wind, if Winter comes, can Spring be far behind?"*

She shook her head as if to scold herself for living, for looking ahead. Barbara had a husband and child, when Leah had neither; why should Barbara be the one to die? Anyway, she should be recalling comforting Bible verses, not the yearning words of one of the worldly Romantic poets she'd treasured.

The door swung wide and warm air rushed out. Mary Yoder, looking drawn and gray, held it open for her.

"I came as fast as I could," Leah said, stepping in and yanking off her gloves. "She's not—"

"Still hanging on, barely," Mary told her through trembling lips. She took Leah's cape. "Waiting to see you, she says. Family said their goodbyes today, but something's still fretting her bad, *ja,* that's sure."

Leah's legs went weak. Surely Barbara did not have some previously unconfessed admission to make. Could she know something about Joseph, Barbara's brother and Leah's runaway betrothed, that she'd never told before?

As Leah and Mary hugged, Leah glanced past the older woman's shoulder. She heard men's voices from the kitchen, so some of the church leaders must be here to pray and comfort. "I can't—can't really say good-bye," Leah tried to explain to Mary, but realized this was no time to talk about herself. "How's Sam holding up?"

"Still angry. Luke Brand told him he'd better accept it," she explained, gesturing toward the kitchen, "or it'll eat him up, and little Becca won't have either of them. The elders been praying. Wish that fancy new doctor in town had come sooner. Maybe he could have helped. They say, you know," she went on, lowering her voice even more, "he works with those newfangled genes that defected."

That are defective, Leah thought, but she didn't correct Mary. With a hard sniff to keep from crying, Leah rushed up the staircase. She had to be strong to help Barbara, Sam and their baby in any way she could.

From above, she heard little Rebecca, called Becca, fussing. Thank God, the child's test for her mother's genetic disorder had come back negative, though the doctor had said Becca was a carrier. Most Amish had just accepted Barbara's disease as God's will, like other hereditary ailments and illnesses that plagued their people, but Leah, the long-time local schoolteacher, had read up on genes and DNA. Yet all that seemed so useless now.

"Sam?" she called from the narrow landing at the top of the stairs. At her voice, the baby's crying stopped. The single gas lantern in the hall hissed softly.

Looking like a man who'd been awakened from a nightmare, Sam appeared at the open bedroom door. His round face was clenched in a blur of anger and grief, as if he'd been holding back until he stepped away from his wife. His shirt was wrinkled and stained, his brown hair mussed, his hands in tight fists thrust under his armpits.

"Thank God, you're here," he whispered. "She wants to talk to you, and wants me and Becca there too."

Leah removed her black bonnet, keeping her white, starched *kapp* on over her pinned-up hair. She followed Sam into the bedroom, which was lit by two lanterns, one on the chest of drawers, one on a wall hook. Barbara, who had always been petite and slender, seemed to have no body at all under the quilt. Her head and shoulders were propped up on pillows, her hair long and straight. She held Becca loosely, as though her arms had been simply draped around the child. A pitcher of water and an array of medicine bottles covered the bedside table. The doctors had said she should stay in hospital for continued treatment, but since the prognosis was so dire, she had wanted to come home.

Leah's first instinct was to wail and beat the wall, but she summoned the self-discipline that so often waged war with her emotions. Biting her lower lip, she shuffled closer. Sam indicated she should sit on the side of the bed where a hollow showed he had been perched.

"Lee!" Barbara said, using Leah's childhood nickname. Her eyes widened, but her voice was so soft. Her face seemed flaccid, as if it took great effort to move each muscle. She no longer looked like her vibrant, pretty self, but like a flower fading before their eyes.

Leah bent over the baby to kiss her friend's cool cheek, then kissed Becca's warm, downy head before she sat on the bed.

"Grateful...you're here," Barbara whispered. "I'm so exhausted, I can't even hold her, my angel. Take her from me...for me."

Sam choked back a sob. Leah, who had helped Mary and other Yoder relatives with the baby in the first month of her life, lifted the little one into her arms and cradled her close, holding her so her mother could still see her face.

"She always liked you," Barbara said so quietly that Leah had to lean close to catch the words.

"I've always loved her."

"I know," Barbara replied. "Sam, tell...ask her."

A silence stretched out in the room.

"Ask me what?" Leah said, bouncing the baby until she realized she might be jostling Barbara. Suddenly, as the women's eyes met and held, one side of Barbara's mouth tilted in the ghost of a smile. Leah silently thanked God for all the sunny, laughter-filled days she and Barbara had shared, even through their tears ten years ago and in these last, grueling months.

Becca lifted a tiny hand and gurgled. "Ask me what?" Leah repeated.

Sam spoke from the other side of the bed where he sat carefully, one leg bent as he leaned forward to take his wife's limp hand. "We've talked it over, Leah," he said, his voice flat and weak, as if he too stood at death's door. "You and Barbara were as close as real sisters, and were nearly sisters-in-law, till Joseph ran off like that."

Leah's insides cartwheeled. She no longed pined for or loved Joseph Lantz, but it had been so long since she'd heard someone say his name. During their traditional teenage *rumspringa* running-around time, he'd taken off for the world, even after they'd been published in church and their wedding date set. Unlike most Amish fence jumpers, he'd never come back, never written—nothing. It had stunned Leah, but she'd picked herself up and gone on, the extra person at so many tables, teaching and loving other people's children. Though she was close to her own parents and siblings, it wasn't like having a home of one's own. She'd never had another come-calling friend; their ages were wrong, or they thought she was too busy to court, or that she read too many books or…

"Didn't mean to bring him up now," Sam said and cleared his throat. "You know I've got to head up the team of brethren who are building churches, even out of state, and my mother's still broke up over *Daad*'s death and doesn't need another burden, no way."

Leah's heart began to thud. What was he—what were they—saying?

"My sisters are too young," Sam went on, "or have

too many children or… The thing is," he said, his voice louder and faster now, "Barbara and I would count it an honor if you'd take Becca on as your own."

"Sam will sign papers," Barbara whispered, "to make you her mother, even in the eyes of English law."

Leah stared from one to the other. They meant it.

"But—I'm a *maidal,* and one without a man in sight!" was all she managed. She hadn't seen this coming. True, Sam was the foremen of a team of young men who did itinerant construction, for not all Amish could afford farmland or could work in a shop these days. And he was right that no particular family members would make an obvious choice to adopt their baby, on either the Lantz or Yoder sides.

Despite the fact Leah had longed and prayed for a child, she was terrified to accept this one. Part of her dream had come true but at the cost of a nightmare. She began to tremble. She almost blurted out that Sam might marry again, and his future wife would want Becca, but she must not say that now. Besides, to have even a few years as a mother, to have someone of her own to love, would be worth any sacrifice or risk.

"I love her d-dearly and would be honored, but are you s-sure?" she stammered, shaking as if she were still chilled.

"I'm sure, Sam's sure—Becca's sure," Barbara said, straining to touch the baby's head as if she would bestow a blessing with the last remnants of her strength.

"Then I will protect her with my very life," Leah vowed, her voice loud and clear. She reached out to hook her little finger through Barbara's, the way they had when they'd made girlish promises of eternal friendship years ago.

Barbara's finger barely closed around hers, but her voice came stronger, surer. "Then I can let go. But I'll still be close…watching…"

The slight curl of her finger around Leah's loosened. A small smile lifted Barbara's lips, and her eyes lit as she looked at each of them in turn. And then the light went out.

1

March 17, 2003

Winter was hanging on by its fingernails. But Leah loved rising early, even on cold, dark mornings.

After she fed Becca, she enjoyed a relaxed breakfast, holding the baby in one arm and eating oatmeal with the other, talking between bites. By nine o'clock, sunlight streamed in the kitchen window onto the Formica-topped table. After years of teaching school, such a quiet Monday morning was a luxury.

"You do know this is our one-month anniversary, don't you, Becca-my-Becca?"

But, Leah thought, that also made it the one-month mark of Barbara's death. Unfortunately, she saw her dear friend everywhere she looked in these rooms. Sam had traveled often, and Leah had spent happy hours here at the Yoders's house with Barbara. Memories of shared activities and conversations both comforted and tormented her, like the time they'd painted the kitchen, getting more white on themselves than on the walls, and laughed themselves silly.

She was struggling hard to make this house hers when it still seemed like Barbara's. Because Sam and Barbara's bedroom was the only decent-size room upstairs, at first she'd slept in their bed. She'd put Becca in a crib nearby since the nursery was too chilly this time of year. But Barbara's marriage and death seemed to haunt the old double bed, and a new, single one was the first thing Leah planned to buy. Nightmares, as much as the chill upstairs, had driven her to lug Becca's crib down into the living room and sleep on the saggy sofa there.

"In a few months you'll be eating *ser gut,* yummy things like this oatmeal and not just that formula. I've got raisins in the oatmeal too, see? I'll make you raisin-filled sugar cookies someday."

The baby loved watching Leah's face, but right now she was fascinated by her moving spoon. "And there's a woodlot of sugar maples just off the back property line," Leah went on, "and when it gets warm, we'll go out there and see the spring flowers."

Leah heard the distant sound of a train, no doubt the one that picked up flour at the AgraGro Mill, just on the other side of the ravine and a field. With the trees bare-branched, she could see the tops of the mill's two tall silos from the backyard. A few weeks ago, when her mother and younger sister, Naomi, had come to spend a rare mild day, they had insisted she get out for a while, and she'd walked over to take a look at the place.

"Do you hear that choo-choo train?" she asked Becca, as if the child knew a thing she was saying. "Some sunny day we'll go over and see it go by. So many things I want to tell and teach you."

This month since Barbara had died had been more than busy. Leah's family had helped her move from her parents' big farm into the Yoder house. Despite the fact Leah had helped her mother raise three younger siblings and had taught eight grades of scholars for eight years, once she was alone with Becca, taking care of her had been initially overwhelming. Each time the baby cried, Leah had panicked that she might be sick, but she'd learned to interpret her fussing and expressions better now.

And though it didn't seem possible, since Becca was so young and so many others had tended her off and on, she seemed to miss her mother. Occasionally, she unnerved Leah by looking over her shoulder or turning her head to listen as if Barbara stood there or was entering the room. Leah partly blamed these incidents on her own jitters. It was strange being cooped up here for weeks on end, when she was used to mingling with lots of people. Yet Becca made up for all of that.

Also in this past month, with Leah's help, a new Amish woman, Mattie Miller, had taken over the one-room schoolhouse, and Leah had officially retired. Despite a few raised eyebrows over Sam and Barbara's decision, the scholars and their parents had showered her with gifts of baby clothing and cradle quilts. She would soon start working part-time at the Helping Hands Quilt Shop, where she could bring Becca with her. Sam's money for Becca took care of necessities, but a job would give her some extra money to fix up the house and buy a new bed.

It was too bad, she thought, that a man who built

churches couldn't find time to fix up his own home, and Barbara had been too tired to decorate much. Sam was still saddled with medical bills, too, despite the community relief benefit the church had held. Since the Amish didn't believe in medical insurance, they all pitched in to raise funds if there was a special need. Sadly, the needs were great, and they held several such projects each year.

A knock on the back door jolted her. Her heartbeat kicked up. People seldom came this far out on Deer Run Road because it was mostly woodlots and fallow fields beyond. The road dead-ended at a ravine, which was crossed only by a footbridge. Access to the Agra-Gro Mill was by another road. The old pioneer cemetery next door—this had originally been the caretaker's house—was tended by the ladies of the Maplecreek Historical Society, but no new burials were held there anymore. And why would someone come to her back door, instead of the front? Nothing much was behind the house but trees.

She put Becca into the plastic laundry basket she'd padded with a quilt and placed it on the back corner of the kitchen counter where a draft from the floor or door would not hit her. Since the back door was solid wood with no window, Leah peeked out the kitchen window over the sink.

She was relieved to see Seth Kline, now seventeen, a boy who'd been the best scholar she'd ever taught. Blond and freckled, he grinned at her when she knocked on the windowpane and waved. She'd taught all the Kline children, including Seth's six-year-old sister, Susie, who had a rare disease that aged her quickly and prematurely.

Leah and Seth always talked about books, and she'd encouraged him to continue his studies, even though he worked various odd jobs in the community to help pay for Susie's medical needs. One of Seth's part-time jobs was cleaning cages and stalls at the town vet's, so Leah had seen him off and on this winter when her horse had intestinal troubles. She hoped the boy wasn't here with bad news about Susie's health.

"Seth, so good to see you!" she called out in German as she swung the door open.

She saw then that he wasn't alone. Miles Mason, an Englishman who owned a gift shop in town that featured Amish-made candies, jellies, honey and maple syrup, stood off to Seth's side. He was a big man, with hulking shoulders and almost no neck. His fur cap with huge, hanging earflaps, and his brown fake-fur jacket, as well as his jowls and bloodshot eyes, made him look like a hunting hound.

"Hello, Mr. Mason," she said, switching to English, and not asking Seth in as she'd intended. Despite the raw wind, she stepped out and closed the door behind her, pulling her shawl closer.

"We just wanted to tell you," Seth said when the man merely nodded, "that I'm working part-time for Mr. Mason. His crew will be in that back woodlot, tapping trees and checking the sap buckets the next few weeks. We won't be on the Yoders's land, but we didn't want you to hear noises or men's voices and wonder."

"I appreciate knowing. How's Susie doing?"

"Pretty much the same, *ja,* her arthritis acting up in this weather. Since it costs so much to pay for rides clear to Cleveland for checkups, *Maam* thought maybe that new gene doctor could help. I might try to hire on, sweeping up for him, in trade for him taking a look at her."

"I was thinking of meeting him too," Leah admitted. "Maybe he knows something about Becca's *maam*'s fatal disease. Besides, I heard he's a pediatrician, too, so he'll be a good man to know. Nothing against the two general practitioners in the area, but they're in Pleasant, and one of them's getting near retirement."

Miles Mason's fixed stare was making her jumpy, so she didn't try to talk up further education to Seth this time. She felt sad the boy was sweeping floors, because he'd been the only scholar she'd ever had who she wished would run off in his *rumspringa* to get schooling somewhere. Most kids his age were feeling their oats right now, as was tradition among the Amish, until they could make a mature decision to commit to being Amish for life. But Seth was loyal to his family, and they needed him.

Though it was something few Amish women would do, Leah stared back at the English man. Unless he was just squinting against the light reflecting off the remnants of snow, his eyes seemed to be assessing her beneath his bushy, gray eyebrows.

"Last year," she said, "Barbara and I watched you tap the trees, Mr. Mason."

"She was real neighborly. Sent out fresh-baked cookies once." He snatched off his hat, uncovering salt-and-pepper hair as messy as a bird's nest. "Sorry for her loss," he added gruffly.

"Your kind words are much appreciated. You know,

I was just eating some maple syrup with oatmeal. I prefer it to brown sugar." She was sure this man had some other business with her, but she was so chilled she was going to have to step back inside soon.

"I hear you don't own this place," Mason said as his gaze took in the house and yard. "It's got some real good sugar trees in front and on both sides that I'd like to tap this year. I'd give you syrup in trade. Actually, I'd like to buy the land. Maybe you could suggest to Sam Yoder that you'd rather move back into town with your folks, 'stead of being out in an uninsulated old house like this with an infant."

Her eyes widened, and she stifled a gasp. This man knew more about her than she could have imagined. Seth liked to talk and he could have pried all that information out of the boy, but despite that fact, she didn't like it.

"As you may know, though Sam no longer lives here, he comes and goes," she told Mason as she began to shake harder from the cold. "I could write him about it if you want, but I have no plans to move."

"Naw, I'll take care of it later," he muttered, putting his hat back on and heading toward his trees.

"Teacher Leah, I'll see you at Luke Brand and Katie Lindley's wedding tomorrow!" Seth called as he started away. "I'm head hostler in charge of parking all the buggies!" He gave her a jaunty wave and trudged after his boss. Leah noted a pickup truck in the distance, which Miles Mason had evidently driven into the stand of trees.

Right then, she decided to buggy into town to pay the rest of her vet bill and drop by that new gene doctor's place across the street. She'd ask about Becca's status as a carrier and what he knew about Regnell anemia. She could offer a reference for Seth, in case he did ask for a job, and maybe suggest the doctor take a look at Susie Kline.

Unlike some Amish, whom she'd overheard saying they'd steer clear of a man who tried to figure out what "mistakes might be in people's insides," she was curious to meet the gene doctor. She'd heard he was Italian, which sounded pretty exotic for Ohio Amish country. He was sure to have some unique stories. One thing she'd missed badly this past month was learning new things to teach her scholars.

As she turned to go back inside, she glanced at the corner of the old graveyard, which was all she could see from here. No Amish were laid to rest there, for their cemetery was on the other side of town. Though most of the pale limestone markers were worn and tilted, a single statue stood out. On a foot-high pedestal, a five-foot angel—wings partly spread, head down—seemed to hover. Snow etched the folds and creases of the hair, robe and wings. Carved from dark gray granite, the figure was still cleanly cut.

The angel guarded the grave of a young woman who had died at age twenty-six in the late 1880s. On a whim one day, the first year the Yoders moved in here, Leah and Barbara had scrubbed the moss and lichen off her and decked her with a spring garland around her neck. Since Barbara had also died at twenty-six, it seemed to Leah that the angel now guarded Barbara's house and baby too.

"All garlanded with carven imag'ries of fruits and

flowers." Leah whispered the words from one of her favorite Keats poems. Then she added, as if the statue could hear, "Someday I'll tell Becca that you're her mother's angel, too."

Dr. Mark Morelli hated mornings. At 9:00 a.m. he hit the snooze button on his alarm clock so hard the clock skidded off the bedside table. "Mmm—damn!"

Squinting at the sun streaking through the vertical blinds, he forced himself up, righted the clock and stumbled into the bathroom. He'd spent half the night staring at columns of numbers he'd been crunching on his new BLAST computer software. The percentages of probable gene mutations burned in his brain even now.

He splashed water on his face, then made the mistake of looking in the mirror. Dark circles under his eyes and heavy beard stubble. Before stepping into the shower, he checked his PDA for voice messages, then called up his e-mails. Former colleagues sending congratulations for his new endeavor, two online genetics newsletters, business messages and a familiar SOS heading from his longtime friend, Clark Quinn, a patent attorney. He'd call Clark as soon as he thought he could form words.

However obsessed he was with this new project, he had to get more sleep. He looked as bad as he did when he'd been drinking, or what he and Clark had always called *wining and wenching*. That memory made him regret briefly that he'd broken up with Morgan, but she'd been dead set against his decision to move to rural Ohio to study "a stupid disease so rare it might

as well be smallpox these days!" All in all, he didn't
love her and didn't need a woman who couldn't be
loyal to his dream—or at least cut him some slack for
a couple of years to pursue it. Like Clark, she thought
he was an idiot for sinking so much of his own money
into this clinic and giving up a huge salary. He had two
possible grants pending, but nothing had come through
so far—probably wouldn't, until he showed some
progress.

His cell phone sounded with the first notes of *The
Triumphal March* from *Aida,* and he went back into his
bedroom to snatch it up. Caller ID told him it was
Clark, so he punched on the phone as he padded naked
into the kitchen to pour himself some grapefruit juice,
hoping it would serve as battery acid and help him get
moving.

"Are you demented, calling me at this hour of the
morning?"

"Hey, pal, you're just lucky to have any friends
after that exit you made from Metzler-Reich. They
may have been civil and handed you a bundle of sep-
aration pay, but as the fair-haired boy—"

"The day I'm fair-haired, hell will freeze over—"

"Genetically determined color of hair noted. But
you gotta watch Brad Dixon right now, since you've
gone off on your own and may come up with info he
wants."

"Both Brad and Andrea Dixon understand my decision. It's what he did fifteen years ago, when he left
HealGene in Atlanta and started Metzler-Reich. Listen, Brad even sent me exorbitantly priced new software called BLAST that rockets through data to

compare DNA sequences, which I was gonna buy myself. And he e-mailed me that something else is coming my way."

"Better hope it's not a lawsuit, once you turn up something new about treating aging. Thar's gold in them thar hills, boy. But remember, your best bud is a patent lawyer who's gonna make sure you keep the profits from any discoveries you make—though if you had a brain in that brilliant head of yours, you'd have picked a more lucrative disease to study, like cancer or the common cold, not some rare childhood illness that can't be instantly turned into billions for drugs and—"

"Yeah, I hear you, Counselor," Mark interrupted. "Get the dollar signs out of your eyes, and let's not have this discussion again, okay? At least, not right now."

It was well-trod territory between them. Metzler-Reich was a Cleveland-based pharmaceutical megacompany, where Mark, now thirty-three, had begun working as a geneticist just out of the Ohio State University med school and had stayed for eight years. Brad Dixon was its dynamic, Fortune 400 CEO, one of *Time* magazine's "Founders with One Foot in the Future."

Biotech pharm firms like MR and HealGene were the Goliaths of the gene-mining industry in a cutthroat business. Part of the real reason Mark had left was that some pharms were rushing discoveries through the multibillion-dollar world of genetic testing and treatment too fast to be sure they were really safe.

Mark had left MR for another reason too: lab re-

search just wasn't his thing. Besides being a molecu-
lar biology major geneticist, he was also a nonpracticing pediatrician. Fascinated by a rare childhood
disease—natal accelerated aging, or NAA—that he'd
stumbled across in research, he'd wanted to get out in
the field to treat patients. And the nearest "field" that
had the most cases—three living ones, as far as he
knew—was Maplecreek in Roscoe County, Ohio,
among the so-called Plain People.

"All right, new subject," Clark said. "Any good-
looking women under those bonnets and long skirts
down there?"

"It's the least of my worries. I'm hardly going to
chase women, when I need to be chasing lethal genes
in their people."

In their gangly, gawky middle-school years, since
Mark's and Clark's names rhymed and they used to be
as inseparable as twins—fraternal twins, since their
looks were as different as night and day—friends had
jokingly called both of them *Ark,* pronounced some-
what like the sound of a barking seal. What saved both
of them from being branded straight-A nerds in high
school was the fact they were tennis and track letter-
men, good-looking and good with girls.

The two had known each other since Mark was
adopted into the Ioconos family at age five. The backyard of the Ioconos faced the Quinn's property over a
railroad track. Clark's huge Irish family had lived on
the other side of the tracks in more ways than one.

The Quinns were dirt poor and Mark's elderly
immigrant parents not much better off, but both boys

were bright and brazen, and put themselves through undergrad and grad school. Clark conquered law while Mark went into medicine on scholarships and gut-hard work.

Despite his Catholic background, Clark had been married and divorced twice because he was such a workaholic; however, Mark couldn't criticize his friend's work ethic. He'd always been driven too, though he liked to think his motivation was helping people—as well as a hunger to do something unique in medical research, something worthy of fame. The fortune stuff, he'd leave to Clark.

"You coming down to see this place again?" Mark asked, flinching as the sharp taste of the grapefruit juice hit him. "It's looking a hell of a lot better than when I bought it."

"Soon as I can get free. You got it rewired for all your computers?"

"Ready and raring to go, at least in the hardware and software department. Now all I've got to do is make some inroads among the flesh-and-blood Amish. All three NAA kids live less than two miles away."

"Get yourself a horse and buggy and grow a beard."

"Don't laugh. I've already been invited to an Amish wedding by the community spokesman, Luke Brand. He's been pretty friendly, though I know he was check-ing me out."

"His kid's wedding?"

"His. He's a widower, marrying—get this—a former cop who used to work with my uncle on the force in Columbus. Uncle Mike and his wife are coming for the ceremony too, so I'm putting them up here one night."

"The ceremony will be in German, you know. I've read it's Old German too, the language of Luther. Hey, maybe you can teach them *Italiano*."

"You know not to try being cute with me until at least noon. Besides, I'd probably make more progress wooing them with my Umbrian cooking. I saved a few pasta pots when I sold off the kitchen stuff. Maybe I can ply them with penne tartufate, huh? They cook like crazy here, but there's no wine, except for medicinal use."

"Man, I love that pasta of yours with the truffles! If I bring some down soon, you can cook it up, deal?"

As they hung up, Mark realized he missed Clark. Until he'd sold his house and moved here, they'd lived just a few blocks apart in Shaker Heights, a upscale suburb of Cleveland and a far cry from the neighborhood in which they'd started out. Clark's flourishing patent-law firm was not far from MR, so this was the first time in years they didn't live and work close together.

Mark finally showered and dressed. He wore khakis and a long-sleeved shirt under his lab coat, but it was so cold he added a V-neck sweater. He couldn't afford to put in a new furnace after he'd purchased, renovated and rewired this thirty-year-old brick ranch house near downtown Maplecreek. In his vintage kitchen, he grabbed a power bar and poured himself the first of many cups of black coffee, then walked to the old living room—now divided into his reception room and office—and looked out onto the main drag as he gulped breakfast.

Most places in this area were Victorian or good old Midwest clapboard farmhouses. The only two ranches he'd seen were right across from each other on the eastern fringe of town. The second brick one—ironically, another clinic, this one a veterinarian's—was run by Dr. Jesse Cutler, who also used a big shed behind his office for the larger animals. Cutler had dropped in once or twice and been real curious about what was going on. The guy seemed to do a ton of business over there, Amish going in and out all the time, and that's just what Mark hoped would happen here.

"Leah, why do you have to be so stubborn?" Jesse Cutler demanded, his voice rising. "I told you that you didn't have to pay full price. Your Nell bounced back real quick."

"I know what it costs to treat a horse with the gripes, Doctor," she said, not wanting to argue but rushing to conclude this business. It was just her luck that his receptionist was not in and the doctor was. Jesse Cutler, DVM, Animals Large and Small, as his sign out front said, was sweet on her, but that always left a bitter taste in her mouth.

And not just because he wasn't Amish. The town's only veterinarian was Mennonite, a group that had splintered from the Plain People years before and were much more liberal. Jesse's people drove cars, went to college and used churches instead of homes for worship. Some former Amish became Mennonite, and the two groups worked together at times and got along fine, though their members didn't intermarry. Once one was committed to be Amish, courting and wedlock to someone not Plain was *verboten*, and punishable by excommunication.

But despite the fact Jesse was a doctor, he didn't seem smart enough to get the message that she was not interested in him that way. If Nell hadn't taken sick this winter, Leah could have avoided him, and his interest in her might not have kicked up again. He was good-looking, all right, with blond, neat hair cut almost Amish, a nice face and broad shoulders. If he'd been someone she'd wanted to court her, maybe she would have been tempted, but to put it as the world did, he just wasn't her type. Too finicky, too controlling, too... well, possessive.

"Leah," he said, finally taking the thirty dollars she'd laid on the counter, "just let me help you out a little. Is there anything you need for that old house? Can I run you into Pleasant or even Wooster in this cold, icy weather to get something for your darling baby? She's really precious." He reached over the counter in his reception room and bounced Becca's mittened hand a bit.

Leah had her bundled up and was toting her in a baby carrier she'd stitched up, with straps over her shoulders so Becca could hang against her chest, facing out, with support for her head and neck. The top of the baby's bonneted head was below Leah's chin level, and Becca's little legs, all warmly wrapped, dangled. But when Jesse bounced Becca's hand, he stroked Leah's breast with his thumb, right through her cape and dress.

Leah stepped back. She always liked to believe the best in people, and it could have been mere accident, but he was biting back a smirk. It wasn't smart to alienate the only vet in town, and she'd been taught to turn the other cheek—breast?—but she was done with Dr. Cutler.

She turned away. "Enough said and done. Goodbye, Doctor."

"Look, Leah, just give me a chance to court you, take care of you. I know you Amish are thick as—"

He stopped talking; she turned back to stare at him hard as his face went red. She headed for the door again, but couldn't resist a parting shot. "Were you going to say thick as flies or thick as thieves?" she asked as she opened the door.

She could hear him hurrying around the counter. "You're the brightest one of the bunch around here, Leah. You're a beauty, even under all those layers, and I like your tart tongue too—"

"Thanks for taking good care of Nell, but she's the only one who needed it."

She closed his own door in his face. At least he didn't follow her outside. Leah didn't even get back in the buggy but just led Nell—who got as jittery coming to the vet's as Leah did—across the street to an almost identical brick house.

The gene doctor's name, Mark Morelli, was newly painted on the mailbox. Katie Lindley, who had become Amish to marry Luke Brand, knew the man's uncle. That was some sort of recommendation, wasn't it? Amish women didn't walk into places to talk to English men alone unless it was really necessary. And this was.

As she approached, she saw that he'd put a sign on the front door that said, PLEASE USE SIDE DOOR, so she went around toward the driveway in the direction the arrow pointed. Besides two parking places for cars in the driveway—one filled with a small, sporty red car that would stand out like a sore thumb around here and slip all over the hilly roads—there was a hitching post, which she used.

PEDIATRICIAN, read the top line of a small sign posted next to the back door. On the second line, it said CLINIC/GENETIC CONSULTATION AND TREATMENT.

She stopped and gasped. There were also big, bold letters in red paint—or was it blood?—scrawled right on the new-looking white door:

GET OUT JEANS DR!! DON'T PLAY GOD OR YOUR DEAD!!!

2

Mark saw the young Amish woman crossing the street, leading her horse and buggy, her baby strapped to her chest. The sight reminded him of a painting of the Madonna and Child, although this Madonna looked not beatific but either angry or damn determined. When he realized she was actually coming here, he hoped the baby didn't have some disease, especially not NAA. Some mothers noticed a problem with infants as young as nine months, but this child looked younger.

He went around to the side entry, still not daring to believe she was coming here. Except for two visits by Luke Brand and one from Luke's brother, Moses, the new Amish bishop, the Plain People had not yet crossed his doorstep. He was undecided whether to distribute pamphlets explaining exactly why he was here or to just go ahead and call on Amish families. Luke had told him where the three families who had NAA children lived.

He gave the woman a minute to knock on the door before he opened it.

"I'm Leah Kurtz," she said, both arms around the

baby, "and I came to talk to you about some things. But I'm afraid someone has marked up your door real bad with a threatening note."

She gestured with a gloved hand, and he stepped outside to look. He caught himself just before he swore.

"I'm real sorry," she went on. "I could help you clean it up."

"I think it's blood. Hopefully, just animal blood— yeah, see that pinfeather there? I'll report it to the sheriff, then clean up the mess. Please, come inside. That's okay, isn't it—if you step inside, Mrs....?"

"Just Leah Kurtz," she said, speaking quickly and nervously. "I'm not married and haven't had a baby, but Becca's still mine."

Huh, he thought, stunned. A virgin birth indeed. He'd always been amazed by the phenomenon of people who thought they saw the Virgin appear in a factory window or a cobweb. Yet this woman was a welcome vision and maybe the miracle he needed to get started with the Amish here. To top it off, despite the cloudy day, an errant shaft of sun struck them with such sudden, intense light they both blinked.

But he felt both furious and deflated about this hate message. Just when he hoped for so much in befriending the Amish, some stupid SOB—probably Amish— did this.

"I'm sorry if the poor, deluded soul who wrote this is Amish," Leah Kurtz said, as if she'd read his mind. "Especially if he or she is a young person, because I was the teacher the last eight years, and I taught them how to spell words like *you're* or *genes*."

He turned to take a close look at her. An expressive

face, with classic, regular features, emphasized by her tawny hair, which she wore pulled straight back under her cap and bonnet, though a few tendrils had cork-screwed loose. Her creamy complexion was perfection. She wore not one smudge of cosmetics, but her full lips were rosy and her cheeks were either wind burnished or blushing. Her heavily fringed eyes were as clear green as emeralds, the like of which he'd never seen without someone wearing colored contact lenses. He was so surprised at the entire package of smarts and innocence, he almost forgot what she'd said, before he blurted, "You taught them to spell words like *genes?*"

"Well, only this year, when my dear friend became ill from Regnell anemia, which led to fatal acute mye-logenous leukemia, and I heard a geneticist was com-ing to town," she admitted. Surprised again, he opened the defaced door for her and inhaled the scent of pine soap and fresh outdoors as she toted the baby past him into the clinic.

To hell with the hate message, Mark Morelli thought as he closed the door and hurried after her. If there were any gifts from God around this place, he'd bet that one had just walked in.

If Jesse Cutler had made her edgy, this man was worse, only in a different way. Leah needed Dr. Mark Morelli to advise her on several things, but he looked like she'd always thought the devil must. She hardly believed in the red suit, horns and tail version. No, Satan would be smooth, sleek and enticing.

Mark Morelli was darkly handsome, with hair so black it shone bluish in the sun. His eyes were the rich brown of spring soil, and he made lightning-fast but deep eye contact that pulled you in. His mouth was firm, taut and a bit crooked in one corner, and she'd never seen such straight, white teeth. When he frowned, like now, his thick eyebrows almost met over his strong nose, and his nostrils flared when he was angry. He was lean and nearly six feet tall, much taller than most Amish men. But the thing that made her most uncomfortable was his beard shadow. As a woman used either to clean-shaven, unwed men or bearded married ones, his unshaven jaw reminded her of a mask on the lower half of his rugged face.

"Please, let's sit down in the waiting room," he said, indicating a black leather couch. "Can I get you some coffee?"

"Sure, that would be nice," she said as she shrugged the baby-carrier straps off her shoulders.

"Milk or sugar?" he called to her from the other room.

"No milk but I like it sweet. Amish love their sweets, you know." She took Becca out of the carrier and, holding her, walked to look closer at the amazing work of framed art on the wall. About five feet high and two feet wide, the glass-covered print was of multicolored twisting strands of beads. No, not beads. She recalled seeing a picture of this pattern in a book she got from the library.

She propped Becca up in a corner of the couch, then sat down carefully. The sofa was soft, and she sank into it. If she had known this man better, she would have told him the Amish would feel more at home with a hard wooden bench. Through an open door just down the hall before the kitchen where he'd gone, she could see what appeared to be several TV screens, making sounds and spewing colors.

"My lab," he said as he came back in. "Computers, data banks, fax, printers. What do you think of my half-cooked-spaghetti picture there," he asked, nodding toward the print. "My best friend gave it to me."

"I suppose your Amish patients will think it looks like a quilt pattern instead of a double-helix DNA strand."

She saw he almost spilled her mug of coffee, but managed to put it on the end table by the couch. Some musical notes went off in the distance. "Yeah, it is a double helix. Just a sec," he told her, turning back to the kitchen. "That's my cell."

His kitchen looked larger than a cell, and she realized he meant his cell phone. Evidently he didn't take the call, because he came right back in.

"You have a beautiful baby," he said, curling his index finger and gently stroking Becca's cheek.

"My adopted daughter, Rebecca Yoder, but everyone calls her Becca. Many Amish have nicknames—mine was Lee." Why was she rattling on like this? "Becca's mother was my friend who died…" Her voice caught.

"I admire anyone who adopts a child," he said. He sat catty-corner on a matching leather chair from her, perhaps intentionally keeping his distance. His hands often gesturing, he leaned forward, as though he studied her intently. He cleared his throat. "I was adopted myself."

"Oh." Their gazes snagged and held before Leah

looked away at Becca, who seemed content but curious. Dr. Morelli had a deep, soothing voice, despite the fact he appeared a bit jumpy. "Becca's one of the reasons I came to talk to you," she went on. "If you're planning to do any studies on Regnell anemia, I'd be most grateful, for Becca's sake and in memory of her real mother."

"But you're her *real* mother now, and don't let people tell you different. Biology is important, but we've learned that environment—and that certainly includes adoptive parents—affects everything too. To answer your question, though, the defective gene sequence for Regnell has already been discovered and patented. I'm pretty sure they're in the clinical-trial stage with it, though it can have a sudden onset and progress so quickly some patients are lost."

Leah nodded, blinking back tears.

"That must have happened to your friend, especially if she had a pregnancy." He cleared his throat. "Have you had Becca tested?"

"She's a carrier, they said. It was shown in a chromosome-breakage test."

He leaned back in his chair before he sat forward again. "Leah, I've got to admit your knowledge of this surprises me, although I expect the Amish to support my genetic studies once they understand why I'm here."

"And why *are* you here? Not just for the lovely scenery, I assume."

"You know," he said, "it is partly the scenery." His eyes glazed over for a moment, for the first time not focusing so intently on her. "My grandfather wanted to take me in after my parents died, but couldn't really handle it, since he was quite sick. Anyhow, when I was twelve, he took me on a trip to his native Umbria in Italy. My adoptive parents were thrilled I could go, since they never had any money for travel. Anyway, it was the trip of a lifetime," he said with a sigh.

She was instantly curious, about the place and this fascinating man. "Umbria is beautiful?" she prompted.

He nodded slowly, as if seeing it all again. "Rolling hills, small towns, simple lifestyles with genuine people—sausage is even one of their specialties there."

"It all does sound familiar."

"Like here, they appreciate their food, simply prepared. I remember bundles of hay in the fields...well, enough of that. Just let me say that, except for the fact that Umbria doesn't have many tourists, this area in the heart of Amish country reminds me of that place and trip and time."

"Is your grandfather still living?"

"No," he said and his deep voice caught. "He died just two months after our return. I'd gone back to my adoptive parents in Cleveland, and I never—saw him again. I figured out later," he went on in a rush, "that he'd taken very few of his meds—drugs—on that trip so that he could stay alert, and that he'd been in very bad pain. And that he'd spent almost his last dollar for us to go. Now, how did I get off on all that?" His eyes misted; he looked down at his feet and cleared his throat.

"But what wonderful memories of a man and place you still treasure. Maybe it was your grandfather's illness that made you want to become a doctor, too." Their eyes held again.

"That, and losing my parents. I think you're right, and very perceptive, Leah. I'd give *anything* to keep people from aging or dying."

"But that's God's plan, and part of living. Luke Brand says you're a nonpracticing pediatrician. Is that because you'd rather spend time with machines—" she gestured toward his lab "—than with patients?"

"I need to spend time with both. I am a *former* nonpracticing pediatrician. I intend to set up a practice. But, as I explained to Luke, I'm here to study a rare genetic disease that strikes children, natal accelerated aging. It also has the acronym—the nickname—NAA."

"I know what an acronym is, Doctor."

"Touché. And I'll bet the students who were in your classroom the last eight years do too."

"They'd better."

He smiled at her and it lit his whole face, making her feel warmer. He seemed so intense, so passionate. She'd never seen a man gesture with his hands so much or have such sudden shifts of voice tone or expression. Although he wasn't saying anything now, he still regarded her so directly she felt as if he touched her.

Suddenly, he shifted sideways in his chair and reached for a little box hanging from his belt. He glanced down at it, frowned, then ignored it again. "Sorry," he said. "My pager. I'll get it later." But he pulled yet another little device from his lab-coat pocket, took out a little plastic pen and, with the tip of it, tapped away at the small screen.

This man needed some speed bumps in his life, Leah thought, just like the ones they'd put on Main

Street because tourists were driving through so fast it was bad for buggy traffic. English people usually came to Amish country to unwind, but she bet he hadn't really relaxed since that trip to Italy.

Dr. Mark Morelli was a bundle of nerves. Maybe that's why she was so instinctively nervous around him, like it was catching. It was a different kind of thing entirely from how she felt with Jesse Cutler, or with Joseph Lantz, years ago, for that matter. For some reason she couldn't explain, she yearned to help this man, not run from him.

"I know three children who have NAA," she said. "I'm quite close to the Kline family, and their Susie suffers bad with it. Seth, the oldest brother, says they'd like you to take a look at her, but they're already burdened with medical bills."

He suddenly looked as excited as a child. "That's exactly what I'm here to do and for free, if there's financial difficulty."

"I also wanted to recommend that you consider hiring Seth as a helper if you need one. He's only seventeen, but he's the brightest scholar I ever had and willing to sweep up or whatever you need."

"Leah, you've made my day. And if it weren't for that bloody threat on my clinic door, I'd have hired *you* as my assistant."

"Oh, right. With all these fancy, modern devices, I'm sure an Amish wom—"

"Hear me out," he said as he jumped up and began to pace. Becca watched him as closely as Leah did, following with her eyes each time he passed. "Not as a lab assistant. I've had two offers of that already and turned them down because I want to remain independent, even though those offers came from friends. I want an assistant who will be a bridge to your people—a community liaison."

She thought for a moment he'd define that word for her, but he'd evidently learned his lesson and plunged on. "Believe it or not, these are still the dark days of genetic testing. Until technology matures, case histories are of utmost importance. They are as predictive as the tests themselves and more cost-effective."

"The Amish rely on worldly doctors," she tried to assure him.

"Good, but you could be a PR spokesman—spokeswoman—for me, in a way. What I need is someone who knows the Amish families, who can visit them to write up family trees for me."

Stopping by the front window, he spun toward her and stopped pacing. "Leah, I am dedicated to finding out what causes aging, in certain children, seven times faster than normal, so that they have arthritis, strokes and heart attacks at age five and die by age thirteen. Have you known any kids other than the three you mentioned who have that curse?"

"Yes, two others, dead now. But the Amish call such children a blessing not a curse. God wouldn't entrust a disabled or diseased child to a family unless they could love and care for them—and bear up under such pain and grief. And they are such loving, special children, they give back even more than they get."

"Ah," he said. "See how much I have to learn about your people?"

"And you're offering me a job, taking these family

histories?" Her pulse pounded even harder than it had when she'd first come into this clinic. Suddenly, the job at the quilt shop seemed dull and pointless.

"As I said, before that writing on the door, maybe," he admitted, flinging a gesture toward the side of the clinic. "In case that's not just some empty lunatic threat, I can't have you, with a baby, going out for my—"

"I'm not afraid, and I'd like to do it," she said, standing to face him with Becca in her arms. "I know the scholars and their families, healthy and not. Why, I've been teaching for years and had just begun to teach a second generation!"

He laughed, and the sound was deeply musical. "Yeah, you're a real old-maid schoolteacher, all right. I could use your help with occasional German translation, too. But I can't allow you to risk—"

"All life's a risk, Dr. Morelli. Everything worth having's a risk, but you've got to trust God and go on. You just admitted you're taking a risk opening this clinic on your own. I'd like that job, for the sick children. Even for Becca and her real—her first—mother."

"If you'll send your former scholar Seth to see me, and if I can get him to ride shotgun for you when you make your rounds to visit families, I'll consider hiring you. I need you badly."

She knew what he meant, all right, that he needed her to reach her people, but his words—the man himself—moved her deeply.

"But when you said shotgun, you didn't mean that," she said. "You don't think—"

"I know your people won't carry weapons. Just a figure of speech. Let's try a partnership. You come back after I talk to Seth Kline, and maybe we're in business. I'd be able to pay you about two hundred dollars a week."

She just gaped at him, holding Becca tightly to her breasts. That was a fortune, especially compared to what she would have earned at the quilt shop. Why, Sam sent her less than that, though he'd evidently come into some extra money lately. This man must be very rich. "A week?" she managed to get out.

"Right, a week, because I realize with the baby, the job would be only part-time. And if your relationship with me causes you any grief, either with your own people or with whatever moron decorated my door, promise me you'll let me know."

Your relationship with me. The words echoed in her head. *Let's try a partnership...we're in business...I need you badly.*

He extended his hand. Though Amish men seldom shook hands and Amish women never did, she bounced Becca to one arm so she could clasp his. The coffee must have warmed her up, or he must have a really good furnace in here, because for the first time since she'd moved to the Yoder house this winter, Leah wasn't cold.

"Is it hot in here?" she asked.

She wasn't sure why, but he laughed again. "I'm surprised too," he said, "but I'd say so."

"You want me to make a big deal of this and try to scare the graffiti perp off?" Sheriff Ray Martin asked Mark. He had reported the incident after Leah left and the sheriff had driven over to take a look at the bloody threat.

"It's more than graffiti, Sheriff."

"Yeah. Didn't mean to downplay it, but I been up to my eyeballs in so much crap from kids around here lately."

"So you think this is kids?"

"Just a minute, and I'll explain, Doc." He flipped open a small notebook from his shirt pocket and clicked open a ballpoint pen. Mark watched him copy the threat word for word.

The sheriff looked to be mid-fifties, with a military haircut and bearing, though his stomach was going, literally, to pot. He was barely shorter than Mark, and managed to look quite official in his crisp brown-and-tan uniform. His sharp hazel eyes darted from Mark to the door, then to his notebook.

"Gotta tell you," he said, "I don't have any one suspect comes right to mind, but, yeah, it could have been some kid, even an Amish one. During their running-around time, some of them drink or get drugged up on cold pills or cough syrup—robitripping, they call it. Some of them—English and Amish—smoke dope, or even shoot up."

"Amish kids?"

"Yeah, and I swear I'll find the suppliers if it's the last thing I do around here. Used to be a nice rural town, but we got us some kind of druggie pipeline lately. Sorry if I sounded flip at first. I'll look into this best I can. You're an asset to our community, so anything I can do to help, just let me know."

"I appreciate that. I don't want to rock any boats right now, just to report the incident," Mark told him, hunching deeper into his leather jacket.

"So, far's you know, only you and Leah Kurtz saw

it—not counting the jerk who did it. Damn, I thought hate crimes 'round here were dead and gone, if you'll excuse the way I put that."

"Luke Brand said those hate crimes were against the Amish themselves, and they'd been stopped."

"They have been. Luke been extending the Amish welcome mat?"

Mark nodded. "I've been invited to his wedding tomorrow."

"Leah's Luke's niece."

"I didn't know that."

"Amish connections are like one big spiderweb, but bet you knew that. It's half the reason you're here, right?"

"True. An isolated Amish population that tends to intermarry is perfect for genetic study."

"Just keep in mind, in case this threat turns out to be anything, you better not have Leah involved," the sheriff said, snapping his notebook closed.

"I thought the same, but she's adamant, Sheriff, and evidently needs the money for a part-time job I offered her." Mark could tell the man didn't approve, but he went on, "Frankly, with her schoolteacher past and sharp mind, she's perfect to collect the data. She'd do visitations and write up family connections for me, check out what symptoms or diseases people recall their parents or grandparents had. I'm going to hire a local kid to ride with her, so she's not out alone."

"Gotta admit, she's a rare one. Amish girls marry young, but she's stayed single and she's real independent, now more'n ever with this baby she took on. I'll help to keep an eye on her, and you do that too, Doc. 'Sides, she's easy to look at, right?"

When Mark didn't answer, the sheriff turned to study him. The man seemed helpful and friendly, but Mark couldn't decide if he liked this guy or not. But what did it matter, as long as the sheriff did his job?

"I'll file this report and keep my eyes peeled for possible authors of this nice little note. See you at the wedding, then," Sheriff Martin said and touched two fingers to the big brim of his hat in a sort of salute. As he started back for the cruiser he'd parked in the driveway, he called back over his shoulder, "But don't be expecting no fancy doings like you're pro'bly used to. See you."

Leah recognized the English woman who rang her doorbell that afternoon, not from having seen her before, but from her friend Katie Lindley's description. It must be Louise Winslow, the new mayor's wife. Despite the fact she wore a full-length leather coat, a scarf and gloves, Leah saw her patchy-looking pink and white cheeks and chin where the wool scarf wasn't wrapped quite tight around her face. Mrs. Winslow, Katie had said, suffered from psoriasis, and her entire body was broken out in blotches. Although Mayor Winslow was a handsome, social person who was always out and about, Leah had heard that his wife was almost a recluse.

Leah fumbled with the chain lock on the front door. When she opened it, she was surprised to feel the sun had warmed the day. The scarf and gloves the woman wore must be because of her disease. Leah didn't feel so bad about letting in a draft now, for Becca slept in her crib in the far corner of the room.

Mrs. Winslow, a tall brunette who was probably in

her early forties, wore big sunglasses and carried two wrapped presents in her arms.

"I'm Louise Winslow, Leah, and I'm hoping you're going to Katie Lindley's wedding tomorrow and can deliver this bigger box for me. Each day I've felt well enough to go out, I haven't managed to catch her at home, with the wedding plans and all. I know you're a friend of hers."

"Oh, sure, I'd be happy to do it. You want to step in a minute? How did you find me?"

"My Amish maid, Sarah Wengerd, mentioned you lived out here with your baby. I hope you won't think I'm being presumptuous, but I brought a baby gift too."

Mrs. Winslow stepped inside and put the large gift, wrapped in silver wedding paper with a huge white bow, down on a chair. She took her sunglasses and scarf off. Leah tried to focus on her gray eyes, but it was hard, because, as Katie had said, her skin looked grotesque.

"The truth is," Mrs. Winslow went on, "I didn't know if Katie would accept a gift from me, considering that she had a run-in with my husband. But I really wanted to offer my friendship to her—to you, too. It's several large serving pieces of French Limoges china for her ready-made family. But tell her the design has nothing to do with Marie Antoinette—she'll understand."

"I'll tell her, but you didn't need to bring a baby gift."

"Oh, I wanted to. I adore babies, though I never managed to have one of my own—the greatest regret in a life full of them. And to think you had one just handed to you. Why," Louise said as she followed Leah's glance across the room toward the cradle, "is she in there? I'm sorry I was talking so loud," she said, whispering now as she handed Leah the smaller package.

"That's all right," Leah assured her as she began to open the beautifully wrapped gift. The wrapping paper had big pink daisies with a smiling baby's face in the middle of each one. "She sleeps really hard, unlike me."

"Sometimes," Mrs. Winslow whispered, with a pointed glance at the pillow and folded blanket on the sofa, "it's hard to sleep in a house alone. I know."

They approached the crib. Becca slept on her back, her head turned this way. "Oh, she's adorable," the woman said in an awed voice. Leah was touched to see her eyes fill with tears. She completely understood the impact of such wrenching longing. "I'm so happy for you, my dear. Frankly, I'd love to have children, especially without my husband around to screw things up."

Leah's eyes widened.

"Sorry. Mustn't slander the mayor. I'd love to hold her, but maybe some other time, as babies need their sleep. I hope and pray that my face wouldn't scare her."

"Oh, no, I'm sure that wouldn't be the case."

"Well, I'm off—in more ways than one," she said with a little laugh that seemed meant just for herself. "Take good, good care of your precious bundle of joy."

Leah watched her go as she stood at the door and continued to unwrap the gift. It was something called an activity toy, with all sorts of bright, noise-making doodads hanging from it, to tie over a crib. Leah was deeply touched, especially when she saw the gracefully hand-written note included:

*My thoughts are with both of you. I know it must
be a dream come true. May your baby always be
healthy and happy.*

Leah glanced down at the wedding present Mrs.
Winslow had left for Katie. Becca *was* a dream come
true—or half of one, at least. For tomorrow, Leah
would smile and laugh with the others at another wedding of another dear friend, and yet be selfish enough
to still long for one for herself.

Feeling strangely depressed when she knew she
should be counting her blessings, especially after the
offer of that exciting job with Dr. Morelli, Leah bundled
Becca up after her nap and headed out for a short walk.

Spring, she dared to hope, was in the air. Forsythia
and pussy-willow bushes were heavily budded, though
no crocus had peeked through the snow yet. She had
intended to stroll into the stand of maples to see how
much sap the trees, now all tapped with buckets hanging from them, had produced. But two men she didn't
recognize were in the back woodlot, so she went past
the cemetery and down the road toward the ravine. The
crooked stream at the bottom was still frozen, and
snow clung to the shadowed north side, but the foot-
path was clear and gentle—no steep climbs on this end
of the ravine, unlike at the other end. Leah chattered
and sang to Becca as they went, putting a tune she
made up to part of a poem by Shelley:

*"A widow bird sat mourning for her love
Upon a wintery bough:*

The frozen wind crept on above
The freezing stream below.
There was no leaf upon the forest bare,
No flower upon the ground,
And little motion in the air
Except the mill-wheel's sound."

She climbed the path on the other side, as she had on her earlier solitary walk, and saw the shortest train she'd ever seen, an engine and one car, stopped at the AgraGro Mill across the field. That certainly wouldn't haul much newly ground flour away.

She'd heard the mill had been built so far out of town because it could actually endanger houses, if they were built too close. Grain-dust explosions, just like sawdust ones at lumber mills, could be as violent and deadly as dynamite. But this scene looked so peaceful, so rural.

Walking across the stubble-filled cornfield, she shaded her eyes. Some of the older parts of the two storage silos had recently been rebuilt. The place still needed painting. A man was on the lofty silo roof doing some sort of repairs. He hung on a tether like a spider.

As she watched, the train pulled away, heading north. "Maybe that's the little train that said, 'I think I can, I think I can,'" she told Becca as they walked back toward home. "I know you don't understand the books I read you now, German or English, but you will some-day. Lucky girl, to have a *maam* who's been a teacher."

Though the air felt warmer than it had in days, the ravine was shadowed, so she stretched her strides as she crossed it, ever careful with her footing. As she emerged on the other side and hurried past the pioneer cemetery, the Yoder house—*her* house—looked less forbidding to her. Surely it would soon seem like home. As if it had been decorated by the hand of God, melting icicles glittered from the eaves. Though she knew that was one sign of a poorly insulated house, it did look pretty. Just before she went up the walk, she glanced back, as always, at the angel statue.

But what was that on it?

Her heartbeat, already accelerated from her exertion, quickened. Both arms holding Becca tight, she walked toward the iron fence near the statue, but didn't go in the side gate.

Someone had decked the angel in a thick necklace of dried flowers. Had Louise Winslow left them, on some eccentric whim? It surely wasn't the work of the men checking the maples out back, who were gone now. No, more likely it was the gesture of someone who admired the angel—maybe even a descendant of the young woman buried here over a century ago—and had left the floral tribute while Leah had been on her walk.

She was perspiring, but a chill scratched at her spine. She forced herself to look closer. She could see no card or note on the garland or on the ground.

When she'd started her walk about a half hour ago, she was certain the flowers had not been there. And they were so much like the ones she and Barbara had draped on the statue two years ago. Those had been wildflowers, though, not store-bought blooms. And these, rustling in the breeze, were dried and just plain dead.

3

After Seth oversaw the other boys unhitching the horses and turning them out in the pasture, he put David Groder in charge of things and dashed into Luke Brand's house. It was overflowing with a hundred Amish and a few English guests. He figured the *hochzut* ceremony itself was a half hour away, and he wanted to talk to the *auslander Englische doktor* he'd seen park his bright red car and go inside. When Teacher Leah had arrived—earlier than the other guests, since she was one of the bride's sidesitters—she had told him to see the doctor about a possible job.

By tradition, the bride and groom were getting ready in separate rooms upstairs with their closest friends. Seth made his way through clumps of chatting people, including his own kinfolk, though his immediate family was not here yet. They were coming a bit late because Susie's arthritis always acted up in winter weather. She was especially excited about today. It pained him bad that she'd never see her own wedding day, unless this Dr. Morelli could help her.

Seth immediately spotted the gene doctor with an English couple, evidently his aunt and the uncle. The bride, Katie Lindley, had worked with Officer Morelli when she was a cop in Columbus.

Standing beside Sheriff Martin and his wife was one of the bridegroom's brothers, Daniel Brand, who had gone English, He was with his wife, the worldly lawyer Brett.

Dan had gone to the world before he chose to be baptized Amish, so he wasn't under the curse of the *meidung,* the Amish word for shunning. Brett and Dan stood with their two girls. Tall, pretty teenage Jennifer was really Brett's niece, and Dan and Brett's own child, Melanie, was still using a walker until she regained all the movement in her legs. That was the result of a bad fall and a coma. It was the same accident that half blinded one of the groom's children, Eli, though he was fully recovered now. Eli stood with his younger sister, Sarah, at the bottom of the stairs, waiting for the bridal couple to descend and make their four-person family official.

Seth's gaze studied the few other English visitors, but somehow, Dr. Mark Morelli still stood out. Maybe it was because, like Seth, he kept looking around, real curious.

"Dr. Morelli." The three English turned his way, and the doctor nodded as if to encourage him. "I'm Seth Kline. Teacher Leah said I could talk to you about a job. I know this isn't the best place, but—"

"No, that's okay, Seth. Uncle Mike, you mind if I leave you two on your own for a few minutes?"

"Sure, sure. Guess we'd better get a seat, with this big crowd."

Rather than braving the kitchen, which was full of

the young couples in charge of preparing the big noon wedding feast, Seth and the doctor walked out the door onto the front porch. It was chilly outside, but they both wore warm suits. Seth listened intently as Dr. Morelli explained what he wanted from him and why he thought Leah needed an escort.

"Sorry someone left a cruel message like that," Seth told him. "My family, we'd have put out a welcome sign for you."

Dr. Morelli smiled. "The thing is," he said, putting a hand on Seth's shoulder, "I don't want Dr. Cutler to be left in the lurch with a lot of animals if you switch jobs. You'd better either be sure you can do both or give him time to find a replacement."

"Oh, *ja,* I can do both. My friend, David Groder, helps him too. Besides that, I work part-time collecting maple sap. There's lots of *rumspringa* guys like me need extra cash. Till then, it will be easier to have two of my employers right across the street from each other, even if I'm going out in a buggy with Teacher Leah sometimes. I can drive her in my courting buggy, since I'm not using it for that. Got no time. My runaround friends really been after me to party more lately, cut loose a little. But I got years ahead of me for that."

"You're a man after my own heart, Seth. I used to work more than one job when I was about your age, though I can't say I was as self-disciplined as you about not partying." Dr. Morelli pressed his lips together tight and nodded for a moment, as if he was remembering something. Then he went on, "Teacher Leah told me your family will be willing to let me treat your ill sister. I want to explain to you what I'm doing, how the lab works and all, because Leah said you're an excellent student."

Seth knew self-pride stunk, but he couldn't help grinning. "She's always after me to keep up my studies. Even," he said, lowering his voice, "to take off for a while to get more learning, work my way through tech school at least. Gotta go now, Dr. Morelli. I accept the job, and real glad I am about it, *ja*."

Seth hurried down the steps and started toward the familiar large, three-seated surrey turning into the driveway. "It's my folks," he called to the doctor. "My sister Susie too, if you want to come meet them."

Seth was real quick on his feet, so he was surprised how fast Dr. Morelli caught up with him.

Mark had met only one NAA sufferer, and the boy had been another doctor's patient, but it had been enough to make him want to dedicate years of his life to the rare and baffling disease. To have the brain and spirit of a youngster trapped in the body of an elderly, ailing person was beyond belief. And in the back of his mind, he'd always thought that if he could discover the mutated gene sequence that caused the sufferer's rapid aging, he might learn something about geriatrics in general.

"*Daad, Maam...*" Seth rattled off a spiel in German to his parents before he began introductions. Mark could see two bonneted daughters on the back seat of the surrey, behind Reuben and Miriam Kline, but the girls looked normal and too big to be Susie. It wasn't until their father introduced Ruth, Lizzie and Susie that he realized there were three girls sharing the back seat. The two older ones were sitting close with the delicate child between them to keep her warm, even under their lap blanket. His pulse pounded as he glimpsed Susie's wrinkled, wizened face and hunched shoulders, a little old woman at age six.

"Best we get out of the cold, and we're late," Reuben said with a nod at Mark. "Seth says Leah Kurtz is going to do some of your visits, but you come calling too—'less you want us to come in to town."

This was too good to be true. Leah and this boy had brought him good luck, that chicken-blood threat on his door be damned.

"*Danke, Herr Kline,*" Mark said, trying out his first German. "I'll be to see you in the next few days, and I'll bring Leah too."

Seth scrambled up into the wagon next to his father, and Mark hurried back into the farmhouse just in time to stand at the side of the crowded room as the bridal couple, separately, with their supporters, descended the stairs.

Leah spotted Mark Morelli right away as she came down the farmhouse stairs in Katie's wedding party. Despite his black hair, he almost blended in, for the Amish men were bare-headed today and Mark wore a black suit over a black, round-necked shirt, not so far from the cut of her people's Sunday clothes. As she went by behind the bride, her gaze caught his.

Leah thought both the bride and groom looked radiant, so happy and dedicated to building a life together after the trials they'd been through. Katie had blossomed since Luke had fetched her back from Columbus, where she'd gone after helping the Amish community stop the hate crimes against them. She'd found a new, good life here with Luke, his two children, his mother, Jacob Ida, and his big, extended family. Luke had only courted Katie for four months before she'd decided to turn Amish.

Leah took her place on the front bench with the other sidesitters. Turning her head slightly, she could see her mother, Levi Em, holding Becca, and her sister, Naomi, who was eighteen, sitting partway back on the women's side. Leah's mother's name was Emma, but many of the Amish not only had nicknames but went by their husband's names. That kept it clear who was who, among related families and friends. Eventually, the men they wed or a particular trait would differentiate them. Many men had distinctive nicknames like Speaker Luke or Carpenter Dan.

She lifted her gaze to note that, in the crowded room, Mark stood at the back with a few others. She saw her father, Levi, sitting just ahead of him with her brothers Isaac, age twenty-five, who was newly married, and Andy, twenty-three, who was betrothed. She made herself turn toward the front again. She knew she should concentrate on the *hochzut* service, for they were never long.

The bride wore a purple gown with the traditional white apron and cape, which she would never wear again until she was laid out in her coffin. Leah blinked back tears, remembering how frail Barbara had looked in her coffin—and how healthy and hopeful she had been on her wedding day.

The new bishop, Luke's brother Moses, conducted the ceremony. He read the traditional verses from the Book of Tobit, urging that a man "take a wife of the seed of thy fathers, and take not a strange woman to wife." If Katie had not converted, this marriage could never have been celebrated among the Amish. But that charge not to intermarry outside the circle of believers was one reason, Leah realized, that genetic diseases kept popping up among them.

She managed another glance at Mark. Though he wouldn't understand one German word being read, he seemed intent, almost impassioned, even when he was still and silent. She looked back to watch the couple clasp hands and the bishop cover their grasp to speak the final words of blessing. It was that simple, Leah thought, yet such a thing seemed to elude her. A smiling Katie and awed-looking Luke were now man and wife forever.

Things were hardly solemn from then on. After tables were carried in between the benches, the noise level swelled before the short silent prayer and then again as the huge meal began at noon. The wedding party, the bride and groom's closest family and friends, and the *auslander Englische* guests were included in the first of three seatings. Platters of chicken with bowls of sweet potatoes, gravy, coleslaw and the traditional creamed celery were offered, followed by cakes and pies. As one of Katie's closest supporters, Leah sat at the *eck,* the corner table, which was decorated with candles and, because of the season, store-bought flowers.

Leah stared at the arrangement of white lilies, yellow tulips and delicate baby's breath in front of her. Katie had ordered these from the florist in Pleasant. Maybe she should go there or borrow a phone at Mark's clinic to ask the florist if anyone had bought a garland of flowers recently. But it couldn't have been too recent, since the angel's garland had been dead.

Laughter lifted her thoughts as humorous gifts were given to the wedding couple, along with the traditional gas lantern and knotted clothesline that symbolized the knotty problems there would be among the smooth days of their marriage. When the bridal party stood to stretch their legs before the next seating, for those at the *eck* would stay for each group, Mark came up to talk.

"And I thought Italian weddings laid on great food," he told her. "By the way, I hired Seth. Can you drive in to the clinic tomorrow, so we can go over how I'd like the family trees recorded?"

"Oh, sure. What time?"

"Around ten would be good. I'll see if we can get Seth to show up too. I've been invited to the Klines' to meet Susie, and I'd like you to go with me."

"Good for you, but we can talk to her now, if you want—I see her coming in for the second seating. She was probably upstairs with the other girls—they're all giggles and excitement today, how well I remember."

She led Mark toward the three Kline sisters, and bent down to Susie's height. "Teacher Leah!" Susie squealed and hugged her, even before Leah could put her arms around the girl. How slight she felt, this child who looked like a midget in her seventies.

"Susie Kline, I'd like you to meet Dr. Morelli."

"Outside already, I kinda met him," she said, smiling. "And watching him during the service, I was, just like you."

Leah felt herself blush, so she was relieved Mark squatted to look right in the child's face. "Susie, I'm happy to *really* meet you. Leah and I are going to visit you tomorrow, okay?"

"Oh, *ja*. Only one thing. Please treat me like a kid and not just a disease, like those other doctors do."

Mark looked dumbfounded for a minute. His eyes narrowed and his mouth went taut. Was that how he regarded this child—all of them? Leah wondered. Were they just specimens or a means to his end? She didn't think so. She didn't want to think so.

"That's a deal," he told Susie. "And I won't ever forget."

"Can you step outside a minute, and we'll coordinate things with Seth about tomorrow?" Mark asked Leah as Susie and her sisters headed in to eat. "I haven't cooked Italian since I've been here, so I might just fix the two of you—Becca too, of course—a little pasta for lunch."

"She's just on formula," Leah said, before she realized he was teasing. Well, of course, a pediatrician, nonpracticing or not, would know all about that. Somehow, this man made her not think but just feel, and she'd have to watch that. He led her out the front door and around the house instead of plowing back through the crowded rooms and kitchens.

"Speaking of formula," he said, "I see I'm going to have to scrap mine and play it by ear around here with

Susie. Are the other two NAA kids such darling characters?"

"Both sicker than her and both boys," she said. "Ooh, it's looking like snow in those clouds. *'Shadows of the clouds have power to shake me as they pass.'*"

He stopped and turned to her. She halted and faced him so fast, her skirt belled out. Their eyes held.

"What's that from?" he asked.

"Wordsworth. I like his nature poems. I like all the Romantics, to tell the truth, because of their deep emotions."

"I haven't read any of them since high school."

"Too much science? Remember what Susie said— she's a kid and not a disease."

"Leah, your people have the power to shake me as they pass. Especially you."

She almost swayed toward him. Was he flirting? Worse, did she want him to? No, it was probably just a compliment, a heartfelt one. She began to tremble, not from the cold but from the wave of warmth— heat—she always felt near him.

"Here," he said, whipping his suit coat off in one smooth motion and putting it around her. Despite the wind, the jacket smelled of some delicious, tangy scent she could not name.

"Oh, I'm fine," she said, giving the coat back as if it had burned her. "I'm plenty warm-blooded."

"Good," he said, grinning at her as he put it back on.

Outside, near the Brand barn, where they expected to find Seth, they saw David Groder, who was going up and down the rows of parked, horseless buggies, jumping to peek into each. It looked like some strange game at first, for he held a chicken drumstick in his hand.

"David," Leah called to him. *"Was ist die Materie?"*

He turned to see who spoke. *"Ich kann ihn nicht finden Seth!"*

"He can't find Seth?" Mark asked her.

"That's it. David, he probably just went in the house for a minute."

"No," he said, switching to English. "After his parents got here, he said he'd watch the horses and buggies until the third seating. I should go in for the second, he said. Things are running late, so I came back out to tell him and to bring him a chicken leg."

"Maybe," Mark said, "he decided to watch the horses from the barn, out of the wind. Or had to run in to use the bathroom."

"Or to check on Susie," Leah put in. "He's always worried about how she's doing."

But their search through the barn and the house, as well as the nearby smaller house where Luke's widowed mother lived and through Luke's windmill shop, did not turn up Seth. The other boys who'd been assistant hostlers even searched the same places a second time.

As time went on and more people came outside to help look, Leah's stomach began to cramp. Seth's parents were worried now, and he'd never put them through that. The boy's disappearance cast a pall over the wedding. Sheriff Ray Martin, in civilian clothes, came out of the house to look around the barn and pasture where Seth had been in charge.

"You gotta admit he's prime for *rumspringa* fence-jumping," the sheriff told Seth's father, Reuben, as he

faced the cluster of concerned Amish. Leah saw that
Mark stood a bit off to the side.

"Not him," the bearded man said. "No signs of it,
you think?" he asked his worried wife.

"None," she said solemnly. "Some of his runaround friends took off for a while, though."

"There, you see," the sheriff said, lifting both hands,
then smacking them on his thighs.

"Teacher Leah," Reuben said, turning toward her,
"you see any signs of it in him? You seen a lot of them
take off time to time."

"No, absolutely not. Seth was too responsible for
that. He's been working at the vet's for over a year, and
was excited about two new jobs, one working for
Miles Mason tapping trees and gathering sap and a
new endeavor, working for Dr. Morelli."

Hatted and bonneted heads swung toward Mark.
Sheriff Martin folded his arms. His wife, Pam, had
come out to stand in the crowd too. Leah thought she
looked amazingly tanned compared to the rest of them
at this time of year, except for the sheriff, who always
looked ruddy.

Everyone hushed as Mark began to speak. "I don't
think he'd take off. He's a smart kid who could benefit from some further studies, but he's dedicated to his
work and family."

Murmuring in the crowd. "Still," David Groder
piped up, "other times and today, he said Teacher Leah
wanted him to get more learning, outside learning."

Eyes riveted her where she stood.

"That right, Leah?" Sheriff Martin asked, coming
closer.

"From time to time, but he would never have left now. He would not just run away, *rumspringa* or not, his friends cutting loose or not."

"Maybe," the sheriff said, "you just don't want to admit he'd take off, like I heard your fiancé did years ago."

A quiet, collective gasp came from her people. If the Amish had been thinking that, they would never have said it. Tears blurred Leah's vision; it was that nightmare over again, just as sudden. Katie, with her new husband, suddenly appeared and put an arm around her.

"That has nothing to do with this, Sheriff," Katie said. "And back when Leah's Joseph left, I heard the sheriff didn't do much, but I know we can rely on you to look into this."

"Look, Kat—Katie—bride of this lovely day," Ray Martin said, turning as if to face the two of them down, "you're Amish now, so act like it. These Amish kids take off all the time, come and go, since before I was sheriff here. A few don't even leave a note, do it on impulse. Happens all the time. The boy will show up. The parents want to file a missing person's report after a week or so—"

Leah wished Katie and Luke weren't leaving on a long wedding trip. As was tradition, they were going to visit his relatives in western Ohio, then, breaking with tradition, they were going with Luke's two children on a Greyhound bus to visit other relatives in Sarasota, Florida.

Leah saw Mark had come closer to her in the crowd. He mouthed to her, "He'll turn up."

She nodded, but turned away with Katie and Luke to go back into the house. If the sheriff wasn't going to look into this, somehow she was. Maybe Mark would help. She supposed they could be right, that it was the devastation of losing her own betrothed that made her react like this, but she couldn't help it. Something was wrong about Seth's taking off. Very wrong.

Leah couldn't sleep that night. It had started to snow, and a howling wind whipped the flakes in circles. Becca was in her usual deep slumber, oblivious to her mother's unease.

Though the Amish way was to forgive and forget, Leah was angry with the way the sheriff had dismissed Seth's disappearance and upset her people. Though they'd never say so, they too probably thought she'd overreacted because of Joseph's desertion. That's what it had been—desertion, not just some young *rumspringa* come-calling friend going to the world for a while. Very few Amish who went English in their running-around time never came back. And those that stayed English let people know where they were.

What if Mark Morelli wouldn't hire her now, without Seth? She'd already told Verna Spriggs, the Helping Hands Quilt Shop owner, that she had decided to take another job offer. But needing the money was only part of her reason for accepting the position. She wanted to help the doctor discover the defective genes, hidden among the healthy ones.

She stopped walking and stared out the window. The snow seemed to sweep sideways at times, obscuring even the maples near the house, let alone the driveway and cemetery. She pictured the angel there, head bowed, still standing guard, and hoped this wind would scatter those dreadful, dead flowers.

Leee-aah, the wind seemed to cry. *Leeee—aaaah.*

She recalled how the wind had shrieked here the night Barbara died. Shuddering under her long night-gown, she glanced at Becca. Leah was usually obsessed with watching her, awed, yet fearful that something would harm this precious life she'd promised Barbara she would protect with her own. Now, in the dim light of the single lantern, she saw the baby stir fitfully.

Strange, but what popped into her mind was how, years ago, she, Barbara and their siblings played hide-and-seek in the cornfields. *"Leee-aah,"* she heard Barbara's voice through the mist of memory. *"Catch me if you can...."*

Sometimes they'd drag their faceless Amish dolls along and thrust them out between the rows, then run to change positions. Once Joseph had taken their dolls and hidden them in the field, and they'd been panicked, trying to find them.

"Leee-aaah..."

She hugged herself hard to stop her trembling. No, that didn't sound like Barbara's voice. Did it? She walked across the room to glance up the dark stairs. The whine of wind didn't really come from up there, at least not more so than from down here. Maybe if she let Mr. Mason tap her trees, he'd agree to cut a few of the lower limbs for her. The wind whistling through them could be making that weird sound.

Worse, maybe it was all just in her head.

She went back to staring outside. The swirl of snow

made her almost dizzy, as if the big flakes sucked her into a white vortex of blankness. Was death's doorway like that, like stepping over the threshold into pure silent whiteness before heaven or hell?

The sound didn't come again; she felt better now. But she jumped when she heard a crunch, then a crash.

She turned down her lantern until it gutted out. What was *that* sound? It had been from outside, of that much she was sure. Then she realized that melting icicles could have dropped off the roof eaves in this wind.

All night, though she heard nothing else unusual, she kept her vigil, wondering and worrying about Seth. At last, the wind evidently shifted or weakened. She shoved her long hair back from her face. She was going to look like something the cat dragged in when she visited Mark and then faced Seth's poor parents, who must be worried sick too.

The next morning dawned overcast, but the snow had stopped. Though Leah expected to see drifts, the wind had scoured much of the snow away. It huddled in corners or on the northwest side of buildings and trees. She did see some icicles under her windows, so their fall must have been what she'd heard last night. Perhaps the wind howling through them before they crashed had made that strange sound. Then, after they fell, it was much more silent. Yes, surely that explained everything.

It would take her nearly half an hour to buggy into town, and she wanted to stop to see her mother at her bakery shop before she visited the clinic. At eight-thirty, with Becca bundled up, Leah went out to harness Nell. As she approached the shed, which had room for two horses and two buggies, though she only had one, she saw fresh footsteps in the scant snow.

She stopped and stared. Heavy prints, neither large nor small, in a way sexless. They appeared to go directly into the door of the shed, as if someone had just bumped into it—actually, as if they had walked through it. But the snow also showed that the doors hadn't been scraped open lately.

Hugging Becca tight, Leah began to breathe faster, almost to pant. Those weren't her tracks. They were bigger, like Barbara's. Her own tracks, from feeding Nell yesterday after the wedding, would have been covered or swept away by now. Wherever did these come from?

Burdened with both Becca and the diaper bag, she followed the single row of prints backward, until she saw their path. Gasping in a breath of cold air, she stopped suddenly. They began at the angel statue, which was now denuded of its garland. And they led from the statue through the side cemetery gate and—

They first went to the back door of her house, then turned away and headed for the driveway and the shed.

Had someone been at her door last night or looked in the kitchen window? What about Nell? Had someone been here during the storm last night, and taken or hurt her horse?

"Nell!" she cried as she carried Becca back to the shed and pulled one creaky door open. At her panicked voice, Becca started to whine, then wail.

The buggy was there untouched. Nell munched hay. At first glance, nothing was amiss inside. Bouncing Becca to calm her, Leah went farther in to scan the interior, snow crunching underfoot on the concrete floor. She looked down. No, snow hadn't blown or been tracked in. It was crushed, dead flowers.

4

Where was he? Who...? It was so black. Was he dead?

Pieces floated to him. Horses. Something about horses...

Pounding headache. No strength to open his eyes. Numb. Entire body. Floating. Heaven? Angel's voices?

Someone speaking. Nearby. He tried to snatch at words, at meaning.

"Did you use Telazol or Droperidol in that dart?"

"Telazol. It works for exotic animals, it works for a kid. I had to estimate his weight, so I hope I didn't overdo the dose."

"Our timing was great to corner him alone there. Thank heavens for our mole."

"Get a good blood sample before he starts to wake up."

Blood and moles, Seth thought. Dr. Cutler had a good side business killing moles. Tunnels in yards. They made tunnels you could twist an ankle in. Sometimes Jesse Cutler gassed them. But he'd heard he took them away live sometimes...cut them up...kept their blood, David said. Still, the man loved dogs, buried them so careful. Seth feared he was in the ground now, buried.

He tried to force his eyes open, to move his arms. Heavy, so heavy. Tied down? Hurt. Hospital?

Yes, he thought as he peered through leaden, slitted lids. Masks. They wore masks, coming close, bending over him.

If he was paralyzed, he'd rather die. A horse kick? Car? Surely, *Maam* and *Daad* would be here soon, but he couldn't recall hearing their names or seeing their faces.

He tried to say his name, but he only hissed.

"Is he coming to?"

"I'll make sure he doesn't."

Leah's mother, Emma Kurtz, owned and managed the Bread of Life Bakery on Main Street in the heart of Maplecreek. Leah had worked there, off and on, before she took the teaching job, and Emma employed a part-time staff of about a dozen Amish women. The familiar, yeasty smell and the warmth of the place hit Leah the moment she got within ten feet of the back door, where she'd tied Nell.

"I don't think your nose is in top shape yet, my Becca, but when it is and you're eating more than formula, you will love this place!"

She had chattered to the baby all the way into town, trying to calm herself after finding the footprints and the flowers. None of it made sense, except that someone was clearly trespassing. She'd read that, years ago, hobos rode the rails, hopping on and off rural trains to find shelter and food. She guessed she was the closest house to the tracks at the AgraGro Mill. Maybe someone got off a train, found the way to the nearest house. He was intrigued by, or even decided to pray at the angel, then headed for the shelter of the house and shed. But he had changed his mind, or had knocked and she hadn't answered because she couldn't hear him in the wind.

She shuddered. All she needed was some stranger knocking on her door at night. As for hearing her name shrieked outside, surely that was the wind or her imagination. She had to admit the house really got to her at times, but she was determined to make it hers and Becca's.

She wasn't sure if she'd tell about her nighttime visitor, because she didn't want to upset her mother or have her parents try to make her return to their house, even for the winter. She'd lived there far too long as it was. However much she loved her family, there was no way she was going to run back home.

"Levi Em's in her office," Ruth Miller called out. "Oh, that baby is so darling!"

Women who had been mixing, kneading and baking bread came for a closer look. By the time Leah got to the office, wedged in between the kitchen and the shop, her cape and Becca's little black bonnet bore the fingerprints of floury love pats.

"You're in town early," her mother cried as she bounced up from behind her desk, where she was evidently doing the books. Emma was plump, which she always said was good advertising for her shop. Leah herself had once been overweight from nervous eating, not to mention the bounty of Amish tables, but when she'd started teaching school, the weight had dropped off her like melting ice. Emma's brown hair was heavily silvered, but her grass-green eyes, which her daughters had inherited, shone magnified behind her wire-rimmed glasses.

"And how's my little sweetie and her *maam*, my big sweetie?" Emma teased as she lifted Becca out of her carrier to cuddle her.

Emma had once had a nervous breakdown, so she was extremely sensitive to others' problems. Leah knew when her mother asked how someone was, she meant it. As one of the few Amish women who'd been to a worldly psychiatrist, Emma sometimes resembled one herself.

"We're both fine," Leah told her, hoping that wasn't really a lie.

"Not upset about the sheriff's accusation that you urged Seth Kline to fence-jump?" Emma asked, pushing her wire-rimmed glasses up her nose when they slipped. "Forgive a mother for saying it, Leah, but you look like Becca's been keeping you awake at night. Bloodshot eyes, dark circles on that pretty face, *ja*, you can't kid me."

"Don't blame Becca. I just don't like the Yoders's bed, and I've been sleeping on the sofa until I can get a new one—which I will, as soon as I get my first wages from the gene clinic. Don't worry about me," she insisted, probably a bit too loudly.

"I do, though." Emma perched with Becca in her lap on the corner of her desk, while Leah stood against the door, her arms crossed. "Mothers always worry. You'll see."

"I know, *Maam*. I understand that better now."

Her lips pressed in a tight line, Emma nodded. "I know I've been such a mother hen lately, and I'm gonna level with you about why. It's not just 'cause I know how you suffered with Barbara's death. How you felt guilty for having Becca to love when she was gone."

"Yes," Leah said only. No use trying to skirt around that.

"Leah, I worry that you never really grieved for your big sister's death eleven years ago. You stepped in to try to help me, to take Katie's place if you could—"

"Which I *never* could," Leah put in, her voice catching.

"Of course not," Emma countered. "You are two entirely different people. And now you've lost someone else dear to you, a second sister. That's why I worry you're on the edge right now."

"The edge of what? Not a breakdown, like you had. That was because you got dependent on those Prozac pills."

"No, that was only what made it worse. Why, I even worried about the loss of Katie coming back to haunt you when you became friends with Kat Lindley, who took the name Katie. You'd lost your sister with that name, and I thought—"

"*Maam,* I'm not still grieving Katie's death, and I'm working on getting over Barbara's. I'm fine."

"But Katie's loss happened so close to when Joseph took off for the world. And you rose up so strong, so fast from all that. I just don't want these tragedies of your life to catch up with you."

"They won't, *Maam.* Yes, I tried to step in to take Katie's place when she died, because you needed help so bad. But that was the way I grieved. I don't pine for

Joseph anymore. Why, if I ever saw him, I'd give him a good piece of my mind."

"I'll bet you would," she said with a nod. "But Seth's taking off—"

"I can't accept that, but in a different way."

Her mother reached around the baby to grasp Leah's upper arm through her cape, then began to brush flour off her shoulder. "You just take care then. Getting so busy again might be a way of putting off the sadness, working hard with that new doctor, getting involved with those who are suffering, when you are too."

"But if I can help them—Susie Kline, the Esh and Kauffman boys—it will make me stronger, just like teaching did, just like having Becca does. Don't worry a bit about me, because I'm doing just fine."

"So I heard, more than once. All right then," Emma said with a decisive nod that bounced her glasses to the tip of her nose again. "I'll give you a loaf of fresh sourdough bread for your new employer. And you just remember, I can keep Becca here if you go out in weather that's bad or if the trip is too far."

"Ah, now I see. All this was just a ploy to get more time with Becca," Leah teased, hoping her voice sounded light. It scared her how well her mother knew her, maybe better than Leah knew herself.

"Think you've got it clear about how to record all of that?" Mark asked as the two of them sat side by side at his kitchen table. Becca napped, warmly covered in her plastic baby carrier, in the waiting room. "Run the key abbreviations for the chart by me again."

"Brackets go around the name of someone deceased," she said, ticking items off on her fingers. "SB for stillborn, C for carrier—once we find that out. DI means died in infancy. Oh, and a capital F followed by a pound sign before I list the number of family members."

"Good. Seth's not the only one who's a quick study."

They were silent a moment. They'd spent part of their time talking about him.

"I just wonder," she said, "if we should have an FJ abbreviation for someone who fence-jumped. These are large families, and it may come up from time to time."

"Let's add it," he said, resting his arm on the back of her chair. "Anything we can do to keep this many interconnected people straight will help. And, Leah, I want to clear the air about something," he added.

"I don't want you to think," she said, "the departure of my betrothed so long ago is what's making me worry about Seth."

"No, I didn't mean that. I'm sorry it happened, though."

"Water over the dam at this point, but it does seem strange how the guys I care about take off."

She sat back in her chair. Then, when she realized it felt as if he has his arm around her, she sat quickly forward again. They'd been shoulder to shoulder while he'd explained the sample family genetic chart he'd spread out before them. As for his clearing the air, she thought, she loved the scent of the air in this kitchen, a blend of aromas: pasta sauce he had bubbling on the stove, the bread she'd brought, and whatever that tangy citrus scent was emanating from him. He was clean shaven this morning, though she could still see the slightest hint of a beard line.

"One of the reasons," he began, when she'd almost forgotten he wanted to say something, "that the Amish are perfect for genetic studies is that they have, especially by modern American standards, huge families. In reducing all the family members to numbers and codes, I want you to know I'm not making a judgment on the size of the family, beyond its value in my work."

She wasn't quite sure what he meant. "I heard Italian families are big too," she said. "Has anyone ever studied them?"

"Yes, as a matter of fact. It was actually in Sardinia, a town descended from only twenty men and women, a pure gene pool, like the Amish. The Sardinians gave blood to be stored, from which DNA was extracted to study hypertension—high blood pressure—and Alzheimer's."

"So you'll be needing to draw blood to figure out each ill person's DNA?"

"Technically, what's called a reference sample can be taken in many different ways, inner-cheek swab, even off a drinking glass or from a strand of hair. But yes, the preferred samples I want to work with mean drawing blood."

"What about expensive equipment?" she asked with a glance at the computers that seemed to run continually.

"Geneticists can really use MRIs—machines that peer inside the body—but they're way too pricey for me, and I don't want to accept them from my former employer. It's important I stay independent."

"So, besides Italians, have there been other groups studied?"

"Quite a few, because DNA knowledge can be so valuable and profitable. Other 'closed society' target groups studied have been Navajo and Hopi Native Americans, Ashkenazic Jews, and the people of Iceland."

"But not all those groups had huge families, right? Not like the Amish or Italians?"

"The Italian families only *used* to be big," he said, rhythmically clicking the tip of his ballpoint pen in and out. It seemed to her he always had to be in motion; his jumping like a slave to his pager and cell phone and his so-called PalmPilot annoyed her.

"Actually, the current birthrate in Italy is dangerously low," he explained, "because Italian men live a long time at home, without marrying or starting families. You won't believe this, but it's partly because their mothers wait on them hand and foot."

She tried not to look surprised. His pager hummed. He checked it, frowned, then ignored it.

"The population of Italy could decrease by half every forty years if trends don't change," he went on. "But why did I end up telling you that?"

"Because it bothers you somehow, I guess. I never told anyone I read the Romantic poets a lot, like I told you yesterday, though my friend Barbara and my mother knew. You didn't live at home a long time, did you?" she asked, thinking of her own situation—not that her mother ever waited on her.

"First of all, I grew up in Cleveland, not Italy. My biological parents and my adoptive ones were both first-generation Italians, but no, no one ever waited on me hand and foot until I earned enough discretionary money to go to some five-star restaurants."

"Five-star?"

"Fancy ones. But back to the reasons the Amish make great case studies. Or can you tell me?"

"Because we know each other and our families, past and present," she said. "Because of the family trees in the Bible, we all value them. Also, you can more easily keep an eye on your patients and their relatives who might have had the same disease—or be carriers—because they live close together and tend to intermarry. Luke and Katie's wedding's the only time I can recall when someone converted to Amish, though sometimes up to fifty percent of our young people leave. Hence, another good reason for big families. The Amish are still growing in numbers, so someday we may have to take over depopulated Italy."

They shared a laugh as he shook his head. "Another reason," he said, evidently trying to get back on track, "is that Amish groups have a limited number of founders, a common ancestry. The founder effect means recessive genes—in this case, those that can cause rare diseases—were streaked out among the next generations. In large study groups like the general population, finding these recessive genes can be like looking for a needle in a haystack."

"But here, in interviewing and studying just three families with NAA, you can discover exactly who is linked to whom."

"Right. In effect, we're going to do detective work here, Leah, as much as medical."

She propped her elbows on the table and put her forehead in her hands. "I wish we could do detective work on Seth's disappearance. It may be as hard to find him as searching for a needle in a haystack, but I think something's wrong."

"I concur. Even if he had it in his head to take off, he didn't need to string us along about the new job. But with all those wedding guests and the other boys acting as hostlers, more or less in the middle of open fields, I can't fathom that there was any foul play."

"I realize that. I'd like to question some of those kids, because they may know more than they're saying—or saw more than they realize. Dr. Morelli—"

"Let's go with Mark, okay?"

"Mark, on our way to or from the Klines' this afternoon, I'd like to look around near where Seth was last seen. And maybe we can talk his parents into filing a missing person's report when the sheriff's deadline passes, though it just isn't our way."

"Let's eat and head for Klines', with a quick detour by the scene of the wedding."

"Which I pray wasn't the scene of a crime."

"Leah, don't let those Romantic poets let you get too imaginative or too—"

"Romantic?" she blurted before she felt herself blush. This time she was saved by a buzzer. She startled, before she realized it was his doorbell. After all, they didn't have to ding-dong as she was used to.

Mark went to the side door. Leah heard a

woman's voice, light and happy. "All right, Mr. Independent," she was saying, "you won't take a lab assistant or an MRI from Brad, but you certainly can take these."

It was someone Mark knew well, she thought as she checked Becca to see she was still sleeping. Maybe it was someone special to him. If so, she would just meet him at the Klines' later, though she hated to wake Becca right now.

"Leah," he called from the hall, "I'd like you to meet someone."

Curiosity was killing her, but she walked slowly out into the entry hall. Mark's guest was tall, slender—actually, reed thin—and despite a beautiful, young face, she was white-haired. It was cut like a close cap around her head. She looked vaguely familiar to Leah, but she couldn't place her.

"Andrea Dixon, this is my community liaison, Leah Kurtz," Mark said as Andrea stepped forward, smiling. "Andrea's a friend and the wife of my former employer."

Andrea had come bearing gifts, for behind her, Mark held a plastic-wrapped quilt, a big vase of mixed flowers—the dried blooms on the angel flashed through Leah's brain again—and a large green glass bottle labeled Moët something-or-other with a mushroom-shaped cork in it.

Andrea Dixon, Leah thought, was shorter than she looked at first. She wore a soft silver leather coat with a pink machine-knitted furry sweater peeking up above the neck of it. A gold and diamond pendant swung over the neck of the sweater, and diamonds as big as spring peas studded her earlobes.

"You've got to join us for lunch," Mark told Andrea.

"And ruin my figure with one of your Italiano cuisine extravangazas?" she said, looking only at Leah now. "I'm so glad you'll be helping Mark pursue his heart's desire," she said with a slick smile, her lipstick all glossy, as if it was wet.

"That's right," Leah said. "I'll be keeping family charts and introducing him to people hereabouts. That's a beautiful building-blocks quilt."

"I thought it was an appropriate pattern for a clinic-warming gift," she said with a blinding white smile at Mark. "Better than more geneware or an offer of a lab tech that my husband considers apropos, but this stubborn man keeps turning down. San Marco, when will you learn not to look a gift horse in the mouth?" she said, laughing and smiling as if to intentionally flaunt her perfect teeth.

Mark put the quilt down on the couch and the flowers on the table. "The champagne," he said, waving the bottle, "we'll save until you can bring Brad down to see everything."

"And that's another reason I popped by. How about Saturday, late morning? We won't stay long, as I have a quilt auction I want to hit in Millersburg that afternoon. If I hadn't bought a warehouse there that Brad wanted to check out, I doubt if I'd ever get him to leave his new baby."

"Oh," Leah said. "You have a new baby?"

"She means a new on-site testing and treatment facility for genetic diseases," Mark explained, still cradling the bottle. "It's at Metzler-Reich Pharmaceutical in a suburb of Cleveland."

"With fabulous state-of-the-art facilities," Andrea said, "that Brad wanted you to oversee, San Marco. Well, enough of that right now. After all your arguing, I'm just grateful we parted friends, and I'm busy with my own interests, so I don't get caught up in Brad's negotiations and patent wars. As is, he's still worried about that buyout and possible hostile takeover by HealGene, Inc., in Atlanta."

"I thought he had that all settled."

"Don't ask. You think MR's aggressive." She gave an exaggerated shudder. "We're minuscule compared to that Goliath, and if you think Brad's ambitious, it's nothing next to Brad's former mentor, Sinclair Marshall."

Leah understood the reference to Goliath, at least, but buyouts and hostile takeovers were a foreign language. Mark must have realized the topic was flying past her, because he changed the subject. "Andrea buys heirloom quilts in this area and other Midwest communities and sells them in her Cleveland antique store."

Leah realized who Andrea Dixon was now. She advertised in local papers that she wanted to buy old family quilts, the more antique the better. She'd had her picture in the local paper, holding up an heirloom quilt from the 1880s. Leah recalled it had belonged to the Roscoes, a founding pioneer family for whom Roscoe County had been named. She almost mentioned to Andrea that a Roscoe was buried under a beautiful angel statue in the cemetery next to her house, but she didn't really approve of the woman stealing people's pasts, and she certainly didn't want her visiting the cemetery.

As Mark put the bottle away, Andrea eyed the table set for two, then turned to assess Leah again. Leah leveled a look back at her.

"Well, I've got to run," she told them as the cell phone in her purse played a tune. "Oh, it's Brad," she said, staring at its little screen. "I'd let you talk to him if I had time, but I have to get going. We'll see you Saturday, late morning then."

She turned to Mark and took one of the lapels of his doctor's coat in her hand. "Just remember, we are all still friends, San Marco, and Brad wants to keep close tabs on your work. Well, I'm sure he'll tell you the same himself, but you men are so bad at feelings when business calls…"

In a flurry of farewells, she was out the door.

Leah was surprised when Mark said he'd ride in her buggy with her, but she assumed he was still worried about her safety. Becca slept in the carrier between their feet, sheltered by the dashboard. Leah had the clear plastic flaps snapped in place and even had the battery-powered heater going. It seemed like a cozy little box with the three of them inside. Still, as warm as a winter buggy could be, she had decided to take her mother up on leaving Becca with her if she had too far to go in cold weather.

She turned Nell in the driveway of the Brand house, which looked so different without all the buggies and people. She stopped to tell the men in Luke's windmill shop that she was going to the barn to look for something that was lost, then drove out back.

"I love the way you put that, without telling them a thing," Mark said. "Amish selective truth-telling. I have a feeling we're going to learn a lot from each other."

"I thought doctors went by reason, not feeling," she said, then wished she hadn't as he shot her a look that she felt clear down to the pit in her belly. The rhythmic swaying of her arm and hip against his didn't help, either.

After they climbed down, Mark picked Becca up and helped her into the sewn baby carrier on Leah's chest. "She'll want a bottle as soon as we get to the Klines'," Leah said. "Meanwhile, I have no idea what we're looking for."

"Ordinarily I'd say strange tracks," Mark said.

Again, Leah pictured the path of footsteps around her house. It made some sense that a rail rider might get off a train in these parts, perhaps hoping the charitable Amish would feed him, but the whole notion still haunted her.

"But," Mark went on, "there were too many boys, horses and people around here to pick out strange tracks. The sheriff should have cordoned off the area and done a decent search, but he's seen too many kids, both English and Amish, act crazy around here—he told me so."

She felt deflated as she paced the area where the boys had parked the buggies. Mark was right. This was insanity. All she found was the chicken leg David Groder had dropped that was meant for Seth. It lay in the dirt, with a pile of horse apples not far from it.

"Ick. I guess this wasn't such a good idea, and we should head for the Klines'. But what's that orange thing over there?" she asked, pointing. "A little bottle top?"

Mark squatted to look at the object, then took out his handkerchief to pick it up. Leah came closer and stared down at it, stark orange against the white linen.

"Do you know what that is?" she asked.

"Unfortunately, I do, but showing it to the sheriff won't help us to convince him Seth's met with foul play. It's the plunger for a hypodermic needle. It fits on top of the vial with the drug and holds the needle in the tiny hole, see?"

"I see. What kind of drugs?"

"Any kind. Sheriff Martin would probably say the kind kids use to shoot up with."

"Not Seth! No way!"

"If not him, one of his buddies. I'd suggest you show this to the church bishop, but not the sheriff. Having the Klines file that missing person's report next week might be the way to go. But Leah," he said, his voice getting darker as he took her elbow to steer her back to the buggy, "I don't want you to suggest anything to them that might screw up my treating Susie. The patient and the work come first, okay? At all costs, protect the work."

"I hear you," she said, surprised at his switch to such a strident tone. She took his handkerchief with the tiny object from him and stuck it under her floor mat. But she wasn't giving up on Seth.

Still strapped down…drugged…his eyes so heavy in the darkness. No, maybe he was not only tied down now but blindfolded too.

The fragments of memory started to click back in place.

Luke Brand's wedding. An English man and woman, coming closer across the side field, then approaching from behind the barn. The field just snow-studded corn stubble now. They had a camera with a huge zoom lens. He'd already sent the other hostlers inside.

He'd walked past the horses toward them, behind the barn, holding up a hand—"Please, no photos"— the words they all used so often uptown when tourists aimed those mechanical eyes at their faces.

"We just want a shot of the buggies all lined up," the man had said. "The light's great today. No close-up of faces."

Seth could see their vehicle—a van with dark windows—parked across the corner of the field, over by where Reuben Coblentz, Luke's former father-in-law, lived.

"Just one, then," he'd called to the couple. They both wore big hats pulled down over their foreheads and huge mufflers in this weather. He couldn't make out their features from here. "And keep me out of it," Seth had added.

"Sure," the man said, steadying his tripod, then peering through the big lens. He lifted something in his hand. "Sure thing."

That was all he could remember. But for some reason, the words the Amish used if someone took a *verboten* picture kept running through his head: *You have stolen me…you have stolen me.*

5

Though Mark was full from their rigatoni and sourdough lunch, Leah had warned him about an Amish custom. He should expect—and accept—some food when they were barely in the door at Klines'.

He soon saw she was right: Miriam Kline plied them with apple cider and huge cookies called jumbles. Food and family talk first, then, if he passed muster, he hoped to get a closer look at Susie.

As he and Leah chatted with the Klines about the weather, Mark could see Susie fussing over Becca from the corner of his eye. Her sisters were at school, so she wasn't surrounded by them this time. He tried to listen attentively and answer her parents' questions about his family, but he was dying to get to theirs. All he really knew about Susie's parents so far was that Reuben worked at Luke Brand's windmill shop and was in charge of it while Luke was on his extended honeymoon. Reuben had buggied home for a long lunch to be here for this visit. At last, Leah evidently decided there had been enough small talk and cleared her throat.

"Now, Reuben and Miriam, about Susie," she said

with a "tune in now" look at him that would have done a wife proud. "Would you mind if Dr. Morelli chatted with her a bit and then you and Miriam could decide if you'd like to bring her into the clinic? I can surely arrange to be there too, if you'd like."

"*Ja,* good idea all around," Reuben said. "Susie, why don't you show the doctor those drawings you been doing."

Mark followed the child into the sunny kitchen where some papers and crayons were spread out on the large table, as well as cookie sheets with some of the freshly baked jumbles still on them.

Through Susie's small, starched white cap, he could clearly see how white and thin her hair was. In the slant of light, he could tell that cataracts clouded her eyes. Her skin looked parchment thin, and bluish veins webbed her temples. She had brown mottled age spots on her little hands. The way she walked, her body stiff and hunched, told him she had incipient osteoporosis as well as arthritis. But she was as jumpy and antsy as any six-year-old.

"Can you make me younger, like Ruth and Lizzie?" she asked him the moment they sat catty-corner at the oak table. She squirmed in her seat and rolled one crayon into another. "I mean, I'm the youngest of us, but can you make me a girl again?"

He felt as if someone had gut-kicked him. This was going to be the biggest challenge of his life. Lab work had been so…aseptic, but this was, as Leah put it, all tied up with feelings.

"I'm going to level with you completely, Susie. I hope to make your aches and pains feel better and be certain that you live as long and as happy as possible."

"Oh, happy, I'm that. Except for Seth leaving. He didn't take any clothes, but he had payday money from two jobs on him."

"Did he say anything to you about wanting to leave?"

"Oh, sure," she said, twirling a purple crayon with her crooked, bony fingers. "He's extra smart, so he wants to know what's out there, like more school, more books. Hardly had time to read anymore. If you'd come yesterday, I'd have said—" her voice rose to a scratchy pitch "—can you fix me up so Seth doesn't have to work a bunch of jobs to help me get better?"

She was getting to him again. "Maybe you can think of me as stepping in for Seth. Not helping the same way, but I'll do all I can. And then, Susie, what we learn helping you, we can use to help other kids like you."

She squinted at him. "Like the Esh and Kauffman boys? Jonas Esh is my second cousin."

Mark's eyes widened. Why hadn't Leah told him that? Surely he'd be able to find the rogue gene, the SNP, of these NAA kids that was different from their normal family members.

"*Daad* thought it would be real good if you look at my pictures," she went on. "I drew these when I was getting help in Cleveland. I heard them say it's to get us not to hide our motions, like they come out when we draw."

"Maybe they meant emotions. I took a test once where I had to look at spilled ink and say what it reminded me of, and some doctors thought they could tell things about me that way."

She frowned down at the papers. "I'm not a good drawer. Do I have to draw if I come to your office in town?"

"Nope. I can't draw for beans either."

"For beans? Why would you draw for beans?" she asked and giggled. The Klines and Leah found them that way, giggling.

Leah was exhausted as she played with Becca, washed and fed her, then tucked her in. It was barely dusk, but the baby, too, was ready to sleep. Leah was drying her hair after her bath when her front doorbell sounded. Startled, she jumped back into her clothes, wrapped a towel around her head and rushed downstairs.

For once, she wished she had an outside light to click on. Since no electricity came into this property, she had no porch light. What if the person who had trespassed last night was back? Drawing aside the curtains, she lifted the lantern from the table and held it up to the window overlooking the front porch.

She heard someone move out there, then Miles Mason bent down to look in. At least he caught on and showed himself, she thought. Instead of going out, she opened the window about six inches to talk through. Looking annoyed, he bent over but didn't stoop or kneel.

"My hair's wet, and it will ice if I come out," she told him. "What can I do for you?"

"You there when Seth Kline went missing?"

"Yes. You—you don't know anything about it, do you?"

"Just what I heard. And here I thought you people were trustworthy."

She didn't like this man, but neither did she want to get into an argument with him. And cold air was coming into the room. "Is that all, Mr. Mason?"

"Still want to know if I can tap those trees in the yard. Sam Yoder's got a job on the Methodist church extension on the other side of town, and if I wait for him to get back, I might miss a sap run."

"Sam's coming back? When?"

"Maybe you people ought to consider joining the real world," he muttered, still bending farther down to look in. "Send some e-mail, use a phone."

"Maybe you people," she retorted, "shouldn't insult people you want something from."

"Yeah, I'll be seeing Sam about selling this place," he said, missing her meaning. "See, that's my church he'll be working on—that's how I knew. I'm lay leader in charge of overseeing the work of Sam's team. He'll be back in the next coupla days, I guess. But what about these trees? Yoders gave me permission last year. It'll mean three gallons of syrup for you. I have to cook up a hundred fifty gallons of sap to get that much."

"All right, go ahead. And I wouldn't mind if you'd cut off a few of the longer branches—they sway close to the house in the wind."

"Will do. Most of your trees will be getting three buckets. A twelve-inch circumference gets one bucket, but most of your trees are eighteen-inchers, which get two, or even twenty-four–inchers, which get three. Just so you know."

"I think I can grasp all that. I wish *you people* well with your tapping and cooking, then."

She lowered the window, then closed the curtains again. Moving the lantern away so she wouldn't make a silhouette, she peeked out, waiting to be sure he left. Even though it was dark, he walked from tree to tree, maybe deciding which limbs to cut. Finally, he disappeared. After last night, she didn't like the idea of anyone walking around outside. Hadn't he driven out here? Where was his truck? Wouldn't she hear him drive away?

A truck went by on the road, and she assumed that was him. She felt not a little upset that he knew Sam's plans before she did.

The next morning, brooding about Miles Mason's visit, Leah remembered his earlier visit with Seth when he'd called her house uninsulated—as if he'd been inside it. But perhaps some of the house's chilliness could be easily stopped by ensuring there were no chinks in the attic. Cold air seemed to seep from the upper floors, which was yet another reason she'd moved herself and Becca downstairs to the ground level. If she could find some bare places, maybe Sam would put insulation in, especially if she paid for it. After their visit to the Klines', Mark had insisted on paying her one week ahead, so she had two hundred dollars in the house, which made her feel very rich.

Leah got the two of them bundled up early to go into town. Her plans were to drop Becca off for a few hours with her mother at the bakery, then buggy out to the Esh farm to interview them and see how little Jonas was doing. Before they left, since they were both dressed nice and warm, she carried Becca into the attic to look around.

The door creaked and the narrow stairs twisted once before a slant-roof attic opened up before her. She'd only been up here once before. She would never have come up at night, even with a lantern. At least now, morning bathed the dusty wooden floor beams with pale winter light—and came through some chinks in the attic walls.

"Yes!" she cried. This might be a lot of work and take some money, but at least she had some answers. The natural air-conditioning might be great in the heat of summer, but it was so cold she could see her breath now. Slivers of light shot through some of the old wall boards and around one of the four windowpanes. This could well be the cause not only of a cold house but of the shrieking sounds she'd heard. If only she could find some equally logical explanation for those footsteps and flowers left outside.

The window that needed caulking and insulation faced west, toward the cemetery and across the ravine toward the mill. Scraping off the frost from one of the narrow panes with her fingernails, she could see the top half of the silos from here. One of them—the one she'd twice seen the man dangling from—was being painted a dull brown-red. So that's what he had been doing there, despite the cold, scraping or priming the old metal exterior for a coat of paint. It was probably the same man who'd painted AgraGro in block letters across the midsection of the silos in the fall. He'd been foolish not to paint the background first. Her breath misted the window again.

On her way to the stairs, she scanned the items stored here. A walnut bench with a broken back that would be great on the front porch. Why hadn't Sam repaired it? Bending over with Becca under the slant of eaves, she peered into a big cardboard carton that was partly hidden behind the bench.

"Oh, no!" she cried. Empty liquor bottles, lots of them. And not beer bottles but large ones, whiskey. A sharp scent still clung to them. She was certain Barbara had not used whiskey medicinally to stem her pain. Sam must have been drinking and was afraid to have visitors—or even Barbara—know. Had he meant to remove these but became too busy? Leah prayed he wasn't still drinking.

On the other side of the broken bench sat an old trunk that smelled of mothballs even before she lifted the lid. She expected more bottles. But two old quilts lay within.

"Andrea Dixon, quilt bandit, eat your heart out," she whispered.

Were these too old to use? Barbara should have aired or cleaned them, for one could never have too many quilts. Their patterns didn't seem like orderly Amish designs but random patchwork, more American pioneer than Plain People.

Wedged on its side, between the quilts, was an antique book of crackled leather, too thin to be a Bible.

Leah pulled it out, closed the trunk and took the book and Becca back downstairs. She lay the book on the kitchen table, put Becca's plastic carrier next to it and flipped the cover open. In a lovely, if overly fancy, hand, the following was written: *Deer Run Cemetery, Maplecreek, Ohio, Records of Deceased, 1880–1892, Thomas Bricker, Caretaker.*

"That's right," she said aloud as Becca studied her. "This house, Becca-my-Becca, used to belong to the cemetery caretaker. We'll look at this tonight. Maybe we can donate it to the Maplecreek Historical Society. What do you think?"

Becca looked as if she thought it was a pretty good idea.

The Esh family chart was the first Leah had actually filled out, since she had promised the Klines she'd be back another day for their information. She already knew that the ten-year-old Jonas and Susie Kline were second cousins, but she wasn't sure of the connection. She wanted to have the documentation to prove the relationship to Mark, but her interview started out strained.

When John Esh seemed more focused on his sick milk cows than on his sick son, Leah realized they didn't trust the whole idea of an *auslander* gene doctor in Amish country. So she began to tell them about an article she'd read of how a gene doctor had helped the Amish in Pennsylvania.

"This young Amish couple was going to be prosecuted by English law for shaken baby syndrome," she'd told John and Esther.

"That anything like Down syndrome?" John asked as his eyebrows shot halfway up his forehead.

"No. It means injuries that happen if someone

shakes an infant too hard in frustration or anger or to quiet them down."

"Not our way to do any of that," Esther had put in with a sniff.

"That's just the point," Leah explained. "The Plain People wouldn't do that, but some English do, so they suspected it of us. But a gene doctor proved that the baby really had a genetic liver disorder. The symptoms for that are large bruises—"

Her voice snagged. She stopped to take a steadying breath. Barbara had had large bruises from her anemia.

"The baby also had brain and retinal bleeding," she went on, pointing to her eye. "Anyway, the family trusted this gene doctor and it saved them from prison and got the baby the right kind of treatment. That's the kind of help Dr. Morelli can bring kids like Jonas. He may not find a cure soon enough to do all he'd want for Jonas, but he can keep you from having to drive clear to Cleveland with your boy when he's so ill. The doctor will not only study but treat your son."

"Teacher Leah makes a good sale, don't she?" John asked his wife. "I oughta get her to unload those two sick cows for us 'fore having to dose them eats us out of house and home."

Esther glanced upstairs, no doubt where Jonas lay. "If Leah says this Dr. Morelli's to be trusted, I say we go with it. She let both Susie Kline and Jonas come to school when they could, even though it was a lot of extra work for her. I trust Leah."

It turned out Jonas's paternal grandparents (GS) were Susie's great-grandparents (G–GS), as Mark's codes put it. Leah couldn't wait to tell him that two of the NAA children were now his patients.

Though Leah went back out into the cold, she felt enveloped in a warm glow. She loved this job so far because she felt she was making a difference with something important. But working closely with Mark came with a risk: she was strangely attracted to him— not that she'd ever let on, but it made her sometimes too impetuous and daring with him.

She jolted from her reverie when a dark blue van came alongside her buggy, honking its horn and edging her slightly toward the berm just past the Eshes' dairy farm.

She simply froze, her hands gripping the reins so hard her nails bit into her palms. Like most Amish horses, Nell was used to being passed by speeding, honking vehicles, so she moved over but kept going.

Leah hadn't had a bad moment like this for years, not since her big sister, Katie, was killed in a hit-and-run accident. For a few months after that, Leah had experienced screaming night terrors. Somehow, she had gotten over the utter frenzy she felt when a motor vehicle came fast or close.

So why panic now? Because her mother had suggested yesterday that Leah was still mourning Katie? Then she recalled that she'd dreamed last night about Katie and Barbara putting dead flowers on the stone angel and beckoning for her to come help them. But surely that didn't mean she'd been forewarned of her own death.

Leah shook her head to fight her fear. The van

honked again, and its driver rolled down the passenger-side window. Even through the buggy's thick plastic cover, Leah saw it was Jesse Cutler. That jolted her back to action.

"Hey!" he shouted, leaning away from his steering wheel on the double-lane rural road. "I was checking on Eshes' sick Holsteins and saw you leave!"

She did not unsnap her plastic window but just yelled through it. "Dr. Cutler, you're blocking the road. This is dangerous."

"I just wanted to apologize for upsetting you the other day. Can't you stop that thing a minute—pull in at this turnoff up ahead?"

"No. I'm late, as is."

"Rushing back to the gene doctor, right?" His voice rose to a shrill pitch as his car swerved even closer. "Can't give a man who's a fellow churchgoer the time of day but love to spend time in his clinic, huh? And he's Catholic, if not an atheist!"

"My, you know a lot about him! Now, please move that van away from my horse."

"She's not the one who's skittish. All scientists are atheists at heart, you know."

She was getting angrier by the minute. She prayed she wouldn't lose her temper or act unworthy of the peace teachings of the Lord. But she unsnapped the bottom of her plastic side window and shouted, "Generalizations are hardly ever true! I don't know his heart, and you don't either! And there's a car coming, and you're in its path!"

"And you're in mine, sweetheart!" she thought he shouted as he sped up to go around her, then roared away. Leah noted his license was VAN-GO 3, and re-called the previous van he'd owned, a dark brown one, had been VAN-GO 2. As far as she knew, Jesse's idea of art was a far cry from the Dutch painter Vincent Van Gogh. It was more like those pictures of sleeping dogs that were all over his reception-room walls.

Just in case Jesse was waiting for her around the bend, she pulled into the Groder farm as if she'd stopped for a visit. Besides, if David was home, she'd question him on anything he could recall about Seth's disappearance.

The nearby *Englische* voices pulled Seth from sod-den sleep.

"Let's get him in the MRI and then get rid of him."

Get rid of him, he thought. Were his parents here? Would he be discharged? But nurses and doctors wouldn't say it like that, would they?

Hands on him, loosing his arms. He lay still, played possum the way he used to. He'd tease his sisters be-fore he'd jump up and chase them around the yard.

If he tipped his head slightly back, he could see out from under the blindfold. It wasn't like the eye patch Eli Brand wore when his eye was cut by a tree branch. Sure as sin, this couldn't be a hospital. Why would they blindfold a patient even if they might have to re-strain one who was out of his head?

Was *he* out of his head? Why was he here? Who were these people?

He moved before he even planned it. Panicked, he shoved at the hands on him, tried to rip off the blindfold.

The woman had her mask still on, but he glimpsed the man's face before he threw up his hands to cover it.

"Help! Help here!" the woman screamed as Seth tried to fight free of them.

Running footsteps. He was lifted, banged back on a table or bed. Someone threw a cloth over his face.

"Who let *that* happen?"

"Did he see?"

"I'm afraid so."

"Stop the Versed drip then. We can't trust that the amnesiac drug will work, so that he can't recall or ID someone."

Terrified, Seth still tried to struggle. Something was pulled from one arm, but something else pierced his other one. He fought hard against the darkness.

"Looks like he's just graduated to our gene therapy list," someone said. "I wasn't sold on trying to let him go as an amnesiac anyway, not with the work being done in Maplecreek now—and with the Amish girl loose."

"Loose, that's a good one," a man said and laughed. "An Amish girl, loose."

"You'd better be working on that little problem, not to mention the boozer."

"I am. I'll handle it, but we can't just shoot them. It'll take some finesse."

Finesse? What was finesse? The walls closed in, crushing even Seth's hearing, shoving him into a smaller and smaller box of blackness.

"So David Groder was no help at all?" Mark asked. He stood by her buggy as she prepared to get Becca and drive home. "By the way, Susie told me Seth had two paychecks on him when he left."

"I know circumstances don't look good," she admitted. "David Groder was no help—just the opposite, in fact. Since some of David and Seth's friends have gone running around, he thinks Seth secretly wanted to too."

"Leah, I know you don't want to hear this," he said, putting his hand on the buggy, which rocked it slightly, "but Seth might have wanted to cut loose. It's hard to read somebody else's mind—or heart."

It reminded her of her defense of Mark to Jesse Cutler just an hour ago. If she told Mark about that, she could just see him stomping across the street to take Jesse on, and that's all she needed right now. It was her problem, not his

"But," she told him, "I *have* been saving one good thing for last. David told me that Sheriff Martin questioned him and the other hostlers about what they saw, so at least the sheriff really is looking into this situation. It makes me feel a little better."

"Though, if David told him again that Seth was feeling the call of the wild, don't get your hopes up."

At least, despite her fears about Seth, she was excited that Mark had been pleased with Jonas Esh's family chart. He'd said he had big plans to schedule blood tests for both youngsters, their parents and siblings, to get DNA samples. Then somehow—and she hadn't followed him on all this—he ran geneware on his computers, looking for the SNPs. Beyond that lay clinical trials, treatments, maybe even gene therapy, which she guessed was pretty risky. He'd said again it would help him to have access to an MRI at the clinic, but he couldn't afford even renting one.

Mark wanted not only to treat the symptoms of

NAA, but to set up a schedule so the children could spend some time together, sharing and learning more about their illness. He'd asked Leah if she'd be at the clinic or a farmhouse for those meetings when he could set them up.

"So, do you and Becca have a big night planned?" He shifted the subject, surprising her.

"Oh, yeah," she said, rolling her eyes. "I'm going to caulk around a leaky attic window before it gets dark and fix myself some macaroni and cheese, then read an old book I found about the cemetery that's next to my house."

He looked surprised. "Doesn't that scare you?"

"No, macaroni's not that hard to fix," she said and reached down to punch his shoulder. "And then, for a really good time, I'm going to try to figure how many rolls of insulation I need to warm up my attic. Becca's father's due back in town soon, but I can't wait for him to fix things up. What?" she asked, when Mark stared at her, wide-eyed.

"It's kismet," he said, then must have noticed her puzzled look. "Fate," he said, "not that I really believe in that. But I've got about six rolls of insulation in the basement here, left over from when the clinic was re-wired and some of the old insulation fell out. I couldn't afford to spring for a new furnace, but I did buy too much insulation. If it's okay that I stop by, I could easily put it in for you."

"Oh, no, that's fine, though I will buy it from you. I couldn't ask you to take time away from here to—"

"Leah, I don't want Becca getting chilled one more night."

She smiled as she accepted his offer and waited for him to pack four of the six big, wrapped rolls of pink fiberglass insulation in her buggy. As she headed for her mother's bakery, using the back alley in case Jesse Cutler was watching, she marveled how something so boring as insulating an attic could suddenly sound so exciting.

By the time Leah had caulked around the window and filled a few other obvious chinks, it was the baby's bedtime. Sitting on the sofa that would only be her bed for another week before she could afford a new one, Leah opened the cemetery book in her lap. She was smiling so much her face was starting to ache. Mark was coming early in the morning with the last two rolls of insulation. Before they put them in the attic, she was going to fix them breakfast.

But that familiar, stale, old-paper smell that emanated from the stiff pages soon cast a pall over her mood. She got up again from the kitchen table to look outside. The maple trees in the yard looked different since they were pierced by spiles supporting sap buckets. She knew if she went outside, she could actually hear their drip, drip, drip. Their silhouettes now looked as if they carried burdens that sapped their lifeblood.

She shook her head to throw off her strange thoughts. She'd been listening too hard to Mark's talk about taking blood samples today. But how she wished Seth had been here to tap those trees this afternoon instead of Miles Mason.

As she sat back down, she quickly adapted to reading the ornate, nineteenth-century handwriting of

Thomas Bricker. Evidently, the caretaker had been a meticulous person. Each numbered plot in the cemetery had listed the date of death and sometimes the cause. This book should definitely go to the local historical society, for it could be of use to people trying to trace their family trees. If such a book had been kept for the Amish graveyard on the other side of town, it would have been a great help to her and Mark.

Matching death dates, she skimmed the pages to see if she could discover what Varina Roscoe, the woman buried under the angel monument, had died from at the young age of twenty-six. She and Barbara had noted that far too many women back then died young. Several were buried with their infants, who died the same day they did. In olden times, Leah thought, a doctor coming to town could be a godsend to save such women.

And no wonder the angel statue was such a fine one, she thought. The Roscoes had once owned a lot of Roscoe county, so they must have been well-to-do. She ran the tip of her index finger along the writing across from Varina's name to see if her cause of death was recorded.

Thomas Bricker had written in much smaller letters there, than anywhere else, maybe to cram more in.

Death Angel given by townfolk for th' angel
who nursed others thro' th' fluenza. Most
tragically kilt by her throat cut, and the
crime never solved. O Death Angel, pray take
no other so good or so young.

6

Pancakes, honey—unfortunately, she was out of syrup—orange juice and coffee had never tasted so good. Leah loved having Mark at the breakfast table and Becca in her lap. His presence made the place seem brighter, cozy, safer…and almost hers.

She did wish, though, she was better at worldly chitchat when what fell out of her mouth was, "You aren't an atheist, are you?"

He almost choked on a bite of pancake. His fork dinged his plate. Shaking his head, he took a swallow of juice, then said, "What brought that up? Because I'm a scientist and a doctor?"

"More or less." She was still hesitant to tell him about being accosted by Jesse Cutler on the road yesterday.

"Listen, Leah," he said, sitting forward across the table, "I really think that the more we know about genetics—the brilliant complexity of it—that scientists realize that there is a genius creator mind behind it all. No, I'm not an atheist, though I haven't set foot in a church for ages."

"Catholic?"

"Catholic, anyplace. Yes, I was raised Catholic. I've

got to admit I liked that Amish marriage ceremony, though—short and sweet." He went back to forking up pancakes.

"The regular Amish services are sweet, but hardly short. There's a lot of preaching and singing."

"If guests are allowed, I'd like to go with you some-day, though I guess I'd have to sit with the men, right? Still, it might be good for the cause."

The cause. His words echoed in her head to burst her bubble. *At all costs protect the work,* he'd said the other day. So, she wondered, how much of his help-ing in the community—helping her today—was be-cause of the work and not really how he felt?

But she had to accept that, to a man like Mark, the Amish were no doubt a means to an end. After all, she should keep in mind that she was helping him to bene-fit her people and herself. She had to learn to protect her own work, her baby and her life, she told herself as she finished feeding and burping Becca.

When he went upstairs to install the rolls of insula-tion, she cleaned up the kitchen and fretted—though a sampler hung in this very house that said, *"Fret not, it only causes harm." Psalm 37:8.* Mark said he hadn't wanted her to help him because he didn't want Becca around the fiberglass particles, and he'd only brought one medical mask to keep from breathing them in.

As he washed up two hours later, Mark asked, "Mind if I take a look at that angel statue out there close-up? I saw it from the attic window, and it looks like a real work of art."

"It is. It's the guardian of this place, I always think.

Let me show you something first that I found in the attic. This house used to belong to the cemetery caretaker." She lifted the book down from the top shelf of her kitchen hutch. "It's the cemetery records. I'm going to donate them tomorrow to the local historical society. I heard they have their meetings Saturday mornings."

He touched the book almost reverently, she thought. "You wish we had something like this for the Amish cemetery across town, don't you?" she said.

He looked up at her and smiled. When his face lit like that, her insides cartwheeled.

"I'm in trouble if you're reading my mind, Miss Leah," he said, his tone teasing. "So where's the info on whoever's buried under the angel?"

She showed him. His eyebrows rose; he slanted a quick look her way again. "Murdered?" he said.

"Mark, someone left flowers on the angel the other day," she blurted. "A garland of them around her neck."

"But she—this Varina Roscoe—has been dead way over a hundred years. It was hardly someone who knew her. The flowers froze?" he asked, squinting out the window into the bright day.

"No. Before they blew away, they were already dead."

"The flowers?"

"Yes, the flowers!"

"Okay, okay. Bizarre. You didn't see who—"

"No. It happened when I wasn't here."

"Let's go out and take a look at her."

"I doubt if it's really a her. Angels are either sexless or male. It's just the long hair and robes that fool modern observers. In the Bible they all have male names. They're messengers or warriors," she went on as she put Becca's cape and bonnet on her and wrapped her in a crib quilt. Mark put Leah's cape around her, donned his jacket and out they went. The ground was a bit slippery from the thawing and re-freezing of snow, and Mark held on to her arm.

"If this one's a messenger, what's she—he—say-ing?" he asked as they approached the side cemetery gate.

"I do know the message when the angel was first put here. The people of Maplecreek mourned for Va-rina Roscoe's loss after she'd nursed so many of them. *Fluenza* does mean influenza, doesn't it?"

He nodded solemnly. "The scourge of their day and time. What we now call the flu has rampaged through America more than once. Especially before antibi-otics, certain strains of it were fatal."

Mark held Becca while Leah wrestled with the squeaky, stubborn gate. He kept the baby in his arms as they looked at Varina's flat marker. Snow etched her name, birth and death dates and the word *Beloved.* For a few minutes they stood silently study-ing the angel, which seemed to stare fixedly at Va-rina's grave.

"Now that Becca's mother's dead—she died in the house right there—" Leah whispered, "whenever I see this angel, I always think of a Wordsworth poem."

"Tell me," he said, gently bumping her shoulder with his.

"The woman the poet lost was named Lucy," she explained, "but I always put in my friend's name, Barbara. And before she died, I used to put in my older sister's name, Katie. She died in a car accident."

"Too much tragic loss. How does the poem go?"

> *"She lived unknown, and few could know*
> *When Barbara ceased to be;*
> *But she is in her grave, and oh,*
> *The difference to me."*

"So sad," Mark said louder.

"I'd say so, *ja,* I would!" a sharp male voice behind them cried, making them jump. "What's all that whispering?"

Sam Yoder stood at the gate. Leah assumed he'd only heard Mark's last comment.

"Leah, who is this man?" Sam demanded.

"Becca, it's *Daadi,*" she said, taking the baby from Mark and starting for the gate. "Sam, this is the new doctor who's setting up a clinic to study hereditary diseases, Mark Morelli. I'm working part-time for him."

Sam nodded to Mark; Mark nodded back. Sam took Becca in his arms, but she immediately began to fuss.

"Doesn't remember me," he said.

"You've been gone nearly a month of her two-month life and, if Miles Mason hadn't told me," Leah said, trying not to sound annoyed, "I wouldn't have known you were coming back to do a job here. I hardly left this house the first month I had Becca. You could have written or visited."

"He paying you well?" Sam asked, his voice more quiet as he glowered past her shoulder at Mark.

"Two hundred a week."

"For part-time? Sure not just for cleaning for him?" He tried bouncing Becca, then gave up and handed the squalling baby back to Leah. As he did, she was hit with his breath, a powerfully sweet odor, somewhere between peppermint and cherry. Her heart sank. Was he still drinking and trying to cover it up? If so, this wasn't the time to ask.

"I'm his community-contact person, so to speak," she explained, cuddling Becca.

"Contact person. So to speak, huh?"

"Sam, I'm doing visitations to fill out family trees for those he's treating, and eventually, the entire Amish community."

"Why should he know our business? And what's with you standing out here staring at Barbara's angel?"

"Barbara's angel? Did she ever tell you about how we put flowers on it one time?"

"May have." He shrugged and scowled again at Mark, who had stayed over by the angel, turning away to give them some privacy. "The last day she was alive," Sam said, "exhausted as she was, she insisted on being held up to look out the window at it. 'Come into my house and take me,' she whispered. 'Come in, come in.' I thought maybe she was outta her head. Don't that beat all?"

Leah shuddered. Sam looked away as tears filled his eyes. Suddenly, he leaned close to pat Becca awkwardly, then lifted her little mittened hand to kiss it. Again the strong scent of mouthwash or breath mint hit Leah.

"Don't worry," Sam said gruffly. "I'm coming into

some extra money soon for some pick-up jobs I did while I been gone. Give you enough to rent a place closer to town, and might just sell this one to Miles Mason."

"I'll be able to help financially now, Sam. And as much work as it may take to fix this house up, I don't think I want to leave. In a way, it's Becca's heritage from her mother. I'm letting Mr. Mason tap the trees, and he surely doesn't want the house."

Sam's features clenched as tight as a fist. "You'll do like I say on it," he muttered through gritted teeth. "The place is still in my name—even though Becca's now in yours."

He must have realized how mean he looked or sounded, because he seemed to get hold of himself. "Just wanted to see her and tell you I was back and will have some money for you in a few days. I'll be at my cousin's and working at the Meth'dist church 'cross town."

He turned away. He'd evidently left whoever's buggy he'd borrowed on the other side of the house without coming into the driveway. She heard it leave, though she couldn't see it from here.

The Maplecreek Historical Society was housed in two single ground-floor rooms on the main street of town, wedged in between Samson's Hardware Store and the Kut 'n Kurl Beauty Salon and Tanning Spa. Leah figured the society's meeting must not have started yet because two ladies were just going in. With Becca in her plastic carrier in one hand and the cemetery book in the other, Leah followed them in the door.

The place smelled slightly musty and Leah fought a sneeze. Glass cases of documents and artifacts, including Shawnee Indian items, edged the rooms, and several clusters of old furniture and mannequins in pioneer garb—all of which looked not far off modern Amish—filled the rooms.

Five worldly ladies were here. One of them was Louise Winslow. Leah recognized her mostly by the fact she wore a brimmed hat and silk scarf and gloves.

"Leah!" the woman cried, bouncing up from her place at the head of the table. "To whatever we owe this honor, I am so pleased to see little Rebecca—and awake, this time. Do you mind if I hold her?"

"That would be all right. She's pretty bundled up."

"Hmm, aren't we all?" Louise said with a little laugh. "She's just lovely, so alert and bright, I can tell. Ooh, I'd give a king's ransom for a little beauty like you," Louise cooed.

To Leah's amazement, Becca seemed fascinated by Louise, when she had been so upset by her own father yesterday—or maybe by his sickeningly sweet breath. Perhaps it was just that Louise's unusual appearance fascinated her, but at least the baby didn't find her scary.

Still holding Becca, Louise introduced Leah to everyone; the last names were well known in the area. The plump lady with lots of gold jewelry and a tan was Sheriff Martin's wife, Pam. She'd evidently been spending some time next door at the Kut 'n Kurl in what Leah heard was a single tanning bed.

"I don't mean to hold you up," Leah explained, putting the book on the table, "but I have a donation I think is a Roscoe County treasure. This is the care-taker's book from the cemetery out by my house on Deer Run, the very one your society kindly tends so neatly."

She was pleased at how thrilled they were as they pored over the book, though Louise spent more time cuddling Becca. "I'm so relieved she likes me," she confided to Leah as Pam Martin read aloud interesting entries from the book. "And I understand you're working for Dr. Morelli."

"Why, yes. He's here to help the Amish children who suffer from natal accelerated aging, but I'm hoping he'll branch out to study other hereditary diseases too."

"That's marvelous. My psoriasis is actually hereditary, you know. A family association exists in one out of three cases. I've been donating to the National Psoriasis Foundation for years, hoping they get as far as gene therapy with it, though that's terribly dangerous—fatal in some cases."

"Gene therapy can be fatal?"

"The death of a teenage boy in Pennsylvania just a few years ago set it back terribly."

"I didn't know that."

"Anyway, please tell Dr. Morelli I'll be calling on him soon. I'd be interested in helping to fund his work, maybe set up some sort of foundation to help him get expensive equipment or a lab tech, whatever, if there's some need."

"He's trying to stay independent of big drug companies, but I know he needs to rent or buy an MRI machine."

"There, you see? Meanwhile, ladies," Louise said, raising her voice, which made Leah realize she might actually be the one in charge here, "I think we've not only acquired a treasure, as Leah put it, but the perfect opportunity to get some more publicity for the society. We will plumb the book for possible stories for the *Maplecreek Weekly,* and see if we can increase donations both material and financial!"

They applauded as if Louise had made a political speech. "Please," Leah said as Louise reluctantly handed Becca back to her, "if you do publicity on this, don't include my name. Just say an anonymous donor."

"You Amish are so unassuming, so humble," Pam Martin said. "We should all take a page from your book—well, I didn't mean it that way," she added, laughing.

Leah felt good when she went out to get back in the buggy. And, despite the fact Mark had company due soon, she couldn't wait to tell him about Louise Winslow's promise of support.

Mark's car was in his driveway, but, strangely, he wasn't home, or at least he wasn't answering his door. Leah wrote him a note and left it stuck in the side door. It looked so clean now that it was hard to recall the way it had been defaced earlier. Since it had been written in animal blood, she half suspected Jesse Cutler, from just across the street, was the culprit, except he hardly treated chickens.

When she clucked Nell out of the driveway, Leah saw the horse was limping, as if to punish Leah for suspecting a probably innocent man just because she didn't like him. The logical thing to do would be to take her across the street to get Jesse's help.

Instead, leaving the heater on in the buggy for Becca, she got out and led Nell into the clinic driveway. She turned her back to the horse and lifted Nell's front left hoof to take a look, even though that shifted her skirts high and bared her black-stockinged legs. Oh, *ja,* a stone wedged in under the metal shoe. She hoped she could get it out herself.

She put Nell's foot back down and rummaged in her purse and diaper bag for something to pry it out with. A nail file? Could she thread a leather rein around it, then pull it out?

Leah lifted the foot again and tried the file. It broke. Her legs were getting cold and—

"Anything I can do to help?" A man's voice, not Mark's, came from close behind her.

She dropped Nell's foot and turned to face a man about Mark's age and height. He whipped off his sunglasses to reveal clear, wide-set blue eyes. His short auburn hair stood up on his head as if it had been trained with some kind of invisible grease, but she could see he was starting to go bald. He wore creased black slacks and a black leather jacket that was open to show a white shirt and red V-neck sweater.

"Hi," he said, extending a hand. "I'm Clark Quinn, Dr. Morelli's friend and attorney. Actually, I thought I'd surprise him. Crisp and clear day for a drive."

"Oh, right. Hi." Since he'd offered it, she shook his hand. "I'm Leah Kurtz, Dr. Morelli's community liaison, and my horse just went lame."

"I see there's a vet right across the street."

"I know, but I think I can get the stone out myself. Do you have a screwdriver or metal file in your car?"

"A screwdriver. Let me get it," he said and walked toward the street. He was back in a minute with an array of them in a neat plastic case. "So, where's Mark?" he asked as she went back to work. "Let's get Sir Galahad out here to help."

Leah didn't know where that Sir Galahad came from, but she realized the English used nicknames too. Andrea Dixon had called Mark San Marco. But she hated that Jesse Cutler had called her sweetheart.

"Dr. Morelli's not answering his door," she said, "though he has company coming."

"Oh, really? I don't mean to horn in. Do you know who?"

"His former boss and his wife from Cleveland."

"Ah, the great and mighty Brad Dixon, probably laden with gifts, like the Trojan horse."

She didn't know the story he alluded to, but she said, "True. Mrs. Dixon already brought him some things."

"I hope Mark's not taking them up on their offer of a lab assistant."

"He isn't, but why not?"

"Because I don't trust Brad Dixon not to plant a spy to keep an eye on Mark's work."

"A spy?"

"In dealing with rapidly aging children, it's possible he'll uncover some secrets about slowing or halting aging in general. Can you imagine how much that discovery would be worth? Pharm firms like Dixon's are out to find something like that, so just be aware that anything you hear working with Mark is for his ears only, or mine—" he grinned broadly "—his friend and counsel."

"There!" she cried triumphantly as the stone flew out from under the horseshoe. Nell stomped a bit on that foot, and Leah backed away. "No," she said, "I can't imagine how much Mark's work could be worth, at least not in dollars and cents. I can't see people tampering with what the Lord has laid out for the length of their lives anyway, though I'd like to see children who are stricken with NAA live longer. But if scientists discover something that could help all mankind, they ought to share it."

"Remind me not to hire you for my law firm's public relations," he said with an expression that was either a grin or a grimace. "Of course, in an ideal world they *should* share," he went on, jamming his hands in his jacket pockets and rocking back on his heels, "but in the real world they've got to be rewarded for discoveries too. That's why I'm a patent attorney, so I can protect do-gooders like Mark from themselves."

"You say do-gooder like it's a dirty word. I pray Dr. Morelli will do good for people here, especially sick children."

"No, I said it as a term of affection. I kid him about it. Mark and I have been best friends since either of us can remember."

Like her and Barbara, Leah thought. How blessed Mark and Clark were to still have each other. "So, exactly what do patent attorneys do?" she asked, peeking into the warm buggy to check on Becca.

"They protect people's rights and property," he said, his voice proud. "Bring lawsuits if those rights are infringed upon. They make—"

"—make a mint for themselves, even if it does stifle progress," a deep voice from behind the buggy said. "They suck up funding and royalties needed for lab trials and testing from pharm firms defending lawsuits against patent infringements. They talk hotshot researchers into going out on their own like runaway mavericks."

"Now, you two," Andrea Dixon said, tugging on the man's arm she held, "let's not get in this again, and not over San Marco. Counselor Quinn, how are you? Brad, this is Leah Curtis—"

"It's Leah Kurtz, Mrs. Dixon," Leah corrected.

"Oh, yes, Kurtz, a good German name," Andrea said with a nod. "She's Mark's liaison to the Amish community."

Brad Dixon nodded, smiled stiffly, and studied her as if she were some kind of lab test herself. He was an imposing man with a craggy, compelling face and silvered hair. Maybe that was why Andrea had colored her hair silver—to match her husband. After all, today they wore matching suede and sheepskin coats.

Leah hoped Mark got home really fast, because she didn't want to play liaison to these people who obviously didn't get along. As if her wishing for Mark could produce him, he opened the clinic door, sending her note to him sailing to the ground. Clark retrieved it before she could.

"Sorry, I didn't hear anyone ring," Mark said, "but I was taking a shower. Brad, good to see you. Clark, I didn't know you were coming. Leah, is anything wrong?"

She was tempted to inform him that Louise Winslow had told her that gene therapy could actually kill people, that it had killed a teenage boy, information he probably knew and hadn't shared with her. And that she didn't like how his friends were arguing over him or talking about money and lawsuits. Andrea might be ripping off people's family heirlooms, but she just hoped these two men weren't ripping anyone off.

"Nothing's wrong," she said, "unless you didn't fix enough pasta for four people. I was just heading home."

Before he could respond, she climbed up in the buggy. She'd clucked Nell out of the driveway at a good clip before she remembered her note, but surely his friend would give it to him.

As gray dusk descended that night and the sky began to shed huge snowflakes, Leah was in a dark mood. This snow might keep her from going to church tomorrow, and tonight it was going to seal her in with all her thoughts, memories and worries. She was pretty sure Sam was still drinking. And she had to remember Mark wasn't Amish but an outsider.

Worse, Becca kept darting looks toward the stairs each time the old house creaked. That unnerved Leah more than anything. She kept recalling that on her deathbed, Barbara had promised, "I'll still be close... watching." Though Leah cherished her friend's memory and though no one Amish believed in hauntings, Becca's startled glances shook Leah to her core.

The draft from up the stairs had greatly diminished, but Becca still seemed jumpy. At last her little eyes grew heavy. She fell asleep in Leah's arms, so she lay the baby down in the crib and covered her up. The coming night stretched out so long, so silent.

Sometimes she imagined she could hear the life-blood of those maple trees dripping into the buckets outside. She dreaded having another nightmare tonight. She hated waking up alone and wanting to be comforted and protected, when she was the only comforter and protector in this old house.

Even reading her beloved books, including the Bible, couldn't soothe her lately. *The valley of the shadow of death* seemed to hover outside this house in the ravine beyond the angel. Even her favorite Romantic poets now raised a strange dread and longing in her. *How wonderful is death and his brother sleep...Both so passing strange and wonderful,* Shelley had written. He'd drowned at age thirty. Keats died of tuberculosis at twenty-five, Byron of disease at thirty-six. All too young to die, like Susie Kline and Jonas Esh and little Amos Kauffman would—Mark said, by age thirteen. She thanked God she had Becca, Becca to keep safe, because Becca kept her sane.

Leah jolted from her agonizing when bright lights pierced the snow and slashed across the window where she stood. Mark's little red car had driven in. He tapped the horn once and got out. He cut across the fresh four inches of snow, holding something in one hand.

"We've got to celebrate!" he called to her and came up on the porch.

She fumbled in her hurry to open the chain lock and swept the door open. "Celebrate what? Becca's sleeping."

He instantly lowered his voice. "Louise Winslow's offer. The use of an MRI, maybe a local foundation for some financial support, so I don't have to make any promises to Brad Dixon to survive. Besides, I wasn't willing to celebrate the opening of the clinic without you!" He stepped in, bringing with him a gush of brisk air.

"Mark, I don't drink champagne—never have, that is."

"I just saved a little bit for us to toast."

"Toast? You drink it warmed?"

"You're priceless, Leah. I don't know what I'd do without you. All right, you don't want champagne," he said, putting it down on the end table by the sofa. "Let's just have some snow instead."

He pulled her cape off the peg by the door and swirled it around her, tugging her out into the flurries. She began to protest, "But Becca—"

"Will be all right, just for a minute. We're not going anywhere."

Leah thought he might have had a bit too much of the champagne already, but she realized he was just high on excitement. And he'd come to be with her.

She laughed as he spun her around in the cascades of heavy snowflakes. They clumped her lashes together, they melted on her nose and lips. She licked at them and laughed. She didn't even miss her bonnet, but just let her starched *kapp* and hair absorb the heavy wetness.

"I'll bet it doesn't snow in Umbria!" she shouted.

"I think it does on the hills, just sometimes in the winter."

"I have an idea! Let's drink some of this tree sap with snow. I haven't had it for years, but it's so good! Here—"

She took one of the buckets off its tap and spilled a little on the snow, then stirred it up a bit. "It's like a snow cone. It's better if it's the cooked syrup and not just the sap, but what do you think?"

"Nectar!" he said, eating it from her cupped hands. "Ambrosia!" He nibbled at her fingertips, and she laughed again.

"And," she said, trying to ignore how dizzy he made her feel, "I know another way to celebrate the opening of your clinic. If you really came to help Amish kids, you're an angel in disguise."

Because she wanted to hug him, she tried to keep him at a distance. Moving away, she lay down on the ground and moved her arms and legs. "Haven't you ever made a snow angel?" she said, giggling. "Come on!"

Her hair ripped loose of her *kapp* and hairpins, and splayed out under her head. The flakes spun down faster, thicker.

He didn't make an angel himself, but knelt by her, hovering over her, first upright, then leaning forward on both hands. "With that black cape, it looks like you have black wings," he said, not laughing now. He looked not only dead serious but awestruck. "My own dark angel," he said and threw himself down close beside her to flail his legs and arms into a much larger angel than she'd made.

Like kids loosed from school, they went wild making them. And then, before she realized it would happen, they were making one together and he rolled on top of her, though he kept his weight off.

And then they started kissing in the wild, wet snow and didn't stop. She never wanted to stop, tilted her head to miss his nose and get closer, and felt the slight rasp of his beard shadow on her chin and cheeks. She held him as he straddled her, like a protective roof against the dark night sky. She didn't want to let him go, even when they could no longer breathe, and she felt the powerful press of his thighs against her hips and she ached to hold him even closer.

"I didn't mean to…" he rasped out, then kissed her again, harder, so intense they could have fallen through the earth to the other side of the planet. Wet with cold snow, she had never felt warmer. With her clothes and hair in disarray, flat on the ground, she felt she soared.

"Ah," he tried to talk again. When he lifted his head slightly, the soft shadows of the distant lantern lit his features. He looked as if he'd been hit not by snowflakes but by an avalanche. "Leah, I—I didn't hurt you? I don't mean to—" He just stopped talking and stared at her.

"You don't mean to hurt me?" she asked, struggling to sit up beside him. "Or didn't mean to kiss me?"

"No, I meant that. The thing is," he said as he helped her up and they brushed themselves off, "do you have to go to confession?"

"Only if I consider it a sin," she clipped out, retrieving her smashed, sodden *kapp* from the head of another nearby snow angel.

"I just don't want you to be insulted. I don't want

to lose you—professionally. I guess I'm an idiot to mix that up with how I feel about you personally."

"You mean it might get in the way of 'protect the work at all costs'?" she asked as she threw her hair back over her shoulders.

"Don't be angry. You tell me never to do anything like that again, I swear I won't—I'll try not. I know it's a...well, a slick first step on a slippery slope for you. Leah?"

"I'm not telling you *not* to do anything like that again. But it can't go anywhere, Mark. With an *auslander,* an outsider like you, it can't go anywhere. It would mean ruin for me—excommunication, the *meidung* with my people. Then I'd be no help to you. That's what I mean, it can't go anywhere."

Realizing she sounded like her own echo, she made the mistake of looking into his eyes again. She could almost read his thoughts: he wanted to tell her it could go everywhere between them, but he bit his lower lip.

"You're the best thing that's happened to me here," he called to her as she went up on the porch.

She turned back to face him. As the dusk deepened to black night, standing there in the snow, her surroundings reminded her of a snow globe she'd seen once in a store, the kind you shook to make the pieces of white plastic swirl. Only, she felt she was inside it with him, out of control, rolling, riding around under heaven.

"I'm praying you're the best thing that's happened to my people here," she said. "And I want to be a big part of that, of your work."

She wanted to be so much more, but she had to fight it, fight her need for him. "See you Monday," she managed to say as she dashed inside the house. And despite the huge upheaval in her mother's heart, Becca still lay calmly sleeping.

After all that, Leah was too keyed-up to sleep. If those wild moments with Mark seemed like a dream, all she had to do was look out at those seven snow angels, large and small, and the huge one where they had lain together. The snow didn't fall so heavily now but by morning, perhaps, all the evidence would be buried.

Overwhelmed by curiosity, she took a sip of the champagne he'd left. A bit tart, she thought, and bubbly on the tongue. It might be better with a sausage sandwich or taste sweet in contrast to German potato salad; she wondered what Mark and his friends had eaten with it. And she was touched again he'd saved some for her.

She closed the last drape above the sofa and lay down to sleep. Becca's regular breathing comforted her amidst the creaks and cracks in the bones of the old house. But it was warmer now with Mark's insulation. So much warmer…

She was shocked to see daylight seeping through the curtains. She had slept. Becca was still quiet. She had only awakened once to be changed and fed. Stretching like a baby herself, Leah rose and pulled on a flannel robe.

Would the snow angels still be out there, so white in contrast with the dark angel in the cemetery? She pulled a single curtain aside to peer out.

And gasped.

The angels they'd made with the imprints of their bodies were still there. But across the throat of each was a crimson slash, as if someone had cut the angels' throats.

7

Sam was not at church, so early Sunday afternoon, Leah buggied herself and Becca toward his cousin's house on the other side of town. Ben Troyer and his wife, Etta, belonged to the Pleasant area Amish church instead of the Maplecreek one. Ben was on the traveling work team that Sam headed up.

"I thought I might find Sam here," Leah told Etta when she answered the door. "Becca's a bit overdue for her nap, but I wanted her to spend some time with him before he gets busy on that new project."

"Good to see both of you, Leah. Yes, they start working on the church bright and early tomorrow morning. Come in, come in," Etta invited. She was a short, spare woman, friendly but probably lonely, Leah thought, since Ben was gone a lot and her two children's families had moved to western Ohio for more affordable land.

"Isn't she looking like her *maam,* now?" Etta added, clasping her hands together, as she peered closer at Becca.

"You know, I think she is," Leah said as she lifted Becca from her carrier in the Troyer front room and sat in the big rocking chair Etta indicated. "I'm so close to her, I don't even see it sometimes. She's certainly Barbara's gift to me. Sam is here, isn't he? I thought maybe he went to church with both of you today, since he wasn't at our service."

Etta's mouth pursed even tighter, as if an invisible drawstring had pulled her lips together. "He didn't feel to rights," she said with a frown. "Slept in. But I'll tell him you're here with his little one and send him right down."

Leah waited for a good ten minutes, playing with Becca, then walking her back and forth across the Troyers' shiny maple floor. Finally, Sam came downstairs with his hair slicked back as if he'd just washed up. His eyes were bloodshot.

"Wasn't sure you'd show your face," he said, folding his arms over his chest and coming close as if to block her into a corner.

"Because I'm working with Dr. Morelli? I don't understand why you wouldn't want me working for a doctor who's trying to cure genetic diseases, especially after Barbara died from one and Becca's a carrier."

"Working for him's one thing, but rolling all over the ground with him's another!"

"I...where were you? That's twice you've just sneaked up. We were making snow angels."

"That what they call it these days?"

"So where were you? Lurking and just watching from the field or the cemetery?"

"You want to know, I was with Miles Mason in his van."

"I didn't see you or hear you. You must have approached with your lights off and parked out a ways."

He looked both guilty and angry. Had Sam been sneaking around, spying on her other times? He could have put blood on the snow angels, but the footprints and the dead flowers had appeared before he was back in town.

"The snow mighta been falling thick," he blustered, "but I don't think you care who saw you. So where was Becca then?"

"Asleep inside. We were only out about ten minutes and then he left. So are you and Miles Mason the ones who defaced the angels? I looked at the red stuff real close this morning. Even though the snow's melting, it could well have been tree sap, colored red. Or it could have been blood."

"What in kingdom come you talking about? Defaced angels? Red sap and blood? All I know is I came out to see Becca again and found you acting wilder than Barbara ever did."

Leah's chin jerked up. "Meaning what?"

"Meaning nothing," he said, and raked his fingers through his wet hair. But a moment ago his stance had turned momentarily threatening and his tone menacing. This could not be Sam, not Becca's father. Again, he clenched his fists at his sides. She shifted the baby back away from him.

"Meaning nothing," he repeated, "but I won't have you working for that doctor when you should be a full-time mother, and I'm gonna tell him so. Sure, you got the 'ficial papers on Becca, but only 'cause I promised Barbara. Well, she's not here anymore. Maybe Etta can take Becca on, 'cause she's missing her own family."

Leah held Becca closer. "I think you have plenty to worry about with your own problem without suggesting I'm not a good mother," she countered. "Barbara wanted me to have her and you agreed. Besides, I found your whiskey bottles in the attic. And I'd say you're still drinking or you would have faced everyone at church today and been up before now. And that sweet breath you have isn't covering up anything."

She actually thought he would hit her. Still blocking him from Becca, she darted past him. All those purple and brown bruises on Barbara's body that were attributed to her disease—had Sam been drinking and hit her? Surely not once he knew she was ill. And what did he mean about Barbara acting wild? Leah might have acted wild too, if she thought she was dying at age twenty-six.

"You better keep your mouth shut about those bottles," Sam said, turning to stalk her and pointing nearly in her face. "I said I got extra money for you to move into town. You just quit that job or else."

"Or else what? That rattletrap house you never repaired because you were probably drinking will fall completely apart, with Becca and me in it? Or else you'll try to take my baby back? I'm a good mother to her, and I'll provide for her financially too. But I can't have someone who's drinking around her any more than I'll bet Miles Mason can have a drinker up in his church's rafters. I regret, for Barbara's memory and Becca's sake, it's come to this between us."

She was planning a quick exit, but he stormed out first, not only from the room but the house. She saw him, no coat or hat on, dash to the old garage out back. As Leah got in her buggy, she kept an eye on the place.

He likely had more bottles there, and she didn't want him returning to rave at her. Or worse.

"What do you mean, you should quit?" Mark exploded when she hit him with that news first thing at the clinic Monday morning. "We were both of us okay with what happened—or so I th—"

"It isn't that," she explained as she faced him under the large print of his double helix. The glass that covered it was so shiny she could see their reflection in it, like a strange twisting mirror. "Our snow angels...I enjoyed making them. It isn't that."

"What then?" he asked as he came closer and took her hands in his. She didn't pull back. Not one bit did she regret what had passed between her and Mark Morelli on Saturday night. And she wanted desperately to help him in his work.

"Sam came back Saturday night," she explained, "and saw us in the snow. He was with Miles Mason, the man who's tapped all the trees around the house."

"Why was he with him?"

"For transportation, I guess, and Miles is trying to get Sam to sell the house and property to him."

"Just to get his hands on about ten more maple trees?"

"I guess so, I don't know. One of his major stands of trees is right behind the property, so maybe he just wants to expand. Also, Sam and the framing team are working for Mason to add on to the church he attends, First Methodist, on the west edge of town."

"And Mason is one of the guys Seth was working for?"

"Right. Anyhow, I've learned Sam's been drinking, for how long and how bad I don't know, but at least since before Barbara died. Mark, the truth is, Sam doesn't want me working here and made threats about trying to take Becca back."

"Physical threats?"

"More or less. But I'm not afraid of him that way," she said vehemently, despite the new nagging fear that he might have hurt Barbara. "He needs help, and if his cousin doesn't get it for him from the church, I will. He mentioned challenging the adoption papers and said that his cousin's wife would take Becca to raise."

"Like hell—heck—he will! You've met my friend, Clark Quinn. He may be a patent-protection attorney, but he could protect Becca too, make mincemeat of Sam, especially if the guy's more or less deserted his child and is drinking."

"The Amish don't sue each other, Mark. It just isn't done. But then, neither is what else has been happening."

"Meaning us?"

"Yes, but that's not what I was thinking of. I didn't want to worry you about all this, but someone put ribbons of red liquid across the necks of our snow angels Saturday night—as if their throats had been cut."

He squeezed her hands so hard she flinched, and he let go. "It must have been someone who knew how Varina Roscoe died and is trying to scare you out of the house. It could be Sam."

"I don't know," she admitted, hugging herself and starting to pace. "Of course, he could have read about her murder in the cemetery book. It was in a trunk by his bottles. But now that I donated the book to the historical society, lots of people know about that. Soon, I suppose everyone around here will know, because Louise Winslow wants to get some publicity in the paper."

Mark leaned stiff-armed on a front windowsill that overlooked the street and vet clinic. "Jesse Cutler yelled at me from his van before he drove off yesterday," he said, his voice calm. "He said I should only treat sick Amish kids and not ripe young women."

"What? Ripe! He has no right—"

"Has he said anything to you? *Is* he anything to you?"

She explained everything she'd been holding back, with the final explanation, "I just didn't want to get you involved."

"I *am* involved if he's going to try to smear me or scare you. The thing is, that message on my door was left before there was any connection between you and me."

"So, you think it's not Jesse harassing me at the house?"

"Not necessarily," he said, still glaring out the window. "There's a saying that 'Hell hath no fury like a woman scorned,' and I guess that could go for a man too. Especially if he thinks we have something going. But as for Sam," he said, turning back to her, "he's been out of town, so your dead flowers and strange footsteps couldn't be his doing. But maybe Mason's been keeping an eye on more than Sam's maple trees for him. Maybe you're supposed to think that the angel herself—himself—went for a walk," he said, raising his eyebrows. "Or Varina herself."

"Don't say that!"

"I didn't mean it's true. I just don't want it to be the same idiot who smeared up my door with a bloody threat. Someone who's against my work, and, since you're helping, is now trying to hit at you. If that's the case, I'd agree you shouldn't work here."

"I'm not afraid. Whoever it may be is obviously a coward."

"Maybe or maybe not. Despite those chain locks you have, I think we need to put some dead bolts on your doors and maybe latches on the downstairs windows. That old root-cellar door doesn't lead into your basement, does it?"

She was amazed at how closely he must have studied her doors, windows and house in the short time he was there.

"No. Barbara said the root cellar's self-contained and not used anymore. I haven't ever looked inside it. The entry to it is covered by layers of dead maple leaves from last fall, like an unbroken seal."

"Look, Leah, maybe you should move back with your parents until this clears up."

"No, I'm not leaving my and Becca's house!"

"I don't want you leaving the clinic either. I need the Kline and Kauffman pedigree charts and—"

"Pedigree charts!" she interrupted. As her hands shot to her hips, her frustration at everything came pouring out at him. "It sounds like..like you're studying breeding dogs. Jesse Cutler would just love that. You never told me they were called pedigree charts. But then, you never told me that gene therapy killed a teenage boy, either!"

"I wasn't holding back the information as if it was some big secret. It made all the papers and set the transfer of good genes through virus vectors way back. Another attempt like that hasn't been done again—at least, not that anyone's admitting to. The odds are getting a lot better on gene th—"

"Genes transferred through viruses? Viruses are something no one wants. No wonder some innocent boy died."

"Leah, if you want a more detailed rundown on things, okay."

"I just want answers about dead flowers and footprints and slashed angels' throats."

He sat her down on the couch next to a wide-eyed Becca, who had stopped studying her own hands to watch them. He sat too and put his arm around Leah's shoulders.

"I think we're back to square one," he said. "I don't want you hurt, so I can't have you out on the roads alone when you're working for me."

"So that's that? I didn't mean I would quit, but just that I should. You said you needed me, but now you're letting me go?" She tried to stop her lower lip from quivering. She hated crying. When her sister died, she'd been hysterical at first and vowed never to lose control of her life like that again. When Barbara died, she'd held it all inside.

"No way I'm letting you go," he said. "But we'll have to make the trips together to do the charts and visit patients. And leave Becca with your mother when we do, for a while at least, just in case someone tries to do more on the road than just cut off your buggy."

"All right," she said, blinking back the sting of tears before they could fall. "Maybe whoever it is will give themselves away or make a mistake. But I am not running home to live with my parents, however much they'd like that."

"Hmm," Mark said and squeezed her shoulders before he let her go and stood up. "Does that mean we're going to have to put your mother on a list of suspects who'd like you out of that house? Maybe she left me a chicken-blood note to close this clinic?"

Despite the fact her mother still kept poultry at their farm, Leah just rolled her eyes at his attempt at levity. "Don't try to change the subject," she insisted. "What about the dangers of gene therapy?"

"I know this may sound like a strange comparison, but the science of genetics is like exploring space—the space program."

"Don't look at me that way. I've read about it. My people do know man's been to the moon, Mark, and about the space station."

"Then you also know that despite those great successes, there have been disasters," he explained, gesturing broadly. "Valuable lives were lost in the *Columbia* and *Challenger* catastrophes. Likewise, geneticists tried to move too fast and made major miscalculations. But that doesn't mean we should scrap a program with so many future benefits."

"But using viruses on human beings to cure them?"

"Geneticists remove the infection part of the virus but keep the infiltration part of it. Since human immune systems attack harmful viruses, we're now working with harmless ones found naturally in the body. But let's get back to the here and now," he insisted, folding his arms over his chest. "I'm going to talk to Sam."

"No, I don't think that would help. I'll do it. Just one more try, for Becca's sake. He is her father."

"All right," he said, "but make sure others are around. Let's drop Becca off at the bakery on our way out to the Kauffman farm this morning. I only hope they'll be as willing to trust me—actually, trust *you*—as Jonas Esh's parents were. And we'll have to hurry, because Susie and her mother are coming in for blood tests right after lunch this afternoon."

They took Leah's buggy, even if Mark's car was safer, because Leah said the Kauffmans would consider a shiny red sport model prideful. "And," she'd added under her breath, "the Amish never use red, the color of martyrs' blood."

"So I should get a more conservative car?"

"Just a word to the wise," she told him. "In bad weather, your little car will be terrible on these hilly, wet roads."

"You sure seem to know a lot about that. Have you ever driven a car?" he asked, a smile on his taut lips, but his voice challenging.

"Exactly once," she told him, feeling proud, although she tried never to boast. "When my brother, Isaac, was in his *rumspringa* days and showing off. He'd borrowed it from a worldly friend, a Ford, I think it was. I was pretty good at steering, except for curves or turns."

"Heaven help us all," he said and winked at her.

"One thing I've figured out, Teacher Leah, is that this area's full of curves and turns."

She wondered if he was referring to more than the roads, but let the subject drop as she smoothly turned Nell onto the long lane that led to the Kauffmans' house and plant nursery. With several of his relatives, Amos Kauffman's father no longer farmed but had a trade.

"And speaking of a word to the wise," Mark said, "I'd like to explain more about how gene study works, viruses and all."

"You probably think I can't grasp it or it would shock me."

"Yup," he said, which both annoyed and amused her. "It only took me about ten years of intense study to *begin* to grasp the complexities."

She had real trouble staying mad at Mark Morelli. She'd thought doctors were full of self-pride, an anathema to the Amish who believed in cooperation instead of competition, but he wasn't an uppity-up, as her *daad* would say. His friends, the Dixons, were another story. Brad hadn't said one word to her, and Andrea had patronized her. At least Clark seemed friendly.

"Okay," she said, using Mark's favorite English word, "tell me what you think is the thing that would shock me most about genes."

"Here goes. I have a theory that the genetic mutation that causes NAA appears in nearly all instances to occur in sperm prior to conception."

She leaned back away and glanced sideways at him. "Did you think, Doctor," she said, "the word *sperm* was going to shock little Amish me? And it certainly doesn't surprise me one bit that the man's instead of the woman's genes could be behind the problem."

"Miss Leah, I do believe you are an Amish feminist," he said and laughed.

She laughed too as they reined in between the Kauffman house and the greenhouse.

Amos was very ill, his mother, Lizzie, explained. Mark wished he could say something comforting, but the eleven-year-old had had a triple heart bypass at the Cleveland Clinic just before Christmas and was not recovering well. Besides heart trouble, the boy had arthritis and was hard of hearing.

Lizzie took him and Leah upstairs to the boy's bedroom. Because Leah had warned him about the boy's condition, Mark had brought his medical bag, just in case. He put it down by the bed next to an oxygen tank. Amos was breathing through a tube clamped to his nasal septum. A tray of pills also held a baseball, signed by the entire Cleveland Indians team, it looked like.

"Are you the gene hunter?" the boy whispered.

"Yeah, that's me," Mark said, smiling. He tried to talk loudly since Lizzie had said Amos didn't have his hearing aid yet. "Man, an Indians baseball? I'd love to hold it. Can you believe all the talent they've been trading away lately, Amos?"

The child's old-man face lit and suffused with color. "*Ja,* you can hold it. Manny Ramirez, Roberto Alomar and Jim Thome—when's the trading gonna stop, Dr. Morelli? I read the papers *Daad* gets me and sometimes even listen to games on a transistor, but right now they're playing down in Florida. I know all their stats from way back five whole years. You a fan too?"

"I am, but not with my own signed Indians ball," he said, examining it closely.

"They visited sick kids where I was getting tests. They were nice, but they stared at me, partly 'cause I'm Amish, partly 'cause of this. Everyone stares."

"Doctors have to stare to see if they can help," Mark said. "But that doesn't mean I don't see you as Amos, awesome athletic fan, just as much as I see you as a patient."

"I've had lots of doctors."

"But I'm a neighborhood doctor, and I make house calls. You know, if it's all right with your parents, maybe we could have our first meeting of the three of you who have this same problem here at your house. No way should that baseball go anywhere it could get lost, and I think Susie Kline and Jonas Esh would like to see it."

"*Ja,* that's fine, long as I'm not too tired to talk that day. And it's *ser gut* if you want to be my doctor—my last doctor, I think."

Bending a bit to put his hand on the boy's thin, bony shoulder, Mark marveled again at the courage and wisdom of these kids. Like the Amish, they had as much to teach him as he did them. As he straightened, his gaze snagged Leah's where she stood just inside the door with Lizzie Kauffman. Amos's mother's eyes glistened with tears, but Leah's shone with pride.

They stayed longer than they'd intended, for when Amos's father, Gideon Kauffman, joined them, he insisted on taking them on a tour of his greenhouse. It was crammed with sprouting perennials and annuals, which would be for sale in two months. Just breathing the sweet air made Leah hope for spring. Gideon gave both Mark and Leah some creeping phlox, sweet alyssum and salvia starts to put on their windowsills and transplant later.

"*Ach,* I know that old place where you're living," Gideon told her. "End of the line on Deer Run Road. Now, each time you come back to see Amos, I'll give you more plants. You spruce that house up this spring, maybe do some window boxes. You, too, at the clinic, Doctor."

"I miss having Becca with us," Leah told Mark as they started back toward town at a good clip. "I want to stop to see and feed her before Susie and her mother arrive."

"I was thinking we might actually see them along here, since their road feeds in just ahead. But bring Becca over," he said. "She's as good an icebreaker as a baseball."

"You played that just right with Amos."

"I wasn't playing at all. That boy and I are going to talk a lot of Cleveland Indians, maybe the Browns too, though I don't suppose the Amish are into football—too violent."

"Don't the Italians play violent sports? What about in your favorite place, Umbria?"

"My favorite place is becoming Roscoe County, but yes, the Italians play soccer and are passionate about that and all of life. And, of course, love is one of their favorite sports."

"Really?" she said, uncertain if he was teasing. "But no violence in that, I hope, especially not in the beautiful setting you described the first day we met. I intend to get a book on Umbria, though, to see if it is as lovely as it is here and—"

"Look," he interrupted, pointing. "What's that ahead?"

She looked and gasped. A buggy was tipped over the ditch, but hadn't fallen in. A dark-colored van had stopped, maybe to help, but took off as they watched.

"Oh, no, oh, no!" she cried. "Not a hit-and-run!"

She didn't recognize the van and couldn't read the license plate from here, not even what state it was. But she could pick out the buggy now by the jaunty tilt of its triangular, orange, slow-moving-vehicle sign and a bumper sticker that read Honk if You're Amish.

"It's Seth's courting buggy!"

"How can you tell those things apart? Do you think he's back?"

She fought to keep from crying, from shaking. Smacking the reins on Nell's rump and clucking to her, she tried to speed the horse up. Mark was already unfastening the plastic buggy cover on his side.

Leah tried to steady herself. This was not Katie's wreck, she told herself. No freezing up, no frenzy. After all, the buggy didn't look banged up.

The moment she pulled behind it, Mark was out and running with his cell phone in one hand and his black bag in the other. Leah scrambled out and tore after him.

The horse had righted itself, though it had slipped down the slope of the ditch and stood, fetlock deep, in icy water, snorting and stamping. On the grassy berm where she'd fallen or been thrown, Miriam Kline lay, looking dazed, staring up at the sky. Her cape was pulled awry; her dress sleeve on one arm was ripped clear to her shoulder.

And Susie, sprawled face-up next to her mother on the grass, all petticoats and spindly legs, looked dead.

Leah couldn't help herself. She saw Barbara and Katie there and screamed.

8

"Yes, this is an emergency," Mark said into his cell phone. "That's why I dialed 911."

Leah wasn't surprised he sounded terse. Why did this have to happen to poor little Susie of all people, and on the way to the clinic? Mark dropped his black bag and touched the side of the girl's throat with two fingers. He left her in her sprawled position but pulled her skirt down to cover her legs.

"Listen carefully, ma'am," he said into the phone. "This is Dr. Mark Morelli. About a mile west of Maplecreek, I've got an Amish-buggy accident with two injured females…"

Susie must be alive! Leah exulted as she knelt by Miriam and held her hand. Yes, she could see Susie was breathing. Mark was now taking her wrist pulse, even while he talked.

"…southeast corner of Hillfarm and Holtz Roads." His voice was clipped and coldly calm. "The adult victim is conscious but dazed, the six-year-old female, who is in very delicate shape, unconscious but breathing and…"

Leah lost track of his words when Miriam struggled

to sit up. She fought Leah's attempts to hold her down. "The doctor's helping Susie," Leah said. "Just lie still in case you broke anything."

"I'm all right—just hit the back of my head."

"No," Mark was saying, "I'm not staying on the line. Send the sheriff if you have to, but get a squad of medics here ASAP. Leah," he said as he punched off and flipped the phone closed, "open my case. In the top pocket, you'll find ammonia capsules." He lifted Susie's eyelids and looked closely into her pupils as he spoke. "It's a little plastic bottle marked NH3. Let's see if we can bring her to, though I think she's got a fracture of the left humerus."

The arm bone, Leah thought. She prayed that would be the extent of the child's injuries, not a coma like the one Brett and Daniel Brand's little girl had suffered through. And not a fatal head injury they couldn't see, like the one that killed her own sister.

"Here," she said, handing him the bottle. Despite Leah's efforts, Miriam was on her knees across from Mark on Susie's other side, murmuring, praying. Mark shook out a capsule and snapped it open under the child's nose. She startled and opened both eyes. Miriam kept murmuring, "*Danken Sie Gott.* Thank God!"

"*Maam,*" Susie cried, "*mein arm...*"

"Susie," Mark said, "I'm going to hold your hurt arm still. Tell me if anything else hurts." Slowly, he lifted her legs together, then moved her right arm from under her head down to her side, all the while holding her left arm in the strange bent position it was in.

"Some others are coming to help fix your arm," he

went on. "The buggy tipped, that's all. It's not broken and the horse is okay."

"Seth's horse and buggy," Susie whispered, squeezing her eyes tight shut. "Star needed some exercise, so we brought him. Is my arm hurt bad?"

"It looks broken but we'll fix it. We'll get you a colored cast and have everyone draw flowers on it."

She opened her eyes and looked at Mark. "Just so I don't have to draw. You said I didn't."

"Nope," he said, carefully shrugging off his jacket, one arm at a time, until Leah helped him. "Cover her with it," he said, and she did, tucking it in around the little body, knees to chin, but for that arm Mark still held stable. "And that's a promise, Susie. Neither of us is going to draw, because we can't draw for beans, remember?"

"Oh, *ja.* I remember that, but not how we got on the ground."

Leah put her cloak over Susie too, then darted to the tilted buggy and found two lap robes, one of which she put over Susie and the other around Miriam, who was trembling so hard her teeth chattered.

"Just nerves," Mark tried to assure the woman. "But for a bump on your head and those scratches on your arm, I think we'll find that you're all right. But we'll watch for a concussion."

"*Ja,* somehow I hit the back of my head. And I must have caught my sleeve when we spilled out," she said, frowning dazedly down at her bare arm. It was all scratched up, and the sleeve was ripped from wrist to armpit. "That van…I think they must have scared Star off the berm, but I can't remember."

"That's not unusual in a trauma situation," Mark

said. "It may come back to you, it may not. Are you dizzy or nauseous?"

"No, but my head hurts bad. Doctor Mark, we don't want to go to the hospital if it's not necessary. Can you put that cast on Susie's arm? She trusts you."

"If you're worried about money, I can handle that," Mark said. "Susie's my patient now, and I'll see she's cared for. But, yes, if the medics check you out, I can set a broken arm at the clinic and we can guard for signs of concussion. Still, with Susie, I think she'd better have some X-rays to be certain there are no hairline fractures."

"I...I just can't recall that the buggy tipped," Miriam said again, as if to herself. "A brown van came too close, but wouldn't I remember the buggy tipped?"

Susie piped up, "I think they stopped ahead of us and got out."

"Right," Mark said. "We saw them near the buggy when we spotted you, but they took off. Either they were afraid they'd be blamed, or they saw our buggy and figured they'd better let other Amish people help. Still, they never should have left when they saw you were both down."

The horrible night Katie was killed flashed again at Leah. She hadn't been at that accident scene, but she'd talked to those who had. Buggy parts and bodies strewn across the road...kids in a small courting buggy, just like this one. To stop the nightmare vision, she went to help Seth's panicked horse.

"Come on, Star, come on now," she said, picking up the reins and pulling them taut so he stopped tossing his head. "Come on, Star, come out of there, up the slope, come on."

Seth had loved this new horse and his buggy, she recalled. He would not have left it, any more than he would his family and his jobs.

The horse struggled and Leah had to use Nell, backing up on the road, to help pull him out. Two cars stopped to offer help, but she told them the squad was coming and waved them on. Finally, with Star still hitched to the courting buggy, Leah righted it and pulled it back on the road.

"I hear a siren," Mark called to her. "It's about time."

"You're not in Cleveland or Columbus," she said as she knelt by Miriam again.

"I know," he said, his voice and expression softer than she'd heard or seen this last frenzied quarter hour. "Don't I know."

But it was Sheriff Martin, not the rescue squad.

"Lucky thing you stumbled on this, Doc," he greeted Mark, and nodded to Leah.

"Is the squad en route?"

"It's volunteer, takes a while out here in the boonies. How are they—little Susie?"

"She's a fighter. A broken arm, I think."

"*Ja,*" Miriam said, "but her head's working better than mine."

"Can you tell me anything about what happened here, Mrs. Kline?" the sheriff asked, stooping to assess Susie, then straightening to whip out his spiral notebook.

"I'm not sure," she said, "but we'll tell you what we know—what the doctor and Leah saw."

The sheriff glanced at Mark, then at her. "What you *saw?*" he said, turning to face Leah. "You were here when it happened?"

"Just approaching," Leah explained. "We saw a van, maybe with people trying to help, but, evidently, when they saw us coming, they took off."

"But not a hit-and-run," the sheriff muttered, looking around again. "The buggy and horse look all right. The van didn't hit them, did it?"

"Apparently not," Mark said.

"Can you identify the van or the people?"

"Let's just get these ladies taken care of before we do police reports," Mark said. "I hear another siren."

"Leah," the sheriff said and gestured her over between the buggies. "You or the doc get a good look at that van or its passengers? Or did the girl or her mother?"

"Not really. They're both a little foggy and shaken, as you can understand. They've had a terrible time of it, with Seth disappearing and now this. It's been five days since Luke and Katie's wedding. Have you come up with any leads about Seth?"

At least, she thought, he had the decency to look guilty. "I've asked around, but no one's seen hide nor hair of him."

"Can I file a missing person's report, if his parents don't, or can Dr. Morelli?"

"Leah, I'm real, real sorry, but we just gotta accept some things. The boy ran off, and I can't blame him, the burden he was carrying. Now, I know where you're coming from, but you just let me wor—"

"Sheriff, you may think you know where I'm coming from," she said, raising her voice above the siren as the medics screeched closer—though she couldn't see why they needed to make all that noise way out here. "But if Seth isn't found, you have no idea where I'm going."

"What the Sam Hill does that mean?" he demanded, but she ran back toward Mark and her friends as the medics pulled up.

Seth jerked awake. What time of day was it? What was the weather? The air in here was so fake—not stale, not fresh, just strange, shifting silently. He didn't even know what day it was. Worse, where was he?

He was annoyed something had waked him, because he was having a good dream for once. Since they'd stopped sticking needles in his veins, his sleep had gotten better. In this dream, he'd been driving Star when he was new, just after he and *Daad* had bought him at the livestock auction in Kidron and hitched him for the first time to the courting buggy. Star was smart, and they were going to get along just great. He could feel the steady sway of the buggy as the roads opened up before him under the crisp autumn sky....

He bit back bitter tears for home and freedom. At least he'd been moved to a different room. This was a hospital, all right, though it felt more like a prison. But he was no longer restrained or run through tests like some kind of lab animal at Dr. Cutler's vet clinic. Cutler kept two stray dogs and two cats in cages all the time, in case they were needed to donate blood for people's pets who were sick or injured. *Ja,* he was starting to feel like he was one of those lab animals.

He spent a lot of time pacing his windowless room. He had to put on a hood—they looked in at him through a sliding space in the door to be sure—before his food trays were brought in. He had a flush toilet, and water from a sink, and a bed, but he was going out of his gourd, as David Groder liked to say. He'd been trying to patch things together that he'd heard in a hundred pieces in here, but not much of it made sense.

He only overheard conversations if they were in the hall outside and if he put his ear to the crack under his metal door. Mostly people were walking past, so he only heard parts. He was wary that they might look in and see him sprawled on the floor. Sometimes, though, disembodied voices floated in through the air vent near the floor, or else through the low-hung, Styrofoam-looking ceiling itself. He'd stood on his bed and pushed one of those sections out, but could see nowhere to go in the dead space above.

Someone was walking by in the hall.

"…got the NAA blood sample…"

"Wow, worth its weight in gold…"

"Two normal adult samples, sib, parent and the recessive…"

"Nearly got caught."

Those two voices moved down the hall. A moment later, he heard, "Can't get rid of her but need to quiet her, move her… Some sort of serious warning to stay away…"

"…if she's gone, it might inspire Morelli to keep going in her memory."

Morelli!

Could they mean Dr. Mark Morelli? They had to! Could he be here? He couldn't be in on this. Seth had been so sure he could trust Dr. Morelli. But if this was a gene hospital, Dr. Morelli could be visiting and not know Seth was here!

Seth scrambled up from the floor, ready to pound on the door and scream his name. But one last fragment of a new voice floated to him.

"The doctor says to get rid of the Amish helper."

Did they mean Teacher Leah, Morelli's Amish helper? Or did they mean him? Seth pressed his forehead and fists to the cool metal of the door and sobbed.

In Mark's kitchen at four that afternoon, Leah and Mark shared a pizza they'd ordered while she fed Becca with her free hand. They were both ravenous. They'd missed lunch, since Mark and Miriam went with the squad so Susie could be x-rayed at the county hospital in Pleasant. At Susie's insistence, Mark helped an E.R. doctor there put her fractured arm in a Day-Glo-pink fiberglass cast.

Leah had led Seth's horse and buggy back to the Klines' and explained to Reuben what had happened. He'd taken the family surrey to Pleasant to bring back his wife, daughter and Mark, who'd signed to pay the E.R. bills.

"Sorry you didn't get your blood samples from Susie and Miriam today," Leah told him. "But I actually think you made more progress, as things turned out. The Klines—and so, all the local Amish—will be on your side now that you took such good care of their own, even using your own money."

"Man, that scared me when I saw Susie thrown like that. A child who should be a resilient six-year-old, and all I could think of was how many little old ladies die from falls. But the amazing thing is, but for that arm, her other bones weren't broken." He shook his head.

"Mark, I was thinking, too." She put Becca over her shoulder and started to burp her. "Susie couldn't have seen people get out of that van, like she said she did. The van's passengers wouldn't have stopped or have gotten out if the buggy hadn't been already tipped, the two of them thrown out, and Susie unconscious."

"Unless she blacked out after she was thrown."

"All right, play devil's advocate like you always do. I know you said trauma can stun somebody so they can't recall an accident, but Miriam seemed totally unsure of what happened even before it."

"So what are you saying?" he asked, trying to bite off a huge piece of melted mozzarella before it dragged onto his chin.

"I don't know. I'll just bet that those people moved or jostled Susie, and she came to for a moment and saw them, that's all. Maybe she'll remember more later, or Miriam will."

"I think we'd better concentrate on getting their blood samples, even if we have to go to their farm to take them. I need those before I can move ahead."

"Can I ask you a question about Clark?"

He looked surprised as he downed some of his cola. "Sure. Shoot."

"He kind of explained what he does. He believes patents protect the rights of whoever makes a scientific discovery. But aren't patents for *things* people invent? There's nothing in the human body a scientist invents—well, maybe a tooth filling or something surgically inserted. But God's the only inventor of the human body, and I don't think He's into patents and lawsuits and making a mint, as Brad Dixon put it."

"I've got to admit, that's been a big argument. But in America, ideas and discoveries can be patented and those patents defended. If I discover an antibiotic or medicine, and it's put in the person's body, that can be patented. It's a huge business, and Clark's in the thick of it, very successful."

"But, let's say you discover an NAA gene—something inherent in the body—that causes fast aging. Could you patent it?"

"For twenty years. Legally, I'd 'own' that gene and anyone who wanted to 'use' it would have to pay me a royalty or percentage."

"On people's own bodies—their own diseases?"

"I know it sounds complex—"

"No, it sounds immoral."

"Leah, it takes a lot of money to prepare medicine and treatments to fight diseases. And unless huge companies like Brad Dixon's pharmaceutical firm are sure they have the rights to their discoveries for a while, they're not going to sink time and funding into it. I admit that patents are a problem, though, because they make pharm firms rush too fast to get drugs or therapy to the market while the patent's still theirs. And that means they sometimes skimp on testing and trials."

"And that's part of why you left MR?"

"Part. Look at it this way. If Becca had a deadly disease—say, she wasn't just a carrier but had inherited her mother's Regnell anemia—wouldn't you want a treatment as soon as possible? Wouldn't you want money poured into it, and would you be willing to take a risk to save her life? There are two sides to it, and I'm caught in the middle, but I'm still forging ahead. I hope you'll decide to stay with me on this."

"And Clark's the lawyer?" she said, shaking her head. "I'll bet you could convince anyone of anything in court better than he could."

He smiled and relaxed visibly. "Well, since the Amish don't go to court, I hope I convinced you. Or at least that you'll think about it."

"I will," she said, standing with Becca. "But I've got to head home before it gets dark."

"I'm going to follow you in the car," he said, closing the empty pizza box. "I just want to know you're safe inside the house and have looked around before you give me the high sign. Then, tomorrow, we're going to install some more safety hardware on your doors and windows."

She was deeply touched. And she knew it must be a sacrifice for him to drive that sports car behind a buggy for nearly thirty minutes at nine miles an hour.

Wondering who had been kind enough to have put a copy of the *Maplecreek Weekly* in her buggy— maybe Louise Winslow?—she headed toward home with Mark right behind.

After Mark returned from seeing Leah safely home, he watched the last buggy and then a car leave Dr. Cutler's vet clinic. Locking up, he walked across the street. The office was dark, so he went around back where a large prefab metal structure held cages and stalls for animals being treated. He'd thought Cutler's OR facilities were in the back of the brick building, but he glimpsed an empty operating table through a lighted window in the shed. And Cutler, bending over it.

He knocked on the door.

"Come in, Groder!" he called. Mark assumed he meant David Groder, Seth's friend, who worked here off and on, but he went in anyway.

"Two corpses to be loaded in my van and—" he said and turned to see Mark.

"What is it, Morelli?" He had bloody surgical gloves on his hands and a mask over the lower part of his face, which he tugged down. "I'm busy."

"Disposing of corpses, I guess," Mark said, trying not to sound taunting. To his surprise, he saw two large dogs lying in a single wooden crate at Cutler's feet. If Cutler hadn't called them corpses, Mark would have thought they were merely sleeping, for they were curled up with their heads on their crossed paws, on beds of what appeared to be blue crushed velvet. Although Mark was used to blood and surgical procedures, he was grateful he hadn't had to deal with death for a long time.

"They've been euthanized, since they couldn't be saved," Cutler said. "I've put them to sleep, as everyone likes to call it."

"That must be a tough part of the job," Mark said, suddenly empathizing with this man he'd come to warn to stay away from Leah.

"Not really. Death is part of life—a fascinating part, at that."

"But people losing their pets...I'll never forget when my dog got sick and couldn't be saved when I was ten. It was like a brother or sister had died."

"If I got emotionally involved each time I had to do this…" He shook his head and shrugged.

Mark almost ordered him not to become emotionally involved with Leah either, but he held his temper. On the stainless-steel table in this small room, he saw a discarded needle and the vial it had evidently come from. And the vial had an orange plastic stopper in it, like the one he and Leah had found in the area where Seth disappeared.

That in itself was mere coincidence and meant absolutely nothing, but Mark didn't like what he saw in Jesse Cutler. He was either an emotional robot, indifferent to controlling—ending—creatures' lives, or he was a connoisseur of such power.

"So," Mark went on, "if you don't mind me asking, what do DVMs use these days to euthanize?"

"Is that a need-to-know question?" Cutler goaded as he yanked his paper mask off his neck and tossed it in a waste container he opened by stepping on a foot pedal. "You want to know, it's the same stuff used for anesthetizing mammalian patients for surgery."

"Sodium pentobarbital?"

"It's usually the primary active ingredient."

"Usually? Mixed with what?"

"Look, Morelli, there are a lot of vet drugs that can paralyze and then kill, if the dosage is too large. But I doubt if you dropped in for a nice little chat on barbiturates."

"No, I wanted to tell you to steer clear—literally— of Leah Kurtz. I hear you almost ran her off the road. Someone evidently tried to do that to Seth Kline's buggy with his mother and sister in it too, and I wouldn't want the sheriff to get the idea you're making a habit of it."

He felt he'd overdone it the minute that was out of his mouth. The van he and Leah had seen near the Kline buggy was not Cutler's, or surely she would have said so. But this guy was getting to him, and he wanted to really lean on him.

"So you came here to threaten me? I know Leah wouldn't report me to the sheriff because that's not the way the Amish operate—hey, excuse the pun," he said and began to wipe down the stainless-steel table with a paper towel as if to dismiss Mark.

He just stared at Cutler as he dropped the paper towel in the wastebasket, then stripped off his plastic gloves and tossed them too. This guy's mind and mood—morals too, maybe—seemed really askew. He might get a kick out of scaring Leah, but if the orange plunger was his, what motive would he have to harm Seth?

"Sorry I'm late, Dr. Cutler," David Groder called out as he came hustling in. "Oh, hi, Dr. Morelli."

"Hi, David," Mark said and clapped him on the shoulder as he headed out. But he turned back toward Cutler at the door.

"I suppose you enjoy watching her," Mark said, "but you bear watching too." With that, he closed the door behind him.

Since Sam still had keys to the house, Leah took Mark's advice that night and wedged chairs under the front and back doorknobs. She would feel better when she got dead-bolt locks tomorrow.

She bathed Becca in the sink, then cuddled her, so soft and sweet smelling. Tomorrow she'd have to do another batch of diapers and hang them out. This time of year they froze into solid ice, so she had to warm them inside after they dried. Barbara's old, generator-powered washing machine in the basement worked fine for such an antique, but no Amish had driers in their home.

And that reminded her, she hadn't even read the *Maplecreek Weekly* yet to look for an article on the antique cemetery book. She hoped Louise and whoever wrote the article had kept her name out of it as she'd asked.

Once she had Becca down to sleep, she sat at the kitchen table and spread the newspaper out before her. The article wasn't on the front page, which carried the lead story about an explosion at a grain elevator in Columbus.

Since the photo with the article showed silos similar to the ones at AgraGro, she skimmed the article with a shudder. There had actually been a series of explosions that set off clouds of grain dust. She read one sentence slowly aloud to be sure she understood it. "'In newer mills, the buildings are designed to come apart in a blast, a process called explosion venting, which dissipates energy with the aim of preventing chain-reaction blasts elsewhere in the plant.'" Maybe that's what AgraGro had been doing in its remodeling, she thought. But wouldn't the flying pieces of buildings be a deadly danger too?

The article said that two workers had been killed and two others badly burned in the Columbus blast. In 1977, she read on, over fifty people died from grain explosions, but that had led to strict federal regulations, so deaths were down to one or two a year.

Thank heavens for that, she thought. It sounded as if someone had made the fatal mistake of generating a spark, which set off this disaster in Columbus. But, she noted, those killed or injured had actually been on-site or just outside the mill and its silos, not a good distance away as her house was.

She began to turn pages of the paper. On page three, her eye caught an article—no, an advertisement—featuring Andrea Dixon. The article instructed:

Please phone the 800 number listed, and I will call on you to see your quilt. I will be happy to come to your home if you wish.

In other words, Leah thought, she might run into Andrea in some Amish homes around here. Andrea would be wanting family heirlooms, and Leah would be wanting family trees. She read on:

I ask that you do not bring quilts to my Millersburg warehouse. That is not a store nor a facility open to the public.

The article included the photo of Andrea with the so-called Roscoe quilt, but it still didn't identify the quilt's maker. Now that Leah had an interest in Varina, the next time she saw Andrea she'd ask her what she knew of it. "I wouldn't dare set foot in your precious warehouse, though," she muttered under her breath.

She flipped back for a possible article on the cemetery book and found it on the front page of the Local section, which included the classifieds, obits and births. The photo with it showed Pam Martin and three other women holding the book—but not Louise, which was understandable. Everyone knew she'd been a recluse for years, so Leah was just pleased that she was going out occasionally now. Was it because her husband had become mayor, and she felt compelled to show herself, or was it because she had some other motive?

Leah skimmed the article. No, she had not been named; it said the book was given by an anonymous donor, just as she'd asked. Louise was quoted throughout the next section, which mentioned interesting tidbits from the book, including Varina Roscoe's unsolved murder. She hoped this publicity didn't start a sort of macabre pilgrimage to visit Varina's grave site. She hadn't thought of that.

The last paragraph surprised but intrigued her:

Each week local historians will delve into the lives (and deaths) of various pioneers mentioned in the book, bringing their stories to light and to life. Watch next week for an article on who might have been guilty in the unsolved murder of local heroine Varina Roscoe.

9

A flutter of wings fanned her face. Barbara hovered over where she slept. Had she flown down from her bed upstairs? Leah should never have told Mark that angels were males. She thought this was Barbara, but it might be Katie.

When Leah sat up, she saw the angel was not female flesh and blood, but stone, gray and foggy. She bent her granite arm and beckoned Leah to follow.

"Who are you, really?" Leah asked.

The angel didn't open her stone lips, but Leah read her mind: *Come. Come and see.*

"Should I bring Becca?"

Leah was sure the angel nodded, for she heard stone scrape on stone. She didn't know where they were going, but she felt no fear. Becca was light in her arms, still asleep, her little face so solemn.

Not stopping to open doors or windows, they went outside. Leah could hear the trees dripping blood, moving their wooden limbs to stop the flow. She was certain they were crying.

She was surprised the snow was not cold on her bare feet. Perhaps she flew too.

See. See here, the angel said, and with one whoosh of wings was back on her pedestal. It was only then Leah saw the angel wore a garland of flowers, frozen ones. And they were dying.

See. See here, the angel said again, and pulled her gray robe up one arm and then the other, nearly to her carved shoulders. The stone folds rubbed and grated.

Bruises? Were those mottled bruises from a beating? Leah wondered. No, more like the scratches on Miriam's arm or the blotches on Louise from that disease.

"What is on your arms?" Leah asked the angel. "What should I do?"

But the angel did not move. Nothing moved now but tears of stone, falling from the angel's eyes like the tears of trees. Although Leah was certain the angel had been moving and speaking, the statue had now gone stiff and hard.

Leah was cold, and Becca was crying. She had to go back inside so Becca's tears would not freeze on her face. She couldn't stay here because she didn't want to fall into this grave.

"Don't cry, Becca-my-Becca," she said and brushed at the baby's tears.

With a start, Leah sat up on the sofa bed. Yes, Becca was fussing, but she was across the room in her crib. A dream? It had been so very real, the angel, the trees, the tears…the message.

What was the message?

As she got up to go to Becca, she felt the tears on her own face too. Cold, cold tears.

Though Leah seldom recalled her dreams, this one stuck with her. But she wasn't sure what it meant. Was it a product of her own fears and deep-buried suspicions, or was it a message from God?

At any cost, she intended to find out. First, she needed to speak with Sam. What had he meant about Barbara acting wild? And had her bruises come from her disease as the doctors had said, or had he hit her? And why?

By seven forty-five the next morning, Leah had dropped Becca off with her mother at the bakery and had driven her buggy to the Methodist church where Sam was working. She didn't care if she ran into Miles Mason and he ordered her away; she was going to talk to Sam as soon as he showed up. Barbara had said he always arrived before his work crew—unless his drinking had changed that, too. If Leah hadn't known full well that Barbara was in heaven, she would have thought the angel in the dream was her friend's unsettled spirit. But since Barbara—like Katie—was now at peace, it must have been her own restless soul.

It wasn't even fully light when she reached the Methodist church and tied Nell to a sapling on the street. The addition appeared to be a roofless skeleton so far. Another buggy was tethered just down the way. Maybe it was Sam's, if he'd borrowed one from his cousin. She walked toward the scaffold that sat in the middle of the addition on the concrete floor.

"Sam? Sam Yoder? It's Leah, Sam!"

Daylight suffused the pale sky through the beams above, but it still seemed so dark down here. And then she saw an Amish man huddled on the other side of the scaffold. Had Sam slept here all night? For one moment she thought she heard the angel whisper, *Come. Come and see.*

She hurried toward him. Could he have been so drunk he'd passed out? If so, Miles Mason just might have Sam's head. No one could trust someone to do a job if they were self-destructing with drink, especially someone Amish, who was hired because he was supposedly skilled and trustworthy.

The figure looked like Sam. *Oh, dear Lord in heaven,* she prayed. She had to get him out of here before the others came. Hangover or not, he'd answer her questions and she'd convince him that Becca was meant to stay with her.

She shook his shoulder hard. He'd passed out, all right. He was dead weight. "Sam. Sam! Wake up and get up."

He didn't budge. Yes, he'd been drinking, because he'd spilled some of the liquor under his head. "Sam! Sam!"

But then she saw it wasn't liquor but blood. She smelled the thick, coppery scent of it. She rolled him on his back—and was certain he was dead.

Sheriff Martin and his two deputies went about their business. The same two medics who'd helped the Klines yesterday waited by their blinking vehicle with a rolling metal gurney and a body bag. The county coroner, a doctor from Pleasant, had arrived. Amidst it all, Leah sat, dry-eyed, at the edge of the concrete foundation they said might have killed Sam. That is, a fall from the rafters to the concrete might have.

His cousins Ben and Etta had been summoned and were still speaking with one of the deputies. Sam's work team stood in a clump, talking quietly with Miles Mason. Other Amish arrived bit by bit. Still, Leah sat apart, dazed, under the fluttering yellow plastic police tape they'd wrapped around the site.

Sheriff Martin had already questioned her. She'd explained how she'd run for help when she found him, how she'd come early to talk to Sam about his daughter. Through it all, she silently wished Mark were here. They'd become a team, somehow. She missed him and needed him.

Her worst moments, besides finding Sam, were when the sheriff came over to question her a second time, after the coroner examined the body.

"From the rigor mortis, the coroner's got an approximate time of death," the sheriff had told her as he took his notebook back out. "So where were you in the middle of last night?"

"Home with Becca, of course."

"Oh, that'll be a great alibi if this turns out to be foul play. An infant's a great corroborating witness. You didn't go outside at all last night?"

She thought of the dream. It *was* a dream. "That's right."

"Seems I heard around town that Sam wasn't too pleased you're working for the gene doctor and told you to back off or else."

"Who told you that?" she said, looking over his shoulder at Sam's work team and Miles Mason. Mason would really be after her to sell the house now, because Becca was Sam's only heir.

"Leah, I have some informants now and then. Look, maybe you ought to take poor Sam's dying wishes to heart and do for that baby what her father—mother, too—would have wanted. Get yourself a job somewhere else besides the gene clinic, if that upset Sam, and move so you're not living out in the sticks."

Living out in the sticks. The words echoed in her clogged brain. Living out in Miles Mason's maple trees, that was more like it. She wondered if he and Sam could have had some kind of disagreement about selling the property.

"Becca inherits that house now," she told the sheriff, "though it's not paid off. It's her heritage from her parents, and I can hardly sell it. And I can't grasp why Sam wouldn't want me to help a doctor who is working to cure genetic diseases, since Barbara died of one."

"You do realize your argument with Sam, and your desire to get him out of Becca's life—and get the house—could be cause for suspicion in court—"

"What?" she cried as her stomach clenched. "I most certain would never mur—"

"Just listen to what I'm telling you, girl. I'm only giving you some advice you'd better take. I know the Amish would never murder someone—not intentionally anyway. I'm just saying it wouldn't look so good for you if this was a worldly situation, because of Sam having words with you and you indirectly inheriting his property."

Now, as she sat stunned by it all—including the sheriff's warning—she could overhear him talking to the coroner about an open bottle of whiskey they'd found in Sam's tool chest. His cousins said he didn't come home last night but since he'd been drinking and had been out late other nights, they hadn't thought much of it.

He'd been out late other nights, Leah thought. Putting dead flowers on the angel and tracking footsteps to her door? He'd know that the shed would shelter him from the wind. Was he just checking up on Becca or did he want something else?

"You want to insist on an autopsy, get a blood-alcohol count?" Leah heard the sheriff ask the coroner. "You'll have to fight the Amish on it if you do."

"Yeah, I know. No, I say we let them just bury him. I think it's pretty obvious what happened—though, even with a ten-foot fall onto concrete, that's quite a bash on the back of his skull. It's almost perfectly circular, like a big stone fist cracked into him there."

"So, next of kin's the infant daughter," Sheriff Martin said. "I guess you might as well send the death certificate to Leah Kurtz when you get it cleared. I'm willing to release his body to the Amish if you are. Leah?" he said, coming over to her, evidently unaware their voices had carried.

Though her knees trembled, she stood to face him. "Looks like the coroner's gonna rule accidental death, a fall onto the concrete. I'm gonna go tell the bishop what happened so a funeral can be planned."

He evidently waited for her to say something. To agree, to thank him. But she was deeply disturbed. Angry. Had Sam somehow abused Barbara? She would never know now. She was grieving more for that than she was for Sam.

"In other words, Sheriff," she said, "your subtle threats against me were way out of line."

"Now look, you seeing a pattern here lately?" he

countered, his face clenched in a frown, his thumbs stuck in his belt. "Lately, when I find trouble, I find you. Take my advice, Sam's too, and just tend that cute little baby you got from the Yoders. She's an orphan now, and that's really tragic. Let's not make it worse. You hear me now?"

"I hear you," she said. But she kept hearing the angel's voice louder, stronger. *Come. Come and see.* And that's what she would do. With Sam dead, she might never know what secrets he and Barbara had, but she was going to get some answers to the other questions that had been haunting her.

"Brad! You should have called ahead, because I've got to go out in about twenty minutes. But come on in," Mark told Brad Dixon as he let his former boss in the door of the clinic. It had been three days since Sam Yoder had died. Leah had been busy ever since, so he still didn't have the Kline blood samples or family tree he needed, but they were going to the Kline farm to get them tomorrow. Today the Amish community was burying Sam Yoder.

Brad scraped his feet on the doormat. "I won't stay long, but I smell coffee."

"Let me get you some. What's all that gear?" he asked, gesturing at the leather satchel Brad toted over his shoulder.

"I'm taking up photography," Brad explained as they went into the kitchen. "I kid you not. I needed something besides pills to get my blood pressure down—either that, or Andrea was going to kill me anyway."

"Too much work and worry. You ought to move to Amish country."

"Hardly. I'm a big-city boy—Atlanta, Cleveland. But I thought I ought to take a few photos around here and that you could send me to some good local sites. I don't just like to wander—got to have a plan."

That was Brad Dixon, all right, Mark thought as he poured him a mug of coffee and topped off his own. He'd always admired Brad's drive and determination, and yet they'd had more than one bad argument before he'd left MR. He hoped this was a gesture to bury the hatchet—and not in each other.

"So you're hustling out to make a house call today?" Brad asked, warming his hands on his mug.

"Actually, I'm going to an Amish wake this morning."

"Is that what they call it, a wake?"

"No, but it's along the same lines. The family and church leaders sit with the body for two days while friends make courtesy calls. The coffin's laid out in the home of the deceased. There's a lot of eating, and the burial's on the third day. You're back in pioneer times with the Amish, Brad."

"I'm just passing through on the way to Andrea's warehouse but thought I'd show you this new camera equipment. It's pricey as heck, so I'd better use it. Can I ask you a favor?"

Mark felt his shoulder muscles tense. He knew Brad wouldn't just drop in for chitchat the way his wife might.

"As long as it's not an offer to come back to oversee the new MR clinic. I wish you well with it, but I need to be here right now."

"Damn. You know I would have put you in charge," he said, leaning forward and accenting his words by hitting the side of his hand on the table the way he often did in board meetings. "You should see it, Mark, state-of-the-art patient rooms set around a central control center and lab. If you'd just told me earlier you wanted to actually practice…"

"Practice here on-site with NAA kids."

"We could have brought them to you. But no," he said, throwing up both hands, "that's not the favor. Do you think I could ride along while you go to that wake? Just get a few shots of back roads? Everything's so dramatic around here with the hills and ravines in this windswept snow, like a sepia print or an etching."

"Ordinarily I'd say no problem, but you know the Amish get real nervous around cameras."

"Yeah, I've heard that, so I'll be cautious. They're trying to avoid being part of 'making any graven image,' aren't they?"

"It's more because they think if they pose for photos, they'll become prideful, and they avoid that at all costs. And they do resent it if you take a shot without asking first."

"You're really getting into them, aren't you? Especially your little aide?"

"Meaning?" Mark said, frowning at him over his mug.

"Close to them, intimate."

"If you mean that in a good way, yes. It's a whole different world, and—so far—they've taken me in."

"And you've taken them in."

"What the hell does that mean?"

"You're helping them, sure, but they are *really* helping you. Whatever you discover about NAA or aging in general, they won't say peep if you make a fortune off of it."

"I'm not here to just use them, and certainly not to abuse them, Brad."

"Enough said. I only mean all of that in the 'good way,' as you put it. It's nice to know you've become so altruistic, and I wish I could afford to be too."

"I'm starting to remember why we didn't part the best of friends."

"Mark, the truth is, I'm here to say I regret that on my part, and what I said today—don't take it wrong. I understand wanting to go out on your own. Hell, it's what I did when I left HealGene in Atlanta and started Metzler-Reich, and believe me, I didn't part from their CEO, Sinclair Marshall, on the best of terms. But I don't want there to be the same rancor between the two of us. I know you don't want any strings attached, as you put it, but I wish you'd let me send you a lab tech or loan you an MRI."

"The mayor's wife is underwriting an MRI and may head up the start of a foundation, and I'll take a pass on the lab tech for now. I can manage my own computer work until I get more of a caseload. But I am grateful for that BLAST software."

"You don't trust me, do you? Or else your patent litigator guardian angel Quinn's been badmouthing me to you again."

"Don't blame Clark, and I do appreciate your offers," Mark said, rising and putting their mugs in the sink.

"Look, I don't mean to take more of your time, but I want us to stay friends."

"I'll make you a deal. You can ride along with me—I won't be long anyhow—but don't flaunt that fancy camera while we're parked at the house. Are you sure you have time, though, if you need to get to Andrea?"

"No problem," he said with a taut smile. "I underwrote her whole warehouse project, so she can't get too touchy if I'm a little late. This new hobby," he added as he stood and gathered his equipment, "is an outlet for my working too hard, being too obsessed with the cutthroat business we're in. Mark, I know I've said some tough things to you—even today—and I just want you to know, I'm backing off. You were my best hotshot geneticist, and I hated to lose you, that's all."

"Then we'll say we've smoked the peace pipe, okay?"

They shook on it.

The Amish brought in food for the guests and took over Leah's small kitchen to serve it. They'd helped to plan today's funeral and burial across town in the Amish Shekinah Cemetery. Amish unity and community had gotten her through these long three days.

Leah had moved Becca's crib from the front room and slept upstairs while Sam's coffin was downstairs. It would have shaken her to the core to be alone with that in the house, but the church elders and Sam's cousins had taken turns sitting with the body at night.

Still, she had not slept soundly. As she had emerged from her shocked state, her mind raced through possibilities—probabilities, Mark would call them in what she thought of as his genespeak.

While her sister Naomi tended to Becca upstairs, Leah stood at the coffin to receive guests. She was coping with Sam's death all right, she realized, but what was still haunting her was Barbara's. Her friend's coffin had been right here on these same two sawhorses in this room just about five weeks ago. The same people had come by, saying the same words about poor Becca.

Leah jerked from her agonizing as Etta Troyer withdrew an envelope from her cape and pressed it into her hands.

"What's this?" Leah asked.

"We found it in Sam's things you wanted boxed and brought over," Etta whispered.

Leah nodded. She had requested Sam's belongings in case there was some sort of keepsake to be found for Becca. And she was hoping to discover a clue to some of the strange things he'd said. Etta and Ben had been here each day but just brought the four cartons of the items today, so she hadn't gone through them yet.

"It's money," Etta went on, nodding at the envelope Leah put in her pocket. "Near three thousand dollars."

Leah blinked in surprise. "He told me he had some extra money, that he'd been doing some extra jobs."

"But that's just it," Etta whispered, looking furtively around as if someone would eavesdrop. "He wasn't. Ben asked the men on his work crew, and Mr. Mason too. Mr. Mason didn't give him that for an advance. His crew said he would leave sometimes at night when they were away, but he didn't take his tools. At least this will tide you over, maybe help to fix this place up for little Becca."

"Thank you, Etta. You've been a real support through all this, you and Ben. And I intend to give you some of this back for taking Sam in the way you did."

"No, that's yours, as he paid me for room and board. But one more thing. There's a scribbled note inside that envelope in Sam's writing, columns of figures he was adding up. I'd say he already had more money than what was in the envelope and planned on more to come—that's what it looks like to us." Etta squeezed Leah's hand and went back into the kitchen where the women were laying out food for a lunch before the procession would head to the cemetery.

"An English man coming," she heard one of the elders say.

Mark! Mark had said he would stop by, she thought, and moved to welcome him. But it was Jesse Cutler, dressed in a dark suit.

"Dr. Cutler," she said, moving back from the threshold.

"I wanted to personally offer my condolences," he said, his eyes riveted on her. "To little Becca too, though she'll never remember this day or her father."

"Please," she said politely as Bishop Moses Brand came to stand beside her, "come in." *Come,* she remembered the angel's voice in her dream again. *Come and see.*

Leah scolded herself for the bitter way she felt toward Jesse Cutler. Whatever he'd done, she'd been taught to forgive—but, somehow, she couldn't forget. She wanted to order him out, but she stood with him and Bishop Moses at the coffin and thanked him for coming. Unfortunately, she found herself alone with him again as she subtly tried to steer him toward the door.

"You'll be even more alone now that Becca's father's gone," he told her.

"He was gone a lot anyway."

"If he ever planned to marry you to get his baby back, that's over now." His voice came so quiet she was sure no one else could hear. "The phantom husband is gone."

Leah couldn't believe this man always managed to annoy and insult her so. She bit back a sharp retort and opened the door for him.

"My former offer is always open," he whispered.

"My door is only open because you are going out of it," she muttered and started to turn away, before she saw a small red sports car parallel parking in the line of buggies on the road. But two men were in it, Mark and, it looked like, that square-jawed Brad Dixon. Jesse's eyes evidently followed her gaze because he said, "Your boss—your keeper—is here," before he hurried out.

She wondered if they were coming in. And then she saw Louise Winslow at the corner of the graveyard, standing with her coat and scarf blowing as she gestured to Leah. Mark hadn't gotten out of his car yet. She wrapped her shawl tighter and hurried out to Louise.

"Won't you come in?" she asked.

"Oh, no—you know me. But I wanted to say I was thinking of you and Becca at this trying time."

Leah was close enough now to see her blotched cheeks between the hat shadow and the muffler around her neck. It was pulled up so high that her mouth didn't show. It reminded her of how the stone angel had spoken in her dream without seeming to move her lips. The way Louise had just beckoned to her evoked the dream, too.

"Your condolences are very much appreciated, Mrs. Winslow."

"Please, call me Louise."

"And I appreciate that you kept my name out of the newspaper article, Louise. I'm looking forward to hearing how poor Varina died—well, you know what I mean." They glanced simultaneously toward the stone angel. When Leah looked back at Louise, she saw past her shoulder that Mark was getting out of his car but Brad Dixon was staying put.

"I'm afraid," Louise said, tapping Leah's arm with a gloved hand, "that Varina was murdered by her lover."

"What?"

Louise nodded. "Her father was the longtime town doctor, but the murderer—the one most people suspected, at least—was a newcomer, a young doctor brought in to work into her father's practice, to take it over. And he worked his way into Varina's heart."

"But what went wrong?"

"That remains to be seen, but I have two local historians working on the story, checking various old papers and sources online. We're going with the article on the doctor, though, in next week's paper." She looked past Leah and frowned. At Mark? Leah wondered.

"That's dreadful—the circumstances, I mean."

"Leah, I'm so sorry we got off on that, considering the day. I just came to see if you need help tending Becca, with all you're doing lately. I'd love to help, especially since it's too cold for her to be outside when everyone leaves for the cemetery."

"That's very kind of you but my sister Naomi's looking forward to taking care of her at my parents' house. Another time, then?"

The woman looked so downhearted. "Yes, another time," she said wanly.

"But I am grateful for your gift to her. She loves all those whirligig things. And for your kindness, Louise."

"You must think I'm foolish. A baby's the one thing I longed for I never could buy, you know. And my husband wouldn't have a thing to do with all that fertility-treatment stuff, as he put it. It couldn't be his fault, of course," she said, her voice suddenly bitter. "But I must go. I didn't mean to keep you away from your guests—and Becca. Hello, Dr. Morelli," she called and lifted one arm in a wave.

Mark waved back. "Louise! Don't forget our meeting Tuesday."

"Yes, 2:00 p.m.," she called before she walked away, down the line of buggies stretching along the cemetery fence between the house and the ravine. Leah didn't see the woman's car, but it must be down there somewhere.

"Was that who I think it was, leaving your house about the time I arrived?" Mark asked as they went up the walk.

"Jesse Cutler, I'm afraid. Is that who I think it is in your car?" she countered.

"Yeah. Brad Dixon stopped by unexpectedly today."

"The same with Dr. Cutler. Does Mr. Dixon want to come in?"

"No, and I'm not staying long, Leah. I just wanted to tell you how sorry I am that Becca's lost her second parent. I know how it changed my life to be an orphan, but she has you, and she's blessed for that."

It was, Leah thought, the nicest thing anyone had

said to her. And Mark was an *auslander*—but not to her anymore.

They went in, greeted people, then stood together at Sam's coffin as several of the elders and Bishop Moses joined them. Sam's head had been nestled far into a cutout pillow, for the funeral director who'd prepared him had said he'd needed to hide the crushing blow to the back of his head.

Leah glanced out the side window toward the angel. And saw that Brad Dixon had set up a tripod and was taking its picture.

Sam Yoder was buried—with all his secrets, Leah thought—next to Barbara's grave early that afternoon.

But she is in her grave, and oh, the difference to me. The words taunted Leah again. If she turned her head just slightly to the left, she could see her sister Katie's grave, too.

Gray clouds clotted the pewter sky, and the wind was cold. She was glad she hadn't brought Becca. Over the years, though, she would bring her here some spring or summer days and tell her good and happy things about her mother—Sam, too, if she could.

But Sam was the key to something she had to unlock. Sam and maybe the Klines, who seemed just as cursed as she was lately.

After the last prayer, the Amish elders lowered Sam's simple wooden coffin into the ground, pulled the leather straps back out, then began to shovel in soil. It thudded on the pine boards as if it were completely empty, a hollow sound.

Usually, the Amish hand dug a grave, but, as with

Barbara's, they'd been forced to hire a mechanical hoe to bite into the frozen winter ground.

Her people did things the Amish way when possible, Leah thought, but then used whatever method was necessary. And that was how she was going to proceed from now on too.

10

"It's hard to know what demons haunted Sam," Mark told Leah as they headed for Klines' farm the next morning.

"Don't say it that way!" she protested. Her voice was shrill; he hadn't realized she was still so strung out over everything.

"Sorry. I know you're still on edge."

"That's what my mother says, but I can't help it. Nothing makes sense. Not only is there something fishy about Seth's disappearance, but about what happened to Miriam and Susie."

"Could the van that stopped near the Klines' buggy have been Jesse Cutler's?" Mark asked.

He felt her shudder and put his arm around her, tugging up the lap robe they shared. He thought she might protest the embrace but she didn't. It always drove him nuts to be bouncing along so close to her. A quick hug might steady her nerves, but it wasn't helping him, as her hip against his seemed to vibrate clear through him. Or was that his damn pager going off again?

"This darn thing," he said and tossed it on the back

seat of the buggy with his free hand. It bounced onto the floor, and he didn't try to retrieve it.

"You don't need to be its servant, you know," she chided. "Not here in your new life."

She was right, and that annoyed him. But her soft thigh rubbing against his through their layers of clothing was more of a turn-on than if she'd been in a bikini. Even though she was always fully covered, he'd taken to imagining her white skin, the shape of her legs under those black cotton stockings. He used to find silk stockings sexy, but the ones Leah wore were driving him to distraction. He shifted sideways on the hard seat, wanting to turn her toward him for an embrace but fighting the impulse.

"I've been thinking about that," she said when he'd forgotten what he'd asked her. "The van certainly wasn't what Jesse drives now, or has for a couple of years, but it is like one he drove before. I don't know if he kept it, but maybe it's out at his house."

"Where you are *not* going, and where he'd probably shoot me for trespassing, so we're back to square one." He hadn't told her he'd confronted Jesse at his clinic. "Leah, I know you're thinking of the hit-and-run that killed your sister, but this van-buggy thing wasn't like that."

"I know it wasn't, but what was it like?" she demanded, turning to him, which nestled her shoulder even tighter under his arm and anchored her warmth against his ribs. "If the people in the van weren't guilty of anything, why did they take off? And something just doesn't fit about Susie and Miriam being pitched out forward onto the ground and then both hitting the backs of their heads—like Sam's head injury, only his was fatal."

"I think you're grasping at straws, seeing connections where none exist," he told her. "It's one of the hazards of being a scientist and wanting desperately to make a discovery. We need data, proof, facts, not feelings or mere intuition. Still, a couple of things have been bothering me too. Susie's osteoporosis should have made her vulnerable to more fractures. As for the Klines' failure to recall anything, even before they fell out of the buggy, I can't explain it, other than general trauma."

"And you know what else? I don't think that the tilt of that buggy would have spilled them out. Scientists are allowed to have theories if they try to prove them, aren't they? Some piece of all this is missing, something just barely out of reach…"

"Leah," he said as they turned into the Kline driveway, "about being just barely out of reach…"

She turned to him, emerald eyes wide in anticipation, full lips slightly parted as she wet them with a tip of pink tongue. Her blend of naïveté and knowledge, sensibility and sensuality, absolutely swamped his senses.

"What?" she asked, blushing as she looked away from his intense gaze and reined Nell in. "Anyway, we're here."

"Right. I'll tell you later," he muttered, relieved he hadn't blurted out more. He wasn't sure how she'd react, and he didn't want to blow his professional relationship with her because he desired a personal one.

He shook his head as they climbed down. He'd actually missed her these last three days, when he'd seen her so briefly. He'd never missed any other woman in his life like that. That both sobered him and scared him. Tonight, they'd planned for him to eat at her place and put extra locks on her doors and windows, even though Sam was gone now.

Tonight.

Leah watched Mark work quickly and calmly, drawing first Miriam's blood and then turning to Susie. "My veins are pretty hard to find," Susie said. She lay on a couch in her living room, and Mark worked from a chair pulled up close.

"You're a real veteran of this, aren't you?" he asked the child. "Okay, make a fist for me."

"Are you going to take blood from my broken arm too? Right through this concrete cast?"

"That's plaster," her mother said, hovering.

"Actually," Mark said, "it's fiberglass, Mrs. Kline."

"That sounds breakable, too," she protested. "And I thought it should have been white, but you and Dr. Mark outvoted me for that bright pink, Susie."

Leah saw Mark's gaze dart back toward the table where she and Miriam had been working on the Kline family tree. Miriam was getting in his window light. Leah knew Mark intended to take more blood from Susie's one arm, since he wouldn't take any from the other. He probably wanted Miriam to back off but didn't want to say so.

"Let's just let the doctor and Susie see to that, Miriam," Leah said and led her gently away. "On our chart, we were back to your paternal grandparents and—"

"Did they do this to me at the hospital the other day?" Susie asked, her voice suddenly strident. Leah wondered if she was going to balk. Poor Mark. He desperately wanted that blood sample and was hoping to come back Monday evening to take blood from Susie's father and sisters too.

"No blood work was done," Mark assured her. "Okay, let your fist open now."

"But I had this done not long ago!"

"No, Susie," her mother said. "It's been weeks since we were at the doctor's in Cleveland."

"You said you had it done a lot," Mark reminded her. "You're just remembering that."

"No, 'cause I was looking up at the sky and I wanted to move but I couldn't. And 'cause I have a mark on my arm—under this cast right now."

"I didn't see that, and I helped with the cast," Mark said.

"Susie," Miriam put in, her voice stern, "I'm the one who was all scraped up, not you for once."

But when Susie said the word *sky*, Leah and Mark had just stared at each other. Susie's memories, however fragmented, had to mean something.

"Miriam," Leah said, "did you ever figure out what scraped your arm and tore your sleeve?"

"All I know is I wish I'd taken our bigger buggy instead of Seth's and that his had side protectors. I never should have taken Susie out in that one, no way, but Star needed a run and Susie wanted to ride in her brother's courting buggy."

"Let's go back to what Susie said earlier," Leah insisted, coming to stand over her, despite Mark's warning frown. "What did you say about the people getting out of their van *before* you blacked out? Could it even be before you fell out? Could you have been lifted out?"

"What?" Miriam demanded. "Lifted out?"

Mark capped the blood he'd drawn and pressed a cotton ball against the needle mark on Susie's arm. "Just bend your arm up a second and *relax,*" he said.

Leah knew he meant her too, but she just couldn't back off now. And that look he'd shot her suggested he realized they were on to something. Memories of her dream intruded again. Had the angel reached down to roll up its stone sleeves to symbolize that Leah needed to get to work on whatever was going on? Or had Leah's own deep-seated thoughts surfaced to prod her into finding something out about Miriam's scraped arm?

"I know it's been four days," Leah said to the woman, "but you didn't have any pinpricks on your arm amid all those scrapes, did you?"

"Only from hitting the ground after my sleeve tore."

"You did have a pinprick?"

"I'm not sure. Something like it, maybe from a little stone."

"Can I look and see?"

"Why, sure, if you want to come upstairs with me."

Come, Leah heard the angel's haunting words again. *Come and see.*

"Mark, we'll be right back."

He nodded. Leah followed Miriam upstairs where she unpinned her dress and drew out the arm that had been scraped. Leah's hopes fell. She was greatly healed; no needle mark, as Leah was hoping for, was visible.

As Miriam slipped her sleeve back on, Leah saw the dress that had been torn on a hanger stuck on the top of the closet door. Miriam's gaze followed hers. "I didn't mend it yet because I wanted to see if it was worth saving or just good for filling my scrap bag."

"Can I show this to Dr. Morelli?" Leah asked, looking closer at the damaged sleeve.

"But he's seen it."

"He hasn't seen that it isn't torn along the seam— or even torn at all. It looks neatly slit, right along here," she said, tracing a finger up Miriam's arm over the exact place they'd been looking for a pinprick.

"What are you thinking? I'd like to know, because I still can't recall a thing about that buggy tipping, no matter how hard I try. That blow to the back of my head might not have led to a concussion, but it must have stunned me bad."

What was she thinking? Miriam's words snagged in Leah's brain. She was positive Seth hadn't run away. And the buggy accident might be no accident at all. Worse, that Sam's cause of death might be doubtful too. She sure didn't want to rile the sheriff up over any of this, or he might accuse her again. But even that was not going to stop her.

"So what are you thinking?" Mark asked the same question of her when they pulled away from Klines' in her buggy.

"I hate to put it this way, but I'm thinking vampires."

"What in the h—?" he said, then cut himself off.

"Mark, what if someone else was after Susie's blood, but we stumbled on it and they took off—probably after they did something to daze their victims and took their sample?"

He looked, she thought, both angry and afraid. "Well?" she demanded.

"I…I don't know. But Susie's blood, at least, has to be in storage in every Cleveland hospital she's been in."

"But it's not accessible, or you could have had your precious sample of it months ago."

"But I knew I was coming here. I planned to get a fresh sample when she was my patient and I had parental permission to treat her."

"Well, maybe somebody else wanted to take a shortcut."

"But how could that somebody have known to drive by at the exact time the two of them were out on the road? It would be too obvious if they were lurking around or cruising back and forth. I'll bet Miriam and Susie seldom go out alone."

"I'm not sure, but we're going to stop and go over the area with a fine-tooth comb."

"I've got to get this blood back."

"Then I'll take you to the clinic and come back on my own."

"No, you won't."

"Because you think it's dangerous for me to be out in a buggy alone? But that must have been true for Miriam and Susie too."

"Do you think Jesse Cutler is involved? You said he stopped you once."

"I don't know!" she cried and pulled over on the berm where the Klines' buggy had been tipped.

She scrambled down. "I won't be a minute."

He climbed down after her with his black bag in hand. "Nell won't run off with that," she said and started walking the sloped, grassy berm above the ice that had refrozen crookedly after the Klines' horse had broken through it.

"What are you thinking we might find?" he demanded, but he too walked along, head down, brushing snow away with the toe of his shoe if it clung too deep in the grass.

"How about a drug vial or orange plastic plunger like the one we found where Seth disappeared? I still have it under the rug in my buggy. I know you think I'm crazy, but—"

"Crazy like a fox," he said, his voice shaky. "There are drugs that not only knock someone out for a while but act as amnesiacs afterward. Only how would someone get the drugs into two females in a moving buggy so they wouldn't recall being stopped and having blood taken?"

She lifted both hands, palms up, as she peered down into the slick grassy ditch. "How about," she said, "stop them for directions, then hold Miriam down and slit her sleeve and jab a needle in her. Then scrape up her arm, to hide that. Susie tried to fight, and they broke her arm trying to hold her down. They laid them both on the ground, gave Susie the knockout and amnesia drug too and took Susie's blood—"

"Or took samples from both of them. Man, that scares me, if that's what happened. If someone else besides me is doing gene work on NAA, they could use Miriam's blood. That's why I want samples of her entire family—not just cheek swabs, but blood."

"And Seth?" she went on. Mark looked stricken. He nodded, then squinted at her.

"What?" she said. "Why are you looking at me that way?"

"Because I recognize that snake you're almost standing on."

She shrieked and scrambled up the bank. "Snake? Where?"

"Sorry the way I put that," he said, pointing. She looked toward the ditch and saw a butterscotch-colored rubber tourniquet she, too, recognized, because she'd seen one earlier today. It lay partly frozen in the ice and partly coiled in the grass on the berm. Someone, no doubt in a rush, had lost the tie that held the blood back in an arm from which a sample was about to be taken.

Seth couldn't believe his ears. He was sure he heard a baby crying. Not in the hall maybe, but through the air vent.

It made him miss his sisters so bad, especially Susie. He'd been eleven when she was born. He remembered everything about Susie's early life. She had been special, and then to see her growth slow at nine months, even as she seemed to age before their very eyes...

It had made him age fast, too—grow up, that is.

He heard the baby's muted cries again. That hadn't been his imagination. It was double sad if a baby was here, a child who was sick.

Voices came close outside his door.

"This is a terrible risk," a man said, a voice he'd heard before.

A woman said, "Not compared to the possible rewards. As soon as we find the SNP, we'll clone it. What if it can be engineered to affect lifespans in a significant manner? We'll move on it as fast as we can, to learn whether normal people have versions of this gene that can extend their lifespans. I'd be the first to volunteer for a trial—after we try it out on the Amish boy."

Seth shot to his feet. They were going to try something out on him that had to do with aging? To make him live longer? They were really messed up, he thought. They needed Susie in here, because she was the one who needed a longer life, not him. Were they going to experiment on a baby's genes too?

He kneeled by his bed and started to pray. He thought of all those times David in the Bible had been chased by King Saul. Saul wanted to kill David, who had despaired for his life and hid in a cave.

This room felt like a cave, all closed in. Seth only hoped God would get him out, the way he saved David. The valley of the shadow of death seemed so, so close here, as if it was somehow right outside that door.

In the hour she had before Mark would arrive, Leah got dinner under control—ham loaf and baked beans with a salad and biscuits, to be followed by frosted brownies. Then, carrying Becca, she went back upstairs, where she'd been going through Sam's things.

She'd found nothing else that tied into the list of money from the envelope Etta had given her. No mention of an employer, no IOU, no unusual correspondence, nothing.

Leah put Sam's spare clothing and books—she'd even fanned through all their pages—back in a carton to put in the Goodwill bin uptown. Was it possible that he had mentioned to Miles Mason that he'd hidden money in the house, and Miles thought he meant a lot of money—enough to want to buy the place and search it? Or scare her out of it? Or, since Mason knew the place had been poorly insulated, had he already been inside to search it?

Mason and two men were out in the back woodlot even now, emptying sap buckets and evidently preparing to cook some of it up in a big kettle on the spot. That would take hours, so was it his way of keeping an eye on this house?

"We'll keep your *Daadi*'s Bible and his *Ausbund* hymnal for you, Becca-my-Becca," Leah told the baby, "and his copy of *The Book of Martyrs* too. The rest we'll give away. We're going to be so busy this spring, helping Mark and fixing up this place just the way we want it. You're going to have to help me decide on some new furniture..."

Babbling on to Becca as she always did, she changed the baby's diaper and powdered her carefully with talc and cornstarch for her diaper rash. She carried her back downstairs and set the table. Out the window over the sink, she could see the men pouring buckets into the kettle while one stirred it with a big wooden paddle. Seth should have been out there helping.

And then it hit her. What if other kids who went missing during *rumspringa* were taken for their blood? Even Joseph, all those years ago? Most of the kids came back or at least let their families know where they were, but not him. Seth was the older brother of an NAA child. Joseph had been the older brother of a Regnell anemia sister.

But no, that couldn't be right, she reasoned. No one even knew Barbara had that disease until recently, and Joseph left way before that. As Mark said, she was grasping at straws. She tried to calm herself before he came, but just the fact they were going to be together got her going.

She tried to sound calm and cheery when she and Becca greeted him, laden with a sack of hardware, at the door.

"I'm probably the only woman in the country who has a gene doctor for her handyman," she said, smiling.

He grinned back. "Just call me Mark-of-all-trades."

"Then I would like to ask you a pediatrician question. Any suggestions for Becca's diaper rash? I'm using cornstarch and trying to air her out, but it's tough in this cold weather."

"Just get some over-the-counter vitamin E capsules. You punch a couple of holes in them with a pin, squeeze the liquid out and rub it on the affected areas and *voilà!*"

"You *are* a handy man to have around."

"Anything for Becca."

Her mood lifted just to have him here. As he washed his hands in the sink for dinner—she noted he had a habit of scrubbing them thoroughly—he glanced out her back window.

"What's that fire under a pot out there?"

"Miles Mason and some guys making syrup from sap."

"Yeah, well, one of them is coming this way. Does it bother you that they'll find us together?"

"Of course not." As she opened the back door, she saw it was Miles Mason himself.

"Don't mean to keep you from your guest," he told Leah.

She was surprised he'd picked up on that, but he must have seen Mark in the window or recognized his unique car. With Becca in his arms, Mark came to stand behind her as she invited Mr. Mason to step inside. She introduced them to each other.

"We keep losing people we have in common," Mason said to her, his voice gruff. "Seth, then Sam."

"You haven't heard anything about or from Seth, have you?" she asked.

"Naw, but what I wanted to ask you has to do with him. I promised the boy that when it came to sap-boiling time, he could have some of his Amish friends out here for a sugaring-off party, and I know he told some of them. It's pretty soon after Sam's funeral, but life goes on. It'd be fine with me if you—or someone among your people—asked some young people out here for the party. I'd provide hot dogs and the fixings if they could use your bathroom facilities."

"So you've given up on Seth's returning? You can't wait for him?"

"The sap's ready now, though there will prob'ly be

a couple of runs later. And, to tell the truth, I'm hoping to hire on some other Amish kids from time to time, so I'd like to meet them. Besides, I want to honor what I told Seth I'd do."

"Should I ask boys *and* girls?" she asked. "It's been a while since there's been an old-fashioned sugaring off."

She'd gone to one with Joseph, Barbara and Sam years ago. It used to be tradition when many Amish families had their own sugar bush, but Miles Mason had pretty much managed to get a local monopoly on that now. Still, he was making a nice gesture, and the Amish *yungie leit* would certainly love it.

"Sure," he said, "boys and girls. The more the merrier, and you being their former teacher, I thought you'd know who to ask. If you want to come out back—you too, Dr. Morelli—kind of like chaperons, that's fine by me. And I'll have your maple syrup for you soon too, Leah. Oh, and I'll saw a few of the lower limbs off your trees."

Leah couldn't believe how polite and kind the man was being, and she scolded herself for her bad thoughts about him.

"When would you want to have the party?" she asked.

"Since this would be for kids who are out of school, how about two days from now, Monday night? In that amount of time, sap should be cooked down toward syrup pretty good. We got good sap flows, since it's below freezing at night, then above freezing in the day. The flow all hangs on the weather, like a lot of things in the winter 'round here."

When he went back to his crew, Leah told Mark, "I feel guilty that I wasn't going to give him a second chance. I might not even have opened my door if you hadn't been here."

"Friendly guys out back or not, I'm putting those locks on the doors and windows as soon as we eat."

"Will you come to the sugaring off?"

"I'm going to draw blood from Reuben, Ruth and Lizzie Kline after supper on Monday, but I'll be here right after."

"I'll ask my mother out to watch Becca, so we can both go outside to chaperon the kids. I'll invite my sister, Naomi, too."

"Leah," he said as he sat down across the table from her, "I'm glad you're not worried about us spending social time together. But you said it's *verboten* for an Amish woman with an *auslander*."

"But we're working together."

"People might think it's more. Sam did. Actually, I want it to be more."

Their eyes held over the steaming platter she'd put on the table. In her carrier on the far end of the table where she could see them, Becca cooed and amused herself with Louise Winslow's gift of bright-colored toys.

"Mark, I told you it can't go anywhere—can't go very far at all."

"I'll take whatever you allow. And if I push for more and get out of line, just tell me."

She felt there was no table between them, nothing between them. It was *verboten* to care for him. As someone had said once about Lord Byron, he was "dangerous to know." But she didn't care. After all, life was full of risks. She couldn't help but smile at him. His eyes darkened as he smiled back.

"We'd better eat before things get cold," she said.

"Remember the first day we met, you asked if it was hot and I said I was surprised, too. Okay, I admit it. I'm more than surprised. I'm intrigued, excited, happy—and hungry."

"We'd better eat then, quick," she said and they laughed together. Too late, she remembered the prayer.

After Mark installed her new locks, they put Becca to bed together, which touched Leah's heart. Barbara and Sam should be here, doing this, not dead at their ages. But then she wouldn't have Becca. She'd be teaching school still, and she wouldn't have Mark either, though she shouldn't think of it that way.

Their growing relationship was uncharted territory for her. She'd never felt this desirous about Joseph. That had all been expected, laid out, comfortable. Was it because she was older now and hadn't really had a come-calling friend for a long time? Was it because she was still a virgin? No, she was certain it was because Mark was so different and yet she wanted to be a part of his life. When he walked into a room, she felt drawn to him like a magnet to true north.

"She looks like an angel," he said, whispering as they watched Becca. They went to sit on the sofa together, which she'd cleared of any signs that it was her bed. She sat next to one arm of it and Mark sat in the middle, crowding her a bit. He put his arm around her shoulders as he'd done in the buggy today.

"I'd like to get you a cell phone to have here," he said, "just in case something happens."

"I can't, really. The bishop draws the line at phones on the property. It's enough you've put all this extra protection in for me, and the insulation."

"I can feel the difference that's made," he said, propping his feet up on the footstool.

As if they were old married folks, she put hers up next to his. She thought he'd say something teasing about it being warmer again, but he just turned her head toward him with one hand. His eyes were such a rich brown with little gold glints dancing in them. They were so close, that even in the lantern light, she could see each black eyelash. The scent of him was tangy, something clean and lemon-lime and utterly male.

She guessed he'd kiss her then and held her breath, but instead he brushed the backs of his curled fingers over her pouted lips. She felt the blood rush to them and to her face.

He touched her chin, her cheeks, her earlobes, brushing back the stray tendrils of hair that had escaped from her starched *kapp*. He ran the tips of his fingers over her throat almost to her neckline and back up.

And so, she ended up kissing him first.

She thought she had control of it, of herself. By starting, she could finish when she wanted. But she was wrong, and his hands took over where his fingers had been and then moved lower to her shoulders and her waist and hips to pull her to him, to cradle her almost in his lap. His thighs were rock hard. She ran her fingers through his hair, crisp and clean. His fingers snagged her *kapp* and sent a heavy tress of hair tumbling free.

And they did not break the kiss.

She could feel him startle when he brushed her breast and realized that Amish women didn't wear bras. He certainly had a lot to learn, she thought through the roaring haze that enveloped her in this long, slow, amazing kiss.

But then, she had a lot to learn too. This was unlike anything she had ever felt or known.

Finally, sometime later but much too soon, they heard men's voices out in front. They broke apart, both breathing hard, in unison.

"Mason's men—the trees," she said.

"We don't need them looking in the windows. I'd better head out of here before it gets too late."

"It's only eight," she blurted, glancing at the battery clock on the mantel.

He laughed richly, though they'd been quiet because of Becca. His laugh vibrated through her entire body, just as his mere presence did. "I mean too late for me to stop," he whispered. "After all, the sap is flowing."

He tickled her as he got up and headed for the front door and took his coat off the peg where she'd hung it. "Kiss Becca good-night and good-morning for me," he added when she came to stand beside him, feeling dizzy. "I'll pay up whatever you give her later, I promise."

She watched him drive out and saw his taillights, like red eyes, disappear down the road. Again, even as she carefully locked up behind him, she recalled the dream of the angel visiting her, not the feelings of dread and awe this time, but because she felt she could have flown.

11

Mark had to search for his cell phone when the notes of *The Triumphal March* sounded just after lunch on Monday. It ticked him off that he'd misplaced it, and the music didn't sound right to him anymore. He'd have to change it to something less strident and grand, maybe something country-western. But where was that damn phone? He'd never misplaced it before.

He found it under the Kauffman family tree next to the computer, where he'd been staring at the screen until the wee hours last night. Caller ID said it was Brad Dixon.

"Mark here. Hi, Brad."

"Hey, I was feeling guilty I abused your hospitality the other day. You asked me not to use my camera near the Amish and I did, though I didn't think they'd mind if I just shot that amazing angel statue."

"I overreacted because Leah did. She's really protective of it."

"Beautiful piece of work, that death angel. I also wanted to invite you to tour the new clinic, if you can break away for a day."

"It won't tempt me to leave my work here."

"That's the furthest thing from my mind—well, maybe not the furthest, but I just want your input on the place. Hell, Mark, I'm proud of it. Just let me know when you want to come so I'm available to show you around personally. I was going to have a grand opening, but I needed to get the clinic up and running, even though Andrea was dying to orchestrate the whole thing."

"If I can play it by ear when I come, I accept. I'm making progress here."

"Great. And even if it's not dinners out, charity galas and fund-raising, I know you have a busy social life," Brad said, back to his baiting tone, which never quite came off as humor or teasing the way it did with Andrea.

"I don't miss any of that. And I do have dinners out and am doing the Maplecreek version of fund-raising. But none of the former society fund-raisers can hold a candle to the sugaring off I'm going to tonight with a bunch of Amish kids, in the woodlot right behind your favorite angel."

"What the heck's a sugaring off?"

"They boil maple sap alfresco to make syrup, an old tradition around here, then make taffy and other treats at a big cookout."

"So, does the bunch of Amish kids include Leah?"

"As a chaperon. She's no kid, Brad. She's twenty-six and a working mother, just like a lot of your staff at MR."

"I hear you. I watched you when you pulled up at her place and caught sight of her. Both your faces lit up when you saw each oth—"

"I'll look forward to seeing the clinic, and I'll call

you to see if your schedule's in sync with mine. Give my best to Andrea in her endeavors."

"Yeah, well, she's in your neck of the maple woods every day this week, acquiring quilts. Talk to you later then."

Mark glared at the phone in his hand, then punched it off. He knew how much it had bothered Brad when Sinclair Marshall, his mentor from his early days at HealGene, hadn't wanted to let him go out on his own. Couldn't Brad take a lesson from that and not keep such close tabs on his own protégé?

If Leah had been a poet, she would have written stanza after stanza about the perfect beauty of this night. It was cold but windless with huge snowflakes falling like powdered sugar. The Amish kids were excited to be together and looked forward to the old tradition of sugaring off, with its taffy-pull and feast.

When Leah glanced across the bare-branched woodlot and her backyard toward the house, it seemed to glow. She had put lanterns in each downstairs window. Now and then she glimpsed her mother's form in the kitchen, walking Becca or just looking out. She could almost smell the baked beans and tart potato salad heating inside. Yes, slowly but surely, the old house, guarded by the stone angel, would become her home.

As more of the party guests arrived and the night darkened, the brushfire under the big black iron kettle crackled and spit sparks that died in the snow. The sap boiled and bubbled beneath the rich amber foam churning on its surface. The crisp air smelled of cinnamon buns, almost as good as those from her mother's bakery.

Leah greeted the last of the guests and introduced everyone to Miles Mason. He'd confided to her that he was not only looking for helpers to harvest the sap— he had nearly eight hundred trees tapped in the area— but to work in his Sugar Bush store uptown.

Leah kept an eye out for Mark. He was going to be late because he was at the Klines', drawing blood from Susie's father and sisters. If only he'd had a sample from Seth, he'd have a complete set of a NAA family's DNA to study.

The specter of Seth's loss loomed over the party, but everyone tried their best to enjoy themselves. Leah's sister, Naomi, was the youngest one here, and she looked excited to be included. David Groder seemed to be glad Naomi was here too, though Leah managed to get him off alone for a few minutes.

"David," she asked, "do you know if Dr. Cutler still has that old brown van of his?"

"I've seen it parked out behind his place on Holtz Road."

"Just parked there, not driven anymore?"

"I'm not sure," he said, frowning. "Maybe Dr. Morelli knows, 'cause he said he'd be watching him."

Her insides cartwheeled. "Dr. Morelli told Dr. Cutler he'd be watching him?"

"*Ja*, 'cause he said Dr. Cutler been watching you— '*watching her*,' he said."

"When was this?"

David shifted from one foot to the other, looking as if he'd been caught at something. "Just a coupla days ago, at the vet clinic…ah, Friday evening."

Leah fought to keep calm. No use putting the boy

in the middle of this. She'd asked Mark not to challenge Jesse Cutler on her behalf, but he had—without telling her, before or after. Yet she felt touched that Mark was being protective. She hadn't leveled with him about Jesse's bothering her immediately, either.

"All right, everybody!" Miles Mason called out. "Gather round here. Now, this snow that's falling is not the final 'sugar snow' I'm predicting's yet to come, but it's real nice. Before we chow down, I want to show you how we know if the sap's ready. I could use a modern thermometer or drip it off a scoop, but I thought you'd like to see the old-fashioned way of checking on it."

At least, Leah thought, he hadn't referred to the crowd of kids as *you people*. Maybe he was learning, changing for the better. She'd certainly altered her attitude toward him lately.

"Now, I've got a twig here and have twisted the tip of it into a loop, see?"

The kids moved in closer. Leah saw Mark pull into her driveway, his headlights slicing through the sifting snow. She heard his car door slam. Through the blur of white, she could see that he came directly across the backyard toward the woodlot as Mason's voice carried in the cold, crisp air.

"Watch now. I dip the twig into the boiling sap—careful I don't burn myself, a'course—and, like blowing soap bubbles, blow through the loop like this."

He blew but the sap just popped. "Not ready yet," he told them, "or it would've blown a big bubble. I'd give it another half hour, so we might as well eat. Your friend Leah's going to bring out the food from the house, and you can get your hot dogs to roast right over here. Got us some fixins, potato chips and marshmallows too, but make sure none of that drops in the kettle."

Crunching through new snow, Leah led Naomi and two other helpers toward the house to bring out the baked beans and potato salad. She met Mark halfway across the backyard as the girls went ahead to get the food from her mother. His dark hair, eyebrows and thick lashes shone with fresh flakes.

"Good timing. You haven't missed one bite," she said, poking him in the ribs through his leather jacket. She wanted to mention his visit to Dr. Cutler, but not now. "Do you want to come in to say hello to my mother and Becca, before she goes to sleep? I'm going to get in a good hug and kiss myself."

"Why, Miss Leah, I don't know if you mean you intend all that for Becca or for my needy self," he said, grinning and laying an open hand on his chest. He wheeled around to escort her toward the house.

She had to laugh. For one moment, she was transported back to the happy, carefree days of the first sugaring off that she'd gone to so many years ago. She didn't miss Joseph or Sam, though, not compared to the way she still mourned Barbara.

"I said, a penny for your thoughts, Leah. Are you okay? If you've been thinking about Seth and what happened to Susie and Miriam, I have too."

"Good," she said, turning to look him full in the face as lantern light gilded his features and lit his dark eyes.

"Let's encourage Seth's friends to have a good time, but not give up on his return or finding out what happened."

The sugaring off passed in a blur of snowflakes falling on happy faces. After their feast of hot dogs and side dishes, they roasted marshmallows and made s'mores. Some of the boys turned their marshmallows to flaming torches and wrote certain girls' initials in the dark night sky. The *yungie leit* gathered fresh snow and made what Mason called toffee slush cones. He poured ladles of syrup onto a cake of ice he'd cut from the stream in the ravine, and they watched it turn to gooey taffy, which they kneaded and pulled with buttered hands until it was deliciously chewy.

Leah watched Mark work the crowd just the way Mason did, only Mark was asking the teens about their families and urging them to tell their parents his shingle was out for treating all children, not just NAA patients. It touched Leah again to see her sister bloom with the knowledge that David Groder had singled her out for special attention. She herself glowed each time Mark shot her a look or smile.

Kids traipsed in and out of Leah's house to use the bathroom and to chat with her mother in the kitchen. Leah had taken her a hot dog and some taffy, and checked on Becca, but the baby was cuddled in her crib, sound asleep, covered well against drafts from the busy kitchen door.

"Don't blame David Groder," Leah told Mark as they leaned against a big tree, away from the kids who were having a snowball fight, "but I learned from him that you had words with Jesse Cutler."

"Yeah," he said, not looking a bit guilty. "The guy's weird, and I'm not sure what he's capable of, so steer clear of him."

"If I can, I do."

"If you can't, let me know."

"Mark, I can't ask you to play protector—"

"I don't want to *play* protector, I want to *be* protector, yours and Becca's. I didn't want to tell you this at first, in case it scared you, but from the minute I heard you had adopted her I felt protective toward both of you."

"You've been wonderful. But I'm the one who promised Becca's mother on her deathbed that I'd protect her with my life. I'm the one who..."

Her voice trailed off. Glancing back at the house over Mark's shoulder as she spoke, she saw a light glimmer, then fade, in the main bedroom upstairs. It had definitely been in the corner room, with its windows overlooking both this back lot and the cemetery. And now, a pale light shone in the attic.

"What is it?" Mark said, turning to look.

"Nothing. My mother or someone has just taken a lantern upstairs, that's all. I'm going to pop in to see how she's doing. I'll be right back."

Leah knew if she had not been recalling Barbara's death in that very room at the moment the light shone there, she would not have reacted like this. Her mother or someone using the bathroom on the second floor had probably just opened the closed bedroom door, and the light had seeped into the room. But then why had the light appeared in the attic?

"Leah," Mark called behind her, "I'll go with you."

"No, I'm fine. Keep an eye on the kids."

"Maam?" she called inside, keeping her voice low since she didn't want to startle Becca. She glanced inside the shadowy crib in the dim living room. As usual, Becca slept like a log under her little quilt, her breathing deep and regular. Soon, Leah thought, she'd be sleeping clear through the night.

Taking a lantern from the front window, she went upstairs. The steps creaked, and a draft of cold air wafted into her face. On the landing where she'd hesitated the night Barbara died, she called out, *"Maam? Wo bist du?"*

No one was currently using the bathroom, for the door was open and it was dark inside. But then she saw the attic door ajar. Holding the lantern aloft, Leah went to the bottom of the steps.

"Maam?"

As a woman's form came to the top of the landing, a black shadow fell over Leah, then a light shone in her eyes. For one insane moment, she almost thought the flitting form was Barbara's—but no, the silhouette was too stout.

"Leah? What is it?" her mother asked.

She breathed again. "I just wondered where you were. What are you doing up there?"

"I thought I'd take a look at those old quilts you mentioned, to see if they could be washed. But they're too delicate, crinkly with age. *Ja,* I bet they'd shred if they were so much as soaked. And, Leah," she said, coming down the stairs, holding the lantern and something else in her other hand—a whiskey bottle— "what about all these?"

"Sam's."

"I'm so sorry. What a shame—a sin, considering how poor off they were and her so sick."

"I intended to get rid of them but didn't have the time—nor did I want to cart them into town to throw away."

"I'll bring your father out here, and we'll bury them somewhere," she said with a shake of her head. Setting the bottle on the step and coming down the rest of the way, she went on, "I've been wondering if that poor soul actually committed suicide. I talked to his cousins at the funeral, and they said he was acting so strange, like he was trapped, being watched."

"Etta and Ben Troyer said that—being watched?"

"Etta did. But Sam evidently didn't leave any sort of note. These empty bottles made me think of notes in a bottle, you know, like wash up on the shore. I was wondering if he might have left a suicide note somewhere in the house, since Etta says there was nothing in the things he left behind at their place, nothing but some money for you. Suicide might be rare among our people, but it's not unheard of, especially when someone is as depressed as Sam might have been over Barbara's loss."

You might know, Leah thought, that her mother was playing psychiatrist again—or detective. She recalled that Mark had said a scientist had to function like that, make discoveries and test theories.

"That's crazy, *Maam,* a suicide note in a bottle. He was drinking and he just fell to his death, and that's bad enough."

"*Ja,* I didn't mean to speak ill of the dead," she said and glanced at the closed door to the main bedroom.

"Did you have that door open earlier?" Leah asked as they crossed the landing to head downstairs. "Did you look for the quilts in there first?"

"I didn't go in there at all. You told me they were in an old trunk in the attic."

"But did you just open the door for a minute? I saw a light…"

"*Nein,* I didn't. The *yungie leit* have been in and out, so maybe one of them opened the bedroom door looking for the bathroom."

Leah said no more. She was fairly certain no one, besides her mother and Becca, had been in the house when she came in to see what had caused the light. Perhaps the bonfire under the sap kettle had been reflected in that window. Surely that was it.

The house was achingly silent after everyone left. Becca slept on in the darkened front room, and so as not to wake her, Leah sat down at the kitchen table.

She was much too keyed up to sleep. The festivities had made this place come to life. Miles Mason had been generous and kind and Mark was…was someone she was falling in love with, even though she would never tell him or another living soul.

She sighed and sank into her place at the table. Mark had brought her notes from Miriam Kline, which would complete the family tree Leah had been constructing. Since she was so wound up, she might as well correlate the information, she decided, but first she'd be sure everything was locked.

She checked each window latch Mark had installed, and assured herself the front- and back-door bolts and safety chains were on. Leah had sent four of the lanterns home with her *maam* and Naomi, but she brought two to the kitchen table to be able to read Miriam's handwriting. She bent over the notes and started to fill in her diagram, when she realized something for the first time.

The Klines were distantly related—through great-grandparents—to the Lantzes, Barbara Lantz Yoder's birth family. Did that mean Becca could not only be a carrier of the Regnell anemia that had killed Barbara, but also have the gene for natal accelerated aging? Was Mark aware of that potentially deadly link yet?

She began to shake. Did that mean she should have Becca tested for the NAA gene when Mark found it? What if Becca failed to grow and began to age like Susie Kline?

Leah knew now, more than ever, that she had to help Mark make progress on NAA. At any cost to herself, she had to support him, encourage, even push him…

She put her head in her hands and felt the excitement from the night drain from her. The Amish had a saying, *It's not all cakes and pies.* Life among their people looked so idyllic to outsiders, but underneath the joys and blessings lay the challenges and difficulties of keeping separate and stable in this dangerous world. Under the facade of family lay the fear of genetic disease from too-close ties. *Blessed be the ties that bind,* but they could be cursed too.

She folded her arms on the table and put her head down on them. Intermarriage and big, close families were what saved the Amish, but it was what might doom them too. That must be the message her people should learn from Mark's time here with them, a message she must help to spread.

She blinked back tears and sniffed hard. Would Mark help her convince her people of the risks of intermarriage, or would he want to keep them the way they were so he could study them? So the complicated family trees could open up the patterns of the twisted double helix to his understanding, the same helix that hung on his office wall that Clark had given him, patterns like the one on Amish quilts and those pioneer ones in the attic...patterns to solve about Seth...

When Leah jerked awake, she was shocked to see she had slept slumped over the kitchen table all night. Dawn lit the sky, though both lanterns on the table still hissed gently, casting wan light.

She stood and stretched, pressing her hands to the small of her sore back and rotating her head one way and then the other. She could not believe Becca had slept through the night. That was a first. She was so proud of her. It was a milestone, but she would surely be wet by now, and that diaper rash would be worse again. Mark had brought her several vitamin E capsules last night, but she hadn't wanted to wake the child to rub the liquid on her.

Still stretching out the kinks, Leah went into the living room and peered into the crib. Becca slept as if she'd been partying all night. Smiling, Leah pulled the curtains open on the window that overlooked the angel. The first thing she noticed was that the *yungie leit* had scuffed some words in the new snow, though she couldn't decipher them from this angle. She'd have to carry the baby upstairs to make out the words, probably just another thank-you.

"Becca-my-Becca, are you going to sleep forever?" she cooed and lifted the quilt slightly from the little head.

The early-morning light was so funny in here. It made Becca's hair looked slightly darker, fuller. The child stirred and stretched, sucking in a big yawn Leah could hear but not see, since she was facing away. Usually, at the mere sound of her mother's voice, Becca turned immediately toward her.

"Come on, lazybones. Got to get you changed and fixed up with something Mark brought to help your rash."

The moment Leah lifted her, she gasped. Heavy—too heavy. Bigger? It couldn't be.

She held the baby out at arm's length, then jolted so hard she almost dropped her. Quickly, she lay her back down in the crib.

Leah peered closely at the sleepy face—a stranger's face.

It—this baby—wasn't Becca!

12

Leah screamed.

Was she going crazy? This was a baby about the same age and general size, but the hair…the face…

It wasn't Becca!

Shaking, Leah pressed herself against the wall to stop the house from tilting.

When she got hold of herself, she looked at the baby again. Hair too brown and too much of it. Eyes blue but not tilted quite right. The face wrong, all wrong. With trembling hands, she undressed the child in the crib.

No diaper rash. No tiny birthmark on the left hipbone. Thighs way too chubby.

No, no, no! This was impossible. Was this another nightmare? She had to wake up now.

This baby seemed drugged. She had hardly reacted to Leah's screams. The irises of her eyes were dilated. Dear God in heaven, someone had taken Becca last night and left a changeling in her place. But how? When?

And worse—why?

I will protect Becca with my life, she'd vowed to

Barbara on her deathbed. She'd told Mark the same thing.

Where was her baby? Who had her baby?

God is a very present help in trouble... Therefore we will not fear. The words popped into Leah's head. But she did fear. *God shall help her, just at the break of dawn.*

"Please help me, Lord God. Please..."

She looked through the sheets and quilts in the crib. No ransom note, nothing. Did someone want her to think this was all in her head? There had to be a note, some explanation somewhere.

Like a madwoman, she tore through the house. Maybe Becca was here, somewhere. Maybe this was just a ploy to scare her, but scare her to do what? Not ask questions about Seth? Or about Sam's death? Not help Mark? Move out of this house? What...*what?*

She ran to the cellar stairs, for they went down from the back door where so many had traipsed in and out last night. But her mother had been here the whole time, and none of those kids would have hurt Becca.

But what if someone else had slipped in while her mother was in the attic? That was around the time the light had shown in the bedroom. Had someone almost been trapped and run upstairs? Maybe the intruder had just moved Becca to that bedroom to scare Leah.

She ran up to the second floor and opened the bedroom door with such force it slammed back into the wall. No Becca on the bed. Nothing disturbed. She should stick with her plan for an orderly search, she told herself, and headed for the cellar again. She was halfway down into the darkness when she realized she had no lantern and dashed back up for one.

"Becca? Becca!" she shouted as she thudded downstairs. She searched everywhere, then hurried back up to the main floor.

She looked behind the sofa, in the pantry, in closets, then rushed upstairs, breathing hard, panting in her panic. Whatever someone wanted of her, she'd do it. Anything to get Becca back. Maybe some sort of ransom note, some instructions, had been left somewhere.

She searched the main bedroom again, willing Becca to be there, praying that Barbara's deathbed promise that she'd be watching didn't mean she'd know how Leah had failed her. She rummaged through the closet, rifled through drawers she hysterically ripped out and left tumbled on the floor. She checked the bathroom, the other rooms, then ran upstairs to the attic.

How could her mother have let someone sneak in and switch Becca for another baby? But this person—people—they were very, very clever. They obviously had someone spying on Leah, maybe on Mark too.

Could Miles Mason have set up the whole sugaring off to distract her so he or his cronies could abduct Becca? She was quite certain the man himself had never left the back woodlot.

She burst into huge sobs when she saw nothing was disturbed in the attic. Yanking the trunk lid open, she felt through the two quilts there. Her mother was right—stiff and crinkly. Thank God, there was nothing under them.

Before she could stop herself, she seized one of Sam's whiskey bottles and then another and heaved them across the room into the eaves. A note in a bottle! Her mother was crazy as well as careless! No, she couldn't fault her mother.

Leah began to shake uncontrollably, but she kept throwing bottles. She was furious with Sam, furious with the entire world. Joseph left her, her sister Katie left her, Barbara, then Sam. Now Becca. Mark had distracted her. And she was so stupid to fall in love with him.

Some of the bottles shattered, some hit Mark's insulation and bounced onto the floor. Her breathing ragged, Leah collapsed to her knees and sobbed so hard she couldn't breathe.

But she got hold of herself again. She'd take this child to the sheriff and demand he search for Becca. Mark and her mother could testify the child wasn't Becca. Mark could do a DNA comparison with Becca's distant relatives if no one believed her. She'd rouse the entire community to search for her baby. She'd put up posters in town. *Meet at the angel to search for my angel.* She'd ask Louise to help her get the word out through the newspaper.

A verse from Psalms popped into her head: *The angel of the Lord encamps all around those who fear him and delivers them.*

She dashed to the attic window overlooking the angel and glared down at it. The guardian angel had not guarded Becca. It had not delivered Becca or Barbara from evil.

Leah pressed her forehead against a cold pane of glass. She was losing her grip on reality. The angel had walked and talked only in her dreams. An angel made of stone to commemorate a tragic death had not decked herself in dead flowers, nor had she dealt Sam a fatal blow to the back of his head because he threatened to take Becca away. But now she feared someone had killed Sam. If someone was desperate enough to kidnap a child, someone might have murdered Sam.

Leah stared at the angel again. Something small and black dangled from its folded hands. Glancing away from the statue, she read the scuffed words in the snow she'd noted earlier but had then ignored in her frenzy: *DON'T TELL! DON'T TELL! DON'T TELL!*

Mark heard buggy wheels crunching gravel in his driveway. He was getting good at noticing little things he never used to pick up on. In a way, he felt he was slowly unwinding inside, though his pulse quickened now. Leah hadn't come in yesterday because she'd wanted to clean her house, since her kitchen and bathroom would be in demand for the sugaring-off party. But maybe she was here bright and early today.

He saw it was Miriam Kline in her big buggy, and she had Susie with her. Mark opened the door and hurried out into the cold. "This is a nice surprise," he called to them. "Is everything okay?"

"My broke arm itches bad!" Susie piped up. "Can you help me scratch it under this cast?"

He tied their horse to the hitching post while Miriam climbed out, then they both helped Susie down. "It's a problem," Mark admitted, "and the solution isn't very high-tech. Do you have a knitting needle around?"

"So, it is safe to poke around in there?" Miriam

asked as they went inside and Susie took her cape off. "I quilt but don't knit. None of the sisters do. It's not our way."

"Then we'll improvise," Mark said, going to his vertical blinds in the front room and lifting the long, clear piece of plastic that hung on a cord to turn the slats. "Susie, come over here and let me lift you up on this chair so the doctor can perform an operation with this magic wand."

Miriam smiled and Susie giggled as he lifted her up.

"I couldn't even sleep it was itching so bad. But I knew you'd fix it, Dr. Mark."

His heart almost melted. "Now, you just tell me where to guide the rod," he told her.

Susie held on to him with her good arm around his shoulders while he carefully slid the plastic shaft down into her pink cast. "Oh, *ja,*" she said with a sigh and rolled her eyes. "Right there. Oooh, *ja.*"

"Then I think I'll have to unhook this rod and send it home with you," Mark told her. "We'll just call it 'scratching edge' technology."

"I am so glad you're my doctor, and we're friends!" Susie said and Miriam nodded.

In all the years he'd studied and researched, interned and practiced, it struck Mark that he had never had a better day.

Leah tore back downstairs, made sure the baby was still in the crib and ran outside.

She could tell what was wrapped around the angel's wrists the moment she got through the cemetery gate. Becca's little black bonnet strings held the headpiece that blew forlornly in the wind. But it was empty, no message within.

She snatched it from the angel and ran back inside, noting that the message in the snow was only along the edge of the cemetery, not around the front of the house where the Amish kids had parked their buggies. And the footsteps that had made those words had begun at the angel's pedestal, just the way they had that other day someone had peered in her back window.

Shaking so hard her teeth chattered, Leah fought back another bout of hysteria. She had to keep calm to find Becca. The message was clear enough: if she went to the sheriff or perhaps anyone, Becca might be…might be…

She pinned up her wild hair and donned her *kapp*. She splashed cold water on her face, then forced herself to pick up this baby. Where had the demon kidnapper gotten this poor child? Was there another mother agonizing over her loss too? Leah was going to find out, and when she did, she'd find Becca. Her baby's abductor was insane if he—or she—thought an Amish mother would accept such as God's will or turn the other cheek. She might not tell, but she surely meant to act.

Leah changed and fed the baby, burped her while she paced, then put her carefully back in Becca's crib. All the while, her mind was churning.

Her first instinct was to question Miles Mason about setting this up, but if he was at all involved, the abductor would know she'd told. She longed to run to Mark, but it was obvious someone was watching her—perhaps the same menace who had put that sign on his clinic in animal blood.

Would Jesse Cutler stoop this low? Perhaps he meant to keep Becca a while, then say he'd found her to become a hero in her eyes.

What about Brad and Angela Dixon? They didn't like her, and didn't want Mark in Amish country. They wanted him back at their precious MR labs and clinic in Cleveland. And, if they were researching NAA themselves, they would need blood from NAA families. Seth, Susie, Mrs. Kline—and now Becca was distantly related.

Or had her baby been taken simply to shut Leah up or stop her? But why?

Louise Winslow was driven by passion to possess a baby. She'd said it was the one thing she could never buy but that she'd pay a king's ransom for. She'd been to the house twice and knew exactly where Becca's crib was and that she was a sound sleeper. But whoever had switched this child for Becca had a baby they were willing to give up, and Leah could not fathom Louise doing that if she had her hands on one. Louise was the only one—besides Mark—that Leah felt she could trust.

Leah realized she desperately needed someone to care for this child so she would be free to find her own. Maybe, since Louise had only held Becca once and seen her briefly twice, she wouldn't even realize the baby was not Leah's. Louise was enough of a recluse— Katie had said she didn't even live in the same house with her husband anymore—that she could keep this baby for a while and no one else would know. Whoever was watching Leah would certainly be more suspicious if she ran to Mark than if she went to Louise.

Leah dug out clothes she'd saved for when Becca got a little bigger. She dressed this baby in them. The poor little thing was starting to look more awake. If she had indeed been tranquilized, didn't that point to someone with access to drugs, someone who had left that drug vial top behind where Seth disappeared and who knew how to draw blood and inject people with an amnesiac?

It certainly couldn't be Mark, so Jesse Cutler and Brad Dixon, maybe even Andrea, were at the top of her list. None of these people would expect an Amish woman to come after them, so she was going to start with Andrea's so-called quilt warehouse, which she insisted no one visit. It was only about a forty-five-minute buggy ride to Millersburg.

But first, she had to solve the money mystery about Sam, and search around here more carefully. Perhaps Sam had left some clue behind about who had given him that mysterious money. His note had hinted he had even more. Maybe someone was planning to ransom Becca for money Sam had hidden. Surely he hadn't promised to sell his own baby daughter to someone who had come to claim her after he died.

Leaving the baby lying in Becca's crib, Leah tore upstairs to the attic again. Her feet crunching broken glass, she grabbed the two antique quilts from the trunk and carried them downstairs. She wrapped them in a large, dark green garbage sack so she could use them as bait to get in to see Andrea's warehouse if her more thorough search here didn't turn up anything helpful. She was not thinking straight; she had to calm down, she lectured herself as she peered at the baby in the crib again.

"Sorry," she told the still-drowsy child. "We'll be going out, but I've got to look around here first. Don't you worry, now, because I know someone to take care of you who will just love you."

She stood for a moment in the center of the living room and pressed her hands to her head as if it would explode. Yes, search this house first—*really* search it for any clues Sam might have left about who was funneling money to him and why. Then take the baby to Louise Winslow and see if she'd watch her, either telling her the truth or maybe trying to pass the child off as Becca. Then take the quilts to try to check out— or psych out, as her mother would say—Andrea and her warehouse of quilts. Next, Jesse Cutler. Then... then anything she had to do to find and rescue the daughter of her heart.

Seth heard the baby crying again, but this time he was sure it was right outside his door in the hall. And somehow, it didn't sound like the same baby as before. Having three younger sisters had made him able to pick out different kids' wails.

"Isn't it nice of her to visit so we can build our DNA bank?" a woman's sarcastic voice said, the voice Seth had come to think of as Nurse Snobby Snotty, until he'd heard someone call her "doctor" the other day. Even without listening through the crack under his door, he could hear them clearly, so they must be right outside. The man was speaking now.

"You know, I think you look quite...ah, what's the word I want?...fetching in that bonnet and long dress and apron. I used to love *Little House on the Prairie* when I was a child."

"Very funny. It wasn't that easy, you know. Not that they would have been turned me in even if they'd caught me, but it was damn risky. I would have changed clothes hours ago, but this get-up seemed to keep her calm, until now."

"Maybe she's hungry."

"Do you think I'm an idiot?" Snobby Snotty demanded. "I fed her but darned if I'm going to baby-sit her. Keeping the older Amish kid around's bad enough."

Another Amish kid! They had another Amish kid here. At least it wasn't Susie. Could it be Teacher Leah's baby?

"As for the risk," the man said, "it'll pay off, believe me."

Their voices were fading. Seth threw himself on the floor and pressed his ear to the crack under the door. He could still hear them. The man was talking again.

"One genetic-drug cure recently netted a pharm firm thirty-one billion dollars," he said, "so can you imagine what antiaging genetic therapy or drugs would be worth? The fountain of youth, discovered right here!"

Seth racked his brain for something he'd learned about the fountain of youth. It had been in one of the books Teacher Leah had suggested he read about the history of America, but he couldn't think of where that fountain was supposed to be. Oh, *ja,* way down in Florida, but he couldn't recall the name of the Spanish explorer who was looking for it. A pouncing lion or something like that.

But he couldn't believe anyone thought they could make a fortune in the heart of peaceful Amish country, so where was this prisonlike hospital he and the Amish baby were in? Maybe clear down in Florida. But if so, why would Snobby Snotty be dressed Amish? Sure, there were a few of their people in Florida, and Luke and Katie Brand were going to visit there, but he had a gut feeling he was still in Ohio. And that made him more homesick than ever.

Leah was soon dripping with sweat. She'd pulled every drawer in the house out and turned it upside down; she'd peered under furniture; she'd looked under every mattress and rifled through the linen closet. She'd crawled under eaves in the attic, gone through every inch of the shed, even emptying some barrels of nails and tools she could hardly lift.

Then she remembered the root cellar.

Mark had asked about it, and she'd told him it hadn't been opened for months. Last autumn's leaves had plastered themselves to it like an undisturbed wax seal. Donning her cape and bonnet, Leah got a butcher knife and rushed outside. The sun was out; the snow was melting. Soon, perhaps that dreadful message—*DON'T TELL!*—would melt, though it was ingrained in her brain forever.

Leah bent over the slanted, wooden root-cellar door to free the sodden mat of leaves along its edges. When she heaved the door upward, she nearly wrenched her back. The door slammed itself open against the house. But she was rewarded with proof that Sam had used the dank area for a storehouse: more whiskey bottles, lots of them, piled haphazardly. She knelt in the leaves and snow and tried to reach down into the cellar, but decided she'd have to descend the four steps into its depths.

Carefully, she stepped down into the bottles, ankle deep, and began to check each, then tossed them toward the empty depths at the back of the cellar. If her mother's note-in-a-bottle idea was starting to make sense, she knew she was really desperate.

Under the pile of empty, smelly bottles was a tin coffee can she almost kicked in her frustration and fury. It was corroded with rust. As she reached for it, Leah imagined it was like poor Sam's soul, once solid but crusted over with some sort of sin, hiding things. She pried open the simple plastic lid and gawked at what lay within.

The can was jammed with rolled bills, mostly twenties, some fifties. And a note in Sam's handwriting, like the one with the bills Etta had handed her at the funeral.

Leah put the lid back on the can and peeked out of the cellar to look around the yard. She saw no one, clear to the bare trees edging the ravine where the very top of the distant silos peeked at her. But she felt someone staring. How she longed to raise a fist in defiance, but she knew better. Unable to contain her curiosity about what Sam had written in the note, Leah hunkered down in the root cellar to read it.

Nearby—too near—some horrible, screeching noise started. It drowned her thoughts and cloaked her shriek. Suddenly, above her, blocking her escape, stood a massive gray form, leaning close.

Leah grabbed the butcher knife and held it before her. For one awesome moment, she thought the death angel had come to life again. But it was Miles Mason, with a chain saw in his beefy hands, stepping closer, bending toward her.

13

Mason was behind the kidnapping and had come to kill her!

Leah knew her knife was no match for the chain saw, so she threw herself back into the root cellar, tripping and rolling on the whiskey bottles. She grabbed one to throw at him. Mason stood, frowning down at her, the roaring saw held horizontally across his body. He took a step toward her, hovered over her, blocking out the light.

Then he turned off the saw.

"Sorry if I scared you," he said. "I knocked on your back door to tell you I was gonna cut your limbs now, but you didn't answer. Figured you were gone."

Her heart pounding against her breastbone, Leah remembered to breathe. "Cut my limbs... You—you really scared me. I was looking for something in here."

"I was surprised to see the cellar door open and just thought I'd look inside."

Bruised by the bottles, Leah righted herself as some of them clinked and slid away. She got unsteadily to her feet and retrieved the coffee can. Mason put the saw on the ground and extended a hand to help her out of the cellar. She took it. Unless he was a very good

actor, she was crossing Miles Mason off her list of possible baby abductors right now. He could have easily
been rid of her and hidden her body—unless he'd just
been assigned to watch what she did next.

"So, you mind if I cut the limbs now?" he asked. "I
don't need my sap bleeding out of big scars on the
trees, but you want them off, I'm willing."

The way he put that almost made her sick. Too
often she'd pictured the tapped trees as dripping their
life blood into the buckets, and the idea of huge cuts,
like surgery on limbs… Was he subtly threatening
her? She didn't think this man did subtleties.

"No, that's all right, Mr. Mason." Her voice was
shaking so hard it didn't sound like her. She was starting to feel dizzy. She hadn't eaten for hours. "I—I
don't want you to have to do it right now, if it bothers
the sap flow. I didn't think of that. It's fine with me if
you wait until later."

"I'd rather, but you been real helpful to me. Hired
on four of the kids last night. They're the best workers, your people. And I'm still real sorry about Seth."

As he spoke, she was aware he was eyeing the mess
she'd made of her dress, hair and bonnet. She must
look like a wild woman. He probably thought the
whiskey bottles were hers, but she didn't want to take
the time to talk anymore. Before she went to see
Louise and then to Andrea's *verboten* warehouse,
she'd have to clean up and change.

"I'm real sorry too," she said and hurried back into
the house to check on the baby. The poor little thing
was starting to fuss. With tears streaming down her
face, Leah changed the child's diaper again—she'd

come in a store-bought one—then lifted her out and walked her for a few minutes. She put her back in Becca's crib with one of the bright toys from Louise, all the while keeping an eye on Miles Mason out the window. He'd gone to the woodlot out back, but so that no one could possibly see what she was doing, Leah tore upstairs to the bathroom and sat on the closed toilet seat to study Sam's scribbles from the coffee can.

The note wasn't just about money. It was a list of dates and times, ranging, as best as she could tell, over the months Barbara had been ill at home, not in the hospital. This couldn't be a record of the money from the Amish relief benefit, because that would have been a onetime gift, not money dribbled in like this. Stranger yet, next to the dates with money recorded, were abbreviations about *mgs.* and *ds.*

Milligrams and doses? Maybe Sam had recorded Barbara's medicine on those dates too, but the entries seemed so random. Leah knew for a fact that Barbara took all her medicines on a regular basis, not just on certain days. And what were these other numbers next to the *mgs.* and *ds.*? The times when he was to give her that medicine? But these were erratic entries too.

What did it mean? What had Sam been doing to earn all this money he was too ashamed or scared to spend? And worse, did it mean he had killed himself over what he'd done, or had been killed to keep him quiet? Perhaps someone had threatened him with *DON'T TELL,* too.

Leah knew exactly where Louise lived, not just because her husband was the town mayor and owned the largest English farm in the area, but because the Winslow acreage abutted Sam Yoder's parents' place. As kids, she and Barbara had played hide-and-seek in the fields in the area. A fragment of memory jumped through Leah's brain: they'd been in the field next to Winslows' the time Sam had taken their dolls and hidden them and they'd looked all over before they got them back. She slapped the reins on Nell's back. She had her going at a good trot already, but she had to hurry, hurry to find Becca.

Katie Brand had visited Louise when she was an undercover cop trying to solve hate crimes against the Amish. She'd told Leah that Louise lived in the small, picket-fenced, gingerbread-trimmed house behind the big Winslow farmhouse. Leah could see from here that the charming, whitewashed fence made a big contrast to the newly installed electrified-wire cattle fences her husband had recently put up along this road. The Amish farmers had all been abuzz about it because it seemed as if the new mayor liked to keep not only cattle in but people out.

How Leah wished Katie were here instead of on her way to Florida, but she had to do this on her own, even without Mark. She looked back over her shoulder again as she turned Nell through the wire gate onto the lane that led from the main road to Winslows' spread. If she was being watched, so be it. She wasn't just going to stay home with this baby while someone else had her daughter and, perhaps, ran amok among her people.

Leah prayed Louise had enough room in her little house to take in a baby for a day and a night; she'd brought clothing, diapers, bedding and formula. But as well prepared as she was, she still wasn't sure what she was going to tell Louise.

Although the woman was apparently both exasperated with and estranged from her husband, the last thing Leah needed was for the mayor to know that an Amish child had been mysteriously switched for another. Who knew what Becca's abductors would do with her if they panicked? People might never understand why Leah hadn't gone to Sheriff Martin. But after the way he'd treated her when Seth disappeared, when Susie and Miriam Kline were hurt in the tipped buggy, and especially when Sam died, she didn't need all his questions right now. No, as much as possible, Leah's investigation had to be done undercover, just the way Katie had operated.

Thank you, Lord, she breathed when she saw Louise was not only home but running out to greet her. Despite the chill wind, she was without the usual scarf or hat or gloves to cover her scarred skin.

"Oh, what a nice surprise!" Louise cried before Leah even stopped the buggy. "I hope baby Becca's in there too!"

Leah prayed that greeting meant Louise had nothing to do with any of this—she was risking everything on that. "I was hoping I could ask you for a huge favor," Leah said as she got out and lifted the baby down in Becca's plastic carrier. "You volunteered to look after Becca during Sam's funeral, and—"

"Oh, I'd love to," she said as she bent over to look closely at the baby. Leah held her breath. "My, she's growing bigger every day, aren't you, sweetie?"

"I realize this is sudden, and you might be busy."

"Not too busy to have a little visitor for as long as you want."

"That's so good of you." Leah had calculated she'd be back from Millersburg by nightfall, unless something else went very wrong. Tonight, she wanted to sneak out to Jesse Cutler's place after dark. She hated the idea of going there in the evening, when he was home, but she couldn't chance being seen by anyone there in the light of day, especially since she intended to examine his old brown van to see if it had been driven lately.

"The thing is, Louise," she said, "I have to buggy to another town, so could I pick her up tomorrow morning? I've brought everything you'd need, and I realize it's a big imposition, but—"

"Leah, this is the best gift I've had in years, that you trust me with her. I'd be honored," she insisted, lifting the child out of the carrier Leah still held. She switched instantly to baby talk, which the English seemed to use but the Amish never did. "This is a wittle house for a wittle girl to visit, just like in a fairy tale, wittle Becca," Louise crooned.

Leah breathed the first sigh of relief since she'd seen Becca was missing. This woman was a blessing, more than she'd ever know.

Leah used Louise's phone to call Mark and tell him she wouldn't be in today either. She hated to lie to him and prayed he'd forgive her later when she found out who had Becca.

"Wild party life too much for you?" he teased when she told him she'd see him tomorrow.

"I just need to get caught up on some things, that's all."

"Will your mother have Becca over at the bakery?"

"I—no, she's here with me."

"Where are you calling from?"

She tried a flip answer. "My cell phone, of course." The moment that was out of her mouth, she realized he had caller ID and had known when he asked her where she was. Was he trying to trick her? Turned away from Louise, who was playing with the baby, Leah pressed the heel of her hand to her forehead.

"Actually," she told him, "I've dropped by Louise Winslow's, as she's been so kind. Then I have some other errands. By the way, next time you talk to Brad Dixon—or Andrea—please tell them I wasn't upset that he photographed the stone angel."

"He called it a death angel. Actually, he apologized already, since I'd asked him not to take photos near your house with so many people going in and out that day."

She was hoping to turn the subject to Andrea, to whether he knew her whereabouts this week. "I'm glad you and the Dixons are getting along," she said. "I sensed some bad blood between them and Clark, though Andrea tries to keep things civil."

"I've had some rough times with Clark, as well as Brad, over my move here, my work. But yeah, Andrea smooths things over. Brad said she's going to be around the area all week, so she may drop in again."

Leah's pulse picked up even more, but she dare not ask any more without giving her plans away.

"I still want to get you a cell phone, Leah. I know other Amish workers use them in their places of employment, and I'm going to insist you carry one in the buggy and keep it at home while you're working with me. I don't even like you buggying around with Becca to see friends in broad daylight."

She had a terrible vision of Mark driving to her house to see her today or this evening and she wouldn't be there. But Becca's abduction changed all the rules.

"I'm beginning to think it's a good idea. Talk to you later."

"Tell Louise I've ordered the MRI. Thank her again for her help. And be careful."

"Sure. Sure, I will." She longed to tell him everything, that she was desperate for his help. That she was terrified she'd betrayed her best friend by breaking a deathbed vow. That she'd lost the baby she loved more than life itself. And that she loved him.

But she did none of those things. As crazed as she felt, she calmly punched the "end" button on Louise's phone, then turned to her and forced a stiff smile.

"Mark said to tell you he's ordered the MRI and thank you for your help. Louise, I really owe you a big favor, too, because I know you'll take good care of— of Becca."

It took asking four women on the street in Millersburg before someone knew where Andrea Dixon's quilt warehouse was.

"It's on South Mad Anthony Street near Killbuck Creek in an unmarked building," the woman said. "It's an old barn, all redone inside, I hear. You can't miss it," she assured her, pointing.

Leah had heard that promise before—you can't

miss it—and then had been promptly lost, so she hoped she could find the place. She drank some of the water she'd brought and forced herself to eat two cookies to keep up her strength. The pecan crisps tasted like sand, and she had trouble swallowing. Her stomach was tied in one big knot.

The facade of the place was aged and authentic: weathered boards, faded red paint. The building seemed worthy of blending in with other antique barns in the area until she saw its windows gleamed with metal frames and glass, and the new tin roof shone in the winter sun. Leah knew resurrecting old barns was expensive and risky, but it was obvious the Dixons were wealthy. And anyone who sank their fortune and future into genetics was willing to take big risks for possible big payoffs.

Leah tied her horse and buggy behind the building, just off what appeared to be the property line, near Killbuck Creek. The creek water was frozen, but she heard it rattling beneath the opaque surface, threatening a torrent of snowmelt.

Why, she wondered, looking at the warehouse, was such a huge space needed to house the quilts that Andrea must be selling? And why, when the advertising said not to come here, were at least ten cars parked in the lot surrounding the building, as well as two buggies? Surely not that many people worked inside warehousing antique quilts.

Leah'd had the strangest feeling about Andrea Dixon since she'd first glimpsed her shiny lips and sophisticated, shrewd ways. Just today Mark had said, *Andrea smooths things over.* If the woman was here,

Leah would ask for a tour; if she wasn't, besides looking around inside, she'd try to find out as much about
her and her husband as she could. This building could
be a perfect facade behind which to hide a stolen
baby—and maybe a teenage boy—for medical studies.

Still sitting in her buggy, Leah hastily removed the
two musty old quilts from their sack and looked them
over. She'd considered asking Andrea about the owner
of the Roscoe quilt, which she featured in local newspaper ads, but using these was better. Yet she'd been
so frenzied she'd hardly paid a bit of attention to them,
and she ought to at least know what she had, before
she pretended to seek advice from Andrea about them.

One had a patchwork design done in faded muslin
or calico squares, some with sprigged designs. Though
the muted colors were totally haphazard, the quilting
stitches were intricate, even and fine. The other quilt,
frayed on one edge, was in a blue-and-white drunk-
ard's-path pattern.

"In Sam's honor," she muttered and climbed down.
Cradling the quilts but longing for Becca in her arms,
she strode toward the big building.

A sign was posted there, but not one anybody could
read from the street: Antique Quilt Warehouse. It had
a phone number, not with a local area code, so perhaps
it was Andrea's number in Cleveland. Leah memorized
it in case she needed it later. Holding the quilts so
tightly they pressed against her throat, she knocked on
the wide wooden door.

No one came. She tried to lift the iron latch; the
door was locked. The two small downstairs windows

she could see from here were covered by dark blue curtains. The largest windows were on the second floor.

She was so tense she nearly burst into tears. Perhaps
there was another way in. Or was this a sign she was
to turn back? Had she been insane to suspect the
Dixons of something underhanded?

She heard a bolt slide inside. The latch lifted, and
the door opened. A young Amish woman peered out.
"Hello," she said, eyeing the quilts. "I'm sorry, but
Mrs. Dixon asks no quilts be brought here. If you leave
an address, she'll find you."

"Actually, I'm a friend of Mrs. Dixon, and I just
happened to be in town. If she's here, I'd like to see
her."

"Oh, she went out for lunch. A friend of hers?"

"Yes, from Maplecreek, Leah Kurtz, a friend of a
friend."

"Well, if she said you could come by, please step
in. You can wait with me until she comes back."

At least she'd made it this far, Leah thought as she
followed the young woman in. Her first impulse was
to throw the quilts down and dash past her to search
the entire building, but she didn't want to get this sister in trouble. Of course, Becca wouldn't be here if this
really was a quilt warehouse. She'd been clutching at
straws again. If only she could search Andrea's office
or ask this woman the right questions.

Leah's pulse pounded even harder. The room just
off the entry, in which they stood, looked like a med-
ical-storage room. It was bright with lights recessed
into a Styrofoam-type ceiling. On stainless-steel
shelves sat large glass canisters of scissors and swabs,

rolls of gauze and needles, among other things Leah could not name. She stepped closer to the door to skim the canisters for vials of drugs or blood-drawing equipment.

"Just supplies for quilt cleaning and repair," the young woman said. "I'm doing one now, if you want to watch."

"Oh, yes, that would be fine."

The woman led Leah down a short corridor into another room where an Amish woman was vacuuming a quilt through some sort of screen with a hose-and-brush attachment. "That one's too delicate to even soak or wash," the woman said loudly, over the roar of the sweeper. "This way."

The next room had a shallow tray of water about the size of a ping-pong table resting on an elevated pedestal. Like the area with the woman vacuuming, it was actually a cubicle, lit by sunlight though the high windows.

"But where are all the people who have cars parked out in the lot?" Leah asked, putting her quilts on an empty chair.

"Oh, that's just extra parking for people who rent apartments down the block."

Feeling deflated, Leah watched the woman test the fabric of the quilt with swabs dipped in some sort of solution, then submerge the entire piece in the shallow water. "The less water, the easier it will be to lift out the quilt and dry it," she told her. "An old quilt can shred with the weight of water. It's a good thing you didn't try to wash yours on your own."

Since the corridors and inner rooms had no ceilings,

Leah could see clear to the top of the barn, which at least meant nothing was hidden in rooms up above. Still, there could be a honeycomb of areas in here.

"Mrs. Dixon certainly has a going concern," Leah observed.

"She sure does. She's a very smart lady. I think she likes getting to meet our people too."

"It's kind of sad to see Amish or American heirlooms lose their history, though, if you know what I mean."

"*Ja,* I agree. Just art pieces to worldly folk, not a family memory anymore."

"I wouldn't put it that way, Clara," came a distinctive voice behind them. "It's just that a new family will now make new memories of owning such a beautiful, important piece. Hello, Leah. What a surprise to see you've dropped in," Andrea said with her trademark smile.

"I was in town on other business and thought I'd ask you about these quilts," she said, gesturing toward the chair where she'd placed them. "I live so far out of Maplecreek, you'd probably have trouble finding me."

She studied Andrea as she said that, but no flicker of nervousness or guilt crossed her face. She was attired in an elegant black pantsuit with a severely cut white blouse, perhaps in an attempt to blend in with her Amish workers, though her short silver hair and colorful cosmetics doomed that effort.

"I'm sure," Andrea said, moving to the quilts Leah had put down, "Mark could have given me directions to your house, and my husband said he was there the other day."

"That's right," Leah said, drawing out each word. "He was."

"My, from the looks of these," Andrea went on,

"I'd judge them late 1800s. Not your family heirlooms, I'd assume, since they look more American than Amish. They're fragile but excellent folk art."

"I told her you didn't really accept quilts here," Clara put in as she gently swished her quilt around in the shallow water.

"For friends, rules are made to be broken," Andrea declared, smiling as she picked up both quilts in her arms and started out. Leah hurried to keep up with her.

"Come on into my office and let's look at these. You didn't bring that little baby of yours along today, did you?"

"She's with a friend," Leah said, trying to watch Andrea's expression again, but the woman kept her face turned away. Leah fought the impulse to demand if she knew anything about her baby, but she was already treading on thin ice here.

"She's not with Mark, I assume, though he certainly seems to be enjoying his work with flesh-and-blood children, instead of just their DNA reference samples. I think Amish country is changing him, don't you?"

Flesh-and-blood children, Leah thought. What a strange way to put that. "Yes," she said, "and I think it's changing him for the better. He's slowing down a bit and enjoying life more."

"But Mark's a driven man with a cause, and I'd hate to see anything—or anyone—change that or slow him down. How's he doing with his research, do you think? Making strides already, and with your help, I take it."

That, Leah noted, had begun as a question but quickly turned to a statement of fact. Still stretching her strides to keep up, she followed Andrea through fabric valleys of quilts hanging on wooden dowels, past a vast array of screens where damp quilts were drying. Leah was amazed at the number of them. Perhaps that's why potential sellers weren't welcome here: Andrea didn't want them to see the land-office business she was doing, marketing other people's pasts. But surely that didn't mean she would have anything to do with taking people's children—their futures.

"I'm amazed that both of these quilts are so stiff and crinkly," Andrea said as she carefully unfolded one and then the other onto the cleared worktable in the spartan room she evidently used for an office. "Why, look. This one actually has Do Not Wash embroidered on its border—and the other quilt too! You'd seen that, of course."

"It is unusual," Leah said only.

Andrea was feeling along the edge of each quilt. "You know, I think there's something actually sewn in here, and not just for stiffening."

Leah bit her lower lip. What if Sam had inserted more money or notes in these quilts and stashed them in that trunk? Or what if Barbara had left some message within? She should have examined these more closely instead of just using them as bait, though if she thought she could get Becca back with them, nothing else mattered. But she was starting to think what had happened to Barbara—dosages and money changing hands—could have had something to do with Seth's and Becca's disappearances, maybe even with Sam's death. Like these squares all stitched together, there had to be some pattern here.

"Yes, I know about the stiffening," Leah lied, hastily folding up the quilt Andrea was not touching. "It's only paper the maker put in—I've cut a part of it open and checked."

"But how unusual. Let me get one of my girls to slit the edges. I promise you, they'll whipstitch it back so smoothly, you'll never know the paper's gone. Leah, this isn't some practical joke, is it? I mean, it is April Fool's Day."

Whether that was meant as a tease or an insult, Leah wasn't going to let her cut open or have these quilts. "No, really, I can do that myself, thanks. I've changed my mind about selling them." She began to fold up the second quilt, though Andrea still held its opposite border.

The truth was, Leah feared she *had* made a fool of herself and a mess of things. Had she really expected to find her baby here, spirited away to a warehouse for quilts? But she didn't trust this woman and didn't like her husband, who wanted to buy and sell human genes.

She finally managed to get the second quilt away from Andrea.

"Are you sure you're all right, Leah? Is there anything I can do?"

"It's just that I agonized over whether to bring these quilts in, and I've changed my mind, that's all," Leah explained as she took the quilts and walked out of Andrea's office. Leah had noted she had no filing cabinets, not even a real desk in there, nothing that seemed worth searching. She probably kept all that back in Cleveland.

"Won't you reconsider?" Andrea asked. "I can make it very worth your while."

"Seeing all the quilts you have here," Leah said, "makes me realize I don't want to part with these right now, but then, I suppose that's the reason you try to keep this place off limits."

Andrea stayed right behind her. "The truth is, I don't want amateurs getting in the way of serious, professional preservation," she replied, with an edge to her voice.

Good, Leah thought. She'd finally put a rough patch in the smooth surface of Andrea Dixon. The woman walked briskly to catch up with her down the deep valley of hanging quilts toward the door she came in. As Andrea reluctantly opened it and Leah stepped out into the cold winter sun, Andrea said, "Have a safe trip back to that darling little baby of yours!"

Leah spun to face her. Although she wanted to burst into tears, she said, her voice deadly calm, "Andrea, I'm sorry if I seem on edge, but I've recently discovered Becca is distantly related to families with NAA children. I haven't even discussed it with Mark yet and suspect he hasn't picked up on it from the family trees I'm doing. Would you do me a huge favor and ask your husband if that means I should have her tested, perhaps at his new clinic in Cleveland? I don't think Mark's far enough along to test her, but I'm sure he'd be willing to take me there."

"I—I'm sorry to hear that," she said, crossing her arms over her chest as if against the cold. "I believe she's a carrier for her mother's disease, Mark said. MR isn't working with NAA at all, but if there's anything Brad says he can do, I'll let you know. And if Mark's too busy—Brad's invited him to tour the clinic more than once and he's put him off—I'd be happy to drive you to Cleveland."

Leah's mind raced. Mark had turned down visiting the clinic she was dying to see? "That's very kind of you. I'll call you at that number you have on the sign here."

"It's my cell phone. Yes, that will be fine. And, Leah, if you decide you want to sell those quilts to help build up a medical fund for Becca, I'll be very generous, I promise."

The last thing in the world Leah planned to do was trust Andrea Dixon's promises, but at least she knew a way to get into the MR clinic, even if they were prepared for her. She might be bold enough to talk her way into a quilt warehouse in Millersburg, Ohio, or sneak onto Jesse Cutler's rural property, but she had no knowledge of huge Cleveland nor of a medical clinic that would likely be very security conscious. If Andrea thought Leah would go to Cleveland with her, though, without Mark along or at least following close behind her, the woman was more naive than she probably thought Leah was.

"I'll certainly ask my husband about a clinic visit for you," Andrea said. "Brad thrives on challenges," she added so deliberately and with narrowed eyes that Leah was suddenly certain the woman knew something.

Leah longed to pursue that last comment, but Andrea quickly closed the door in her face.

14

Mark heard someone pounding on the clinic door. It wasn't just a knock but a panicky demand. He jumped up from staring at the columns of SNP correlations on his computer screen and ran to see who it was. He only hoped it wasn't Leah who was that distraught, or someone who'd come to tell him she was in trouble.

He didn't recognize the red-bearded Amish man who stood there with his buggy pulled up behind him. Mark yanked the door open.

"Can I help you?"

"*Ja*, Doctor. We not met, but Teacher Leah said you could help my boy, Jonas Esh. He's took bad."

"I'll get my things. Do you want to go in my car?"

"*Ja*, sure. Our farm's not far out, but that little thing'll go faster than my horse."

Mark grabbed his jacket, cell phone and medical bag. By the time he ran out to the driveway, Mr. Esh had tied his horse to the hitching post and was folding his legs into the passenger seat of the low-slung sports car. Mark jumped in and backed down the driveway to the street.

"What happened, Mr. Esh?" he asked as he headed out of town.

"Funny thing. We got a big dairy farm, you know. Somehow the herd got out and went all up and down the road. Took both of us and our two oldest boys to get most of them back in. When the wife went upstairs to check on Jonas, his eyes were open but he was kind of dazed. Guess you know, kids like him can get strokes, so she was real scared, *ja,* she was. Teacher Leah told us you could help, so we are praying you can check him, help us decide what to do. Turn right up here on this road. And be careful, in case there's still a coupla cows loose."

Inside, they ran up the stairs of the Eshes' big, old farmhouse. Esther Esh stood by a bedroom door.

"How is he?" her husband asked.

"More alert, but so pale," she said, nodding to Mark as she gestured him into the room.

Mark was grateful to be here, but he regretted it was under these dire circumstances. To perhaps lose Jonas before he even had a chance to work with him, or the boy had a chance to grow up...

"Jonas," his father said as they reached the bed in the dim room, "this here's the doctor Teacher Leah told us about, Dr. Morelli."

"Hi, Jonas," Mark said, putting his bag on a bed-side chair and bending close to the boy. "Could we open the curtains to get some light in here?" he asked.

Even when his mother opened the curtains and light spilled in, the boy's pupils remained dilated. Another child shrouded in a fragile body, another victim Mark desperately wanted to help and save.

"Jonas, how old are you?"

"'leven."

His voice was a mere whisper, his word slurred. Maybe it *was* a stroke he had suffered. His face looked flaccid, but one side of it was not drooped more than the other, as Mark had expected.

"How many fingers am I holding up?" Mark asked.

"*Eine*—one."

"Right. Can you move your hands and feet? Let's try the left foot first."

Slowly, Jonas complied, moving each limb. Not a stroke, Mark decided, however sluggish the boy appeared. He pressed his stethoscope to the bony chest. Heartbeat slightly slow but not erratic. Mark uncovered the boy's right arm to take his pulse too, and saw a quarter-size spot of blood on the sheet under his elbow. Mark turned the arm over and saw the dull reddish mark of a recently applied rubber cincture. And in the pale blue ribbon of a varicose vein was a clear crimson puncture mark with some dried blood around it.

Mark's pulse accelerated faster than his patient's. He checked Jonas's other arm for an injection site and found it in a similar position. Perhaps just one intruder had been here, but one who could have both administered a drug and drawn blood.

"Do you have to give any of Jonas's medications intravenously?" Mark asked the hovering parents. When they hesitated, he reworded his question. "Does he need shots in his arms?"

"Oh, *nein*," his mother said, twisting her apron in her hands. "You mean, like insulin? My father had diabetes, but that's one thing Jonas hasn't had yet."

Someone could have let the cows out deliberately, Mark theorized, then when the family went after them, sneaked into the house where this boy was weak or sleeping. He didn't want to alarm the Eshes by questioning Jonas about what he recalled, but *he* was sure as hell alarmed. He'd bet this kid was drugged too, like Miriam and Susie Kline had been when their buggy supposedly pitched them out on the road.

Damn, he had to get to Leah and tell her to be even more careful with what she had once called vampires. They were dealing with someone insidious who was after NAA blood—and, in another way, maybe after his and Leah's too.

Leah felt light-headed and weak as she buggied back into Maplecreek. Her neck was sore from continually craning it to be certain no car followed her for long. Nell, too, seemed nervous, as if she sensed someone was watching them. Leah could imagine Andrea or Jesse Cutler driving up close behind to bump her off the road—or, the way things were going lately, bump her off permanently. But vehicles passed with a whoosh of air and speed. Some passengers looked back at her, but she prayed it was just the usual rubbernecking to get a glimpse of whoever was in an Amish buggy. At least she saw no brown vans on the road.

It was nearly five o'clock when she arrived in Maplecreek, because she'd stopped at a quilt shop in Millersburg, bought a pair of scissors and slit the edges of both quilts. Sitting in her buggy in the alley behind the quilt store, she'd pulled out nearly fifty pages of stiff vellum paper covered with old-fashioned writing. The script was flowery and the brown ink so pale the words were hard to decipher.

But she could tell a few things about her discovery. The pages were too old to have anything to do with Sam or Barbara. And the last page, numbered forty-seven and labeled The End, was signed by Varina Roscoe.

Leah's eyes had nearly crossed trying to read the diary, which went on and on about how much Varina loved Dr. Adam Barlow, whom her father had taken in to learn his practice. Varina, *overwhelmed by his ardor, his covert pledges and promises,* had written that she had *committed her body and her life to him.* Too late, she'd *discovered to her abject horror and eternal shame* that he was married and had a wife and child in another town.

There was much more to read, but Leah's already shattered heart ached for the woman. She prayed something worse wasn't yet to come in the tragic words, for Varina had written, *I have made the difficult determination to expose the doctor's perfidy, even at the cost of my own ruination and demise in this community that has honored my work among them during the vile disease.*

Leah feared, if poor Varina had gone to Dr. Barlow and threatened to ruin him, he had a motive to kill her. Or, if he had simply fled, could Varina have been distraught enough to kill herself?

Mark rang Leah's doorbell and knocked on both her back and front doors before he realized he should look in the shed to see if her horse and buggy were there. They weren't, so she must still be running errands. But it was getting dark. Maybe he'd meet her on the road to town, but he decided to leave a note for her, shoved under the kitchen door:

*Jonas Esh had blood covertly taken and may
have been drugged. I'll be back later. Don't open
the door to anyone but me. We need to do a lot
more digging.*

Leah had no intention of heading out to Jesse Cutler's place until it was quite dark and she had a clearer
head, so she hitched Nell behind the Maplecreek K & S
Restaurant and went in the back door. It was an Amish
family-run establishment, doing big business now that
the restaurant across the street, the Dutch Table, was
up for sale. All the local Plain People knew the real
name of the K & S was *Katsche und Schmatze,* "talk
and eat," but most tourists couldn't pronounce that.

Leah wasn't a bit hungry, but she knew she had to
eat. She used the rest room, then sat in the back booth
and ordered chicken and noodles and coffee, longing
to have Becca cuddled in her lap or in her carrier on
the seat beside her.

Leah knew the waitress and most of the kitchen
staff, for she'd taught them in school, but she answered
their questions by rote when they popped out of the
kitchen to see her. Hoping some strength would kick
in, she ate and drank mechanically. After she left here,
she desperately wanted to see Mark just down Main
Street, to have him hold her and tell her she'd find
Becca, that he would help, but she dared not. Until she
needed him to get to the MR clinic in Cleveland or
until she got a lead, she had to stick to the kidnapper's
threatening ultimatum, *TELL NO ONE.*

"Hey, Leah, I thought it was you!" a jaunty male
voice said. It was Mark's friend, Clark Quinn, with

earphones around his neck. Evidently, he'd been listening to some music on a small radio that protruded from his jacket pocket, but all she could hear was muted static. He'd probably just come in or was sitting at the counter and spotted her.

"Oh, Clark, hello."

"Mark's not joining you, by any chance?"

"No. Just going to eat and run."

"Mind if I sit down for a minute? I thought maybe you could tell me where he is."

"You can't find him?"

"He's not at the clinic, and he left his cell phone at an Amish farmhouse where he was treating a child. I called him, but someone named Esther Esh said he forgot it, and she had no idea where he was."

"Did she say what happened? Is her son all right?"

"She said Mark helped her boy. Is he one of the local NAA kids?"

She nodded. Evidently thinking that was permission to sit down, he slid into the other side of her booth. At least he hadn't meant that Mark had truly disappeared.

"You've done a great job getting Mark in on the ground floor here," Clark said, folding his hands and leaning slightly forward. "And you've helped him to be happy."

"Wasn't he happy before? I know you're very protective of him, especially with the Dixons. Do you think they wish him success here or not?"

"That's the multibillion-dollar question. I think they want him in their hip pocket, so to speak, on anything he learns about NAA or an aging gene. If they thought he'd go elsewhere with his finds, they'd consider him not friend but foe."

"Do you think there's any chance they are actually doing their own similar research in case he doesn't share what he finds with them?"

He looked alarmed. "Frankly," he whispered, leaning even closer, "I don't put much past Brad Dixon. Genetics and medicine mix to make a cutthroat environment."

"And he sounded like he's totally against letting you patent what Mark learns."

"You've got that right, but Dixon can't stop me," he vowed, and knocked once on the wooden tabletop. "Listen, Leah, let me just level with you. I've been trying to get it through Mark's thick skull that he needs to be wary of them. For all I know, that BLAST software Dixon gave him has a cookie, worm or virus in it."

"Those things…in a machine?"

"A cookie means someone besides Mark could find out what Web sites he's visited, possibly not only track him but have access to his work. A worm is something embedded in his machine that could destroy his work. And, for all I know, they could have infected his work with a virus that would funnel all he's doing to the supercomputers they use at MR."

Leah realized she had a lot to learn about the machines on which Mark spent so much time. She must have still looked confused, because Clark added, "In other words, Mark might have a spy device in his machines. But once he's patented anything he finds— *anything*—it's his to bargain with to the top bidder, the pharm firm that will support him and his success, be that MR or some other. Leah, anything you can do to urge Mark to look out for his own interests, as well as those of his patients, will be invaluable for him.

"Excuse me for bringing this up, but I understand you lost your best friend, the mother of your baby."

She was surprised at the sudden shift in subject and blinked back tears. Becca, she had to find Becca, not sit here talking about machines or anything else, even Mark, even saving those NAA kids. She managed a nod as she groped in her purse on the bench to pay her bill.

"Like I said before," Clark said, dropping his voice again, "Mark and I have been best friends for years. I'd do anything to help him. Since you had a friend you lost and took her child on, you'll understand how I feel about helping him. Deeply dedicated."

Leah's teary gaze snagged his, so intense, much like Mark's.

"Yes," she said. "I do understand. Now, if you'll excuse me. And if you see Mark—"

"I hope to. You sure you don't want to come along?"

"No, I have to see a friend. But I'd appreciate it if you don't tell Mark, because he worries about me being out on the roads. I'm fine, though."

"Sure. As long as you don't tell him I asked you to help me keep an eye on him. Deal? One best friend to another?"

"Deal," she said and slid out of the booth before he could see tears in her eyes again. She prayed that Clark would never feel he'd let his best friend down, the way she had Barbara.

Wishing she didn't have to hang a lantern in the buggy and have the red, reflective, slow-moving-vehicle sign on the back like a bull's-eye, Leah headed out Holtz Road toward Jesse Cutler's. As the roads got more rural, other vehicles became scarcer. Trying to steady herself, she breathed in the crisp, cold air outside town. Unless a car coasting behind her had its headlights off, she could tell better than in daylight that no one was following her out here.

She'd like to think that the clear, black sky with its pinpoints of stars heralded spring, but she knew that early-April snowstorms were, if not common, at least possible. Yet she didn't care if she saw another spring if she didn't get Becca back. She'd even bargain with that despicable Jesse Cutler for her baby's return.

Gutting out her side lantern, Leah turned Nell down a narrow farmer's lane just one small field away from Jesse's spread. She drove way back in, past the best view of his house, beyond a woodlot that might be Jesse's or the farmer's. Jesse didn't farm, but he owned about fifteen acres, land the Amish would love to buy and plant.

A line of trees edged the back of Jesse's land; neatly cut lawns surrounded the house. It was a white-pillared colonial he'd built on a site where he'd torn down an old farmhouse. Everyone knew Jesse had made money more than once by purchasing and reselling rural property after razing run-down buildings, but, unlike Miles Mason, Jesse had never shown an outright interest in her land—only, unfortunately, in her.

Jesse had kept the small barn on his land. She figured that somewhere between the house and barn she'd find that old brown van David Groder had mentioned, the one that could have stopped to "help" Susie and Miriam Kline after their buggy "accident."

You might know, she thought as she tied Nell to a tree in an old apple copse beyond the woodlot and the nearly full moon rolled over the horizon like a ripe peach. The moonlight made it easier for her to see, although she would still take the flashlight she kept in the buggy, but it would also make it easier for someone to spot her. She blessed her dark gown, bonnet and cloak. Years ago, when her people were hunted for religious reasons in Europe, had their attire helped some to escape hunt hounds, prison and a martyr's death? What if Jesse kept guard dogs? The artwork in his clinic suggested he loved dogs of all kinds.

As she headed through the woodlot toward his house, she noted maples with sap buckets that looked like Miles Mason's. All around her, she could hear their *drip, drip, drip.* The sound came in rhythm with her footsteps, thudding in her ears as she left the shelter of the woodlot.

She stood trembling, trying to decide whether to risk going closer to the house. Unlike in facing Andrea, her instincts told her not to beard Jesse in his own den. But for Becca, she'd risk it.

Holding her skirts up to move more easily, she crept closer to the house. It was well lighted on the ground floor; no closed curtains shrouded the windows. Did that mean he had nothing to hide? She wanted to be sure he was inside, then look for any hints he had a small visitor he or someone else had kidnapped. Her plan sounded desperate, but she was that.

She could see the silhouette of the van out back near the barn. Though she'd fully intended to check it out first, she felt drawn to look in the house. Bare-limbed fruit trees lined the driveway; perhaps she could hide behind them, or climb them to look inside. If she did see a sign that Becca was there, she'd go to Mark or even Sheriff Martin for help, although she'd have to keep herself from breaking through the glass with her bare fists.

She darted behind a tree but needed more height to see in below the level of his ceilings. Hiking up her skirts, she climbed several feet into the tree. At least there were a lot of gnarled branches to hold on to.

Her view from here was of a wide brick fireplace with large paintings both above and beside it of sleeping dogs, similar to the pictures he had in his office waiting room. Oh, no, he might indeed have dogs. If so, she hoped he kept them inside at night when it was cold. But she'd glimpsed no doghouses out back, and no fence for a dog run.

She nearly fell out of the tree when Jesse walked by the window, but he didn't look out, and with his lights on inside, probably wouldn't see her anyway. He appeared to be talking on the phone. Soon he paced by again, from the other direction, this time appearing to glance out before moving on. Leah jumped from the tree and ran toward the back of the lot. As she glanced toward the house again, she saw what must be the dining room, where there were more large paintings, maybe photographs, of sleeping dogs, all on some sort of background that looked like blue, wrinkled velvet.

She longed to peer in all his windows, but she was afraid to now. Blessedly, the van was parked at the corner of the small barn, so it probably couldn't be seen directly from the house. But to be sure, she went around to its far side.

Still with her flashlight off, she realized it sat to one side of a tall, corral-type gate that led to a fenced-in area. A sign hung high from the gate, and she'd probably have to use her flashlight to read it.

As she neared the van, along the corral fence, a voice came from somewhere nearby. Leah let out a little cry, dropped her flashlight and hit the ground, facedown.

"Welcome to Pet Haven, the portal to Pet Heaven," the gentle, almost crooning voice said. Jesse's? "If you wish to visit your departed best friend, you are most welcome. If you need information about cremation or burial, a funeral service or an eternal resting place, please contact Dr. Jesse Cutler in Maplecreek at the phone number or Web site listed on the information posted on the gate."

It took Leah a minute to realize that Jesse's voice was actually fake, recorded. The brown van, which she could see from here, had stuffed animals peering from its windows. And it appeared to guard a pet cemetery!

Once she got hold of herself, she stood and trained her flashlight into the van. The side window acted like a mirror, so that her own face appeared superimposed over the vehicle's interior.

The scene within reminded her of one of the three movies she'd ever seen, with Barbara, Joseph and Sam, during their *rumspringa*. It was about an alien from outer space called *E.T.* Some darling English kids had hidden him in a pile of stuffed animals in a closet, and he'd blended right in, so their suspicious mother couldn't spot him. Were these stuffed animals toys or real, mounted the way hunters sometimes did to flaunt their dead prey?

The van not only looked well kept, but she saw that its gas tank read three-fourths full. The license, VAN-GO 2, had a current sticker on it, so it was still valid. Even better than all that, tire tracks through the remnants of snow and refrozen mud suggested it had been driven recently.

All that was evidence against Jesse, at least when it came to the drugging of Susie and Miriam. And if he'd done that, he could have also been the one who'd drugged the baby left in Becca's crib. If so, he might have Becca, or know who did.

But it was all still too patched together, too circumstantial.

She needed more on him before she risked confronting him or running to the sheriff or Mark. Though she'd proved part of what she'd hoped to find, she felt dread about the proximity of the pet cemetery, which lay beyond the fence and gate. Could there be something else hidden out there, some other clue to Jesse's strange behavior?

She wondered if pets were actually buried, just like their English owners, with caskets and ceremonies. Perhaps Jesse knew that the Amish and the practical farmers of the area would think spending money on pet burials was frivolous and fancy. Had David Groder or Seth known about this cemetery, or was this some sort of secret? If so, what others did Jesse Cutler harbor? As Mark had said, the man bore watching.

Glancing nervously back at the house and careful to

keep her slender beam of light blocked by her body, Leah stepped a short distance inside the fence. The burial markers were flat, so they couldn't be seen from the road. Several graves had plastic animal toys, a few had fake or even real flowers, frozen, dying. She shuddered as she recalled the ones draped around Varina's death angel.

Etchings and some glossy pet photos on the metal or marble tombstones gleamed in her light. Had those large paintings in Jesse's house been of dead animals?

She scanned a few epitaphs. *He would lick the hand that had no food to offer,* read the words beside a cocker spaniel's photo. *A pet is not forever, but its loving memory is,* was etched in another stone. *Goodbye, Sparky, running through green fields, forever chasing Frisbees,* said another.

She stared agape at the one that said simply, *Goodbye, Baby.*

Leah sucked in a sob. *Becca.* She had to find Becca.

As she swiped tears from her face, she heard the buzz of men's distant voices, not the soothing tones of the recording she'd somehow tripped. In a crouch, she ran for the gate to get out. Just then, she realized the voices were emanating from the woodlot she'd come through. Mason and his men, checking their sap buckets? She'd tied Nell not far from there. But worse, she saw Jesse come out of his lighted back door and start walking toward her.

He had a large light with him and swung its broad beam back and forth across the snow-etched ground in front of him. If the cemetery voice had made noise that summoned him, Jesse might see or hear the sap gatherers and think it was just them.

It was too late for her to try to make it to the barn or even dart behind it. Hiding behind the van was her only choice. She prayed she could keep the vehicle between her and Jesse until he passed by.

But as she darted past the fence, she triggered the recording again. "If you wish to visit your departed best friend, you are most welcome..."

Jesse started to run. She could see his light bouncing and hear keys jingling as he jogged. If only she could get inside the van, hide among those animals the way the alien had in the movie. She tried the closest door. Locked.

No way could she afford to face Jesse Cutler on his land, and she didn't like the way Miles Mason kept turning up either. She hit the ground and scooted on her back under the van.

"Hey, Mason, that you in my woods?" Jesse called, his voice shrill as he stopped running. Leah held her breath; she could hear him panting. "You haven't been over here, have you?"

"You kidding me!" Mason's voice boomed back. "That place gives me the creeps. I'm sticking to these trees."

"Then it was someone else—twice," Jesse muttered as his booted feet stopped inches from Leah's head.

15

Above her, Leah heard Jesse unlock the door of his van, then open it. Evidently without relocking it, he slammed it shut. His boots crunched gravel as he went toward the cemetery, setting off the recorded voice again: "Welcome to Pet Haven, the portal to Pet Heaven…"

Leah tried to edge farther under the van, away from Jesse. If she could scoot out the far side, could she run toward his house and around it to the road? Or would her dark form be silhouetted by the lighted windows?

"…If you wish to visit your departed best friend, you are most welcome…"

No, Jesse was coming back. With the flat tombstones and his light, he must have quickly realized no one was hiding in the small, fenced area. Her heartbeat, which already seemed to vibrate the mud- and slush-covered undercarriage of the van, accelerated. But Jesse walked away toward his small barn and looked out behind it.

She could see him clearly. In case he did turn the bright beam her way, she shifted sideways and pulled her knees up, trying to hide in the shadow of the back right-side wheel.

She heard him curse.

"Mason," he shouted so loud Leah jerked and hit her head on the tire, "you got Amish kids with you? David Groder over there?"

"Not tonight," Mason shouted back. "What's your beef?"

"They like to look around in here, I know they do. Just thought they might have come over."

"I've got a buddy with me, but no Amish kids tonight. What's it to you?"

"I just don't like anyone sneaking onto my land," he shouted. "The trees, I gave permission for, but that's it. I put up with people all day and like my time alone. Someone broke the eye beam on this fence, according to my meter in the house, and I heard the voice when I came out again. It sure as heck's not the ghosts of these dead dogs!"

"Well, maybe the meter just malfunctioned, you think of that?"

Jesse swore again, under his breath, then came closer to the van, his soles spitting gravel through the thin layer of snow. He opened the van door again, driver's side.

The chassis dipped as he got in. Leah prayed he was just cold and wanted to get out of the wind. Maybe he had decided to sit inside to see if the recording went off again.

But he started the engine. It roared to life above her, around her. He was going to drive!

When Mark picked up his cell phone at the Eshes' farm, he asked to check on Jonas again. The boy looked much better. As Esther Esh went out to get them some cake and ice cream she insisted on, Mark sat carefully on the edge of the bed.

"Do you remember anything about your family going out to chase the cows?" he asked Jonas.

"I think *Maam* called up to me they were out. I felt so bad."

"You were feeling sick then?"

"No, bad, because I wasn't strong enough to help. I used to herd the cows into the barn and help with the milking, 'fore I got too sick."

"And while the family was out of the house, did you sleep?"

"I didn't want to. The cows never got out before like that, on the road. But I think I fell asleep or something, can't remember. The next thing I remember was you were here—*ja,* that's it. *Maam* brought you in and said the doctor was here."

Mark gritted his teeth. If he had the capability of doing a blood test for drugs, he'd bet this farm that the puncture mark on the boy's left arm was from the administration of an amnesiac drug. Damn! Did someone actually think he wouldn't pick up on this? Either someone was racing him for the NAA findings, or was sending him a subtle but threatening message. But was it to hurry up with NAA research because someone was breathing down his neck? Was he to lay off, or what?

Whatever was going on, he had to find Leah and figure it out. Someone was willing to play with people's lives, and it scared him to death.

Leah wondered if Jesse had seen her and wanted to flush her out—or crush her.

Terrified, she half scooted, half rolled out from

under the van as he put it into gear; he drove away. Sweating in the snow, she lay on her face, then lifted her head to watch it go. She was shaking so hard she could not get to her feet to flee.

As he drove out of his driveway, she rolled clear over to the corner of the barn, leaned against it, then stood shakily. Jesse could look back or come back; Mason might see her from the woodlot. She would have to circle clear around to get Nell and the buggy and find another way to leave the area.

Bending over, she headed for the back of Jesse's land. When she approached where she'd left the buggy, she saw he had pulled onto the road where Mason's truck was parked. She peered through bramble bushes, listening to the two of them arguing, but could not now catch their words. At least, she thought, as she reached Nell and led the poor horse and bumping buggy down the frozen ruts of a farmer's plowed field, she had learned several things tonight.

Jesse Cutler was even stranger than she'd thought. More importantly, his brown van could well have been the one she saw near the Klines' tilted buggy. And if Jesse had anything to do with drugging, kidnapping or killing people, he was probably not working with or for Miles Mason.

Leah felt battered and utterly defeated when she put Nell in the shed that night. She couldn't bear to face her house without Becca. If the place had haunted her after Barbara's tragic loss, it would be so much worse now. Exhausted, she staggered toward her back door, fumbling with her key. But she heard a sound behind her, from the direction of the angel.

She turned to look, peering into the depths of darkness. Through the spikes of iron fence, moonlight etched the angel's silhouette. But the statue moved. It spoke.

"Leah, where in heaven's name have you been?"

Mark! It was Mark. She saw he was between her and the angel, walking up the driveway on the outside of the iron fence. Where had he come from, so suddenly and silently?

She burst into tears, ran to him, and hurled herself into his arms. "I wanted to tell you," she sobbed, "but I was so afraid to. I need your help, but if I tell you, they might hurt her…"

"Who? Where's Becca?"

"I don't know. I have to find her, but I don't know, don't know…"

He swept her off her feet, bounced her once in his arms to get a better hold, and started toward the house. "Leah, calm down. Where's Becca?"

"Someone took her. I'm trying to tell you I don't know where she is!" But she did know one thing. She needed Mark's help desperately.

Leah told Mark everything in bits and pieces as he washed her face and hands as if she were a child, then fixed her toast with honey and herbal tea in her kitchen.

"When I saw that other baby, I went just wild," she said as she explained everything she'd done in the house, then about taking the child to Louise. She saw he got more upset as she related her trip to Andrea's quilt warehouse; he looked livid when she told him what happened at Jesse Cutler's.

"You don't listen, do you?" he said, slamming a cupboard closed. "I could have helped you with all this."

"No, you couldn't. I shouldn't have told you now. But—where's your car?" she demanded, suddenly realizing she hadn't seen it.

"I left it down by the ravine behind some bushes. I decided to wait for you to get back, all night if I had to. And it's a good thing I hid it, because I'm staying all night. And I don't care if that melted message in the snow said *DON'T TELL,* we're in this together."

She nodded. Hearing that helped some. "There's something else," she said. He looked wary, wide-eyed again, as he had when she'd told him Becca had been abducted. "That Kline-family information you brought me from Miriam," she went on, her voice trembling again. "The Klines are distantly related to the Lantzes."

"Barbara Lantz Yoder, your best friend, Becca's birth mother?"

She nodded again.

"So you panicked that Becca may have NAA."

"Of course I did! She could, right?"

"Yes, but the odds are slim. How slim, I'm not sure, because I don't have the percentages down yet, any more than I've found that damn gene. I know where it isn't, in a lot of DNA, but not where it is, where it's hiding…" His voice trailed off and he sat back down, putting his head in his hands and his elbows on the table as if to prop himself up.

"Mark, when Andrea showed me out of her warehouse, I told her that about Becca, the possible NAA tie," she admitted. "I asked her if, since you weren't far enough along yet, I could bring the baby to their MR clinic—if Brad could do anything. I was just desperate to get into the place."

"And she said?" he asked, looking up and narrowing his dark eyes.

"You know it could be them, don't you? I'm sorry, but it could be."

"Yeah, I know. What did she say?"

"She said she'd check with her husband, that she'd drive me there if you were too busy."

His fist hit the table, bouncing the spoon off her plate. He explained to her what had happened with Jonas Esh and let her read the note, still on her floor by the door. "It's way beyond coincidence or misinterpretation," he said, shaking his head. "I was furious at first that you acted so quickly, almost confronting Andrea and spying on Cutler, but I think that's exactly what we have to do." When he went on about wanting to help and protect the NAA kids, she remembered she'd seen Clark tonight.

"I forgot to tell you I saw Clark at the K & S Restaurant," she told him, sipping her now-cold mint tea. "He wanted to talk to you, help you to protect any of your findings. But did he find you?"

"I missed him, probably when I went back to the Eshes'. He left me a note. He's got a client in Columbus, and he's been able to pass through here a lot lately, so he'll be around. I tried to call him when I got my cell phone back, but he didn't answer.

I know he's been worried about me," he said, raking his fingers though his hair. He'd stopped the pacing he'd done earlier, but now he jumped up and poured her more hot water on a new tea bag, gave her the cup back, then slumped down across from her again.

"Best friends can sense things sometimes," she said, "just like twins do." Leah arched her sore back. She wasn't sure she was making sense anymore, so floaty, dizzy. "Mark, you didn't put something in this tea, did you?" she asked as she stared down into its darkening depths.

"No, but I've got sleeping pills in my bag in the car I can get. I'd never give you something unless I asked. Besides, with the shape you're in, a bed should be all you need to sleep. Tomorrow we're going to ask Louise if she'll keep that baby longer and go calling on the Dixons and their clinic. We'll tell them we came to look around before bringing Becca in."

She reached across the corner of the kitchen table and grabbed his wrist. "But if they have her, they'll know we're bluffing."

"They *can't* have her. I can't believe it of them. Brad's invited me to see the clinic more than once. He told me to let him know when I was coming, but let's not. Let's just show up on his doorstep, and see what we can shake loose there. Now, you get to bed, and I'll stand guard."

She loosed her grip and rose slowly, then started toward the living room. He followed, evidently thinking she would obey, but she protested, "I couldn't sleep, and not upstairs in a bed. I've been sleeping on the sofa in here almost since I moved in. I'm going to buy a new bed, but I just couldn't sleep in Barbara and Sam's bed, and it was too cold upstairs before you put in the insulation."

"Do you really think you could go to bed in the room with Becca's empty crib?" he challenged when she stopped at it and lifted its little quilt in her hands. "With windows someone could look in?"

"I close the drapes, of course."

"Let's not argue. I'm not leaving you alone tonight, and you have got to sleep."

"I'd have nightmares. Mark," she said, cuddling the quilt, "I don't want a sleeping pill. I want something to keep me awake. If you don't have anything, I'll switch to coffee and—"

He turned off the single lantern in the room, pulled her over to the sofa and collapsed on it with her in his lap. She sat stiffly at first, then wilted against his strength with her head on his shoulder, clasping his arms he wrapped around her. Becca's quilt was pressed between them; the top of Leah's head tucked perfectly under his chin.

"Leah, we'll figure all this out and find Becca, hopefully Seth too. But if I'm going to help you, you have to get some sleep tonight, and I do too. You said you weren't thinking straight today, and I'm not taking you anywhere tomorrow if you're in worse shape than this, because you could jeopardize our efforts."

She turned her face up to his. "Then do you admit the Dixons could be checking up on your work—testing what will eventually be your conclusions and discoveries."

"I'm scared to death that's it. Maybe it's not them doing the hands-on stuff, but someone on their staff, maybe even someone who was a former colleague of mine. But still, kidnapping—no. I keep telling myself the Dixons and the MR staff are the obvious choice, but they are very smart people. And very smart people don't make themselves the obvious choice for something like that."

"But they may think they've warned us off. You didn't react to that sign on your clinic door, so they took Becca and threatened me with that *DON'T TELL* message. Hopefully, it only meant I'm not to go to the authorities. I don't trust Sheriff Martin anyway."

"Though money is not why I'm in the hunt for NAA genes or cures, I do know there can be billions of dollars potentially involved. Clark's repeatedly warned me about that, even if Brad and Andrea have barely alluded to it. And where there is that much money, as well as prestige and power, on the line, people can do insane things.

"But enough agonizing until tomorrow," he added, shifting her in his arms so that their faces were inches apart. "I'll sit up a while, keep an eye on things, then get some shut-eye too."

"I was thinking, maybe we could hide a camera in the attic and train it on the angel," she said as he hugged her hard, then sat her on the sofa as he got to his feet. "Then the next time someone tries to leave something there, or make it seem as if the angel's come alive, we'll have them on red film."

"Infared? It may come to that. But, no more talking, Teacher Leah, or you're going to be given a detention. You insist on this sofa, fine, but it's lights out."

Feeling boneless from fatigue and grief, Leah obeyed. With Mark, she had hope. Still, as she stretched out and he covered her with a quilt from the back of the sofa, she thought about filming the angel, and she recalled how Brad Dixon had already captured it on film.

Seth never quite knew what time it was in here, not even if it was day or night. His sleep cycle was all screwed around. He figured he slept many more hours than he used to. But he had the strangest feeling it was night now and not only because they'd dimmed the lights in his room.

He had a theory he'd been studying that, when it was dark outside, the air vent in the wall that was next to the floor by his bed brought in colder air. It was a subtle shift, but he could tell the difference. Could that be possible, or was he starting to really crack up?

But the thing was, what did that mean? It didn't make sense that they'd turn the temperature of the air down in the colder nights. Maybe the air was linked to the outside. Then it would be naturally colder during the night than the day.

If he could unscrew the vent from the wall, would it lead to the outside? He'd seen those large, mushroom-shaped, rotating things on the roofs of buildings that pulled in or pushed out air.

The air vent in his wall was nearly two feet wide and one foot high. Would it connect to a shaft through which he could crawl or climb to a roof or outlet? Since his room was shaped like a triangle, did it mean the vent or shaft would be weird-shaped too?

He got out of bed and knelt by the vent, running his hands along it. When the lights were brighter, he could study it better. Three—no, four—screws, imbedded flush into the metal.

But what could he use for a screwdriver? If it took him a long time to loosen the screws, he had the time. At least he hoped he did, before they tried what he'd heard was some kind of gene transplant they had planned for him.

Leah woke and started to stretch languorously before reality crashed in. Becca was gone. They had to find her. They were going to Cleveland.

Though the curtains were all closed, daylight seeped through to dust the room in grays and golds. She startled to see that Mark slept sitting on the floor, his dark head on the sofa between her stomach and her knees, where she'd curled on her side. She could see each separate mussed, crisp strand of his hair from here, and longed to touch him and hold to him.

"Mark."

"Mmmph." He jolted instantly awake. "Mmm, daylight. We've got to get going. I'll fix us coffee and something to eat."

"I'll do it, then run upstairs to wash up and change. Did you see anything outside last night?"

"I thought the moonlight would be enough, but clouds came in. I'm not used to no outside lights to turn on. I nodded off staring out that window—" he gestured toward the window by Becca's crib "—and finally gave in. I'll go upstairs to use the bathroom first, then." As he started away, he added, "You're very quiet when you sleep."

"That's only because I didn't have a nightmare for once. I think sleeping with you helped, so—"

She realized what she'd said and cursed herself for being no match with him in the ways of the world. Of all the crazy things she'd done lately, falling for him was surely the most insane.

"So, let's hold that thought until we have Becca back," he said as he headed upstairs. But she had seen his swift smile.

Leah had never ridden in Mark's little red car before. It sped around other vehicles on I–77 as they headed north toward Cleveland. She seemed so close to the ground, compared to sitting up in a nine-mile-per-hour buggy. She had no idea how fast he was driving and was afraid to ask. The road roared at them, a huge gray ribbon of pavement with broken, white dividing lines that mesmerized her, if she stared at them. It was disconcerting not to have Nell's bouncing, swaying rump ahead instead of the back of others' cars and the fast-flying road.

Louise had been delighted to keep "Becca" for another day. She'd remarked again that the child seemed to be growing by leaps and bounds, but apparently had no idea it was another baby. Leah didn't feel too guilty misleading her friend, since she knew Louise loved babies in general. Perhaps, she thought, as Mark turned on his clicking turn blinker and went around another car, if no one claimed that child after they got Becca back, Louise could try to adopt the little changeling.

Mark looked and drove like a man possessed. She knew he was holding in barely leashed rage. He was furious yet hurt that his friends might have betrayed him, that Clark might be right about the Dixons. And he was enraged that the children he had vowed to help and protect, including Becca, were being hurt.

"We can't just walk in and demand things," she ventured in the silence that had fallen between them. "Do we have a sort of cover story?"

"Since you already asked Andrea to talk to Brad about testing a possible NAA baby, we'll say we've come to discuss the possibility, but that I'm getting so close I'll be able to test Becca myself in a few weeks."

"Really? That's wonderf—"

"And not true. If they've been bluffing me, it's the least I can do to them. But I just can't believe it of them," he said again, hitting a fist on the steering wheel, "I just can't."

"I remember something else Clark said last night. He's been worried that the BLAST software Brad gave you might have cookies, worms or a virus."

"Idiot that I am, I never thought about Brad giving me a Trojan horse. Damn it to hell!"

She'd never heard him curse like that, though she'd guessed he probably did from time to time. God forgive her, she felt like it too.

By the way Mark seemed to be driving almost automatically as they left the freeway and turned onto a wide, urban street in a suburb of Cleveland called Shaker Heights, Leah could sense they were getting closer to Metzler-Reich, the pharmaceutical giant she now pictured as her enemy. The name was German, which had pleased her when she'd first heard it. But now she pictured it as a Goliath, and herself as the rural shepherd boy David. David had killed his enemy, she reminded herself.

"Where did the two names for this company come from?" she asked.

"Two small pharms Brad bought and merged after he had words with the firm he was with in Atlanta and struck out on his own."

"Why Cleveland, if he had ties in Atlanta?"

"When I say he had words with his former firm, HealGene, I mean he had a real falling-out with its CEO, a very ambitious, brilliant, if aggressive man, Sinclair Marshall. The sad thing is, Brad also married the boss's daughter."

"Andrea is the daughter of his former boss?"

"Right. Talk about bad blood after Brad disagreed with how his father-in-law was running things. Sinclair Marshall evidently believed Brad, however talented and educated, should practically work his way up from the mailroom, if you know what I mean."

She nodded. "Poor Andrea, having to choose sides between her father and her husband. They don't have children of their own, do they?"

"Neither of them seemed to want any. By the way, it also irked her father that a huge hunk of her inheritance went to set MR up in competition with Heal-Gene. One thing that's bothered me is that Brad always felt that HG—HealGene—was pushing too hard for cures, taking shortcuts. But he's been doing some of that himself to stay competitive lately, and that's one of the reasons I left. Still, I can't believe he'd do something as unethical as what's been going on in Maplecreek. It's like someone's using your people as unknowing lab subjects, without permission, without caring one bit about what they think or feel or their freedom."

"Like guinea pigs or lab rats!" she blurted. "But they don't realize we won't run their mazes or meekly submit to their immoral practices."

He reached over to squeeze her hand, then drew it to his mouth and kissed the back of it. His lips seemed to brand her skin, but she felt it was a gesture that went deeper than just support, or even of friendship or desire. Her stomach flip-lopped, and not just because they'd turned into a cul-de-sac with huge buildings that Leah suspected were their destination. Mark had always done that to her.

"Are we here?" she asked.

"Thar she blows," he gritted out between clenched teeth, nodding toward a massive complex. Over their little car loomed a huge, new building with a stylized sculpture of a double helix and the big words METZLER-REICH in front, surrounded by a manicured lawn.

It was the style as well as the size of the building that awed her. It was curved and looked as if it was made entirely of glass, which reflected the sky. That, in turn, seemed to flow along its shapely silhouette.

"Glass-and-flash architecture, they call it," Mark said as he turned into a winding driveway toward the monster building. "Nothing with corners anymore but lots of tinted windows. Brad made a point of getting the same architects for it that had done HG in Atlanta. Before MR had several huge moneymaking medications okayed by the Food and Drug Administration, this place was just a two-story, brick building. It was like that when I came—the good old days. You're not even looking at the new clinic. It's built in a circle, around treatment rooms and with ORs out back, near a man-made lake."

She nodded mutely and turned her head to both sides to take it all in. Signs pointed people toward Administration, Research and Development, Clinic, Marketing, or Receiving and Distribution.

And she'd been right: the place was guarded. A muscular, uniformed man stepped out from a small stone gatehouse near a metal bar that blocked their way in.

Mark rolled his window down and stuck his head out into the brisk breeze. "Hey, Ken, remember me?"

"Dr. Morelli? Yo, good to see you," the guard said and gave Mark what the English called a high five. "When I was the night guard, half the time it was just you and me here 'til the wee hours."

"Brad Dixon's been asking me to drop by to see the new clinic for days, so I thought I'd do just that. He in today?"

"Oh, sure, but you should have called ahead. You know I have a pass sheet, and I'm not 'sposed to deviate from it. Seeing as it's you, though, I'll just call his secretary and clear it. Who's your companion?"

"Leah Kurtz, also an acquaintance of the Dixons'."

As the guard leaned down to look her over, Leah

leveled a stare back at him. His referring to her as
Mark's companion irked her and reminded her of the
canine companions Jesse had buried practically in his
backyard. The guard's eyebrows went halfway up his
forehead when he saw how she was dressed. Whether
or not he recognized her as Amish she didn't know and
didn't care. She just wanted to get inside and look
around for Becca.

The man disappeared into his little house. Mark
rolled the window back up.

"What's our plan?" she blurted, trying to fight the
butterflies in her belly.

"Whatever works. Let me take the lead, and keep
your eyes open."

The guard stepped back out, pushed a button to lift
the bar, and waved them through.

"And don't panic, okay?" Mark added.

"Okay. Sure."

If Mark's vague, play-it-by-ear plan didn't work,
Leah was ready to do anything to find and free Becca.
She pressed her hand against her thigh to assure herself she still had the kitchen butcher knife taped tightly
in a sheath there.

16

The Metzler-Reich Care Clinic awed Leah, but she tried not to let it scare her. Though only one story, it was perfectly round, with curved glass gracing the front; the stone walls on the rest of its circumference had no windows, so she gave up hope of later peeking in the rear rooms from outside. The reception area was vast and silent with two young women behind the long, free-form desk. Teal carpet, potted plants, framed photos of smiling families on the walls—none of them Amish. The place breathed peace and safety, but Leah's stomach knotted even tighter. Where were the patients, their families or friends?

The two women at the desk pretended not to stare at Leah. She was used to that, yet she sensed their surveillance went deeper than usual. Hadn't they ever seen an Amish woman before? If they hoped to treat patients with genetic disorders, they'd best get used to her attire, though she could not fathom her people coming here voluntarily. She blessed Mark for giving up all this opulence to practice near his patients.

"Dr. Morelli and Ms. Kurtz," the blond woman said—which meant the guard at the gate must have called ahead, "please have a seat. Brad Dixon is coming right over from Administration to join you."

Leah sat ramrod straight in a chair with nubby green upholstery; Mark walked to the windows beside her and looked out at the lake. The hard length of the knife sheath pressed against her thigh. She felt so pent-up she could explode. Why didn't Mark have an exact plan? Why hadn't he prepared her for what she might find in this world he knew was so alien to her?

Reeking confidence and power, Brad Dixon burst through the door at the back of the waiting area with a big smile on his face. He was, Leah admitted, an impressive, if austere, man. Pulling a white lab coat over his dark suit, he went directly to Mark and shook his hand, nodding at Leah as he looked over Mark's shoulder at her.

"Didn't you bring your baby, Leah?" Brad asked. "Andrea said she might need a blood test for something Mark wasn't ready to deal with."

Leah stood to face him more at his height. She had no intention of being intimidated or cajoled. "Family trees have suggested that my daughter is very distantly related to at least one NAA sufferer," she said, meeting his piercing stare. "But *my* question is whether Metzler-Reich is prepared to deal with an NAA blood test for her. Have you tested any other babies here?"

Brad looked surprised at her response, and, behind him, Mark frowned and gestured with a slash of his hand across his throat. Was he reminding her of their snow angels' slashed throats or of Varina's fate?

"Leah is understandably upset by her discovery and nervous about Becca," Mark told Brad. "We'd like to take a look around before we bring the baby in some-day soon, and you've been after me to take a tour for weeks."

"That I have, but you're just lucky I'm not tied up with something this morning. You should have called ahead so I could have had a few things ready for you."

And maybe have some things hidden, Leah thought, hoping they'd be able to get something damning out of this man. She didn't think she'd overstepped, but Mark obviously did.

"The truth is," Mark rushed on, "I fully intend to take blood samples from Becca and her distant cousins, but I thought you might want to double-check my work."

Brad's eyes widened, then narrowed. Again she read surprise on his face, but was that guilt or guile that had also flitted across his features?

"I thought," Brad said, frowning so hard his brow furrowed, "you were adamant about going it alone. Of course, if you'd come back under MR's aegis, I'd be pleased to put our vast resources at your disposal to study NAA. But is it your concern for Leah's child that's made you reconsider so suddenly, or something else?"

So much implied in so few words, Leah thought. Brad Dixon might be on a fishing expedition to learn how much they suspected about him. The man might smile and sound supportive, but maybe it was because he needed to study and then patent NAA genes for a huge profit, a profit that built these sprawling build-ings on land the size of at least six Amish farms.

"I'm just starting to realize," Mark explained, "that this gene search and its huge implications may be bigger than me or Leah's people. I may have to rely on the biotech power of MR to make progress fast enough to help the Amish NAA sufferers."

"And, as you mentioned," Brad said, "the huge implications that could lead to. The sky's the limit!"

The man had become completely animated and yet his eyes seemed glassy and transfixed. He must have realized he sounded like a zealot, because he seemed to get hold of himself as he went on, "But as for NAA itself, any help you need—if you're willing to play ball—just let me know. And if you do, I'll expect you to keep Clark Quinn off my back with his accusations and lawsuits."

Brad turned away and gestured they should follow him. Standing by a distant door, as if he'd appeared from nowhere, a bald, burly man in crisp slacks and a knit shirt, whom Leah had not noticed before, waited. Brad didn't introduce him, and Mark merely nodded to him, so she didn't ask who he was. The man pressed his open hand to a glass square on the wall, and the door opened inward.

"We've gone to state-of-the-art palm-print ID technology since you've been gone," Brad said, "but we'll circumvent that for you right now."

The three men waited for Leah to precede them. Feeling she was entering a foreign land, she stepped into a curved corridor with cobalt-blue carpeting. Farther down the hall, a few workers in white lab coats worn over their daily clothes went about their business. The entire edifice seemed built around a hub, as if it were a giant buggy wheel.

"It's quite a layout," Leah observed. "Are the examining rooms and patients' rooms similar to a regular hospital?"

"I'll show you later," he promised. "The on-site lab is in this section, Mark, though we've still got R&D in the main building."

"R&D is research and development of drugs," Mark explained to her.

Brad did not open the door labeled BIOTECH, but gestured that they should look through a long, tinted window that ran along one wall of the corridor.

Leah stifled a gasp. Within a curved room stretched three rows of glowing, moving screens that dwarfed the two Mark had. Multicolored graphs danced across some; others had columns or numbers spinning by. Workers sat at some, typing away, while other machines were untended. And in a separate room next to this one, white-coated workers moved among large machines. Some wore goggles, some squeezed drops of something from what looked like tiny turkey basters into vials or test tubes and others peered into huge microscopes.

"I see you have BLAST running," Mark said, still staring into the computer room. Leah could only hope that he'd noted the tops of the vials appeared to be like the one they'd found where Seth disappeared. "I've really appreciated that geneware you gave me," Mark went on. "If we work together, I could use all your memory here to boost it, do a faster search for the SNPs."

"Only one of several reasons you should come back," Brad said with a broad smile as he clapped Mark on the back. Leah could see their faces reflected in the window over the shift and smear of colors on the screens. Behind the three of them, the bald man had tagged along and stood back, watching, arms folded, against the far wall.

"Let's face it," Brad said to Mark as they began to walk toward the hub again, "your clinic is light-years away from this one. If you want progress made—to help Leah's baby and kids like her, whether it's NAA or something else—I'd suggest you move on it fast."

"I'll think about it, that's for sure," Mark said. Despite feeling so tense, Leah smothered a smile at that. Amidst Brad's push and the rush and power of this place, Mark's answer had sounded absolutely calm, conversational and controlled—so Amish.

"And, Mark," Brad added, "until we've got the ink dry on our new contract, tell no one—including Clark."

Leah stubbed her toe on the carpet and almost stumbled. *Tell no one?* Brad Dixon *must* be behind Becca's disappearance and who knew how much else. He was playing with them, subtly threatening them.

Almost before she realized she would speak, with a pleasant voice and careful expression, she asked Brad, "So, do you have any children or babies being treated or studied here right now? Not for NAA, of course, but I'd very much like to see an examining room and patient's room."

"No infants or juveniles right now. You do realize, Leah, we have a very select patient list and focused research here. But I'll show you a sample patient's room in a few minutes."

After they passed through the busy central area, where Leah finally saw nurses and doctors, he took them down another carpeted hall, the opposite spoke in this giant wheel. The rooms didn't even have windows in their doors, nor were any open or ajar. A few of them had little one-way windows for observation, which Brad explained when asked. Finally, they came to a door he unlocked with what looked like a plastic card. How she wished she could get her hands on it, but that desperate desire seemed another dead end.

"Oh," she said when Brad hit the lights in an empty room, "it's shaped like a piece of pie."

He smiled at her, but no warmth reached his gray eyes. "I think the architects call them triangular, but I like your description better. And the mention of pie reminds me, it's almost noon. Will you two stay and have some lunch with me? Mark, if you want to come back some other day, I'll set you up to see what's going on with our latest fast-track projects. But if you want to head back to the country and bring the baby—or any of the NAA kids—here later, that's fine by me."

"We'll discuss it and get back to you ASAP," Mark said. "About everything."

"Great. Whatever's made you come around, I'm grateful for it. But I don't want it leaking out to other marauding biotech pharms. I repeat," he said, looking at Mark, then directly into Leah's eyes, "don't tell Clark or anyone what we have going."

Leah dropped her right hand to feel the handle of her knife again through her skirt and slip. She'd been crazy to bring this in here. She was just lucky they didn't have a metal detector. This time she was not facing a chain saw with a kitchen knife, but she might as well be. What could she do? Beg him? Accuse him? Draw her pitiful weapon on Brad Dixon with his bodyguard right behind them?

No, she'd have to play it his way—Mark's way, too—at least for now. She was completely out of her element and it would betray her Amish heritage to use any sort of violence. Somehow she and Mark needed to lure Brad Dixon back to Amish country to deal with him there. Still, right now, she wanted desperately to draw her knife and hold it to this demonic man's throat until he told her exactly what he knew about her beloved Becca.

"So what was that slash-throat sign you gave me?" she asked Mark on their way home. "You know, when I asked him if he had other NAA blood-reference samples."

"That was a cut-what-you're-saying sign. Don't go there, change the subject."

"In other words, shut up and let you handle it. Why didn't you tell me that *before* we went in, when I was asking you what our plans were? Mark, with our snow angels' throats being cut and with how Varina Roscoe died, that sign was as threatening to me as the bloody sign on your clinic door or the *DON'T TELL* in my yard."

"I wasn't thinking about that. The signal was just instinct. I guess it started as a silent sign for moviemaking."

"Oh, great. I guess I just forgot what it meant from all the movie sets I've been on."

"Leah, I forget the gaps between us sometimes. Most of the time. I just didn't want you to give our motives away until I could feel him out."

"You don't think pretending to go back to work for him is going to make him tell all, do you?"

"Yeah, I'm hoping if I go back to him alone and tell him I'm ready to sign on the dotted line, he might give me something to work with."

"We have to act now!"

"By doing what? How about we kidnap Brad or Andrea and put their feet to the fire, or get some truth serum and inject that squirrely Jesse Cutler until he talks, or put Miles Mason on the rack to find out if he saw someone sneak in during the sugaring off to take Becca?"

All the way home, even while they were arguing, Leah was haunted by words from a Shelley poem, a section she'd never understood before but did now:

> *'Tis we, who lost in stormy visions, keep*
> *With phantoms an unprofitable strife,*
> *And in made trance, strike with our spirit's knife*
> *Invulnerable nothings...*

At the quilt warehouse, at Jesse's place, and at the clinic, she had wanted to learn and do so much. So far, all her efforts had come to nothing—less than nothing. *Becca.* She had to find Becca.

"Leah, are you listening? I said, I hated to lie to him about wanting to go back to MR, but it was the only way I could think to get him to give himself away."

"Yes, and he did."

"If you mean that he said, 'Tell no one,' that could be pure coincidence."

"He said it twice! Once at the beginning, and then

again at the end, just to remind us to quit playing games with him!"

"Maybe. But I'm a scientist, and theories need to be tested and proved. Do you have a better idea than making him think we'll play along? We can hardly accuse him outright—though you came close today."

"I know, I know," she said, leaning forward against her seat belt to prop her elbows on her knees and put her head in her hands. *Unprofitable strife...strike with our spirit's knife...* Had she run out of options? Dear Lord, there had to be something else she—they— could do to find Becca or make her abductors give her back.

"Of course, we could go to the authorities," Mark said as they turned down the road toward Louise's to pick up the baby.

"I don't trust Sheriff Martin." She leaned back and turned toward him in the narrow seat. "Katie Brand didn't trust him when she went undercover for him, and he wasn't much help to her in the end. And he's made no real progress on checking into that threat on your clinic door, or Seth's disappearance, and he more or less threatened me with a murder charge when Sam died."

"Be careful you don't start suspecting everyone," he said and reached over to squeeze her left knee. His hand felt so warm, so steady, but maybe that was because she was still so shaken. "Before I know it," he went on, "you'll have me on your list. Okay, how about we try bringing in my uncle from Columbus, Katie Brand's former partner? At least he'd be an objective but trained police professional to consult."

"But if we're being watched, whoever has Becca would panic if we bring in an outside officer."

Mark heaved a huge, forced sigh. "Leah, no one in Maplecreek knows Mike Morelli but Katie, and she's in Florida on her honeymoon."

"He came to Luke and Katie's wedding," Leah countered. "I saw him talking shop, as they put it, to Sheriff Martin."

"I didn't realize they'd met or were conferring. I must have been outside with Seth then. Then I can bring him in incognito, undercover, like Katie was working here among your people. At least, I can e-mail or phone him, explain things and ask his advice."

"What if Clark's right, and there're some kind of cookies to trace your e-mail? Or a worm in your phone?"

"A bug," he said, sounding even more exasperated. "I don't think you can bug cells, though conversations can be picked up with the right recording devices nearby."

"Cells—that's what those piece-of-pie-shaped rooms reminded me of," she said, shaking her head as they turned in the lane that led back to Louise's little house. "A bed, a sink, a toilet, but no windows, only an air vent…" She shuddered and broke out in goose bumps again.

"There's a second car at Louise's," Mark observed, pointing ahead. "She must have company."

"At least it's not someone Amish who might realize it's not Barbara Yoder's baby."

"Not your baby, you mean." He parked but left the engine running. He turned to her and seized her left wrist in his right hand. "You haven't let Barbara down, if that's been haunting you. We are going to find Becca."

"The night Barbara died, the last thing she said was that she'd be close, watching…"

"You don't believe in ghosts, do you?"

"At this point, I should. First, the dead flowers around the angel's neck were so like the live ones Barbara and I put there once. And then those footsteps from the statue, as if it looked in a back window and later wrote the *DON'T TELL* message. And that blow to Sam's head, like he'd been hit with a huge stone fist, the coroner said. Mark, I have dreadful dreams that the angel comes alive!"

"Leah…"

"No, of course I don't believe Barbara's really haunting me—any more than I believe that angel comes to life and talks to me!" she cried, gripping his wrist in return.

"Then let's go get the baby Louise has back and…"

She shook her head so hard her bonnet strings flew. "I'm going to tell Louise I don't feel well, that if the baby's settled in here, could she please keep her. I realize Louise may think the request odd, but I need just a few more days."

"To do what, exactly?"

"I don't know!"

"You can't go after that weirdo Cutler! And Miles Mason's evidently got a temper. You can't endanger your life—"

Louise Winslow knocked on Mark's window, jolting both of them.

"I don't mean to get in the middle of something," she

called to them as Mark rolled his window down, "but welcome back. She's just fine, and we've had the best time!"

"We were just discussing," Mark explained, "whether Leah should take Becca back yet, as she's running a slight fever."

"Oh, I'm so sorry. I'd be happy to keep her for a bit longer, if that would help. Why move her in this chilly weather, even though you've got the car instead of the buggy? Now, you just listen to the doctor, if you don't feel well, Leah. And, I must say, you do look a bit feverish. But I know you'll want to see her, give me the good-parenting seal of approval."

"Oh, yes. We'll be right in."

"A friend is here visiting, so don't you think I've left that little sweetie alone for one minute. Come on in now, both of you," she said and darted back into the house.

When they went inside, Leah saw that Louise's visitor was Pam Martin, the sheriff's wife. She realized the two women knew each other from the historical society, but she was surprised that the once-reclusive Louise had guests stopping by. Pam looked as hearty and tanned as ever.

"Mark," Louise was saying, "do you know the sheriff's wife, Pam Martin?"

"I saw you at the Brand wedding, but didn't have a chance to meet you," Mark told Pam and traded what the English called small talk with her.

Leah went over to the baby and took one of her chubby hands. She knew she should make an effort to pick her up. If it really were Becca, she'd be cuddling her, but Mark had glibly given her the perfect cover story. "I don't want to chance passing anything on to her, if I am coming down with something," Leah said when everyone looked her way. "Mrs. Martin, I just wish I could stay as healthy as you in the winter."

"And," Louise said as she came over to pick the baby up, "it's not from that tanning booth at the Kut 'n Kurl, either, though I've used that to help my psoriasis from time to time."

"Now, never mind—" Pam began to protest, but Louise was not to be deterred.

"Pam's been down to Florida again, keeping an eye on the place the Martins are building in Sarasota. You just can't trust architects, you know. I learned that when I had this little house put up."

"Oh," Leah said, "Sarasota's the same place Katie and Luke Brand went for part of their wedding trip, to see relatives."

"It's not much of a place we're building," Pam put in quickly, looking suddenly nervous. "Just a little retirement getaway we've saved for for years. And I know, Dr. Morelli, I shouldn't get as much sun at my age as I do, but it just makes me feel much better."

"How's the sheriff lately?" Mark asked her. Leah could have kicked him. She'd like to know a lot more about the Sarasota house.

"Busy, always busy," Pam said. "Maplecreek isn't 'Mayberry RFD,' like some folks think, you know," she said with a little laugh that seemed forced and fake to Leah. Maybe Mark was right. She was getting absolutely paranoid.

"In other words," Mark said, "the sheriff and his deputies have more than one bullet in their guns."

Everyone but Leah laughed. She had no idea what they were referring to and didn't care. Probably some English movie they'd all seen. But it did strike her as strange that she hadn't heard anything about the sheriff possibly retiring to a place he was building in Florida. The community gossip was that the Martins were barely getting by, because they had three kids in college at the same time.

Leah's mind raced. Unexplained money had come to Sam, perhaps tied to Barbara's medications. And now, maybe secret money might be coming to the sheriff, too.

Seth had found that the end of the handle of his spoon was the best—the only—screwdriver he could come up with. But that meant he could only loosen the screws from the air vent during meals, because he had to give the spoon back or his captors would notice. Worse, he'd lost some time, because they'd come in and drugged him for some reason. He was pretty sure he'd been out for at least a few hours. Other than that shot, though, he saw no other puncture marks on his body.

But after two meals, he had the four screws out far enough that he could turn them with his fingers the rest of the way. He planned to crawl out through the vent at night. But he was going to have to risk opening it and looking inside the first time in daylight, to be sure there was no drop-off inside. Still, he was so desperate to get out of here, he'd risk just feeling ahead and crawling into the darkness.

Holding his breath, he lay the loosened screws on

the floor. He braced himself in case the vent was heavy, then lifted it out and away.

Ja, thank God, the space was large enough for him to get through! And it went horizontally. It curved, though, probably to fit the outside of the building. As far as he could see, there were pools of dim light at regular intervals. Those must be where the vents from other rooms joined the shaft.

He had no idea if the narrow space eventually went up or down, but it had to go to the ground or to the roof. It just *had* to.

17

While Mark was making the rounds of her property and checking on Nell in the shed, Leah picked up his cell phone from the kitchen counter where he'd left it next to his car keys. She rifled through her junk drawer next to the sink to find the phone number where Katie and Luke could be reached in Sarasota—just in case, Katie had said. Leah didn't want to ruin their wedding trip, but she was desperate for help.

She talked to a woman who said she'd fetch Katie to the phone. "Tell Katie it's nothing to worry about," she said, "but that Leah Kurtz would like to speak with her."

"Sure thing," the woman, who managed the motel the couple was in, said. "It's so nice to have newlyweds here, and their kids are so cute. They were visiting relatives yesterday, but they're in today, only Amish family who ever stayed here. They went walking on the beach in swimsuits, real conservative ones, but—"

"I really need to speak with her."

"Oh, why, sure. Didn't mean to rattle on so, but it's just so nice to deal with their kind of people."

The phone clunked down as the woman went to get

Katie. Leah knew she was becoming impatient, angry—she even felt violent. But even the Lord himself showed righteous indignation in the temple when he turned over the money-changers' booths and told them it was not a den of thieves. And neither was Maplecreek!

Mark came in and she put the phone back on the counter without hanging up, praying he wouldn't grab it. It wasn't that she meant to keep this idea of hers a secret from him, and she should have asked permission to use his phone first, especially for a long-distance call. But she didn't want him suggesting they should bring in the sheriff again, just because she was willing to ask Katie's advice. She smelled a rat there, a big one.

"Okay, as I said," he told her, not even looking at the phone, "I'm going to check the bedrooms and attic." He went out and she heard him go up the stairs.

Finally, Leah heard someone pick up the phone. "Leah, it's Katie." Her friend's voice sounded so good. "Is everything all right?"

"I told the woman to tell you not to worry."

"She did. She talks all the time."

"I just need a favor, a local one for you right now."

"What do you mean?"

"Did you know that Sheriff Martin and his wife are building some kind of retirement home in Sarasota?"

"Go on! He's always said they're barely scraping by. With his kids away at Ohio State and that nice house they have, I believed him."

"It's a long story, but I need you to find out if it's a small place or what. I heard they have architects working on it, so that sounds pretty grandiose. Do you think you can find the house, if that's all the information I have?"

"Hey, I wasn't a police officer for years for nothing. I might have been on cloud nine the day I got married, but I do recall that Mrs. Martin looked as tanned as George Hamilton."

"As who?"

"Never mind. Sure, I'll look into it, and I bet I can do most of it over the phone. If not, Luke and I will take a taxi to check out the place. I'll do it right away, but how should I let you know what I find?"

"Can you call my mother's Bread of Life and just leave the message with her? Her number's 555-412-6731."

"Got it. Leah, what's going on? Is Becca all right? Are you still working for the new doctor?"

"Yes, and he's making progress. We both are."

"But you seem upset. This sounds urgent, so I'm going to treat it that way. Am I right about that?"

"Katie, you asked me to trust you more than once when you were here trying to help my people. Just trust me now, and I'll fill you in later. And have a wonderful time."

"I am. I've never been happier, but I sense you need hel—"

Leah punched off when she heard Mark coming back downstairs. Katie Brand might sense that she needed help, but she was too far away to really give it. At least Mark was here. She loved him, but all that had to be put aside for now, Leah reminded herself, maybe forever. She had to rely on her own strength and resources to find and save Becca. And that's just what she was going to do.

"I've got a couple things to do at the clinic," Mark said, taking his cell phone from the counter, "and then I'm going to drive into Pleasant to get you one of these. I don't care if it's *verboten* for the Amish, you need a cell phone now. If you won't take it and use it, I'll be forced to camp out here every night."

"No, I agree. If you get me one, I'll use it."

"Okay. I'll be back as soon as I can. Meanwhile, don't open the door to anyone but me."

He kissed her cheek and hurried out. She didn't even watch him drive away. As the setting sun streamed crimson through the side windows, Leah stared at the silhouette of the angel. The bare-limbed trees lining the ravine made its silhouette seem that of a frenzied person with wild hair. And the AgraGro grain silos peeked above it like an extra pair of tall, heaven-bound wings.

If only that angel were real, Leah thought, and could lead her straight to Becca.

Mark drove into Pleasant and purchased Leah a cell phone, then hurried back to his clinic. Before he returned to Leah's, he had something important to do.

He scrutinized both doors and all his windows, outside and in, just the way he'd done Leah's nearly two weeks ago. He hadn't taken that "Jeans Doctor" threat on his door seriously enough. He'd been dead wrong, because things were escalating. He had to turn his training to tracking and testing of another kind.

"Doors and windows A-okay," he muttered. "Not tampered with, inside or out."

He dreaded going into his computer room. What if Clark was right and Brad had sent him software that damaged or destroyed data? Or funneled it straight to those monster computer banks at MR?

He sat at the computer and ran a virus- and cookie-checker on BLAST, then all his geneware. Nothing. But any techie worth a damn would realize he could check this out. And if they were doing parallel research by eavesdropping on his plans, they would be running their own data, hoping, with their vast resources, to beat him to the answers and the ultimate prizes.

So maybe the Dixons had planted a good old-fashioned listening device instead. He and Leah had discussed key things in this clinic that their enemy might have used to do dirty work. They'd talked about Miriam and Susie Kline coming in by buggy that day they were hurt. The listening device could have picked that up, so the Dixons knew when and where to strike at them.

He racked his brain for what else the Dixons had given him or touched. The champagne bottle Andrea had brought was long gone, but he rummaged in the top kitchen shelves for where he'd put that vase she'd brought with roses.

"Idiot!" he told himself as he examined it. "Glass. There's no bug here. You can see right through it."

He searched everything around the path that Andrea had taken in from the clinic door that day when he'd introduced her to Leah. Nothing on or under the pegs for coats and capes, or the hall table. But how about that quilt she'd brought, the one Leah said was the building-blocks design?

He pulled it off the back of the couch in the waiting room and flapped it open. Just as Leah had found Varina Roscoe's diary in her quilts, Andrea could easily have stitched a bug in here. But although he felt all along the quilt, even held it up in front of a light, he found nothing.

He searched the kitchen, under the table and chair where Brad had sat when he'd so conveniently dropped by on the day of Sam's burial. Nothing but a few spiderwebs. Both Andrea and Brad had used the bathroom different times they'd visited; he went over that room with care.

Mark raked his fingers through his hair. He had to get back out to Leah with the cell phone. His own clinic was creeping him out now, almost as much as that old cemetery caretaker's place where she lived.

Leah still stared at the angel as evening grayed the scene outside. Hearing horse's hooves and buggy wheels, she looked over to see a surrey pulling into the driveway. She exhaled a sigh of relief. Even in the twilight, she recognized the horse and her family's biggest buggy. It looked like her father, Levi, was driving, and her mother sat ramrod straight beside him. Leah ordinarily would have run out to greet them. But, silently cursing whoever was tormenting her and those she loved, she pressed her face to the window to be very certain it was them.

The surrey stopped in a position that blocked her

view of the angel. Well, she couldn't spend the time they were here watching it, or they'd think she'd taken leave of her senses. And maybe they'd be right.

She shook her head as she rushed to the back door to let them in. What if someone had harmed them? Or what if her mother had somehow found out Becca was gone and blamed herself?

"*Maam, Daad,* this is a surprise, so late," she said as they came in. He was carrying four empty bushel baskets, stacked together. In an open paper sack, her mother had a fragrant loaf of cinnamon bread she put down on the counter. "Is everything all right?" Leah asked. "Is Naomi all right?"

"*Ja,*" her father answered, putting the baskets down on the floor. "Just going through her first wide-eyed time, now that David Groder wants to come calling."

"How's Becca?" her mother asked, glancing toward the front room. "She asleep already?"

Leah was tempted to throw herself into their arms to sob out her fears. But they'd bring in the bishop, if not the entire Amish community, for a search. Word would get out everywhere, including to Sheriff Martin, which could attract the worldly media, like when her sister was killed in the buggy accident. No, she still had to try to do things her way, at least for a little while longer.

"I've been running a fever," Leah told them, "so she's staying at my friend Louise Winslow's for the night. Louise has been so kind and adores babies."

"The mayor's wife?" her father asked, his voice rising.

"Now, Levi," her mother put in, touching his arm,

"you remember she came to pay her respects to Sam, though she wouldn't come in the house. And she gave both Katie Brand and little Becca gifts."

"What are the baskets for?" Leah asked, hoping to change the subject.

"Sam's booze bottles," her father said, still frowning. "Told your mother the ground's too frozen right now to bury them. We'll drop them off at the city dump in the dark. No good speaking ill of the dead."

"Your father and I still want you to know," her mother said, "that you can come home anytime. We're both out during the day, and Naomi's going to be working in Mr. Mason's Sugar Bush store this spring. So, during the days, the big house would be pretty much yours and Becca's. And, if you still want to work for Dr. Morelli, we're a lot closer to his clinic than you are."

"Well," her father cut in, "'nough said about that old topic. Em, how about you come help me load those bottles in the attic? You got an extra lantern, Leah, or should I bring the one in from the buggy?"

"I've got an extra, but it will be very dark up there. Let me just pop out and bring in the one from the buggy, too."

Mark would have a fit if he knew she was rushing outside, Leah thought. Darting around the side of the buggy that faced away from the house, she lifted the lantern from its hook. She took a step toward the cemetery's iron fence and lifted the lantern high, so it caught the statue of the angel in its wavering light. Its shadows shifted, and the angel seemed to move and breathe.

"Don't make yourself completely crazy," Leah whispered to herself and turned back toward the house. Then she remembered her father's binoculars, which he always carried with him. Though he was an avid bird-watcher, those closest to Levi Kurtz knew that he was secretly fascinated by airplanes. He'd stop plowing and look up to watch one go over. If no one but the family was around, he'd gaze through those binoculars for hours at jet trails or small planes buzzing Amish country.

Leah reached into the buggy and lifted the binoculars out, then hurried back into the house and closed and locked the door behind her. She heard her parents already upstairs, clinking bottles. She locked up again, and hurried up to join them.

"*Daad,*" she asked, "would you mind if I borrow your binoculars for just a few days?"

"Not you sky-gazing, too," her mother said with a smile.

"Not at birds or airplanes, but I'd like to watch spring burst close up when I'm in the house with Becca, and out on the roads visiting families for Dr. Morelli."

"*Ja,*" her father said, "coupla days fine by me. Wonder how long that poor soul took to drink all this stuff."

"You won't believe it but there's more in the root cellar," she told them. "But it's cold out tonight and that can wait."

"Another snow coming, heard uptown," her father said as he started to load a second basket. "Some winter, *ja,* worst we had in years, and hanging on."

"Miles Mason calls it a sugar snow that will bring a

big sap run," Leah said. From her lofty vantage point of the attic window, she adjusted the focus of the binoculars. It was getting black out there, too dark to see the angel.

"Oh, Leah, almost forgot," her mother said and fished a folded piece of paper out of her apron pocket. "Katie Brand called clear from Florida for you with a message. Here, I wrote down what she said. At first, I thought she meant she and Luke were going to buy a big place down there," she said and laughed.

Still holding the binoculars, Leah bent near a lantern to open and read the note. Her mother had jotted down ideas rather than sentences:

Prices in that neighborhood $800,000 for land alone. Large home, custom-built. Boat-dock space, country-club membership. A bonanza of bucks? More later.

Leah's heart raced. Sheriff Martin had come into a windfall. And his wife had looked guilty about it and did not come up with any believable explanation, such as a wealthy relative had died and left them money, or even that they'd won the lottery. Sam Yoder had hidden a very small fortune, and now it sounded as if Ray Martin was willing to spend a large one.

"Leah?" her mother's voice startled her. "Other than asking how everyone was, especially you, that's all Katie would say. What's this all mean?"

"I honestly don't know yet, *Maam.* Katie's following up on whether we're able to trust the sheriff, that's all."

"Any Amishman worth his salt that's read *The Book of Martyrs* could tell her that," her father groused as he started to fill the third basket. "Never trust worldly government and its military or civil authorities. Trouble is, can't even trust all the Amish, this day and age," he muttered and tossed another bottle.

But Leah was only half listening. Somehow she had to confront Sheriff Martin, to blackmail him or panic him into giving himself away, into revealing whomever he was working with or for. As soon as she got that cell phone from Mark, they'd make a plan.

"I saw a big surrey on the road and almost stopped it," Mark told Leah as he came in the back door, smacking his wet gloves together.

"Good thing you didn't, because you would have made my parents more suspicious than they already are," she said as she locked the door behind him. "They came to take Sam's bottles out of the attic."

"And they wondered where Becca was."

"I told them she was with Louise because I felt feverish. The way I look and feel, that half lie even got past my eagle-eyed mother."

He took off his jacket and threw it onto the back of a kitchen chair, then drew her over to the table. "Cell phone lesson number one," he said, producing the small, gray device. "I've already programmed my number in here, so I'll show you how to access it quickly and how to redial fast. And it's charged."

As he explained everything to Leah, he seemed brusque and hurried. "All right, try it now," he said, scribbling a number on a scratch pad and taking his phone into the other room. "That's my phone number," he called to her, "but you can get me fast by just hitting #1. Okay, call me," he shouted.

She started to punch the number in, then saw he'd turned the phone off again. Finally, she heard his number ring in her ear and louder in the other room. It was not his old strident tune, but one she recognized called "Take Me Home, Country Roads." Like her, Leah thought, even in these worst of times, Mark Morelli was changing for the better. But if he had any plans to slow down or relax his old pounding pace, it better not be now.

Again, Mark checked her windows and doors to be sure nothing had been tampered with, then searched her closets, under the beds, and went into the cellar and the attic, though she'd just been up there. All the while, Leah fingered Katie's note in her apron pocket. Should she tell Mark that Sheriff Martin might be taking bribes?

Mark hadn't approved of her direct approach with Brad Dixon at the clinic, so he surely wouldn't want her to confront the sheriff in his office tomorrow, as she had planned. Katie had said months ago that the sheriff's office was a well-staffed place; not everyone could be on her enemy's payroll. She'd decided to walk right in and try to get Ray Martin to realize he had to come clean or she'd go to the newspaper, to the mayor, to other law enforcement officers. If she had Mark along, he'd probably try to take over or give her that cut-throat sign again.

"You're so quiet now, when you were argumentative and angry earlier," he said as he stood ready to leave. He'd told her he'd searched the clinic for a bug the Dixons could have left, but he was going back to look everywhere a second time. She'd promised not to buggy into town tomorrow without being on the phone to him all the way.

"And call me anytime, even in the middle of the night," he told her as he took his cell phone, gloves and car keys off her kitchen counter. "Leave the phone turned on and sleep with it."

"I will," she promised as she joined him by the back door.

"In lieu, that is, of not having me here, with my head practically in your lap, like the other night." His voice was soft and suddenly seductive. "Leah, I'd like to come back later or just take you into the clinic with me, but I know we can't—you can't. Not yet."

She nodded. But for the wind outside, which had started to swirl more snowflakes, the earth seemed silent. In the house, the only sound was the steady, gentle hissing of the gas lantern on the table. And their breathing.

"We'll find her," he whispered, "as well as who took her and why."

She nodded. They moved together at the same time, clinging to each other. With her mouth pressed to his cheek, her lips rasped against his beard stubble. They held hard to each other, her arms clamped around his waist, his clasped behind her shoulder blades. It was only when her body pressed full length to his hard sinew and muscle that she recalled she still had a knife strapped to her thigh.

He tilted his head and kissed her hard. "I need you, more and more," he said as he set her back and turned the lock to get out. "Call me, and I'll call you."

She locked up behind him as he disappeared into the darkness toward his car, which he'd parked down the road near the ravine. As dragged-out and distraught as Leah felt, she suddenly realized that, for the first time since she was young, she had a come-calling friend to love.

Mark crunched through two inches of deepening snow. As he unlocked his car, he thought he heard another vehicle start nearby. And was that noise windshield wipers thumping back and forth, or only the wind through the trees?

So as not to make a sound, he closed his car door just enough to make the dome light go out, then sat inside, straining to listen, barely breathing. Large flakes had piled up on his windshield, but he didn't want to start the wipers. He'd parked behind a screen of bushes along the ravine. Had someone else done the same?

His breath was steaming up the cold glass, even under the screen of snow. A sugar snow, Miles Mason had predicted. The flakes were so big they looked like spun sugar. He couldn't recall whether his dome light would momentarily come back on if he closed his door completely. If so, and if anyone else was out here, he'd be a sitting duck.

And someone was!

How long had they been hidden here? If it hadn't been dark when he pulled up, would he have noticed? And had he been seen?

In total darkness, a square-shaped vehicle crept out from the dead end of the street and coasted past the cemetery, then Leah's house. For a moment, Mark hesitated. What if that was a decoy to lure him away from Leah? Damn, but he was going to get this guy for good.

He turned on his ignition, then cracked his window to hear the other vehicle better. Only when it sped up after passing Leah's did Mark slam the door shut, hit the windshield wipers and pull out.

At first he feared he'd lost the other vehicle in the snowfall. Could it have turned off somewhere already? What if it was behind him now or doubling back?

But there it was ahead. The driver had turned his lights on, illumining the vehicle's silhouette and the blinding snow blowing across the road. A pickup, SUV or van? For once, Mark wished his car didn't have running lights that were perpetually on.

Before his prey got to town, it slowed to make a right turn off Deer Run Road. Its headlights slashed across the snowswept intersection.

As the vehicle turned, Mark was close enough to tell it was bulky and dark-colored. An old, brown van.

18

Almost as soon as Mark had left, Leah wanted to call him.

Whatever else happened, she wanted to thank him for helping her try to find Becca. She still felt his kiss on her lips and his arms around her. He'd said he needed her more and more. Was that his worldly way of saying he loved her? Though her Amish world had accepted him as a doctor, they would never accept him as her suitor or her husband. Yet—once she had Becca back—she desperately wished it could be so.

Besides that painful yearning, she was feeling guilty that she hadn't told Mark about Sheriff Martin's bonanza of bucks, as Katie had called it. Most of all, though, she needed to hear Mark's voice, his calm, rational voice.

For again, the house was creaking and groaning. As it had two weeks ago—and the night Barbara died—the wind was starting to shriek around corners and howl under the eaves. She felt so fearful that she was tempted to ask Mark to come back. It didn't take much imagination to think that wail of wind was an unearthly voice crying, *Leeeahh...Leeeeaaah.* Or was the voice too shrill to be an adult's? It haunted her heart, like a baby's wail.

She looked out the side window, but swirling snow obscured the cemetery and the statue. *Beloved* was the word on Varina Roscoe's grave. Too young to die, from a slit throat as well as a broken heart.

Leah's hands flew to her throat. Varina had loved a young doctor, and he'd betrayed her. She had helped nurse her neighbors through a pestilence. *Beloved.* Becca was beloved too, and Barbara. If Leah could find Becca and bring her home, perhaps the memory of Barbara's loss would lessen.

Leah dashed into the kitchen and grabbed her phone. She turned it on and punched in #1 as Mark had showed her. It rang and rang. Could she have done something wrong? Why didn't he answer?

After an eternity, she heard a click and a voice, a desperate but distant voice.

"Leah? Is th…you?…can't read…ID number… now…okay?"

His voice kept cutting out. And why couldn't he read her ID number on the screen? Even if he was on his way to the clinic and it was dark outside, the numbers lit up.

"Yes, it's me," she told him, raising her voice level.

"I said…you okay?"

It sounded as if he was shouting, though she had to strain to hear him. She began to yell too.

"Yes! I can barely hear you!"

"I…both hands on…wheel."

"Where are you?"

"Tailing brown van…was parked…your place."

She gripped the little cell phone so hard her fingers cramped.

"Can you see the license plate?" she shouted. "Jesse's old one is VAN-GO 2."

"Can't...almost...whiteout."

"But *where* are you?" she repeated.

"Right turn...Deer Run...onto...road toward... mill. Blowing snow..."

Could the snow or wind be interfering with his voice? And hers too? She tried to enunciate each word. "The van may lead you to Becca! Can you stay back but keep it in sight?"

"Leave...line open... Keep talk..."

She held her breath, picturing how hard it must be to chase a dark van into the night through a screen of snow. She stared out through her back window, seeing her reflection as if in a mirror darkly. Yet in her mind and heart, she saw only him in that little car he drove too fast, gripping the steering wheel, trying to help her, to find Becca.

"Mark, can you still hear me?" she shouted so loud her ears rang.

His voice came even more distant and tinny. "Yeah!"

"There's a narrow, covered bridge over the ravine along that road! Be careful!"

"How close to...mill...? Haven't been...here... Lost them. Bridge...spinning out!"

She was certain she heard a squeal of brakes—or was that the shrieking wind outside again?

"Mark? Mark!"

Nothing on the other end, though the line still sounded open. No busy signal, no one punching off.

"Mark! Mark, can you hear me? Mark!"

Still holding the phone, she ran for her cloak and bonnet. She jammed her feet into boots, then quieted to listen to the phone intently. Nothing. Dead air.

"Mark?" she cried into it again, but her voice came out a squeak.

If he'd gone off the road, she knew about where he would be. There was no way she was going to call the sheriff's office for help. Sheriff Martin had been no help when the Kline buggy went off the road and it would be just like him to want to arrest Mark. She could be to the spot in less than fifteen minutes, and if Mark was hurt, she'd call the hospital in Pleasant.

She was panicked that Mark could be spirited away as Seth or Becca had been. Or harmed, like Sam. Storm or not, she was going out to hitch up Nell and find him—and that brown van.

Seth guessed it might be dark about now, because he'd had his biggest meal of the day a while ago. When it became quiet in the hall outside, he decided it was time. *Ja,* he was going to risk crawling through the vent, at least to explore it. If he could escape to the outside, he would. If the crawl or climb was too long, he'd remember his route and come back, then try again later.

He had rolled his single towel the long way, then bent it once. It might pass for his legs, curled up. His pillow was going to be his body, and the new roll of toilet paper his head. If someone looked in, he hoped they didn't realize how small the form was under the single blanket on the bed.

He knelt and, by feel in the dim room, removed the four loose screws and lifted the air vent out. He leaned it against the leg of his bed where he could get it and, he hoped, move it back into place from the inside behind him.

At first, the curved, horizontal shaft looked pitch-black. But as his eyes adjusted, he saw the lighter areas where air vents from other rooms connected to it. How was he going to go in headfirst and pull the vent to the wall? He'd have to risk leaving it off. And, if they saw that, the dummy on his bed would be pointless.

But he had no choice. He was scared and was getting a bad stomachache, but he had no choice.

When he got completely in, he saw the top of the shaft was not as high as he'd thought. He'd have to drag himself on his elbows, rather than crawling. But he knew he'd never manage scooting to get out again backward. He had no choice but to go ahead.

"Now or never," he whispered. "*Ja,* can't turn back now."

Leah left the long knife taped to her thigh. Locking her back door, she hurried out into the dark, cold night. The wind buffeted her skirt and cloak and ripped at her bonnet as she ran for the shed with an unlighted lantern in one hand and a flashlight in the other. The strap of her father's binoculars bounced over her shoulder. If the snow let up a bit, if the stars came out, they might help somehow.

In the shelter of the shed, she lit the lantern and spoke soothingly to Nell. "I'm so sorry, girl, but we've got to go out in this. You know the road, at least part-way."

The light let her see the traces and reins used to hitch the horse hanging on pegs on the wall. She harnessed the buggy fast despite the cold that stiffened her fingers, even in gloves. Yet she perspired as if she were in the heat of day. All the while, she kept an eye on the half-opened door of the shed, praying for protection, that whoever had evidently parked nearby in that brown van had not somehow circled around. But Becca needed her—Mark too. There was no turning back.

She didn't even stop to close the shed doors against the snow as she started out. Light from her safety lantern, bouncing on the side of the buggy, caught the iron spikes of the cemetery fence and reflected slightly off the snow caught in the angel's garments, hair, wings and neck.

Startled, Leah stared at what appeared to be a shiny, thick necklace on the statue. She reined Nell in with a quick, "Whoa!"

Was that why the van had been lurking outside to-night? The demon inside it had evidently painted a scarlet band around the statue's neck. The threat was unmistakable: it looked for all the world as if some huge hand had cut the angel's throat.

Dark. It was suddenly so dark, and his head hurt ter-ribly. Pain flamed when a light shone in one eye and then the other.

"I see his air bag deployed. He out?"

"Pupils aren't dilated, but yes. At least he's breathing."

"Thank God, or there'd be hell to pay from the pharm. They still want him to make good here, and come around."

"Don't talk about that. You can never tell what unconscious people hear. Give me your flashlight. Damn, it's getting late."

Dark. It was so dark, and he was hungry. Didn't they know twelve-year-old kids were always hungry? Why did they always eat so late here in Umbria? At home in Cleveland, they ate at five-thirty. Maybe all Ohioans did, but not these Italians. And Grandpa had said, 'When in Rome, do as the Romans do.' Still, they weren't in Rome, but a little hill town called Trevi.

"Let's call the counselor. He can be here in five minutes. Here, use Morelli's cell, in case he checks it later. Go over there and call, while I give him a quick shot. I'm going to put it in his hip because he's already suspicious about our drugging the others."

"Just hurry up, would you? I've got to go back to the girl's house, now that we know Morelli won't get in our way tonight. If that slashed throat on the angel doesn't scare her, we're going to have to burn her out."

"Quit doing your own thinking and make the call. Just tell him we're about half a mile from the mill on the east side of the road. And tell him not to use his headlights, even though it's so damn dark."

The one giving the orders was a woman. Maybe she was the Italian cook his grandfather said was so good. *Dark.* The cook said it was dark.

"Is that dark celery, Grandpa?"

"Black celery's what they call it, my boy, sì. *Sedano nergo, a specialty here in Trevi. And you're going to*

eat this pork-stuffed celery with me, aren't you, my lit-
tle American boy? No hamburgers and fries here in
Umbria. You have to become a part of this life, eat and
see and love it all like an Umbrian, sì?"

"Sì, Grandpa. Okay, here goes. It's not bad—good,
but kind of strong."

"Kind of strong, like life, eh? See, Marco, don't you
be afraid of different places and people. Bravo, mi
Marco, bravo..."

Bravo to Leah, Mark thought. She was so brave and
beautiful. He loved her, and little Becca too. He
couldn't bear to lose them as he had his parents and
his beloved grandfather. He'd only just found Leah in
Amish country, but he wasn't sure where to find
Becca...

He surrendered to the dark serenity of the Umbrian night...

Seth froze where he was in the shaft. He'd passed
two rooms, shaped just like his, in the curved path he
was crawling. But he heard a voice in this third room,
a man's. Holding his breath, he inched forward and
peered upward through the slitted grate. He had to
move his head up and down to get the whole view. It
was like looking at the old TV set Mr. Mason had in
the back of his store, when the picture was flickering.

A man was alone in some kind of office, talking on
a small hand phone. He was real upset. Seth hadn't seen
him or heard his voice before. And this didn't look like
a doctor's office. Maps were on the walls, instead of
lighted X-ray boxes or those framed certificates Susie
always liked. The books on the wall were a huge

matched set. This man wore no doctor's coat or those pale green pajama outfits folks in here wore. Even at night, he had on a fancy suit with a vest, white shirt and tie.

"He *what?*" the man demanded into the phone, his voice rising. "Is he hurt? Was Leah in the car with him?"

Seth startled and bumped his head on the ceiling of the shaft. The man evidently didn't hear the dull, echoing thud. "Did our doctor inject Morelli with Versed too?"

He was talking about Teacher Leah and Dr. Morelli! But what was Versaid?

"Yeah, you're right," the man went on, grabbing a dark overcoat from the back of the door and pulling it on one arm. "I'll take care of him. No—no, we don't want her burned out yet. That's a last resort—or the next to last, if we have to *really* get rid of her."

Still on the phone, one arm in his coat, he rushed to his desk and picked up a ring of keys. "Just get in the van, go back and keep an eye on her—that is, unless she gets in your way or becomes more of a liability. I think the big man would pay to have her taken out, but not if he thought Morelli would be too distraught to continue his work here. Now, if they thought the loss would inspire him to work all the harder—listen, I'll leave her up to you. I'm on my way right n—"

Still talking, the man rushed out into the hall. Seth caught a glimpse of a lighted work area with a nurse at a desk before the office door closed slowly and quietly behind him.

Seth rejoiced that he was still somewhere near home. But his friends were in bad trouble. It sounded as if Dr. Morelli was just being watched, but that Teacher Leah might be killed.

The moment Mark moved, pain seemed to cleave his head in half. Where was he?

Opening both eyes slowly, he felt stunned. He was in his own bed at the clinic. And Clark was standing over him.

"You all right, pal? You spun your car out and phoned me for help, remember? Thank God, I wasn't far away. I was heading into town, hoping you'd put me up for the night, but now I'm gonna take care of you."

Mark frowned, but that hurt too. His brain was like black celery soup with gnocchi bobbing in it. Now, why had he thought of that?

"Leah," Mark managed to get out through a dry throat. "Where's my phone? Gotta call her. What time is it?"

"It's about 10:00 p.m., but I'm not sure where your cell went. Sorry, but I might have left it in your car. I'll make sure it's towed into town in the morning."

Mark lifted a hand to his head. "How bad is it?"

"You wrapped the front of it around a tree near the most picturesque covered bridge I've ever seen. Do you remember any of the accident or its aftermath?"

"Not really. I gave Leah a cell phone, though, and I was talking to her. Where's yours? I can use that," he said, trying to sit up.

"Just stay put," Clark insisted, pushing him back onto his pillows. "I'll go get it and call her for you, while you rest. If you don't, I'm going to run you into the hospital in Pleasant—it's the nearest one, isn't it?"

"Yeah. How'd you know that?"

"You want something from your medicine cabinet or doctor's bag?" Clark asked, not answering the question. "Painkiller? Sleeping pill? You're going to be sore as hell in the morning, and really in pain when you see that sweet little car of yours."

"Leah told me to get something better for the roads around here. I should have bought a truck or van..." Something swirled through his thoughts like snow.

"You got Leah's number?" Clark was saying. "I'll go get my phone and call her for you, but you've got to rest."

"Just get the phone, and I'll remember it—if I can."

"Sure. Be right back."

A van, Mark thought. He'd been following a brown van, which he figured might be Jesse Cutler's, through the snow. He'd wiped out. Before that he'd been talking to Leah about where he was, but Clark had appeared, as if he'd been listening in...

Damn, he couldn't remember anything about calling Clark. It was tantalizingly out of the reach of his memory, just the way Susie and Miriam had described...

Mark got to his feet. His head pounded, and he was already sore, especially his left hip. Staggering a bit at first, running his hands along the walls, he left his bedroom and glanced out the side window at Clark.

Clark's car was sitting in the driveway, but he was walking up and down alongside it, talking into his phone. He couldn't be calling Leah because he didn't know her number. No one would tow a car at this time of night. Was he phoning the hospital in Pleasant?

Mark's hand, leaning heavily on the wall by the front window, bumped the print of the double helix Clark had given him, swinging it slightly.

He fought to clear the fog from his brain. Clark had been his best friend for years. Clark, patent attorney, had been so fiercely protective of his medical work here. Clark, who had always believed that money talked but everything else in the world could take a walk, who had come and gone here at the strangest times, as if he knew exactly what was going to happen next...

As badly as he was hurting, Mark lifted the large, framed print off the wall and leaned it against the end of the couch. The back of the print was covered with brown paper to keep the dust out. His hand shaking, he reached out, punched a hole in the corner of the paper and ripped it entirely away.

The screaming sound hurt his head. But the tiny, black listening device, securely taped in the lower left corner of the frame, hurt his heart.

Her heart was still thudding from the sight of the angel, but Leah struggled to calm herself. The leaden sky spit snow, but she was grateful the blizzard had abated—the whiteout, as Mark had called it. Deer Run was slippery and icy in spots, so, though she hurried Nell along, she was careful that they didn't skid off into a ditch.

He'd been spinning out, Mark had said. She wasn't sure if that mean his tires had spun on the ice or his entire car. She was terrified he'd gone off the road near the bridge.

Leah was so cold she was shaking. Just up ahead
was the turn Mark had said he'd made—toward the
AgraGro Mill, if she'd heard him correctly. Nell nav-
igated the sharp corner well. Leah's spirits began to
lift. She was praying he'd only broken his cell phone
or dented his car and that he was not hurt himself.
Wouldn't it be a funny moment, she tried to buck herself up, when she'd let him borrow her cell phone to
call a tow truck?

But the next moment, her hopes crashed. Mark had
said he'd lost the van, which she wished desperately
they could find and trace to Becca. Would the driver possibly return to watch her house? Maybe she could leave
a note on the angel, saying she'd do whatever was wanted
to get Becca back. But first, she had to help Mark.

Despite the fact she knew she was breaking the law,
Leah unsnapped the plastic window on her side and
reached out and around to gut the safety lantern hanging there. Years ago, after her sister's accident, she'd
vowed that whenever she buggied anywhere at night,
she'd have it lit. But if that van was still in the area,
Leah wanted to sneak up on it. She might not be able
to keep up with it in a buggy, but, if she could confirm
her suspicions that the license plate was VAN-GO 2,
she'd have enough evidence to bypass Sheriff Martin
and bring in other police authorities.

Leah slowed Nell as the road began to narrow near
the bridge. Both tree lines crept closer. Those on the
left guarded a shallow ditch before fields began. But
on her right, denser trees edged the same ravine that
stretched for miles, even past her property. Mark must
have been near here when he called.

She unsnapped the front of her plastic window and shoved it off to the side. Turning on her flashlight, she began to sweep its meager beam ahead.

She gasped as it reflected brightly off the back of a blood-red fender up ahead. Yes, he'd hit a tree! And then, she realized the light illumining the scene was much too bright to be just hers.

19

Even as Leah snapped the reins to urge Nell on, she heard the hum of an engine close behind. As she looked back, widely spaced headlights blazed even brighter, blinding her with magenta and yellow spots before her eyes.

The first nudge the vehicle gave her bumper almost jolted the carriage into Nell.

Leah saw no way to outrun her tormentor. The nearest building was the AgraGro Mill across the bridge and a wide field, but would there be a night watchman to help her? Or should she jump out of the buggy and hide in the ravine?

The vehicle revved its engine again. She'd bet all Sam's money it was a brown van and that the driver meant to shove her into a tree, maybe just as it had wrecked Mark's car. But no, from what he'd shouted over his cell phone, he'd slid into the ravine.

Metal butted the back of the fiberglass buggy. It shoved into Nell; the horse snorted and shied. Leah braced her feet, holding on to the side of the buggy, frozen. She prayed Mark was still alive in his wrecked car, but she remembered how her sister had died, hit from behind like this, on a black, black road.

His heart thudding, Mark stood behind the door and waited for Clark to come back inside. When he stepped in, Mark shoved the door into him, slammed him face-first into the wall and twisted his left arm behind his back.

"What the hell! Have you gone crazy?" Clark demanded, his face pressed against the wood-paneled wall.

"What's crazy is how things are starting to fit together, *pal*. And I still want to borrow that phone."

"You probably have a concussion. Let me run you to the hospital."

"How about giving me another amnesiac shot and running me clear into Dixon's MR clinic? I'm certain you're on his payroll, though you've been putting on a real good show about not getting along with him. I just hope, for your sake, you're not into a few other, little things like harassing, kidnapping and maybe worse."

Sweat poured off Mark. It was taking every ounce of his strength to hold Clark's wrist. He'd bent Clark's arm up nearly to his shoulder blade. Clark held his cell phone in his free hand. Mark couldn't figure out how to take it without easing up on him, so he marched him down the hall.

"You want the phone to call Leah, fine," Clark said through gritted teeth. "But you've got it wrong about Dixon. And what was that about kidnapping or worse? What are you talking about?"

"Anything for big bucks, right?" Mark accused. He forced Clark to his knees beside the ripped backing of the helix print.

"Why is that torn up?"

"Recognize your thoughtful gift? How about that little black circular thing in the lower left corner?"

Damn, he was getting dizzy, and his head was thudding like horses hooves. He found himself praying for once, praying he wouldn't black out.

"It looks like a bug," Clark said. "And because it was in the back of the print, you're blaming me? Man, that head injury's making you flip out. All our years of friendship, and you think I'm bugging you? I swear I had nothing to do with that. Are you telling me you don't think someone could have gotten in here and planted that *after* I gave the print to you?"

Mark wavered in his fury. "You've been spending one hell of a lot of time in little Maplecreek, for a hot-shot patent attorney with clients in Cleveland and Columbus. Why do you keep turning up in town, like when Brad and Andrea Dixon were invited here? And what a coincidence you were so handy to help me out tonight. Not to mention how you tried to charm Leah in the restaurant yesterday."

"Oh, now I get it. You think I've been moving in on your woman—an Amish woman? Just like the old days, right, the macho jealous thing, even though we were best friends?"

"Stop throwing the best-friends thing at me! What we *were* may not be what we *are,*" he insisted, though it cut deep to say that. "And the thing with Leah's not like that at all."

"I can tell you're a goner over her. Okay, she's bright, different, naive, even sexy, but she's a virgin—or is she, now that she's been so tight with you? Aaagh, let me go!"

"Just shut up and hand me that damn cell phone, nice and easy." As if he were raising his hand in a holdup, Clark lifted the phone so Mark could take it. He had to call Leah right now, to be sure she was safe and tell her he was okay. But keeping pressure on Clark's arm while dialing her number one-handed wasn't easy.

"Look," Clark said, "if you think I'm up to something, call the sheriff and let him lock me up, but you're breaking my arm. God knows I'm telling the truth, Mark. I think Dixon's hired someone to keep an eye on you, but it sure as hell isn't me. I've always had your best interests at heart—"

As Mark lifted the phone to his ear, Clark kicked out backward at him. Mark tried to sidestep, but Clark, still kneeling, gained enough space to throw his body backward into Mark. He lost his hold on Clark's arm and the phone dropped and skidded away. They sprawled together, wrestling, shoving, knocking into the glass-covered print, which tipped over them and shattered on the floor.

Mark closed his eyes against flying glass. When he opened them, he was staring into the bore of a small, snub-nosed gun inches from his face.

"Let's talk sense, buddy boy," Clark gritted out as he gasped for breath. "Dollars and sense."

Leah could hear her cell phone, but it was muted, muffled. It had to be Mark calling. At least it meant he was alive, safe somewhere.

But her phone must have fallen off the buggy seat. She bent to feel for it on the floor, but the next nudge of the vehicle shoved the buggy and Nell off the road toward the trees at the top of the ravine. Snorting, shaking her head, the horse tried to hold back on her own, despite the fact Leah was pulling on the reins.

Leah wondered if Miriam and Susie had been shoved off the road like this and then, because of the injections someone gave them, couldn't recall it.

The buggy tilted and she nearly pitched out. Fury filled her, for the Klines, for Becca, for Seth and even Sam. For herself and Mark. That had to be him on the phone, but she couldn't scrabble for it now, because she refused to be smashed into a tree or pushed into that ravine.

The phone finally went silent. Standing precariously on the front fender of the buggy and holding her small knife, she leaned over Nell's rump and sawed at the heavy strap traces that held the horse to the buggy. Her first thought had been to abandon the buggy and try to ride Nell to the mill, but it was still a long distance across an open field. And buggy horses were never ridden. Nell could throw her, for all she knew.

But if the horse ran off in the dark, her pursuer might think Leah was on her back. And if the vehicle chased Nell, that would give her time to find her cell phone, check Mark's car, and hide in the ravine.

"Whoa, Nell. Stand still, girl."

Leah freed one of the traces and started on the other, just as she heard the engine rev again. She braced herself, hanging on the back strap and cupper. This hit shoved the buggy askew on the road. The headlights illumined her, like a butterfly pinned to a lighted board.

She yanked the knife through the last trace, and it gave way. Pulling the reins free from the twisted buggy, she threw them over Nell's back and hit her flank hard with her free hand.

"Nell, go!" she cried. *"Schnell!"*

The horse lunged from the buggy shafts and ran free, straight for the covered bridge. The buggy jolted again, wobbling toward the line of trees. Leah jumped off the side, away from her attacker. Bending low in the thin shaft of shadow the battered buggy afforded, she ran for Mark's car.

She was almost there when she heard the vehicle hit the buggy again. The headlights caught her, disorienting her for one moment, but at least they lit up the interior of the car.

Empty! Thank God! He had gotten help or had walked away. Her tormentor's vehicle turned toward her, bumping through the grass on the berm toward the trees. In that moment before its headlights washed over her again, she saw it was a van, a brown van. But neither the style nor the license was Jesse Cutler's.

She ran to the edge of the ravine.

There was no path. She sat down and slid through the snow; her skirt and slip rode up, baring her legs, and the rough, snowy ground scraped and chilled her. The sheath with the knife she had taped to her leg pulled at her flesh. Her cloak caught on tree bark, but she yanked it back. Twigs tried to snag her bonnet, but it was held in place by its ties around her neck. She grabbed at saplings to stop her speed, then wrapped her arms around a tree and held on tight. She'd lost the flashlight, but was surprised to feel her father's binoculars still suspended from her shoulder.

Above, she heard a car door slam shut and feet crunch snow. The van's headlights were still on; light streamed through the trees, making them look like black bars in a cage high over her head.

"Leah, it's Sheriff Martin! You all right down there?"

She was only half surprised, but she was completely terrified. Not answering, clinging to the tree, she tried to get behind it, in case he had a searchlight. She pulled her bonnet up to cover her head and white *kapp*.

"Leah, I didn't know it was you in that buggy till I saw you cutting the reins. Thought it was whoever the doc said's been harassing both of you, maybe the same person painted that hate message on his clinic door. The doc's all right—just hit his head. You down there, girl? Come on, now. You can trust me."

"Get up!" Clark ordered, leveling the gun at Mark. "And get back."

Feeling as shocked as he was dizzy, Mark righted himself and scooted back on his butt. Though the weapon was small, it looked as big as a cannon up this close. The fact Clark had a gun cleared his head faster than realizing his old friend had bugged his office and sold him out to the Dixons. Or was it to the highest bidder? Despite the fact the Dixons looked as guilty as hell, Mark couldn't shake the certainty that Brad and Andrea didn't like or trust Clark and that he returned those sentiments.

Totally exhausted, Mark sat on the floor with his legs bent and his back against the leather couch. He was going to have to play Clark's game to have any chance here. "What about dollars and sense?" he asked.

Clark got off the floor and slumped on the chair directly across the coffee table, still pointing the gun with both shaking hands propped on his knees. He seemed to have gotten the worst of it: a split lip, one eyelid swollen already, and his hair and suit—a suit, in the middle of the night—were a mess.

"You don't get it, do you?" Clark goaded. His voice was deadly calm, but his eyes were alight, almost feverish in their intensity. Why hadn't he realized that Clark was totally driven by wealth, not so much by the things it could buy, but by the passion of pursuing it?

"Get what?" Mark countered. "That you've got the upper hand?"

"Listen up, buddy boy, because this may well be your last chance to have everything in life you've ever dreamed of. For you, that means the kind of fame that comes with curing a terrible childhood disease, with isolating the aging gene and leading the development of its potential. Mark, your medical discoveries could mean miracles. The therapies could bring longer lives, if not eternal life, to all mankind."

"I'm deeply touched by your benevolent motives. Clark Quinn, prophet to and new savior of all mankind."

"I'm trying to tell you this is big—so big. Our next step is to lobby Congress to redefine aging as a disease, rather than a natural condition. If aging's a disease, we can try to cure it. That's the way to get billions poured into research and development. I'm convinced

your NAA work will lead to a patent for the aging
gene. Everyone will want a piece of it, but *you* will
own."

"Me and who else? My patent attorney and Metzler-
Reich?"

"Mark," he said, shaking his head as if Mark was
an idiot, "I'm not working for Metzler-Reich. Brad
Dixon's clout and vision are minuscule compared to
my employer's."

"Don't tell me the U.S. government or a foreign
government's behind this."

"Hardly," he said with a sharp laugh. "They're the
ones—John Q. Public, worldwide—who are going to
ultimately pay the bills. In a way, it's like a pyramid
scheme, where the most profit goes to those at the
top—you, me and the sponsoring pharm firm, Heal-
Gene."

"HealGene? You're working for Sinclair Marshall?
Then the Dixons know nothing about all this."

"Bingo. And if you refuse to accept reason, and the
moola doesn't move you, maybe you'll be happy to
help us, just so your little Amish squeeze can get her
baby back. What do you say?"

Mark's stomach went into free fall. They had
Becca. They'd no doubt drugged and taken blood sam-
ples from Susie and Miriam. They might have taken
Seth too, but could they have killed Sam?

"Did your people take the baby to get blood samples or to keep Leah in line?" Mark demanded, getting angrier with each revelation.

"So you do know the baby could have NAA too.
Barbara Yoder's DNA must have had the defective

gene hidden in it somewhere. But if they'd just wanted her blood, they'd have found a covert way to get it. The word came down to take the baby until Leah learned to behave, so to speak."

"To stop helping me?"

"Not exactly."

Mark decided he'd better try another tack. "I am impressed with HealGene's thoroughness. We only just found out that Becca could have the disease. I assume you're holding Seth Kline too?"

"Look, *I'm* not holding anybody. That end of things is not my doing at all and—"

"Oh, right, I can see you're lily white in all this. The thing is, I have no choice but to accept your dollars and sense," Mark said, praying he could see this through. "I expect Leah to be reunited with Becca immediately, and I want to phone her right now to tell her and be certain she's okay. Now, where's your cell phone?" he asked, starting to get up.

"Not so fast. You just stay put. Since HealGene's been duplicating all your work, I've got to be certain they still want to deal with you—and trust you. I'm going to get an HG lab tech in here to work with you. Don't think I'm trusting you yet," Clark added, wagging the gun at him again.

"You know, pal," Mark said, emphasizing that last word, "considering how deceptive and dirty Heal-Gene's operations are, maybe you'd better not assume they trust you, either."

There was no wind in this abyss; it was the darkest nightmare of the soul. The ravine showed itself in hues of gray, black and blacker, but Leah knew she had to go farther into it. No way was she going to trust this man, comforting words or not.

"I can't let any harm come to you, Leah," Sheriff Martin called down to her. She could see the long shadow he cast above. "So if you don't sing out, I'm just gonna have to come down after you. Believe me, you could get really hurt down there."

A pause, perhaps so his implied threat could sink in. Wind shifted through the tops of the trees.

"Like I said, if you're worried about your friend, Doc Morelli, he's safe. Just hit his head when he skidded into a tree. He's back at his clinic, and I'll let you call him there. Bet he could use some tending."

How long and how closely had Ray Martin been watching them? Had he tampered with the death angel to try to scare her away? But why? And on whose pocketbook, as her *daad* always said.

"Listen up now, girl," he called out, his voice becoming harder, angrier. "If I gotta come down there, I'm not gonna be too happy 'bout that. I'm real tired of you bucking me, especially since I still got it in the back of my mind you might have been involved in some foul play in Sam Yoder's death."

His shadow, thrown by his own headlights, grew as he evidently stepped back from the edge of the ravine. Leah heard his car door open and a strange metallic sound. No, she knew what it was. A rifle being loaded. Both of her brothers hunted, and that sound was unmistakable.

Trying to find firm footholds, she went farther down the steep slant of heavily treed ravine. Saplings shuddered their snow on her from their shaken branches.

Rocks protruded erratically. No path through the ravine here, as there was near her house. She was making her own trail. At least he couldn't bring his big headlights down here with him.

But Leah soon saw a broad beam of light playing through the trees as he came over the lip of the ravine. She heard his weight snap a sapling and he cursed. In case he was following her initial slide through the snow, she headed sideways so she wasn't directly under him.

It was tough going, as she was nearly swinging from the saplings above the rocky drop-offs to the frozen stream. Again she was grateful for her black clothing. When he shifted his search beam in her direction, she turned away from its jerky path through the trees, bracing her boots against protruding roots or rocks.

"Since you're not talking, girl," he called out into the quiet night, "I'm gonna have to make a judgment on one of two things. Either you're hurt real bad, so you can't talk, and I'm gonna find you down in this rocky ravine. Then I can help you, see? Or you're guilty of Sam Yoder's murder, and this is gonna become a hunt for a suspect who's fleeing the law, and that's me. You better cooperate now, so I don't think you killed poor Sam."

When she didn't respond, his voice went up another notch higher, shriller.

"Got a rifle here and I know how to use it. I wasn't a marine sharpshooter for nothing. Your friend, Cop Katie, ever tell you that? I'm real good at tracking prey, especially human prey that make themselves my enemies."

The sapling she was gripping bent. She lost her balance, fell to her knees, and started to roll. She hit her hip hard on an embedded layer of rock that stopped her. But she'd made too much noise.

For some reason, her brain filled with images of Mark holding the baby as all three of them looked at the angel, that day Sam found them standing together like a family. Had the sheriff, or whoever Sam worked for on the sly, killed him to shut him up, or because he demanded more money for whatever he'd done for them? If so, they were good at making things look like accidents, from tipped buggies to Sam's smashed skull. And she wouldn't let them or this man get away with it again.

Leah froze as the light swept over her, past her, then darted back and settled on her, before flitting off again. The sheriff came closer, the metal parts of his rifle hitting on bark as he went from tree to tree. She could hear him taking big breaths as if he was out of shape. Had he spotted her?

She was on the edge of a drop-off above the frozen stream. Like the day she'd visited Andrea Dixon's quilt warehouse, she could hear water rattling below the surface, trapped beneath its icy ceiling. How far below? she wondered. Should she risk jumping if he trapped her on this ledge?

A sudden noise broke her thoughts. For one moment, she thought he'd shot the rifle, but it was not a bullet pinging off a distant rock. It was his cell phone. He turned his light off and answered it. If he hadn't been so close, she might have used the time to crawl farther away. Instead, she fixed her feet more firmly on the stone outcrop and clung between two saplings.

"Sheriff Martin here," he answered the call. "Oh, hi, hon. Working late on something." It must be his wife, Pam. "Got a call from who? Oh, yeah, the builder."

The builder. Could that be a code for whoever the sheriff was working for? If so, his wife was in on it too—but then, with that huge home down South, she'd have to be.

"That right? Now, what a coincidence. No, don't worry about it. I'll handle everything. See you later, hon."

Seth found the vertical section of shaft that must go to the roof for fresh air. A wire-mesh grate was between him and it, but he found that it simply lifted out. Was he dreaming? Even though it was night, some light grayed the narrow metal tunnel, a straight shaft for once. And best of all, it had an attached ladder he could climb!

He was going to get to the roof and escape or at least call for help. He was going to be free and warn Teacher Leah that evil people were after her.

He climbed easily and steadily. It felt great not to have to crawl. Still, he tried to keep quiet because this air vent echoed. He expected to come up inside of one of those large, mushroom-shaped things that rotated on roofs he'd seen. He prayed he'd be able to work his way out of that. But when he reached the top of the shaft, he was amazed to find himself looking up at the open night sky. The pinpoints of a couple of stars even poked through the clots of clouds.

It was windy up here. He filled his lungs with free air.

But as his eyes adjusted, he saw he was too high to escape easily—sky high. It seemed impossible, but he was on the top of a tall, wide silo. Another one loomed right next to it, attached as if they were Siamese twins. Below lay other buildings and then black fields.

He knew where he was! He was at the AgraGro Mill, which overlooked Mr. Mason's big maple stand and Teacher Leah's house just across the western side of the ravine. If it weren't so dark, he could probably see for miles.

He also saw a small platform just outside this shaft, but he knew he'd never get down from here. The top of the silo was so curved and steep—no doubt slick with ice or snow that must have just fallen—he'd plunge right off if he left this cubbyhole.

Seth nearly jumped out of his skin when he heard a metallic, unearthly voice behind him. He turned to see a humanlike creature with bulging eyes sprawled almost flat at the very edge of the platform, looking out and away from him.

"I read you, Sheriff," the monster said in perfectly clear English. "I've got my night goggles trained that way. She darts out across the field, you want me to shoot her right away or let her get on the property first?"

After talking to his wife, the sheriff had made another call, but Leah wasn't certain to whom or even what he'd said. He'd turned slightly away and muffled his words.

Silence again. Leah's pulse picked up even more. Frozen in place, she huddled, still as a statue, not daring to breathe.

"Got to level with you now, Leah," the sheriff said, talking loudly. Maybe he didn't know she was this close to him? "I got standing orders from the folks I work for that they don't want you harmed, only reined in a bit. You been making me pretty mad, defying me and getting in the way, but the thing is, I think you'll listen to reason about your baby. Hey, she's just five minutes away and needs you real bad."

Leah's heart both thrilled and feared. Was this just another ploy to make her give her position away? No, if he knew her baby was gone, he had to be in on the crimes.

"Don't let this gun scare you now. I'm putting it down against this tree, leaving it here."

She heard him put it down and turned her head, squinting in his direction around the edge of her bonnet. He shone his light down as he wedged the rifle against a tree. Then he walked away from it, heading toward her.

"Now you just listen up, Leah, and maybe we can make us a deal here. You know," he went on, "all you had to do was clear out of that old house so you weren't so close to what was going on at AgraGro. They couldn't trust your spying on it, coming over to stare at the place, watching the train come in with supplies and test subjects on board."

Test subjects at AgraGro! The flour mill? Her walks to look at the remodeling and repainting of that place had started all this? Then that building must house the clinic she had thought she'd find hidden at Andrea's warehouse or at MR in Cleveland! And Becca was there?

"But then, you made things even touchier by getting in with Mark, the golden boy I had to keep an eye on. All of us had to treat him with kid gloves, see? Now if both of you swear to work with your competition, not fight us, we'll give you Becca back and let bygones be bygones, that's my orders. And one more thing. There's money in this, Leah, big money, enough to treat all the Amish who are ill, both kids and adults, money to cure these tragic genetic diseases that plague your people."

He paused again. She could hear him breathing heavily. The ravine was silent, but for the sheriff and the unseen stream below, rattling rhythmically. Two terrible lines from a haunting poem by Byron darted through her thoughts: *For the Angel of Death spread his wings on the blast/And breathed in the face of the foe as he pass'd.*

"Whatever happens," the sheriff's voice rang out, "I want you to know none of this is my fault. I helped them for money, sure, but like I said, I think they will help your people in the process."

They. The Dixons must be bribing the sheriff. The money Sam had was probably theirs too. Since their clinic in Cleveland was so far away, they'd set up a local one here, checking Mark's work, looking for a way to make him join forces with them.

"I didn't want to ride herd on Morelli at all, but they insisted," the sheriff went on. "I tried to warn him off with that sign on his clinic door, tried to make it look like some illiterate Amish kids did it. I wanted him to be careful, just like I want you to be now, thinking over the choice you have. To keep quiet and get Becca back—or not.

"I could have just burned your house down so you had to move out, but I tried to warn you by using that angel to psych you out. I kind of enjoyed that, thinking things up, using brains instead of brawn for once. See, Sam and I worked for the same employer, and he told me about the flower necklace you and his wife had put on that statue. I even tried to scare you about Varina Roscoe. My wife told me that sad story before it was even in the paper."

He chuckled at that. The man Maplecreek trusted to keep order was the defiler of it. He had profited and pleased himself through it all. Was he just playing with her now to get her to give away her position? Or was he really under orders not to hurt Mark and, since she was Mark's assistant, not to hurt her, either? And would he really reunite her with Becca?

"I had plans to hang an Amish doll with a noose round its neck from the angel's throat, but I thought that might be a bit over the top." He shouted a sharp laugh. "Now that *might* have sent you running. But you just wouldn't bite, wouldn't budge. I admire your spunk and smarts, girl. I'll enjoy working with you, instead of against you."

She heard him take a breath and shift his position. "Talk to me, dammit!" he shouted. "I've got orders to take you to the AgraGro place to talk to the powers that be and get your baby back! Believe me, if you try to get outside help and get into that place on your own, Becca will be gone with all the rest."

What did he mean by that? Maybe they could quickly evacuate everyone in the clinic on one of those trains? Tears squeezed through her eyelids. From her house, from that window next to Becca's empty crib, she could actually see the place her baby had been taken. So close but yet so far, these two desperate days she'd searched for her.

"Your baby's been crying a lot lately, ailing, I guess. It gets on a lot of people's nerves, know what I mean? I'm sure you could quiet her so they don't have to."

Another veiled threat. But could Becca really be ill? Leah didn't trust this man, but she couldn't bear for Becca to be without her one moment more. The sheriff was so close he'd probably find her anyway. She was almost ready to fall off this ledge, and if there was any chance at all that she could have one more moment with Becca, she should seize it. If he took her to the covert clinic at AgraGro, she'd find some way to escape with Becca.

And if they kept her there too, Louise would soon discover she was gone. Maybe she'd look into things and learn that the baby she tended was not Rebecca Yoder.

"All right," she spoke up, trying desperately to sound strong. "I'll go with you, Sheriff, if I can have my baby back."

"Now that's more like it," he said with an audible sigh of relief.

She held her breath, praying, as he shuffled closer on the stone ledge. Hanging on to two saplings, she stood and turned to face him.

"Most of what I told you is true, Leah," he said, sounding angry yet apologetic. "But the thing is, I just got a call from my wife, telling me Katie Brand is on my trail down South. You overstepped, girl. I'll have to tell my bosses that you ran into the ravine and fell off a ledge before I could bring you to the mill like they want, like when I had to stop Sam for wanting more money. Honest, I'm real sorry… The boss said not to hurt you, but I got a wife and kids to think about."

Too late, Leah knew she'd made another mistake, a fatal one this time. He wasn't going to put a bullet in her, but he wasn't going to let her see Becca one last time, either. He was simply, easily, going to shove her off the ledge to the rocky streambed below.

20

Mark listened intently as Clark held a quick, furtive argument with someone on his cell phone across the room. He could only pick up a few occasional words, but *another chance* and *Leah's baby* had been among them. All the time, Clark kept the gun pointed in Mark's direction.

He'd been rehearsing his options but they were few. At least until Clark let him talk to Leah and make sure she and Becca were okay, he had to cooperate.

He suddenly realized he'd sacrifice anything for them, including his life. He'd always told himself that his work had to be protected above all else, but he'd found things that meant more. Leah. Becca. The generous Amish of Maplecreek whom he'd come to care for. Yet the needs of those people brought him right back to his work.

"Sinclair Marshall must think a lot of you if he lets you call him this time of night," Mark said when Clark punched off the phone.

"I was talking to his...ah, let's say his lieutenant, who oversees local operations. He says he doesn't like or trust you, but as long as you agree to have a combination lab tech and watchdog live here with you, he'll give it a try."

"Who is this lieutenant? Is he or she from here or was this person brought in to work—oversee operations—here?"

"Not a need-to-know for you yet. Everyone takes orders from above now, including you."

"And I'll be rewarded for this?"

"Royally. You can start adding onto this piddly place tomorrow or build a high-tech lab from scratch somewhere around here. We will work with you now, Mark, not against you."

"And here," he said, sarcasm sharpening his voice, "I thought you and I had always been on the same team. But what do I expect from a guy who has dollar signs in his eyes, like some cartoon character?"

"Don't push it! Our past only gets you so far."

"So I see. And it hurts like hell."

They glared at each other for one long moment. Clark looked away first, down at the gun he held as if he couldn't believe it was in his hand.

"You said I could call Leah," Mark reminded him.

"Yeah, let me check on that."

"I have her number."

"In a way, so do I. Just stay put, because until your new assistant arrives tomorrow morning, it's still me, you and this gun. It's too bad things got so out of hand here. One more wrong move from you, though, and you can kiss Leah goodbye."

Mark watched him make another call. It *did* hurt
like hell that his best friend had betrayed him, but the
fear of losing Leah loomed larger. He prayed she'd
stayed locked in at home, but after his frenzied phone
call to her, he feared he knew better. What if she'd gone
out on the roads to try to find him? Sure, she was
naive, as Clark had said, but she was brave and even
brazen when it came to those she loved. She loved
Becca more than anything, and he hoped he had a
place in her heart too.

"Damn," he heard Clark mutter. "Why doesn't he
answer?"

The sheriff had gone silent, after all his earlier talking. He was intent only on her, Leah thought, like a
hawk ready to hit a rabbit. His cell phone rang repeatedly, muffled somewhere in his jacket, but he paid no
attention to it this time. He reached one big hand toward her; it wouldn't take much to send her tumbling.
He thrust his light in her face, blinding her, and shoved
her left shoulder.

Holding on to one of the saplings, Leah yanked the
other back and let it go.

With a whir and a snap, it whipped him, crotch to
forehead.

He cried out and clawed at her, trying to grab her,
but missed. Leah held to the sapling and stretched to
reach the bare branch of a bigger tree above her head.
She snagged it with one hand.

In a split second that seemed like eternity, Leah held
on tight as Sheriff Martin pitched off backward into
blackness, fanning his arms as if he could fly.

His light fell too, bouncing, hitting. Its beam raked the ravine and then went out. Below, she heard the man's big body shatter ice, freeing the water it held back.

Then nothing. Nothing but her own panting and her sobs.

Seth ducked his head back down the shaft so fast he almost fell off the metal ladder. The man on the roof had a rifle with a big, raised sight. He'd said he could see in the dark with those night goggles. And it sounded as if he was waiting to shoot Teacher Leah, that she might be coming here. Worse, he'd been talking to the sheriff, who must know all this stuff going on and wasn't doing anything to help.

Seth couldn't decide what to do. If he weren't Amish, he'd risk sneaking up behind the man to try to push him off. But then he'd be committing violence and murder, even if it was for a good cause.

He could huddle here and wait until he heard the man get ready to take a shot, then burst up on top and kick his gun away. But the man could throw him off, and he would be too late to save Teacher Leah. And what if the man started down the ladder or looked into the air shaft? He could pick Seth off like shooting fish in a barrel.

Maybe he should go back down. He hadn't noticed whether the ladder went clear to the ground, because the tunnel was darker below. His hands were sweating so bad, even in this cold air, that he was afraid he'd fall the length of the shaft and end up dead after all.

When Leah stopped shaking, she realized she had several choices. She could go down to the streambed

to see if the sheriff was dead and, if his cell phone still
worked, call Mark.

But what if he wasn't dead and grabbed her? And
it was not likely his phone survived the fall, even if he
did.

No, she had to do whatever she could to get to
Becca at the AgraGro clinic—if that's where she was.
And that meant a long climb up, not down.

She considered taking the sheriff's rifle with her,
but she had no notion of how to use it. She was probably going to have to talk her way into the clinic. She'd
be better off using wile than a weapon, though she still
had her butcher knife taped to her thigh.

The climb was long and difficult, sometimes two
steps up and one sliding back. Thank God, maples
grew thick here in the ravine, but most of them were
young and bended easily. Miles Mason evidently
hadn't tapped any yet. She wondered if he tended the
maple trees in the woods beyond the AgraGro Mill.

When she made it to flat ground again, she fell to
her knees, panting at her grueling exertions. Her heart
was nearly pounding out of her chest when she saw her
battered buggy. She must get going now, run to the
mill, but she had one more thing to do first.

When she opened Mark's car door, his dome light
popped on. Gasping, she threw herself into the front
seat over the protruding gearbox. Once she realized the
source of the light, she sat up and looked around.

His now-deflated airbag had been deployed from
his steering wheel. Praying it had kept him from real
harm, she rummaged through the glove compartment
for paper and pen, then scribbled a note:

*Secret clinic inside AgraGro Mill. Gone there to
find Becca. Sheriff tried to kill me and fell into
ravine. Leah Kurtz. April 3.*

She wanted to leave the note on the windshield, but
it might blow away, so she left it on his dashboard. Too
bad, she thought, gripping Mark's steering wheel, that
she hadn't really learned to drive. She'd never backed
up in a car, for the one she'd driven briefly years ago
had already had its engine running and she'd only
made it go forward.

But as she got out again, she stared at the sheriff's
van. It was headed in the right direction, toward the
bridge and the mill. Could he have been in such a rush
he left the keys in it?

Nervously, she approached the dark hulk. It had no
police emblems on its exterior, so it must be his private vehicle—or belong to the people he worked for.
She pulled the handle on the driver's side, and the
door popped open. This ceiling light, too, came on.
Holding her breath, she leaned in.

The keys were in the ignition.

If Leah were out looking for him, Mark theorized, she
would have found his car, assuming Clark was telling the
truth about leaving it where it was until morning. When
she didn't find him in his car, she would have tried to call
him, but either Clark had his cell phone and had turned
it off, or it was lost somewhere. And if she couldn't call
him, it would be like Leah to come looking for him—
unless something terrible had happened to her, too.

He couldn't remain Clark's prisoner anymore. He

didn't have the luxury of time if Leah had been caught or hurt.

"You said I could talk to Leah," he told Clark again and got unsteadily to his feet.

"But I didn't say you could get up and walk around!" Clark said, leveling the gun at him again.

"Let me talk to Leah now, or the deal is off."

Clark crunched through the broken glass on the floor as he came closer. "Sit!"

"I'm not some damn trained dog. Why don't you just go ahead and shoot me? Just call that local lieutenant—the bloodsucker of these innocent Amish—or tell Sinclair Marshall that the NAA gene doctor's blood is all over his clinic floor because you shot him. Maybe they can use my DNA to clone the next doctor they can push around or try to buy off or threaten—"

"Are you going to shut up and sign on with us, or not? I'm telling you, it's the only way to get Leah and her baby back together."

"I don't see any evidence of that!" Mark accused, though he did finally see a way to get that gun. The quilt Andrea Dixon had given him was still draped loosely over the arm of the couch, where he'd thrown it after searching it yesterday. If he could just obscure Clark's vision for one second, even if he fired the gun, the bullet might go awry and he could tackle him.

"Okay, okay," Mark said, holding up both hands, palms out as if in surrender. "Just let me talk to her, and I'm on board for good."

As if to sit on the arm of the couch, he stepped back. He pretended to move the quilt away, then flung it as he hit the floor behind the couch.

The bullet banged somewhere into the room. A second followed. By the third, he'd tackled Clark and had him down again. They struggled for the gun. This time, Mark vowed, he wasn't going to lose.

Leah had no trouble starting the van. She tested both the right and left foot pedals to remind herself which one was the forward and which the brake. She peered through the steering wheel at the dials and numbers, but had no idea how to make the lights come on. Still, maybe this was better done in the dark, in case the sheriff hadn't told them he was coming to the clinic. But why didn't the van move when she stepped on the forward pedal?

She fumbled with the handle on the gearbox beside her. Finally, the van jerked back until she hit the brake; when she moved the handle again, it rolled ahead. She let it go slowly, giving all her attention to steering the big vehicle across the one-lane bridge and then keeping it on the road as she moved past the ravine. She was suddenly scared that Sheriff Martin would rise from the ravine like a ghost and try to stop her. She shook her head to clear it and drove on.

Staring ahead through the windshield at the few lights on at the mill, she saw it with new eyes. Last year, people in town had wondered what sort of rebuilding and remodeling was being done inside, but the hate crimes Katie and Luke Brand were fighting had taken everyone's attention. No one had seen this outrage right before their eyes, like something hidden in plain sight.

She leaned forward and gripped the wheel harder. The sheriff had said that, at first, they wanted her out of her house because they thought she might be watching them at the mill. But she'd only been taking walks. Taking walks and enjoying her new life with Becca.

Maybe Sam had been bought off because he was onto the clinic hidden in the mill. Or had he been selling the Dixons something besides silence, like Barbara's blood?

The van bumped off the berm, but she managed to avoid the shallow ditch that ran along the field and to steer back onto the road. She had no idea what she'd say or do to get inside, but she was going to find Becca, at all costs.

Still huddled in the air shaft at the top of the ladder, Seth heard the man above him talking again. Though he'd been about to retreat, he froze and strained to listen.

"Hey, boss, tell Clark I can't raise the sheriff either, but I gotta assume that's his van heading here. He said she'd be on foot—if she even got out of the ravine. Yeah, strictly tranquilizer darts. No, he knew you said not to hurt her. Far as I can tell, he might be bringing her in. The van's halfway down the field."

There was a long pause. Whoever was on the other end of that conversation was evidently yelling into the phone. Seth couldn't pick out words, but he could hear a raised voice from here.

"Yeah, yeah, got it. Just have the gate guard check out who's in the van then. And listen, I don't care how damn angry you get if things get screwed up, you better give me fair warning if you decide to blow this thing. When Sinclair Marshall sent me here, he swore there'd be no Armageddon unless that was the only way to cover things up. Hey, you swear to it, or I'm coming down there in person…"

Seth skidded down the ladder so fast he felt he was going to fall. He stopped at the grated door where his original horizontal shaft had intersected with the vertical one. Yes, this grate lifted off, and he could feel the top of a ladder to take him down. This must be how the guy with the tranquilizer gun got to the top of the silo from the ground. Though he hadn't seen a rifle, he must have been shot with some sort of tranquilizer the day of the Brand wedding. But all he knew now was he wasn't going to get knocked out again.

But what had the guy with the goggles meant about blowing this thing? What thing?

At least, Seth sure knew what Armageddon meant. In the Book of the Revelation in the Bible, it was the final, bloody fight between the forces of good and evil.

Mark hog-tied Clark with cords he yanked off the vertical blinds in his reception room, then taped him with adhesive bandages, including over his mouth. He took his cell phone and tried Leah's number, but no one answered. Knowing she didn't like or trust the sheriff, and he'd learned to listen to her instincts, he called the State Highway Patrol. He told them that Clark had assaulted him with a pistol and where he could find him.

"No," he told the patrol dispatcher as he took Clark's keys and ran outside to Clark's car, "I can't stay on the line. I'm hoping a friend who's in trouble will call me. But I'm heading out to 1008 Deer Run Road to check on her."

As soon as he was speeding down Deer Run, he realized he should have kept Clark with him for safekeeping, but finding Leah and Becca was all he could think about. When he turned into Leah's driveway and saw the horse shed open and empty, he knew in his gut she wasn't here. His first hunch must have been right. She'd gone out to the bridge to try to find him. But that was a couple of hours ago, so why hadn't she come to his place or back home?

As he backed out to turn around, his headlights caught the angel statue. Its throat was red—bloodied, slashed like the woman whose grave it guarded, with some sort of animal blood, no doubt. He thought of the GET OUT JEANS DR!! DON'T PLAY GOD OR YOUR DEAD!!! sign on his clinic door. But the truth was, HealGene and those it had paid big bucks to were the ones playing God.

Fear churned like bile in his belly as he roared back the way he'd chased the van earlier tonight—no, yesterday now. Clark's dashboard clock read 1:00 a.m.

He braked carefully to take the right turn toward the covered bridge, then sped up again, despite his dread of having another wreck. His headlights caught the gleam of his car, the hood wrapped around a tree trunk. Even with a seat belt on and his air bag deployed, it was no wonder he'd hit his head and blacked out. He was blessed not to have whiplash.

He parked Clark's car but left the engine running and the headlights on. Getting out, he gasped.

Over by the tree line—a battered buggy! He ran to it. One wheel off, dented and bent, but thank God, no Leah inside. "Leah!" he shouted, cupping his hands around his mouth. "Leah!" But all he heard was the wind, moaning through bare tree branches.

When he headed back toward Clark's car, he saw the entire story caught in the headlights, in the new-fallen snow. The narrow tracks that the thin, steel-rimmed buggy wheels had made were erratic. A wide-wheeled vehicle had bumped into the buggy and shoved it around, then toward the ravine. And over here, the horse had run loose alone.

Nell. Had the wreck been so bad it had freed the horse? But he saw footprints, two pairs of booted ones, one set like the old-fashioned rubbers Leah wore, the others heeled, a man's bigger feet. Both pairs of boots went back and forth from the ravine—into the ravine? She'd come back up again, but had the man in the van? The big vehicle had driven off, loopily, toward the covered bridge.

He told himself Leah couldn't be driving the van, but he knew better. To where? It didn't double back toward town.

He knew he had to follow, but first he had to check his car to see if his cell phone was there. He couldn't help hoping that she would still try to contact him on it.

He saw her note on the dashboard, even before he opened the car door. He grabbed and read it, horrified. She must have driven the sheriff's van to the AgraGro clinic. But that was over a quarter hour ago!

He sprinted for Clark's car, fumbling with Clark's

cell phone to call the highway patrol again. His best friend had betrayed him, but he'd also given him the means to get to Leah—if he wasn't too late.

The twin silos of the AgraGro Mill loomed ever larger before Leah. After the brown van bumped over the railroad tracks, she brought it to a stop just outside the wire gate. A man she didn't recognize walked out of the mill building itself where the wheat was ground to flour to be stored in the silos. In what part of the complex, she wondered, was the clinic? Part of it still had to be a working mill, didn't it?

Maybe she'd been crazy to drive in rather than sneaking in, but the thin wire fence was not only high but looked electrified, like the system Louise Winslow's husband had recently installed for cattle fences.

She gripped the steering wheel so hard that her fingers cramped. The guard opened the gate and approached—he didn't look armed, at least. She wasn't sure how to roll the window down when he stopped and looked in at her, so she cracked her door and nearly fell out when he pulled it all the way open.

"This your van, ma'am?"

If this man was local, she'd never seen him.

"Ah, no, it's Sheriff Martin's private vehicle. He's been hurt in the ravine and needs help, and this was the fastest vehicle and the closest place. Can you send someone? I think he's broken his leg, and I've hurt my ankle trying to help him. It's so cold out here, could I come inside until help arrives?"

"You have help coming?"

"Not if you don't call for it."

"Why didn't he call for help on his cell phone?"

"I said he fell down the ravine. He broke it."

"The Amish don't drive, ma'am, and it's the middle of the night. Don't you have a buggy—"

"Of course I do, but the Amish do know how to drive. We can learn before we take our final church vows to renounce modern technology." She had no clue what she'd say next. Desperate and panicked, she only knew she had to get inside to find Becca. "Can't you please help me to help him?" she cried, her voice pleading.

"Sure, sure. It's fine if you come on in, and I'll call for help. We just can't be too careful at night, you know."

Ah, she thought, had he given something away? Why would they need to be careful if this were just a flour mill?

She faked limping on her left ankle. He was letting her inside! But the office they entered gave no hint of being part of being either a mill or a modern medical facility of any kind. Dull walls, a single desk, metal file cabinets, an empty gun rack on the wall. This was a far cry from the Dixons' other place in Cleveland.

"Right in here, ma'am," he said, indicating another door. "Why don't you just wait in here."

She was elated that the room she entered had a second door. As soon as the guard left to make the call, she'd sneak out to see the rest of the complex. They might set off a general alarm for her, but all she needed was a few minutes to hide and a few prayers that this clinic didn't have a palm-print ID entry through its doors. A secret, rural clinic wouldn't have all that security technology, would it?

As soon as the guard stepped out and closed the door behind him in this dim room, she rushed to the opposite door. But as she did, forgetting her fake limp, she heard a man dramatically clear his throat behind her.

She froze, then turned, fully expecting to face a furious Brad Dixon. But, even though the man sat in shadow, she could tell it wasn't Mark's former boss at all.

"Hello, sweetheart," he said. "Doggone it, I knew you'd come around sooner or later." He shouted a sharp laugh as if he'd made the most hilarious joke. Only then did she surmount her shock to realize who it was.

21

"Jesse—Dr. Cutler!" Leah cried. "You—here."

"I'm delighted you're surprised," he said and chuckled again. "It just shows what good work I'm doing on my moonlighting job. And I can't tell you how many nights I've fantasized that Saint Leah would come to me and say, 'I'm yours.'"

She tried the handle of the door she was near. Locked. She'd have to double back. But he emerged from the shadows to stand between her and the door she came in. He stood grinning, legs slightly spread, arms crossed over his chest.

"I don't know why you're here," she said, her voice quavering, "and don't want to. I just want my baby back, then I'll leave without another word about any of this."

"I can see you're thrilled at the prospect of our romantic tryst. Believe me," he said, whispering now, shifting nearer, "no one will ever know you came here to do anything I ask."

"Is Becca here?" Her voice broke, betraying her fear. "I want to see her, or at least talk to Brad or Andrea Dixon."

"Who?" he demanded, looking sincerely surprised.

"Oh, you mean Morelli's former employer? No, Leah, you're here to be with me. And you're going to prove that right now, or I'll have to assume the worst. If I do that, neither you nor Becca are going anywhere."

"Then she *is* here!" She clasped her hands. "Please, whatever you have in mind, just—"

"What I have in mind is you coming over here and proving to me you never meant to slight and insult me. That you've just been playing hard to get. That your relationship with the precious gene doctor, who I have to protect when I'd like to put him permanently in my little cemetery—"

"With the dead dogs, you mean," she blurted, before she realized she should play dumb.

"Were you the one who set my warning device off by Pet Haven Tuesday night? Poor Leah, afraid to knock on my door when Miles Mason showed up. But you wanted to, didn't you? You wanted me then, too."

"Stop saying that! I want Becca and that's all, so—"

He leaped at her, dragged her, pinned her to the wall with his body. The ring of keys he wore on his belt ground against her hip bone. He ripped off her bonnet and *kapp*, loosing her hair in a wild curtain. He tangled one hand in it to tip her head back and bent to kiss her. When she still managed to turn her face away, he nuzzled her neck and jammed a leg between her thighs.

His breath hot, he spoke against her throat. "I know you're stubborn, Leah, but you're not stupid. I'm giving you a way out, a reason not to have you just disappear permanently. I'd hate to have to put you in my pet cemetery with the other failed experiments."

She had started to fight him, but she froze, pressed to the wall. "Those aren't…really pets…buried there?"

"Sure, they are—above the bigger coffins of my employer's gene therapy experiments gone wrong. Those people were mostly from Atlanta, a few from here. People who just disappeared, so let that be a word to the wise."

"People from here? Amish?"

"As a matter of fact, I think you knew one who gave us his all—Joseph Lantz."

She gasped. Joseph! He hadn't just run away those years ago. Even then, some pharm firm had been trolling the quiet waters of Amish country for their own purpose and profit. And they'd killed him! Whoever owned this place, they'd killed him! But she wasn't going to end up in a pet cemetery guarded by this demon—and neither were Becca or Seth.

She fought to keep her voice calm. Maybe she could get to the knife she still had strapped to her thigh. "Jesse, are you really a gene doctor too?"

He laughed deep in his throat. "Oh, they'd love to hear that in Atlanta."

Atlanta again. What was that where they'd taken Joseph before they'd built this place here? Mark had told her about a huge biotech-pharm firm in Atlanta. Andrea Dixon's father ran it, but he was estranged from the Dixons.

"By the way, you got me so excited when you came calling," he said, "I forgot to ask what happened to the sheriff. He was to bring you back, and then you're suddenly driving his van in here. Did he tip you off to this place, or did you figure it out another way? And where

the hell is he? Talk, sweetheart!" he demanded and
ripped open her cloak. With his free hand, he roughly
fondled her breasts through her dress.

She gritted her teeth at his touch. She had to outthink
this man, try to take his keys and get away from him.
Despite her vow to do no violence, she had to get to her
knife.

"I'll tell you where he is if you tell me where Becca
is. If you give me just a little space, you'll find I can
cooperate," she said, struggling not to just spit in his
face.

She freed one hand and started to lift her skirt. But
what if he put his hand under her clothes and felt the
knife? She tried to both shift him away, yet lift her skirt
and slip higher.

"Now you're getting it," he said and laughed at
some private joke again.

"Tell me where Becca is."

"You first." He pressed her harder into the wall and
shoved his hand up her skirt, but luckily, along the hip
that didn't have the tape holding the knife. He stroked
her there, then shifted his hand behind to grab her but-
tock. She let him, just to keep his hands away from the
knife, though she couldn't get to it now either.

"The sheriff is down at the bottom of the ravine, injured or dead," she said, her voice steady now. "He tried
to kill me, though he said his orders were not to hurt
me. If you gave those orders, Jesse, I'm really grateful."

He was starting to breathe heavily. "Now you know
why I wanted you safe," he murmured, clamping her
closer to him. "And I had orders not to upset Morelli.
I wanted you with me—like this."

"And Becca?"

"You prove you're mine, we'll keep her too."

"I mean, where is she?"

"Upstairs, third floor. Don't worry, we'll get her later—after."

"This office building has no third floor."

"In the south silo. Medical hubs—in the center of each floor of the silos. The only wheat grain here is in the big storage bins behind the place."

She began to draw a mental map. "So parts of this are still a working mill?"

"Barely. Just enough goes out to—" His head jerked up and his hand stopped groping her. "You don't have a bug on you, a listening device? The sheriff didn't turn on us and send you in here?"

"Of course not."

"I'll believe you when you strip for me. Fast or slow will do," he said with an expression between a grin and a leer. Still he didn't loosen his grip on her, didn't step back as she was hoping. "Sweetheart, I'm going to have to check you thoroughly for hidden bugs," he said and laughed.

He seemed back in control of himself. Despite her frenzy to get rid of this man and get to Becca, things started to fall into place. Whoever was behind this big, expensive effort had the sheriff and Jesse on his payroll. Jesse must have been the one watching Mark, because their places were right across the street from each other. Since he'd suspected a bug on her, Jesse might have bugged the gene clinic, but Mark had somehow missed the device.

"Look," he said, grinding against her, "let's just

make this a business deal, then. This isn't much of a romantic setting, but you just prove to me here and now that you're dealing in good faith—"

It was too much. She didn't know whether to laugh, cry or scream. So she kneed him hard, the way her friend Katie had taught her to if she was ever cornered by bullies. She shoved him away and ran for the door she'd come in. But it opened to nearly bang into her. The guard who had brought her in stood there with a pistol in one hand.

"Hey, what the—" the man clipped out as Jesse doubled over to retch on the floor. The guard grabbed Leah's arm and flung her back into the room, then bent to help Jesse.

"Dr. Cutler, you all right? I don't know how it happened, but Frank just called from the roof to say our cover may be blown. He can see at least two police vehicles on the dead-end street by the girl's house, so she must have called them."

"I didn't," she insisted. "I want my baby back, that's all."

Both men ignored her, as the guard went on, "And Clark Quinn's car's coming toward us on the access road, but he isn't answering his cell, any more than the sheriff."

Clark Quinn! Now the rest of the puzzle fit. It would kill Mark to learn his best friend had betrayed him.

"If the cops start across that ravine and field on foot," the guard told Jesse, "I say we got us about fifteen minutes max, but you're the one's got to give the word if no one's here from HealGene."

That was it, Leah thought, HealGene, the Atlanta

pharm. But having answers to every question she'd ever asked wouldn't mean a thing if she didn't find Becca.

Jesse stood with the guard's help and wiped the back of his mouth with his trembling hand. He looked as terrified as she felt.

"All right," he told the guard, sucking in a deep breath. "Set Armageddon for twelve minutes. If the cops swarm the place, they go up with it. Sound the alarm for personnel. And you," he added, glaring at her, "can blow sky high with that baby of yours and the NAA girl's brother, you Amish whore!"

"Seth? Seth is here—" Without a backward glance, Jesse, with the help of the guard, staggered to the door, went out and slammed it. She heard him lock it.

A buzzer-type alarm began. It hummed a moment, then was silent, then hummed again. Armageddon? Did he really mean they were going to blow up this place? Maybe they had it rigged with explosives. He'd said part of this was still a working flour mill. The article in the paper about another mill stuck in her mind: a grain-dust explosion had left people inside dead and those nearby severely burned.

With Leah's note jammed in his jacket pocket, Mark sped over the narrow covered bridge and raced toward the mill. The highway patrol dispatcher had hardly believed him when he said to send help there. Mark had never given the place more than a glance, though its presence had always been felt beyond the western town limits, especially from Leah's house. He'd seen it from her attic window the day he'd put insulation in for her. With its silhouette above the trees, it had looked simply antique and picturesque.

Under the two outside pole lights and beyond the train tracks and tall wire fence, he saw people running out of the building and heading around in back. Did they have some warning that he had called the authorities? The gate was closed, so, bracing himself, he ran Clark's car right through it. Sparks flew; he felt a jolt. The damn thing must have been electrified.

At least no one tried to keep him from entering as he got out of the car and ran for the door. It was locked, but a woman in medical scrubs raced out, looking panicked yet dazed, as if she'd been asleep. Jamming his foot in the door to keep it from closing, Mark grabbed her shoulders and shook her once. From inside he heard some sort of alarm.

"What's happening? I'm Dr. Morelli, here to see the HealGene rep on-site. I want to sign on, do what I can here."

"Oh—the gene doctor. But your car wreck was just—" She bit her lower lip. Her eyes were wide with fear. She knew about his wreck just a few hours ago? Could she have been there?

"Talk to me, or you're not going anywhere. What's happening?"

"The guy in charge is still inside, getting some samples that weren't transferred yet. Let me go! That's—that's a fire alarm."

He had to move fast. Shoving her aside, Mark went into the building. He inhaled deeply but didn't smell smoke. The alarm was much louder in here, and a man was coming down the short hall toward him with a rack of glass vials in his hands. He too looked panicked, even more so when he saw Mark block his way.

It was Jesse Cutler!

"You bastard!" Mark cracked out. "Where's Leah and the baby?"

"She's here—being reunited with Becca. Too many people know about this place, so we're leaving it—that's the signal to clear out."

"Not a fire alarm, then, is it? If there's a fire, it could cause an explosion."

To his amazement, Jesse hooted a laugh.

"Cutler," Mark shouted, "you're not going anywhere until I find Leah and Becca safe. Your legal eagle is already in custody, and your sheriff buddy is down at the bottom of the ravine, so the jig is up and—"

Jesse threw the tray of vials at him, shoved him and tried to run past. Mark hit him with an uppercut, then tripped him, sending him sprawling into the glass and blood. Mark dragged him off the floor and slammed him back into the wall, once, twice.

"I said, where are they?" he shouted.

"Upstairs, third floor of the south silo, I swear it," he cried, holding up his bloody hands as Mark drew a fist back to hit him again. "Here, take my master keys."

On the man's belt, Mark saw the ring of keys. When Jesse fumbled with them, Mark yanked them free. "Thanks, but you're coming with me."

"No! No, I'll surrender to the police outside. Someone called them. They're over at Leah's place."

Thank God, Mark thought, they'd come at least that close.

"Let me go," Jesse pleaded. "This place—it's

rigged to blow up in less than ten minutes. To cover everything, like you said, a grain-dust explosion that will set off a chain of blasts, impossible to disprove and—"

Despite the fact Mark knew he might have given him the idea to lie about an explosion, he smelled no smoke that would indicate a fire. And those running like rats off a sinking ship had looked so panicked— and Cutler was frenzied.

He had to move fast, and this guy was dead weight. Mark threw him down on his face in the glass and blood. He ran down the hall into the heart of the complex, praying he could find his way to the south silo's third floor in time to save Becca and Leah.

Seth heard the muted echoes of an alarm. They had probably learned he'd escaped and that was the signal for a full search. The alarm vibrated the shaft. He'd come down all the way to the bottom, so he assumed he was on the first floor. He had to find the way out of here before everyone came looking for him.

Unfortunately, it was pitch-black. The gray light above didn't filter this far down from the top of the silo. He'd taken several turns in the vents. In the dark, besides the rhythmic alarm, he could hear a strange clanking and shouts, maybe a woman's voice.

Could they realize he was somewhere in their air-flow system and were hitting on the shafts to tell him he'd better come out? Was that woman doctor, who had drawn his blood and whose voice he'd often overheard when he was locked up, shouting at him to show himself?

He found the entry from this large vertical shaft and

crawled in the direction of the sounds. He figured he wasn't under the silos anymore. Yes, a woman's shouts, that's what the racket sounded like now, but he was pretty sure it wasn't the evil doctor's voice.

He began to see squares of gray light ahead and passed the grated vents of rooms like his, only these were square and not triangular. They might be offices, but not quite like the one the man in the business suit had fled earlier. No one was in them and the doors stood ajar. If he could only get out into one, he'd be free.

Still, he had to find the woman who was shouting. Strangely, it sounded like Teacher Leah, not that she had scolded her scholars much or raised her voice too often.

Peeking through the third grate, he saw her pounding on a door with a chair, shouting, "Let me out of here! Someone, stop and unlock this door!" He yelled her name three times through the air grate before she heard him and turned around to look his way.

Mark tore up the first staircase he found. He saw two more men running down the first flight toward him. The scene made him think of what it must have been like for the firefighters going up the stairs of the doomed World Trade towers while others were fleeing downward. And that reminded him, he had to warn the highway patrol guys about the coming disaster.

The pair approached him on the stairs. One wore pajamas; the other was dressed like a lab tech. He grabbed the guy who looked sleepy and pressed him back into the staircase wall.

"There's a three-month-old infant up on the third

floor," Mark said, holding the man by the flimsy lapels
of his pajamas. His top two buttons popped off.
"Maybe NAA unit, maybe not. Where is she?"

The other man spoke, though he didn't break stride
down the stairs, "Top door at the right, second floor,
not third. Somebody told you wrong," his words
floated back, echoing in the stairwell.

Cursing Cutler, Mark took the stairs up two at a
time. He fumbled with his cell phone and hit redial.
When the highway patrol dispatcher came on again,
he shouted, "The flour mill is set to explode in a few
minutes. Tell them to grab people fleeing out the back
way, but not to get too close!"

A stitch in his side felt like the thrust of a knife as
he yanked the door open from the landing to the second floor. He could only pray that the tech had told
him the truth, and Leah would be there with Becca.

"Teacher Leah!" Seth screamed through the grate
and banged on it. "I'm in here, in the air shaft, down
near the floor." Squinting through it, he could tell she
didn't understand.

"In the next room?" she shouted.

"No, in here! Down here!"

She ran to him, knelt and looked in. "Seth, the
building's going to explode. You have to get out! Have
you seen my baby?"

"There's a baby on the second floor. There was another one, but she left and this one came."

Becca! The second floor. But surely more than
half the time was gone already. Still, she grabbed the

knife she'd never managed to use against Jesse, and dug its point into the first of the screws on the air-vent grate.

She bit her lower lip to hold back tears as she turned and pried out all four of them. Expecting the building to blow up at any moment, she dragged Seth out, head-first, onto the floor.

"I didn't know you had a knife," he said, taking it from her and rushing to the door. "*Ja*, I was wishing I had one instead of a spoon all this time, 'cause I'd have worked on the lock on my cell."

Gripping her hands together, Leah stood back out of his light as he worked. He stuck the tip of her knife not in the keyhole, as she was expecting, but slid the point of it up and down in the crack between the door and the doorway. Miracle of miracles, it clicked, and he yanked the door open.

"Seth, go outside and run."

"I won't leave you—"

"Go on! Someone has to tell this story, and you're living proof. Tell them to dig up Jesse Cutler's animal graveyard—go!"

She shoved him toward the open front door and held her skirt high to tear up the only staircase she saw. Second floor. She prayed someone had been good enough to take Becca out with them, but if not, she wanted to be there with her, hold her, because they'd never make it downstairs again in time.

A boom? Was that the first explosion and now they would be spreading? The sound seemed to echo deep inside her. No, a door in the stairwell above had slammed open.

And then a baby's cries…someone running, running, coming down the stairs.

"Leah!"

"Mark?" He looked over the banister as he came down, with a small form cradled close in his free arm. "Is it Becca?"

"I've got her. Go down—down! They've rigged this place to blow up. I can run faster if you're not right with me—go on."

She almost defied him in her longing to see and hold her baby. But she trusted Mark. Loved Mark. If everything ended now, Becca would be in good hands and arms.

She flew down the stairs, with Mark pounding right behind. She prayed he wouldn't fall, that the blast was a lie, or that some heaven-sent angel would stop this hellish nightmare.

She nearly slipped in the hall by the door she'd come in. Broken glass, crimson blood. Had windows shattered already?

She held the door open for Mark as he vaulted through with Becca. "The ditch along the road!" she screamed as they felt a whoosh and heard a blast.

The earth shuddered, and the air itself seemed to slap them from behind. They were nearly lifted and thrown as they struggled to reach the shallow ditch.

They huddled there together. The night sky lit with a thousand suns and other booms followed, shaking the earth under and around them.

Somehow, in the chaos, Mark shifted the screaming baby into her arms, and she held her at last while he huddled over them like a bulwark against death itself.

"The silos are ripping up!" he shouted, but she just pressed closer to him, cradling Becca under her, lengthwise between her breasts. Whatever happened, they were together, like a family, *till death us do part*, she thought.

Huge fragments of metal flew and thudded nearby. Grain dust blew like a blizzard, followed by the smell of smoke and crackle of flames. And heat, heat like the July sun trying to sear them, until Mark pounded through the shallow ice in the ditch and threw cold water on them, which felt so good.

And then the whir of wings, fanning cooler air, hovering overhead, so loud, so lovely in the black of night. Leah looked up and saw a huge halo and sweeping, blinding streams of light. She felt dizzy, delirious. Was it real or a vision?

"Look!" she screamed at Mark over the uproar. "The angel's come to save us!"

Reflected in the light, tears streaked down his rugged face. "It's a rescue chopper, looking for survivors, my love—and that's us!"

"Yes," she sobbed, holding Becca and pressing tighter into the safety of his arms. "That's us."

Afterword

The June sun felt warm on Leah's back as she finished planting marigolds around the base of the angel statue. The last two she put at the top corners of Varina's simple tombstone, on either side of the word *Beloved*, then stood back to survey her work.

"What do you think, Becca-my-Becca?" she asked the baby, who watched her intently from the carrier she'd nearly outgrown. "The last of Mr. Kauffman's flowers he gave us for introducing Amos to Mark."

She'd been on a binge of planting, cleaning and cooking lately, anything to keep busy while waiting for the results of Becca's gene test for NAA. Mark had located the gene just a week ago, and Becca's blood had been the first he'd tested to learn her odds of developing the deadly disease. Leah always watched the baby intently to see if she showed any of the signs, though Mark said they wouldn't appear for three more months anyway.

Leah sighed and leaned against the angel as she gazed at the full branches of the maples between her house and the ravine. They seemed smaller and lighter without sap buckets dangling from their spiles. And above the tree line, how strange not to see the silos that had housed all that evil.

"A blessing, Becca-my-Becca, that we went through so much, because it stopped them from hurting others. Mark and the Dixons want to do it right with tests and trials and not just push things through for money—starting with your test."

She'd given all Sam's ill-gotten gains to Mark to hire a molecular-biology grad student to help in the lab for the summer and for Seth Kline to be trained as an office manager. She'd insisted the donation be in Barbara Yoder's name.

Since that contribution—and because the looming presence of the rogue clinic had been erased from the earth—this old house had finally, truly seemed hers. Becca no longer glanced up the stairs as if listening for footsteps; the wind no longer seemed to howl her name. The only thing was that the place needed major repairs she couldn't afford. Mark had bought her a new buggy and she'd purchased an entire new bedroom set, but she needed the rest of her salary for living expenses right now.

Mark, however, had big plans: marriage and moving in here and raising Becca together while they expanded and remodeled the house. Only, marrying him meant she must leave her people—Becca's people—and be shunned. She had known her love for Mark could come to this. For now, she'd put him off, claiming that, until she found out for sure if Becca would develop NAA, she couldn't even consider such plans.

More than once he'd told her, "I know what it would mean to you to give up being Amish."

"But do you know what it would mean to you?" she'd argued. "To no longer have your community liaison, but instead, a wife whom the Amish would no longer invite in, eat with or trust? The *meidung* has always had terrible consequences, and it would separate you and your work from the people who need it most."

"If they won't accept you over time," he'd insisted, "when you have done so much for them, we'll move the clinic to Pleasant."

"You know you need to protect your work. It will never be the same if the Amish won't visit the clinic because of me, whether it's in Maplecreek or Pleasant. Yes, I love you and want to wed you," she'd admitted and never meant anything more. "But Mark, it would not bring healing."

"If you weren't Amish, you could testify against HealGene with me when Sinclair Marshall, Clark and Jesse Cutler come to trial."

"I know, I know…"

And she knew how much she loved him. She knew he would be so good for her and Becca. But his work was essential to the well-being of her beloved people. Could she let him go? Or let her people go? She'd confided to her parents about it and to Katie and Luke. But they'd all counseled the decision was hers, however much they loved and wanted to support her.

She checked to be sure that Nell was still grazing out by the back woodlot. Then, lifting Becca from her carrier, Leah walked around the front of the house and sat in the rocking chair on the porch. She blessed the silence. The worst day had been when the national television reporters, with their satellite trucks, swarmed the town to cover Joseph Lantz's proper burial ten years after he'd disappeared.

Now, the police, media and tourist gawkers had departed, at least until the trials began this winter. Heal-Gene and Clark had top lawyers, but they'd never escape the charges. Though the staff and several gene therapy patients had been successfully evacuated from the mill before it exploded, the vast array of charges included murder for the loss of Joseph Lantz and several others who had been disinterred from Mark's pet cemetery. Leah and Mark only hoped all the negative, sensational publicity didn't set back genetic research that followed moral medical procedures and was being done for the right reasons.

She rocked Becca, remembering how Pam Martin, the sheriff's widow, had come here with her lawyer to apologize for her part in the tragedy. Pam had plea-bargained by agreeing to be a witness for the prosecution so she wouldn't go to prison for complicity and leave her children without a parent. Leah recalled how excited Louise Winslow had been just yesterday, when she'd sat on this porch to say that she was going to be allowed to adopt the child she'd named Hope, whom HealGene had evidently bought through an illegal baby market.

Now Leah hugged her own child and promised, "Whatever happens, Becca, you will always be mine." Lifting her eyes toward town, she saw the white van that Mark had bought, hurtling down the road toward her house.

"He always did drive too fast, *ja,* he did," she said to Becca as she hurried toward the driveway to wait for him. Her heartbeat kicked up and her stomach knotted. He might have the results of Becca's test. Whatever it showed, he'd vowed they would go through it together.

"A beautiful day!" he said as he got out and smiled.

"The test?" she asked.

"Leah, since MR will be my pharm firm, I'm having Brad Dixon double-check my findings, but I couldn't stand a second longer away from the two of you. Seth's manning the computer, and he'll call us with the results."

"Good. That's good," she said, then realized what he meant. "But you've seen your results! You're just having him check them?"

With Becca cradled between them, he nodded, embraced them both and kissed her. His touch was strong and sure, as if he could will all things to go well.

"Tell me, then," she said. "Tell me!"

"I think the news is good, but this is all new territory. And no one's cutting corners anymore."

It wasn't enough for her. Mark was way too optimistic about things. He thought marrying her and adopting Becca would be smooth sailing. Even if Becca had NAA, he'd probably think he'd cure it before she showed the dreadful symptoms, or surely before she died young.

He carried Becca, and they walked toward the porch. "Whatever we find out," he said, "my proposal is still the same. I don't want to go on, professionally or personally, without both of y—"

They startled when the phone rang. Leah took Becca back. His arm around them both, he answered it. "Seth, yeah. It came in faxed? Read me the numbers on the bottom line, exactly, all of them."

When Leah saw Mark's eyes glaze with tears, her heart plummeted and she clutched Becca to her. But he smiled the next moment, nodded, pulling her harder against him. "That's good news, Seth. That's what it means! And that you are going to make a great office manager."

As they huddled together in the bright sun, Becca was the only one dry-eyed.

Leah's marriage to Mark brought the most exquisite joy and the most bitter pain she'd ever known. With him, she had never been happier. Yet her parents were devastated she'd left the faith, and the entire Amish community of Maplecreek mourned her loss as if she had died in the devastation of the mill. Though Louise popped in often, Katie and Luke Brand were the only Amish who visited the first week they were back from a wedding trip to Italy. The weight of the Amish shunning, the dreaded *meidung,* was heavy indeed.

But today was crisp and clear, a lovely autumn day, and Leah had her spirits up. Mark had hired a firm from Cleveland to build a two-room addition onto the old house, before putting on a new roof and making other repairs. The workers were due at 7:00 a.m., but, though Leah kept glancing at the kitchen clock and out the window for their trucks, she saw nothing on the road yet. When no one showed up by seven-thirty, Mark phoned the company.

She could tell something was wrong from the look

on his face. "What is it?" she asked, bouncing Becca on her hip. "They didn't get the day mixed up?"

He looked both astounded and angry. "Some idiot called and canceled everything!"

"What? Who would do something like that? I thought we were finished with underhanded dealings and harassment."

"Luke was the only one who knew. But...Leah, look down the road," he said, pointing.

"Hold Becca a sec, and I'll get the binoculars," she said, retrieving her father's battered pair, which she'd somehow left in Mark's wrecked car the night the mill exploded. Before she was formally excommunicated, she'd bought her *daad* a new pair, and she had refused to let Mark replace these. They worked well enough, despite one broken lens.

They ran outside to the front porch. "Well?" Mark prompted as she adjusted the focus.

"A huge line of buggies. And a wagon with piles of lumber!"

"I think your people have made their decision." He hugged her from behind as Becca looked from one to the other, babbling as if she'd known all along. "Luke told me the church was having a meeting to decide whether they would embrace the clinic and the two people who had saved Seth and helped their children."

"Why didn't you tell me?" she cried as she started down the steps.

"I didn't want to get your hopes up," he said, hurrying after her. "I didn't even know if they'd accept me, NAA cure on the horizon or not."

But what was on the horizon now, she thought,

were the people she had always loved and could never really leave, even if they did ban her from their fellowship. She tore across the yard, daring to hope this was not just an effort for Mark's sake, a thanks to him for the inexpensive care he offered all Amish children at the clinic.

"I've never seen an Amish barn raising," Mark said, sounding as excited as a first-grade scholar. "But I bet this will come close!"

Smoothing her long, navy blue dress down as she ran, Leah blinked back tears. She always wore English clothes now; her head was bare, though she'd not cut her long hair and had it pinned up and back today. It was not an Amish woman who awaited her people, but not an English woman either. Leah had one foot firmly planted in each world, and she and Mark had decided Becca, at least, must be free to walk in both.

Her parents were in the first wagon, with her sister, Naomi, and David Groder in the second seat. Her mother was crying too, her cheeks glistening in the sun.

"Now don't you fret about food," Levi Em shouted. "I've got bread enough for King Solomon's army, and the sisters have plenty else!"

"Is it okay? I mean, can I stay and eat with everyone?" Leah asked, running beside the buggy as it led the long parade past the house and into the driveway. Mark was already gesturing other buggies to park in the front yard. "Is it all right?"

"Won't be quite the same, maybe, but everything changes in this life," her father said as he climbed down and held her shoulders hard. "The bishop and the elders decided, *ja.* If the Plain People can accept and trust the medicine of the future, we can honor those who bring it to us. And that is not only your new husband, but my daughter too."

"I couldn't lose two daughters," her mother said, wiping her fingers under both eyes. Mark put Becca in her grandmother's arms, but, for once, Emma Kurtz was only intent on Leah. "My dear daughter, you were never a replacement for your older, lost sister, but always your best self."

The Amish spilled from the buggies and wagons. Young men who had been her scholars carried ladders and brought tools in their broad leather belts, shouting greetings to Teacher Leah. Church elders began to take planks and roofing shingles from the horse-drawn wagons. Women she had looked up to all her life carted picnic baskets and blankets. Planks and sawhorses appeared, to set up long lunch tables in the driveway near the side of the cemetery.

Susie Kline came by, giggling and riding on Seth's back to hug first Mark, then Leah. Jonas Esh had been too ill to come, but Amos Kauffman's father, Gideon, carried Amos to a blanket where he could watch everything, while his portable oxygen tank helped him breathe.

The boy had brought his autographed baseball and was soon showing it to other kids while his father unloaded flats of red geraniums. He placed the plastic pots down the long stretch of table and across the Morellis' front porch. Soon the air rang with the shouts and sounds of carpenters and roofers, the chatter of children, the clink of tableware and the laughter of women.

Later, when they all sat down to eat and Bishop Moses Brand asked for a moment of silent prayer, Leah peeked through slitted lids because she wanted always to recall this day, this scene. It was then she saw, above the bounteously laid tables, beyond the bowed bonnetted and hatted heads and the cemetery fence, someone had put a bright red geranium in the angel's clasped hands.

Author's Note

Dark Angel is the third novel in a series set in the Amish area of Maplecreek, Ohio, so if you have not read *Dark Road Home* and *Dark Harvest,* I hope you will look for them. They can be read as stand-alone stories, but are interwoven by key characters and the rural setting.

As Leah says in this story, the Amish have a saying that, "It's not all cakes and pies." And, indeed, the life of the Plain People has many challenges today. Hit-and-run accidents, the encroachment of worldly life, the expense of farmland, hate crimes and the challenge of genetic diseases are some of the difficulties they face with bravery and deep belief.

As for the idea of putting a clinic inside a flour mill, last year on a book tour I stayed at the Crowne Plaza Hotel at Quaker Square in Akron, Ohio. This unique building has its hotel rooms built around a central hub inside old grain-storage silos.

The flour mill explosion at the end of the book is entirely possible. In 2003, in Columbus, Ohio, a grain elevator exploded in this manner. Flour dust is not the only thing that can set off such an explosion. A lumber company in New Knoxville, Ohio had a disastrous explosion from sparks igniting sawdust.

The big challenge of researching this book was dealing with genetic diseases, especially as they affect the Amish. Mark Morelli's clinic is inspired by two actual clinics, but was in no way based on them.

There is so much to read about this fascinating new medical field, and information changes daily. Gene therapy, which received several setbacks, is now meeting with more success, such as in the treatment of defective immune systems in children.

As I mentioned at the front of this book, I did fictionalize the two major genetic diseases in the story, but I based them on authentic illnesses. My natal accelerated aging (NAA) was inspired by progeria (Hutchinson-Gilford Syndrome). At the time in which I set the novel, there was no treatment for progeria, although a genetic test was under development. Two Web sites for information about progeria are www.genome.gov/11007255 and www.nebi.nlm.gov.

Barbara Yoder's fictional genetic disease, Regnell anemia, is based on Fanconi anemia. That Web site is www.fanconi.org. Unfortunately, the Amish suffer from other genetic diseases I did not mention in this story.

For those interested in the amazing future of genetics, which will affect all of us, a good book for laypersons is *Beyond Genetics* by Glenn McGee, a bioethicist.

Because I greatly admire and respect the Amish and love to visit their areas of rural Ohio, I hope to write another book set in Maplecreek sometime. I have also written one other romantic suspense novel with an

Amish setting, *Down to the Bone,* set in western Ohio, where some Amish have migrated to find affordable land.

Karen Harper
July 2004